CARTOON NETWORK
BLOCK PARTY!
GET DOWN!

ten by:
bie Busch
lly Fisch
n Haspiel
l Kupperberg
e Roman
n Rozum
k Strom
Willems
Warburton
d Zajac

Illustrated by:
Kim Arndt
Jeff Albrecht
Maxwell Atoms
Angus Bungay
Dan Davis
John Delaney
Jared Deal
Maurice Fontenot
Frank Homiski
Tim Chi Ly
Scott McRae
Matt Peters
Dave Schwartz
Dave Simons
Robert R. Smith
Enis Temizel
Mike Wetterhahn

Colored by:
Digital Chameleon
Heroic Age
Lee Loughridge
Sno Cone
Zylonol Studios

Lettered by:
Ken Bruzenak
Jared K. Fletcher
Jenna Garcia
Sergio Garcia
Rob Leigh
Tom B. Long
Nick J. Napolitano

CARTOON NETWORK BLOCK PARTY VOL. 1: GET DOWN!
Published by DC Comics. Cover and compilation copyright © 2005 Cartoon Network. All Rights Reserved.
Originally published in single magazine form in DEXTER'S LABORATORY 7-8 and CARTOON CARTOONS 9,
11-12, 14, 21, 25-26, 28. Copyright © 2000, 2002, 2003, 2004 Cartoon Network. All Rights Reserved. CARTOON
NETWORK, the logos and all related characters and elements are trademarks of and © Cartoon Network.
The DC logo is a trademark of DC Comics. The stories, characters and incidents featured in this
publication are entirely fictional. DC Comics does not read or accept unsolicited submissions
of ideas, stories or artwork.

DC Comics, 1700 Broadway, New York, NY 10019
A Warner Bros. Entertainment Company.
Printed in Canada. First Printing.
ISBN: 1-4012-0517-8
Cover Illustration by Gary Fields.
Publication design by John J. Hill.

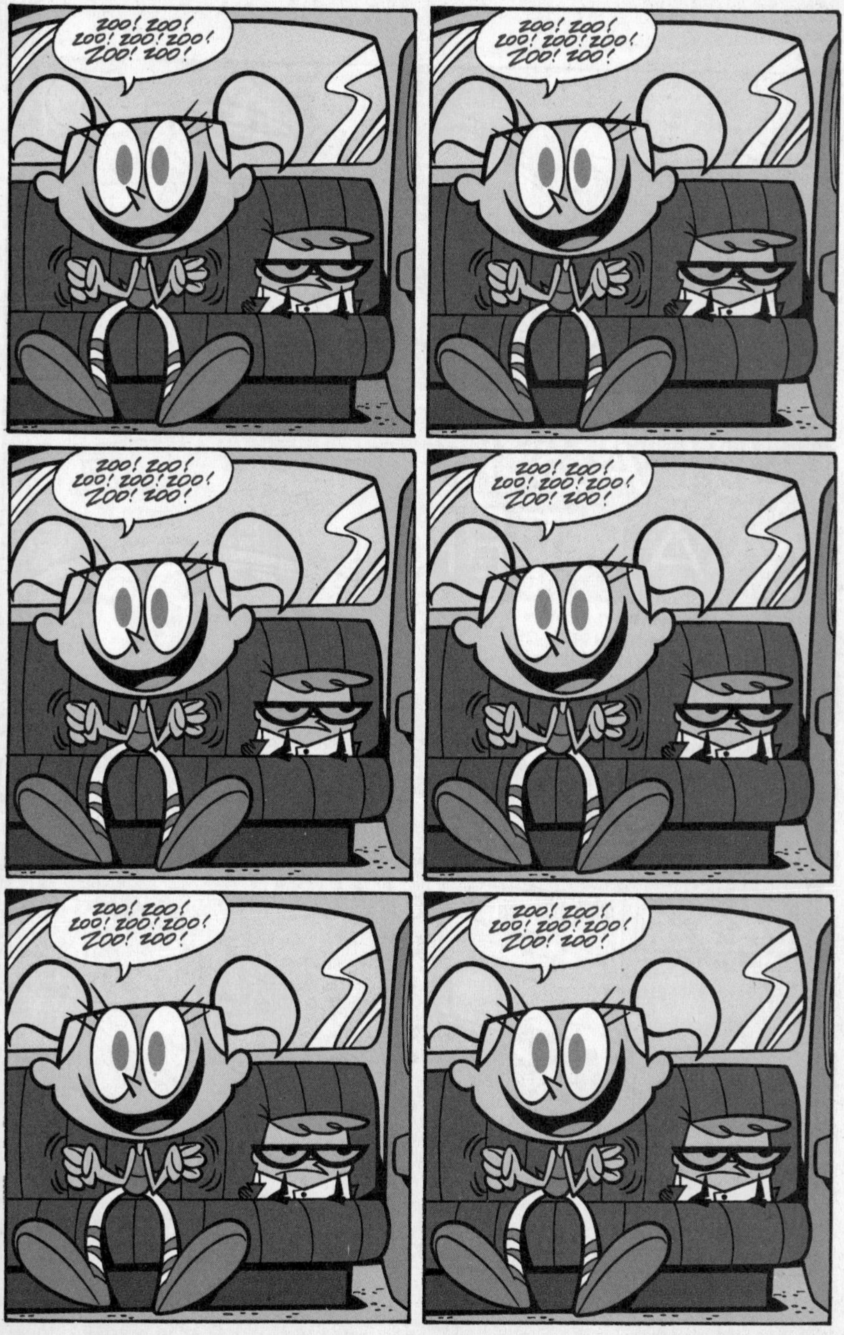
ZOO! ZOO! ZOO! ZOO! ZOO! ZOO! ZOO!
ZOO! ZOO! ZOO! ZOO! ZOO! ZOO! ZOO!
ZOO! ZOO! ZOO! ZOO! ZOO! ZOO! ZOO!
ZOO! ZOO! ZOO! ZOO! ZOO! ZOO! ZOO!
ZOO! ZOO! ZOO! ZOO! ZOO! ZOO! ZOO!
ZOO! ZOO! ZOO! ZOO! ZOO! ZOO! ZOO!

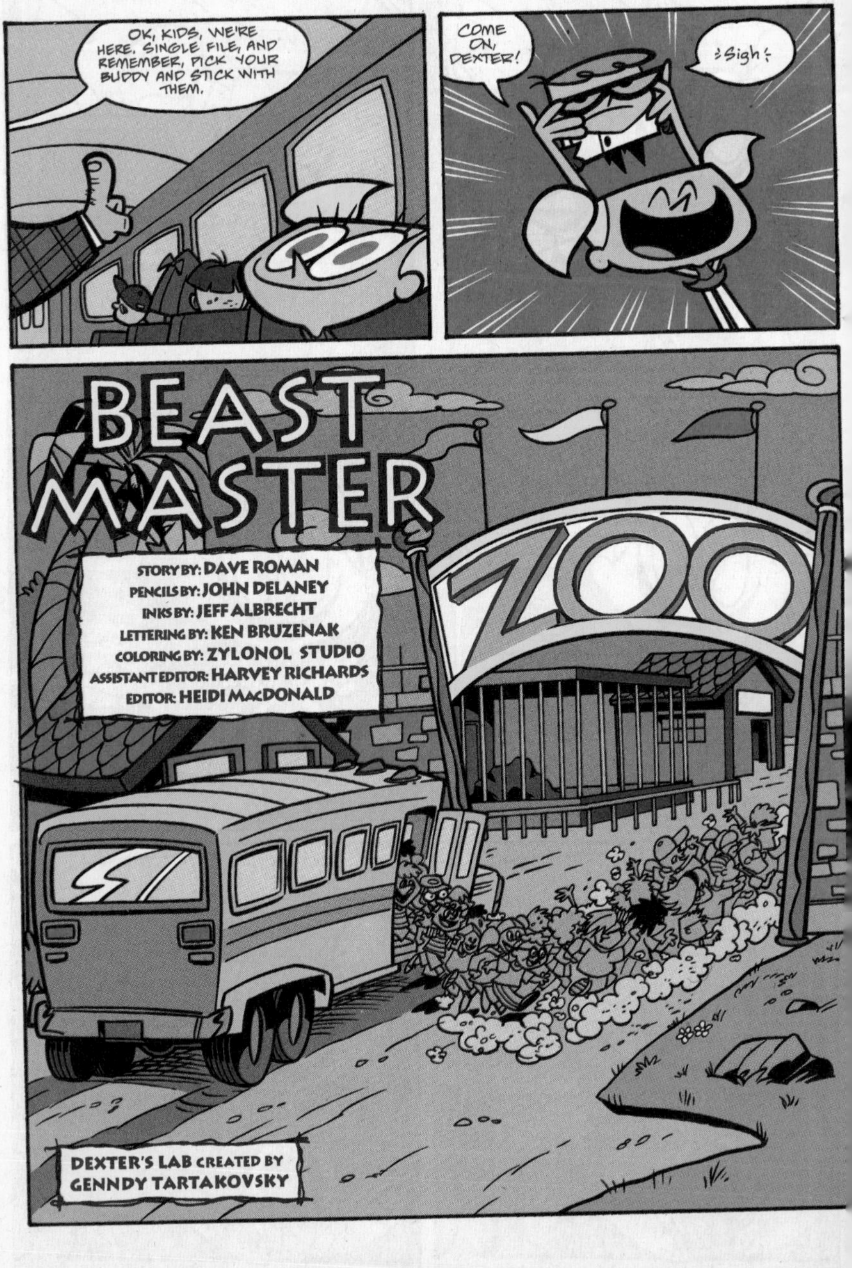
OK, KIDS, WE'RE HERE. SINGLE FILE, AND REMEMBER, PICK YOUR BUDDY AND STICK WITH THEM.
COME ON, DEXTER!
Sigh
BEAST MASTER
ZOO
STORY BY: DAVE ROMAN
PENCILS BY: JOHN DELANEY
INKS BY: JEFF ALBRECHT
LETTERING BY: KEN BRUZENAK
COLORING BY: ZYLONOL STUDIO
ASSISTANT EDITOR: HARVEY RICHARDS
EDITOR: HEIDI MacDONALD
DEXTER'S LAB CREATED BY GENNDY TARTAKOVSKY

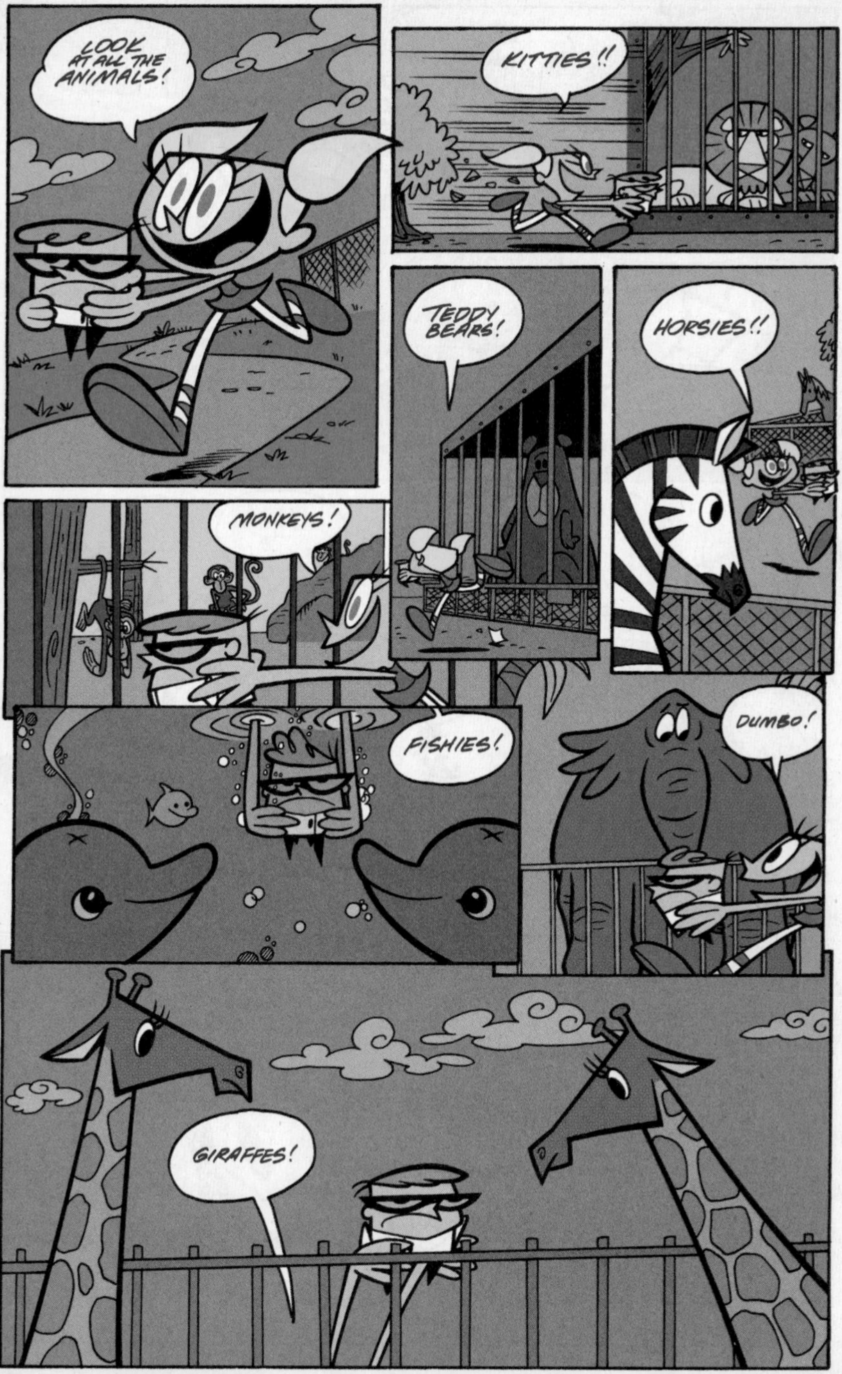
LOOK AT ALL THE ANIMALS!
KITTIES!!
TEDDY BEARS!
HORSIES!!
MONKEYS!
FISHIES!
DUMBO!
GIRAFFES!

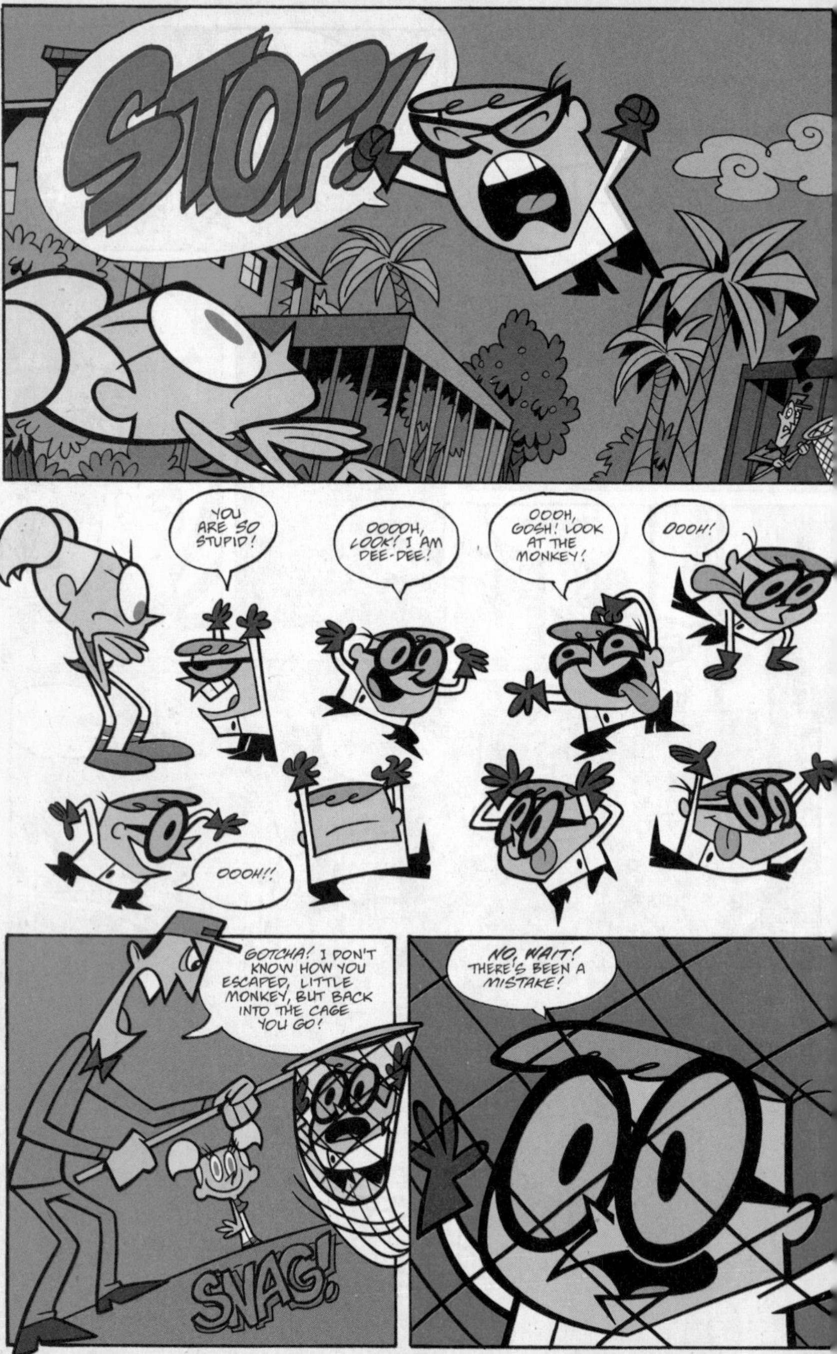
STOP!
YOU ARE SO STUPID!
OOOOH, LOOK! I AM DEE-DEE!
OOOH, GOSH! LOOK AT THE MONKEY!
OOOH!
OOOH!!
GOTCHA! I DON'T KNOW HOW YOU ESCAPED, LITTLE MONKEY, BUT BACK INTO THE CAGE YOU GO!
SNAG!
NO, WAIT! THERE'S BEEN A MISTAKE!

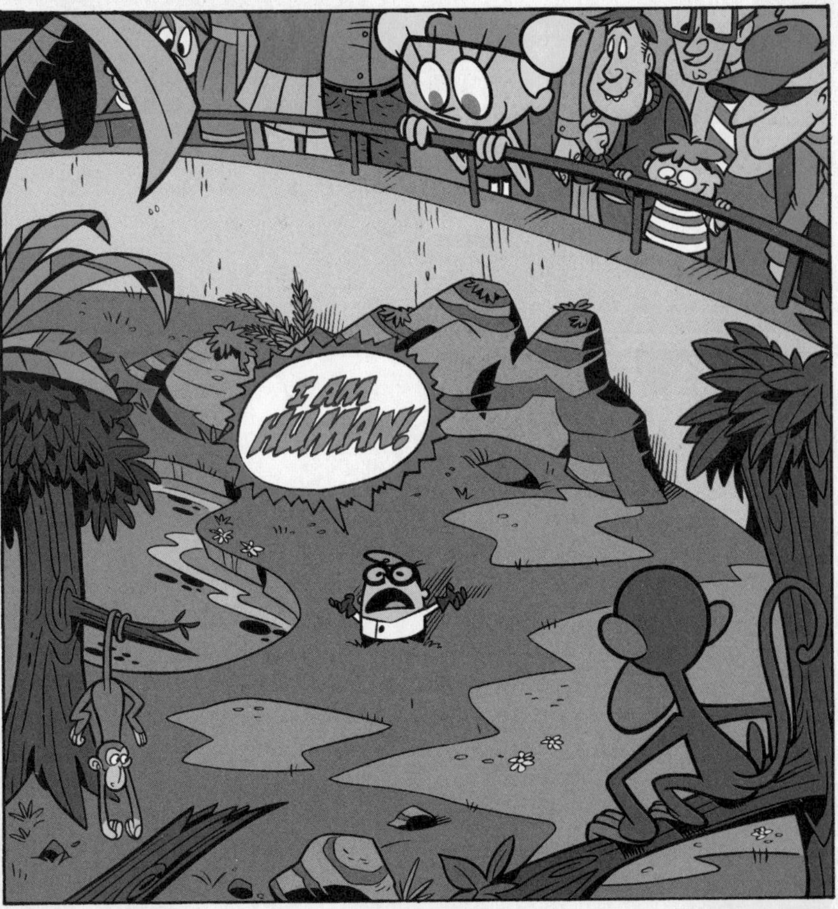
I AM HUMAN!

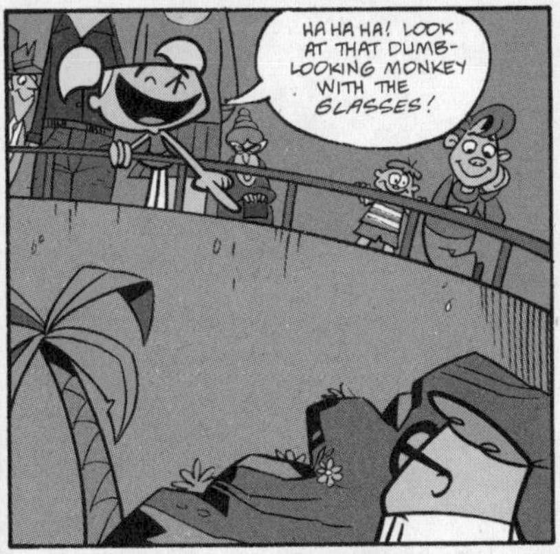
HA HA HA! LOOK AT THAT DUMB-LOOKING MONKEY WITH THE GLASSES!

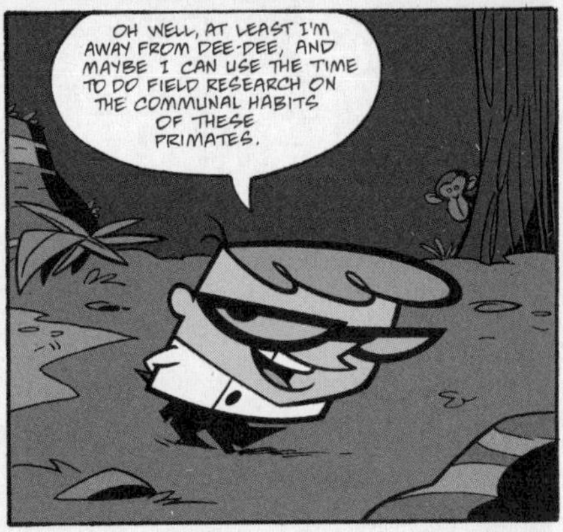
OH WELL, AT LEAST I'M AWAY FROM DEE-DEE, AND MAYBE I CAN USE THE TIME TO DO FIELD RESEARCH ON THE COMMUNAL HABITS OF THESE PRIMATES.

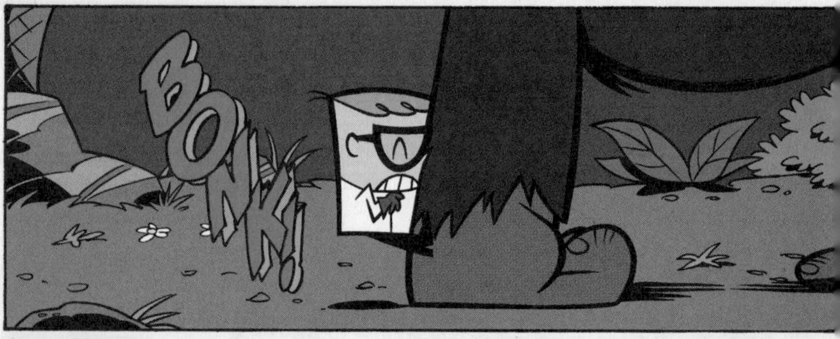
BONK!

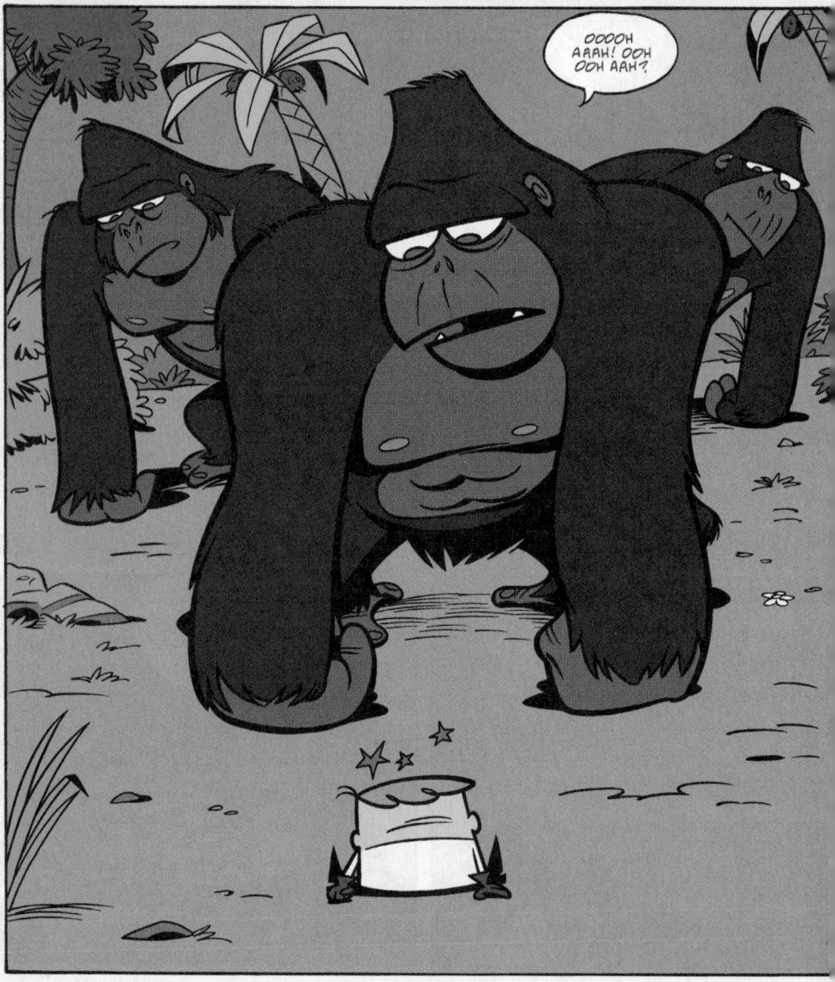
OOOOH AAAH! OOH OOH AAH?

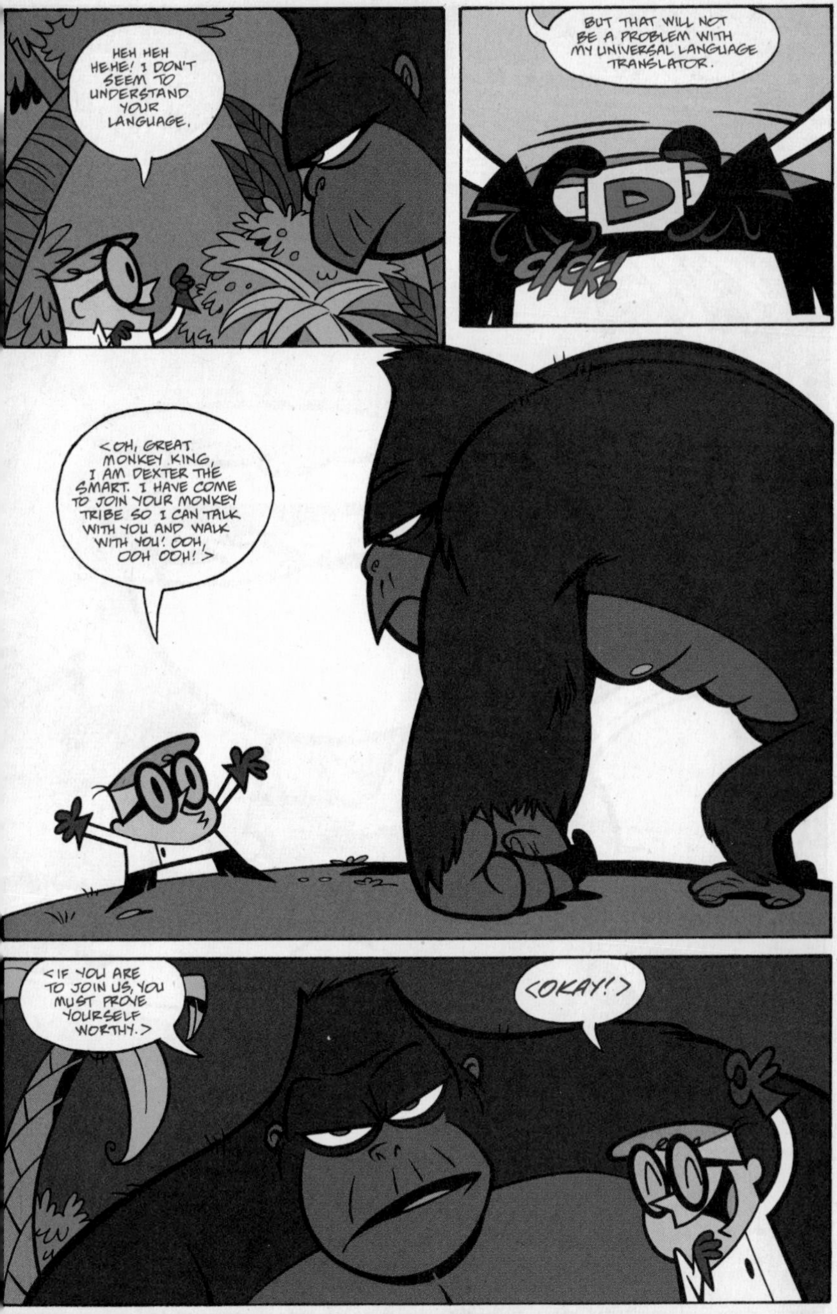
HEH HEH HEHE! I DON'T SEEM TO UNDERSTAND YOUR LANGUAGE.
BUT THAT WILL NOT BE A PROBLEM WITH MY UNIVERSAL LANGUAGE TRANSLATOR.
D
CLICK!
<OH, GREAT MONKEY KING, I AM DEXTER THE SMART. I HAVE COME TO JOIN YOUR MONKEY TRIBE SO I CAN TALK WITH YOU AND WALK WITH YOU! OOH, OOH OOH!>
<IF YOU ARE TO JOIN US, YOU MUST PROVE YOURSELF WORTHY.>
<OKAY!>

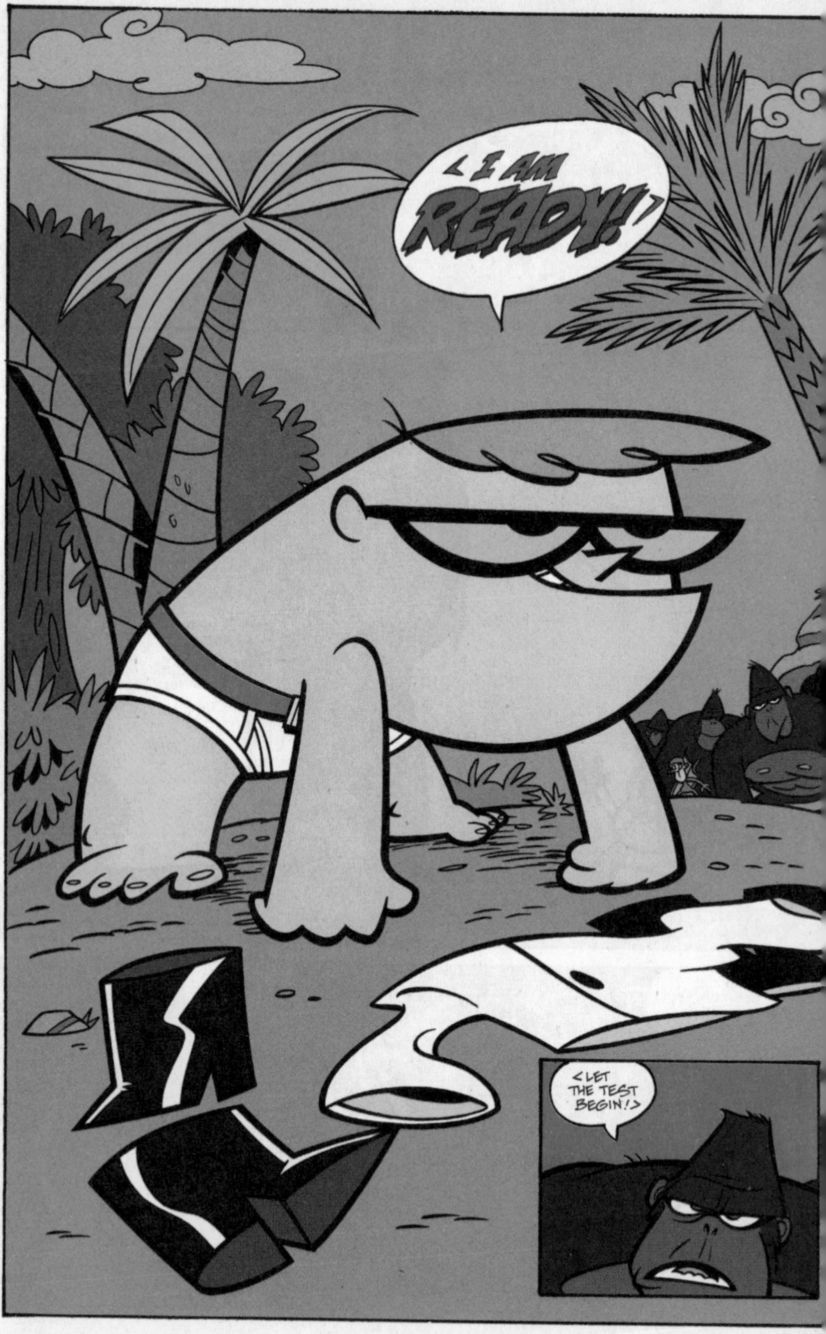
< I AM READY! >
<LET THE TEST BEGIN!>

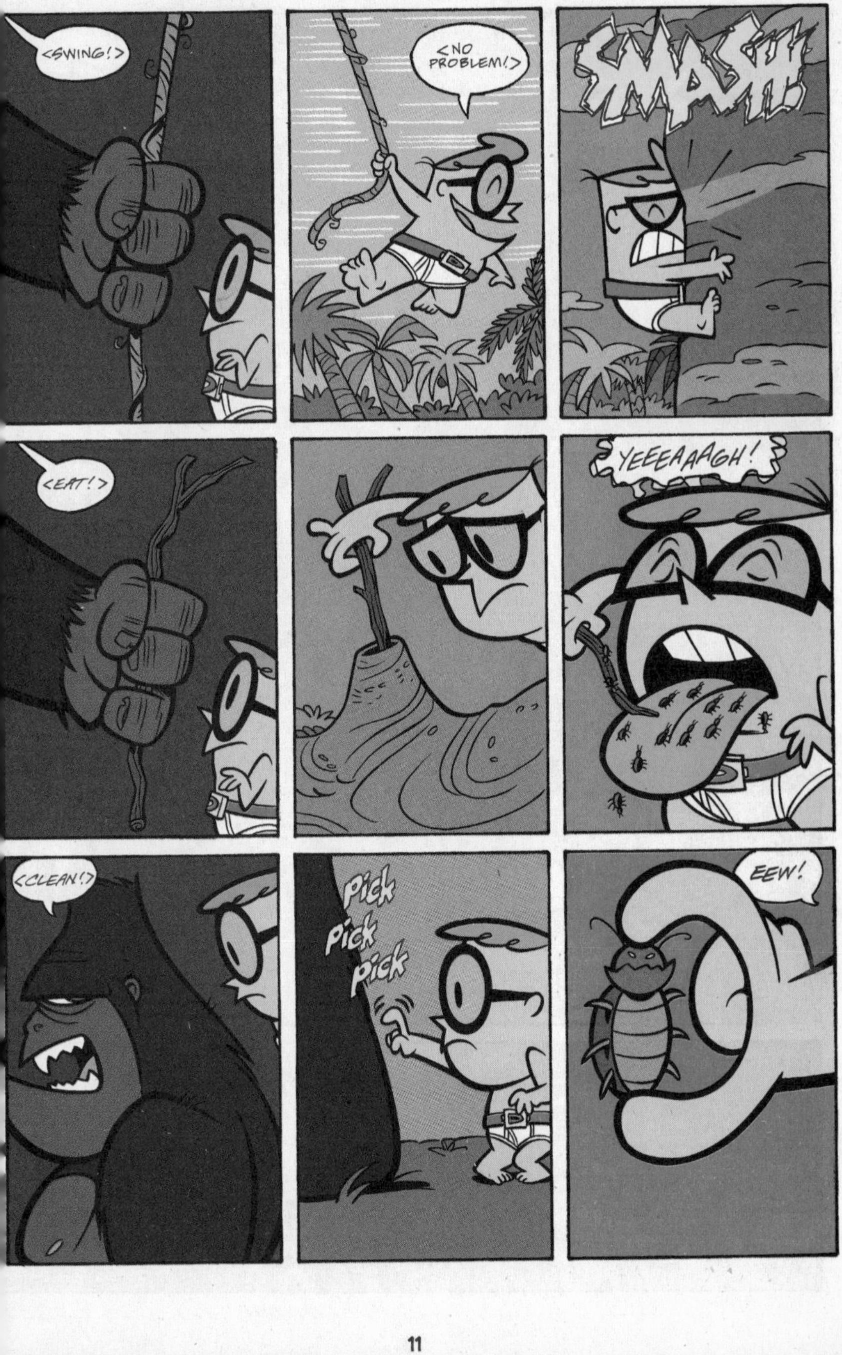
<SWING!>
<NO PROBLEM!>
SMASH!
<EAT!>
YEEEAAAGH!
<CLEAN!>
pick
pick
pick
EEW!

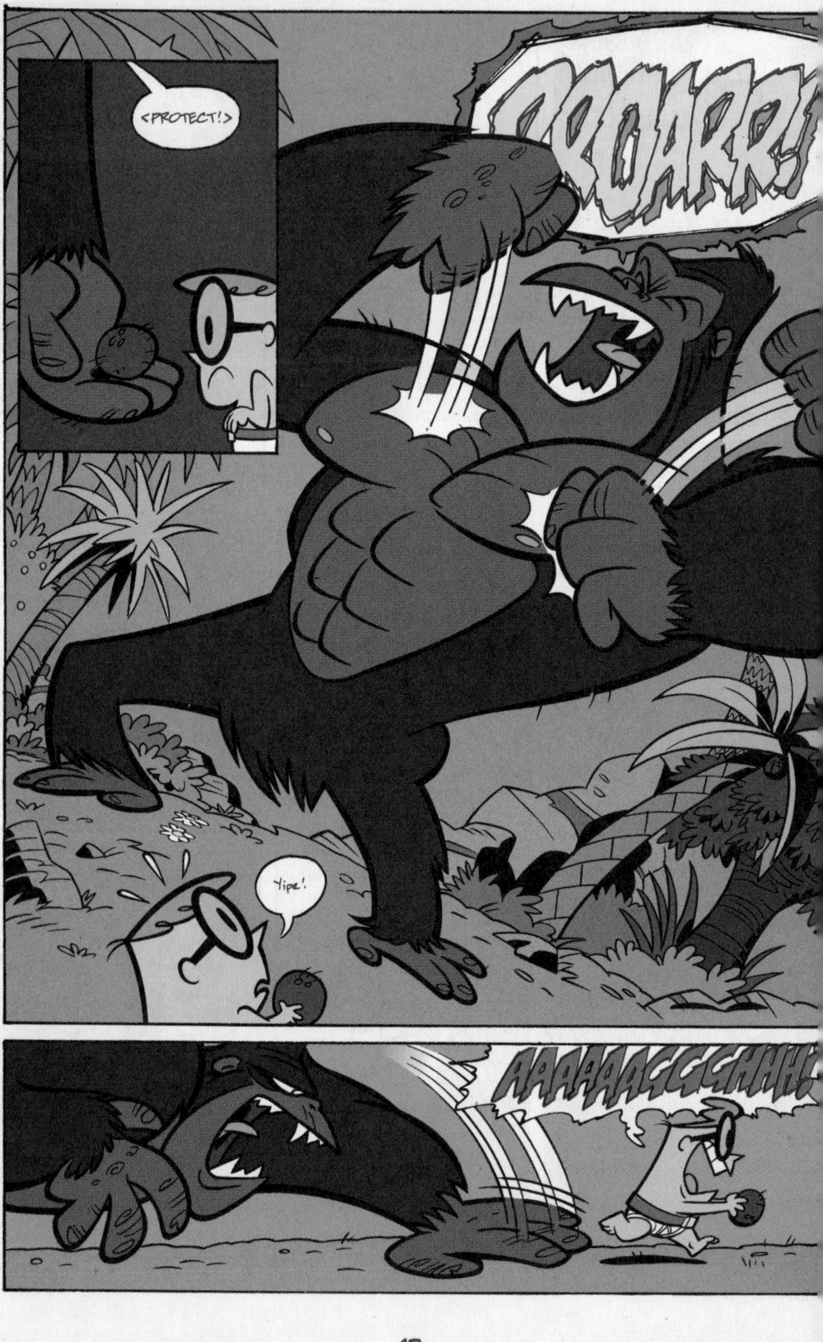

<PROTECT!>
Yipe!

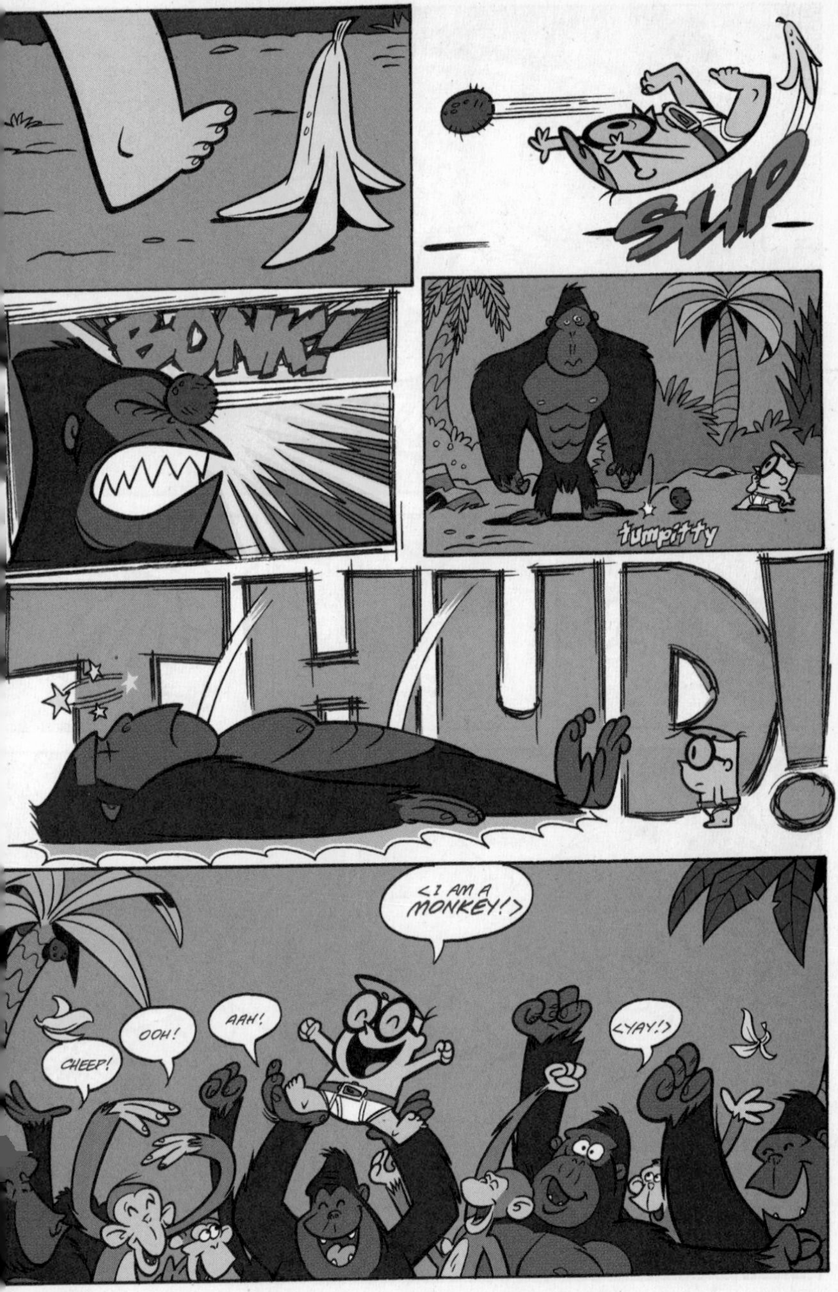
SLIP
BONK!
tumpitty
THUD!
<I AM A MONKEY!>
CHEEP!
OOH!
AAH!
<YAY!>

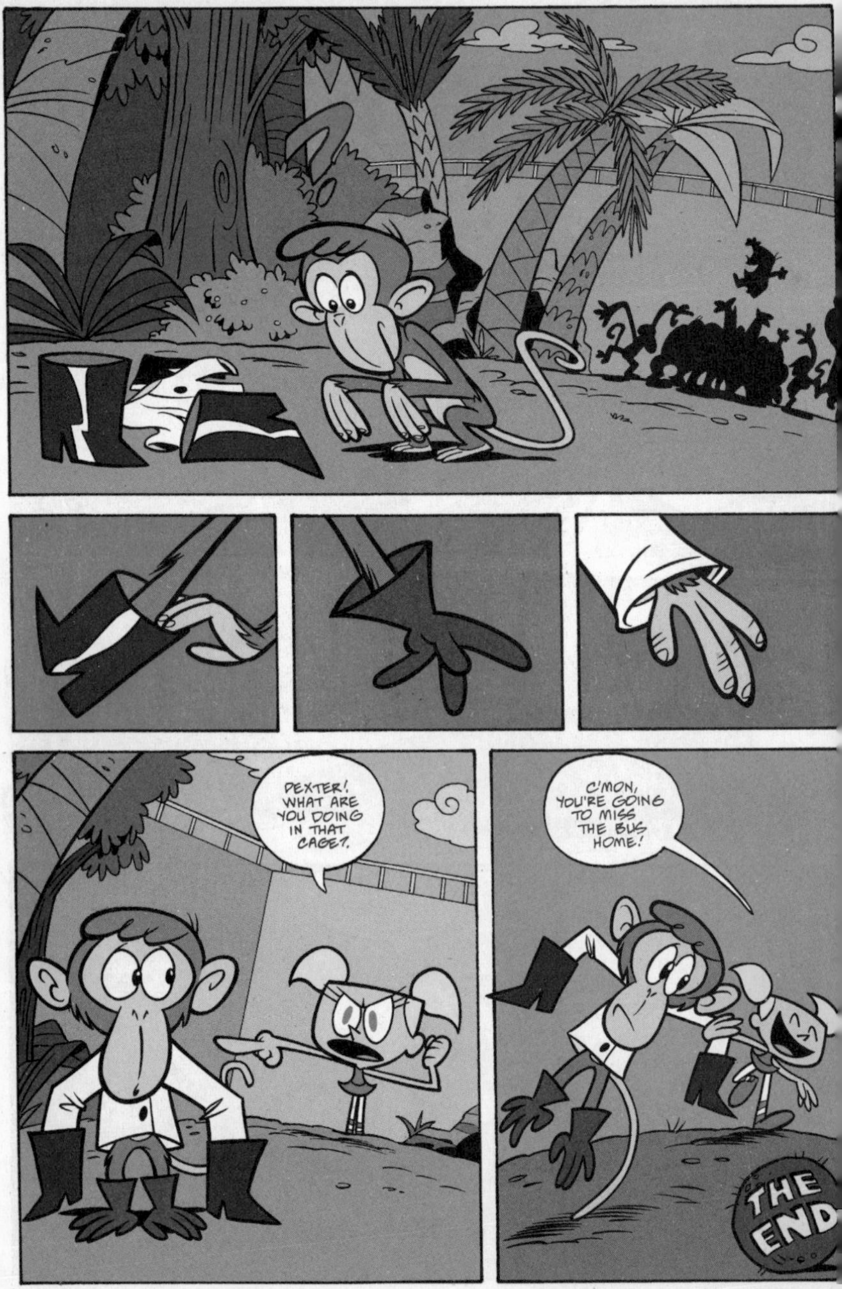
DEXTER! WHAT ARE YOU DOING IN THAT CAGE?
C'MON, YOU'RE GOING TO MISS THE BUS HOME!
THE END

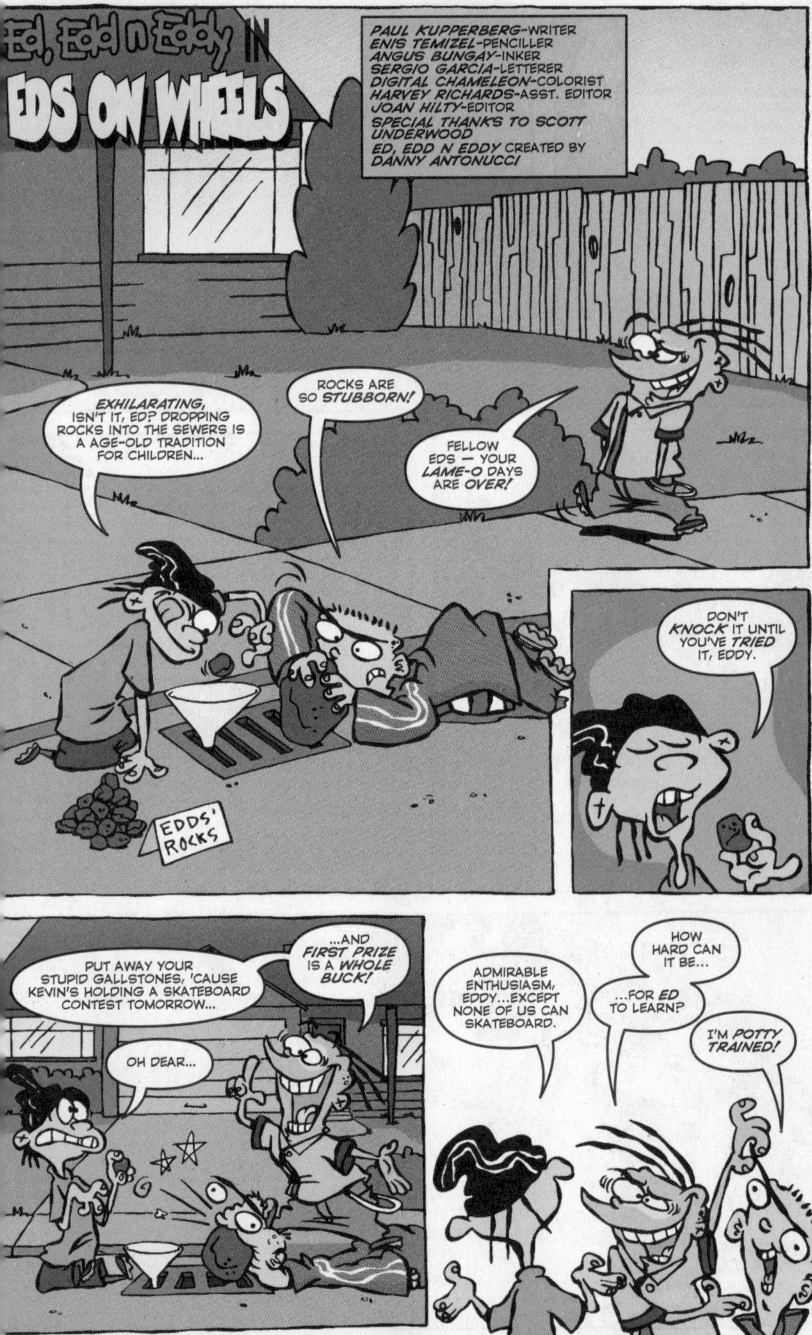
Ed, Edd n Eddy IN
EDS ON WHEELS
PAUL KUPPERBERG-WRITER
ENIS TEMIZEL-PENCILLER
ANGUS BUNGAY-INKER
SERGIO GARCIA-LETTERER
DIGITAL CHAMELEON-COLORIST
HARVEY RICHARDS-ASST. EDITOR
JOAN HILTY-EDITOR
SPECIAL THANKS TO SCOTT UNDERWOOD
ED, EDD N EDDY CREATED BY DANNY ANTONUCCI
EXHILARATING, ISN'T IT, ED? DROPPING ROCKS INTO THE SEWERS IS A AGE-OLD TRADITION FOR CHILDREN...
ROCKS ARE SO STUBBORN!
FELLOW EDS — YOUR LAME-O DAYS ARE OVER!
EDDS' ROCKS
DON'T KNOCK IT UNTIL YOU'VE TRIED IT, EDDY.
PUT AWAY YOUR STUPID GALLSTONES, 'CAUSE KEVIN'S HOLDING A SKATEBOARD CONTEST TOMORROW...
...AND FIRST PRIZE IS A WHOLE BUCK!
OH DEAR...
ADMIRABLE ENTHUSIASM, EDDY...EXCEPT NONE OF US CAN SKATEBOARD.
HOW HARD CAN IT BE...
...FOR ED TO LEARN?
I'M POTTY TRAINED!

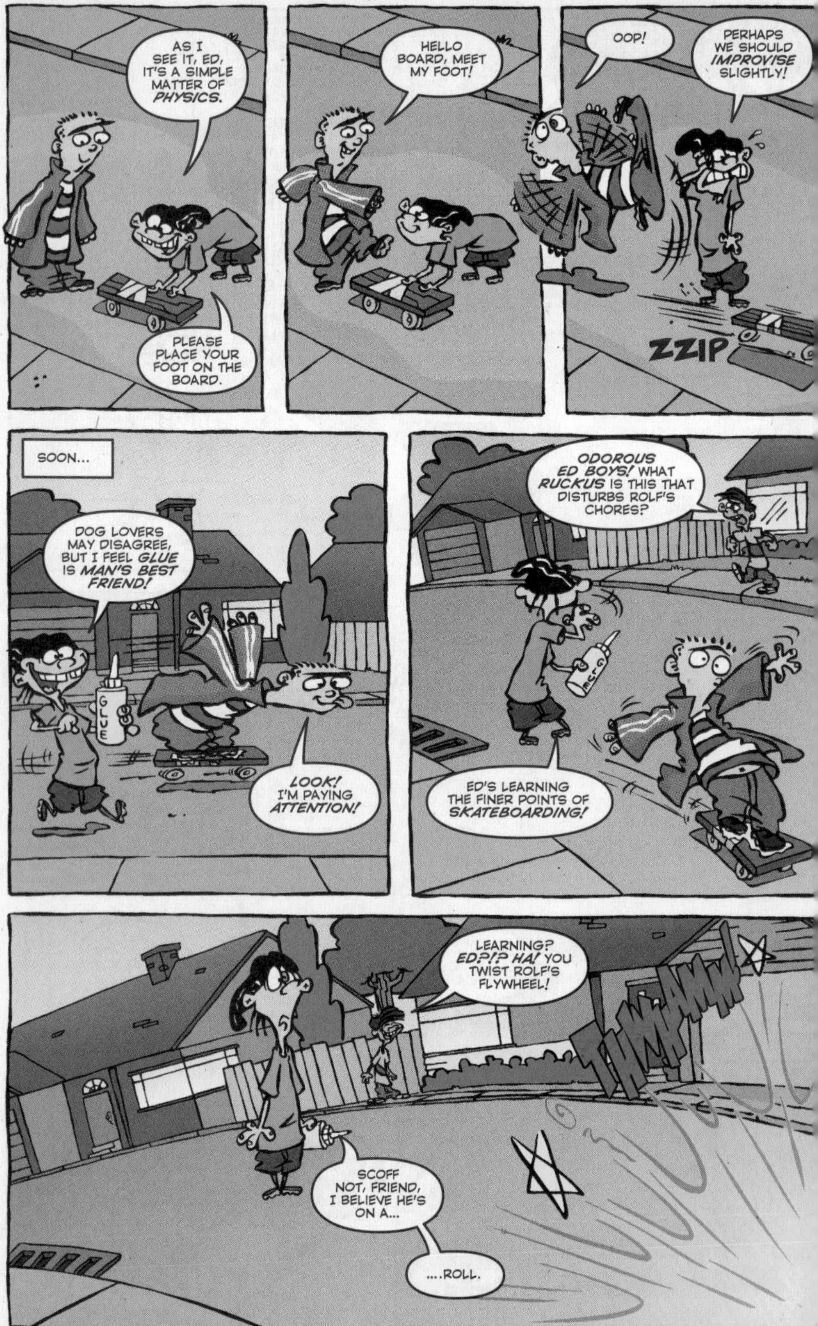
AS I SEE IT, ED, IT'S A SIMPLE MATTER OF *PHYSICS*.
PLEASE PLACE YOUR FOOT ON THE BOARD.
HELLO BOARD, MEET MY FOOT!
OOP!
PERHAPS WE SHOULD *IMPROVISE* SLIGHTLY!
ZZIP
SOON...
DOG LOVERS MAY DISAGREE, BUT I FEEL *GLUE* IS *MAN'S BEST FRIEND!*
GLUE
LOOK! I'M PAYING *ATTENTION!*
ODOROUS ED BOYS! WHAT *RUCKUS* IS THIS THAT DISTURBS ROLF'S CHORES?
ED'S LEARNING THE FINER POINTS OF *SKATEBOARDING!*
LEARNING? *ED?!? HA!* YOU TWIST ROLF'S FLYWHEEL!
SCOFF NOT, FRIEND, I BELIEVE HE'S ON A...
....ROLL.

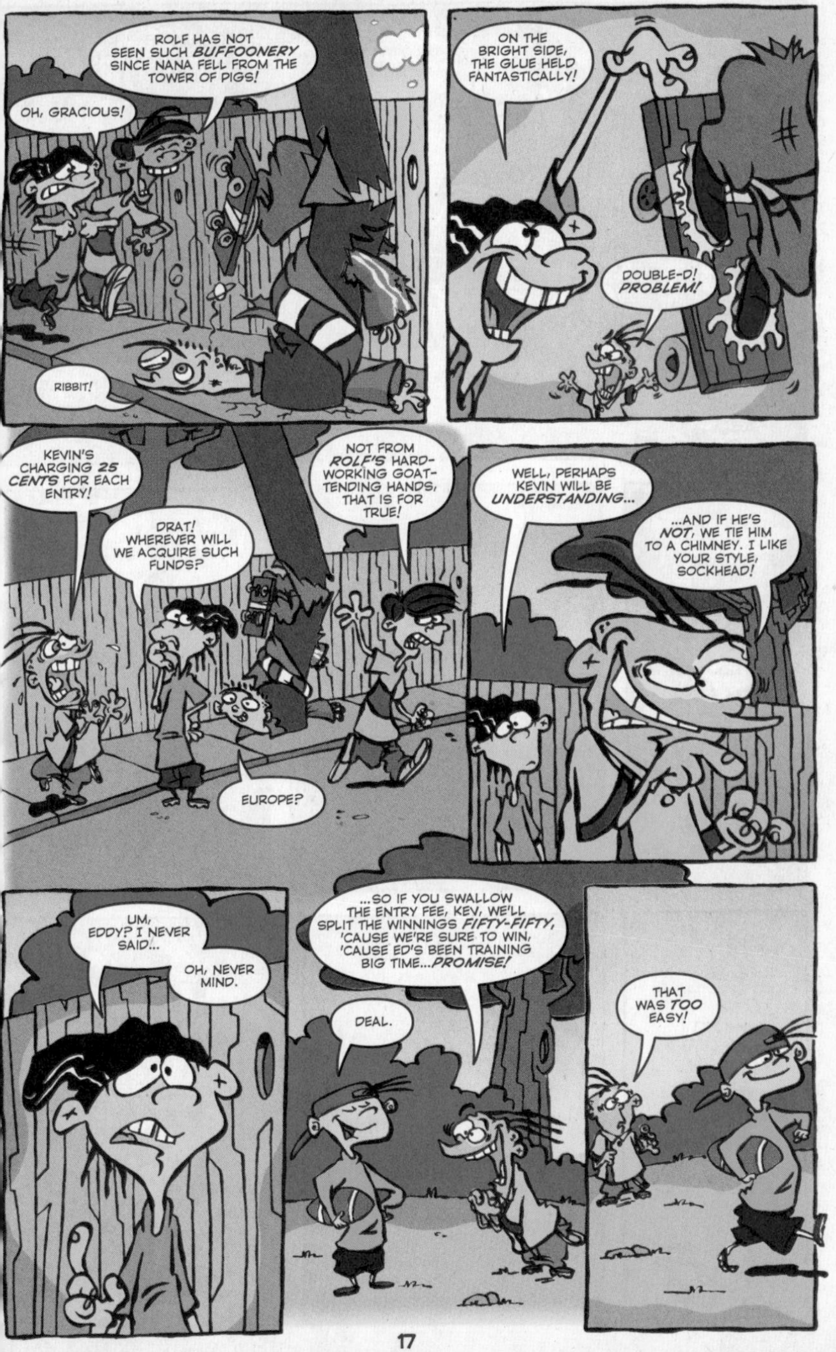
ROLF HAS NOT SEEN SUCH BUFFOONERY SINCE NANA FELL FROM THE TOWER OF PIGS!
OH, GRACIOUS!
RIBBIT!
ON THE BRIGHT SIDE, THE GLUE HELD FANTASTICALLY!
DOUBLE-D! PROBLEM!
KEVIN'S CHARGING 25 CENTS FOR EACH ENTRY!
DRAT! WHEREVER WILL WE ACQUIRE SUCH FUNDS?
NOT FROM ROLF'S HARD-WORKING GOAT-TENDING HANDS, THAT IS FOR TRUE!
EUROPE?
WELL, PERHAPS KEVIN WILL BE UNDERSTANDING...
...AND IF HE'S NOT, WE TIE HIM TO A CHIMNEY. I LIKE YOUR STYLE, SOCKHEAD!
UM, EDDY? I NEVER SAID...
OH, NEVER MIND.
...SO IF YOU SWALLOW THE ENTRY FEE, KEV, WE'LL SPLIT THE WINNINGS FIFTY-FIFTY, 'CAUSE WE'RE SURE TO WIN, 'CAUSE ED'S BEEN TRAINING BIG TIME...PROMISE!
DEAL.
THAT WAS TOO EASY!

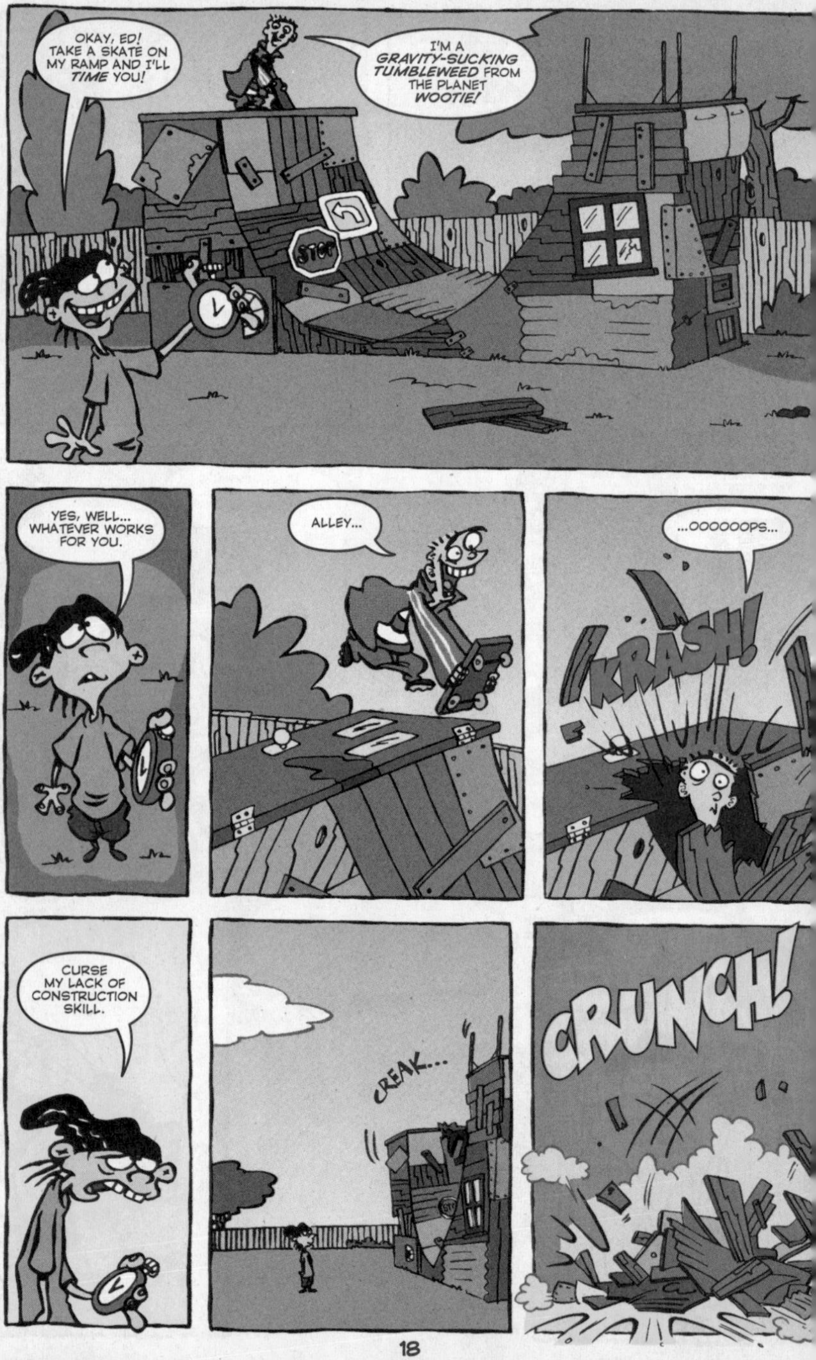
OKAY, ED! TAKE A SKATE ON MY RAMP AND I'LL TIME YOU!
I'M A GRAVITY-SUCKING TUMBLEWEED FROM THE PLANET WOOTIE!
STOP
YES, WELL... WHATEVER WORKS FOR YOU.
ALLEY...
...OOOOOOPS...
KRASH!
CURSE MY LACK OF CONSTRUCTION SKILL.
CREAK...
CRUNCH!

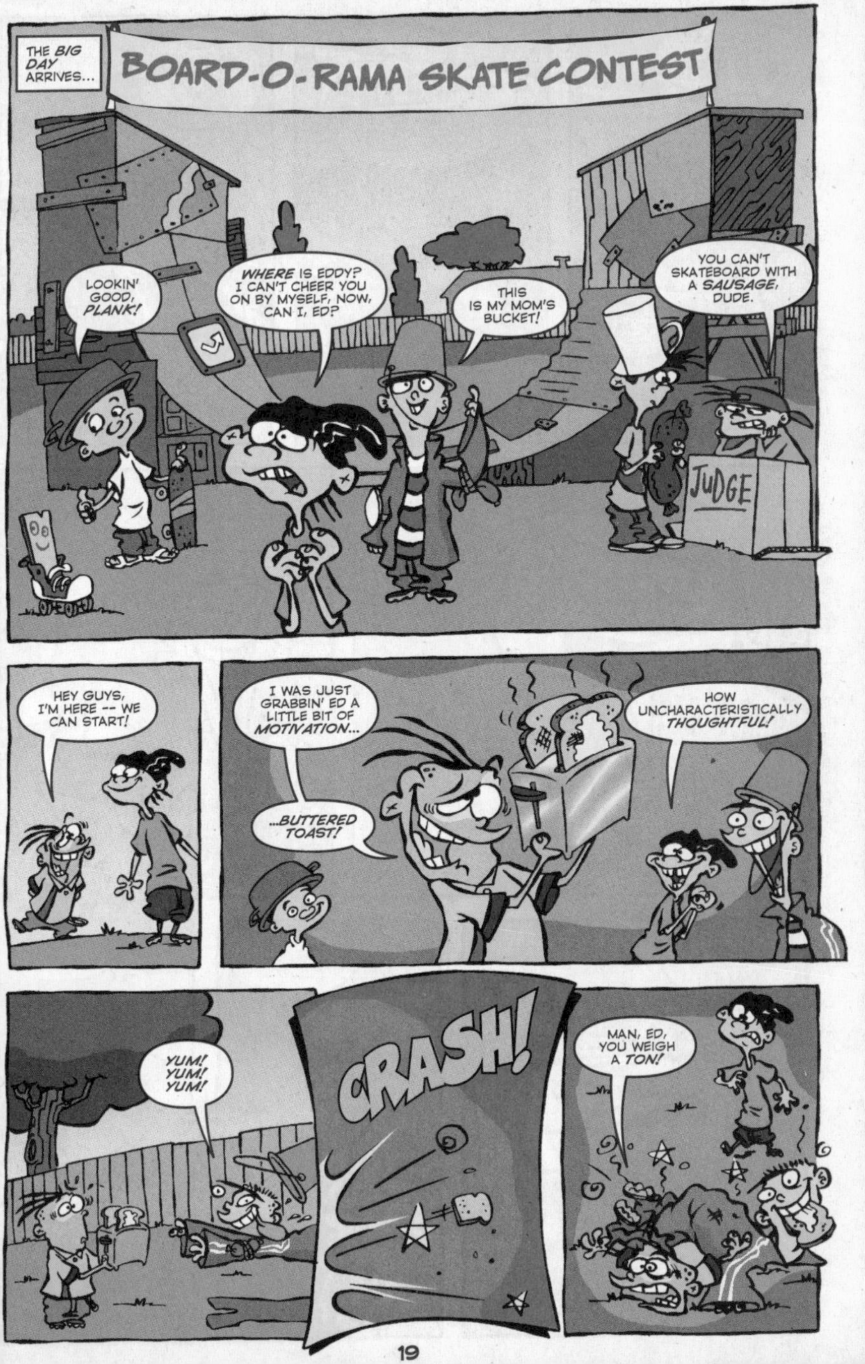
THE BIG DAY ARRIVES...
BOARD-O-RAMA SKATE CONTEST
LOOKIN' GOOD, PLANK!
WHERE IS EDDY? I CAN'T CHEER YOU ON BY MYSELF, NOW, CAN I, ED?
THIS IS MY MOM'S BUCKET!
YOU CAN'T SKATEBOARD WITH A SAUSAGE, DUDE.
JUDGE
HEY GUYS, I'M HERE -- WE CAN START!
I WAS JUST GRABBIN' ED A LITTLE BIT OF MOTIVATION...
...BUTTERED TOAST!
HOW UNCHARACTERISTICALLY THOUGHTFUL!
YUM! YUM! YUM!
CRASH!
MAN, ED, YOU WEIGH A TON!

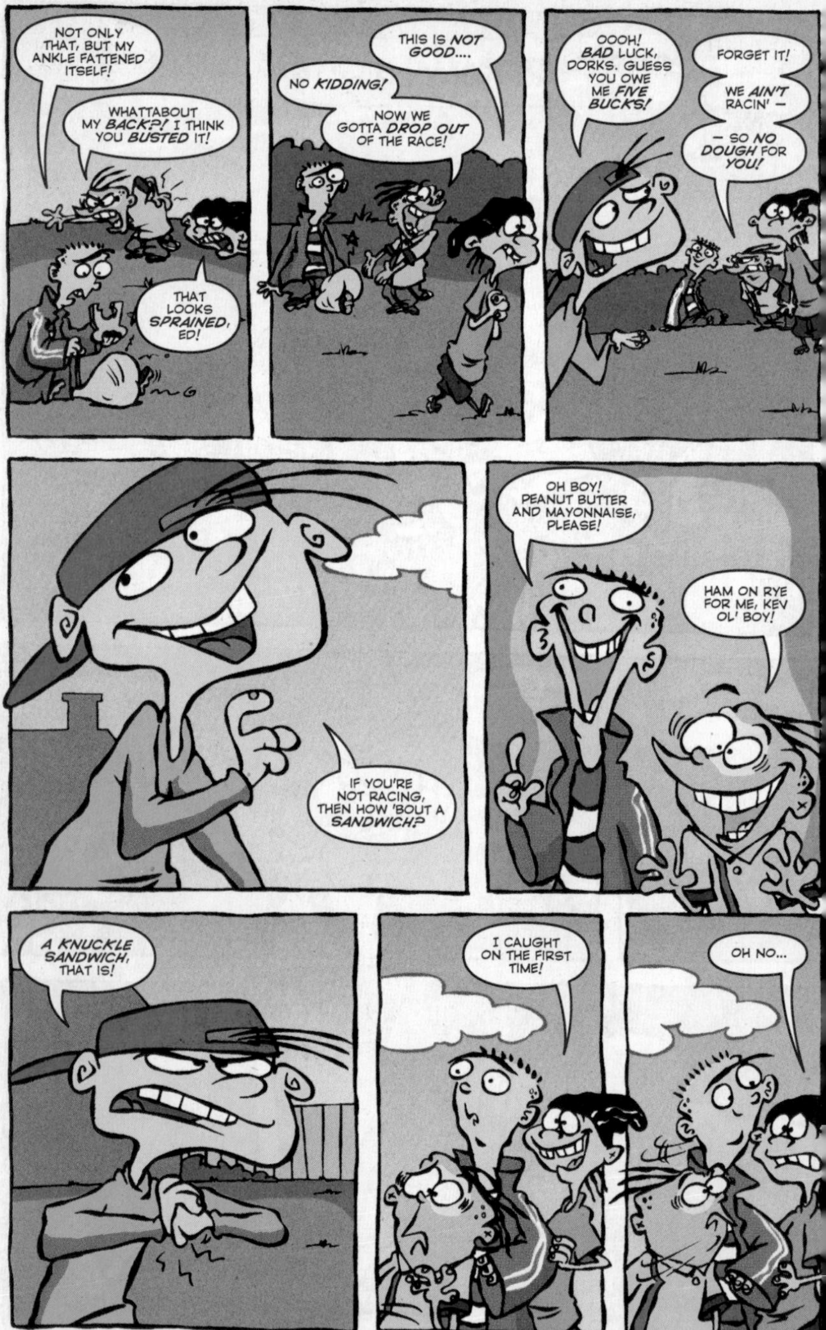
NOT ONLY THAT, BUT MY ANKLE FATTENED ITSELF!
WHATTABOUT MY BACK?! I THINK YOU BUSTED IT!
THAT LOOKS SPRAINED, ED!
THIS IS NOT GOOD....
NO KIDDING!
NOW WE GOTTA DROP OUT OF THE RACE!
OOOH! BAD LUCK, DORKS. GUESS YOU OWE ME FIVE BUCKS!
FORGET IT!
WE AIN'T RACIN' —
— SO NO DOUGH FOR YOU!
IF YOU'RE NOT RACING, THEN HOW 'BOUT A SANDWICH?
OH BOY! PEANUT BUTTER AND MAYONNAISE, PLEASE!
HAM ON RYE FOR ME, KEV OL' BOY!
A KNUCKLE SANDWICH, THAT IS!
I CAUGHT ON THE FIRST TIME!
OH NO...

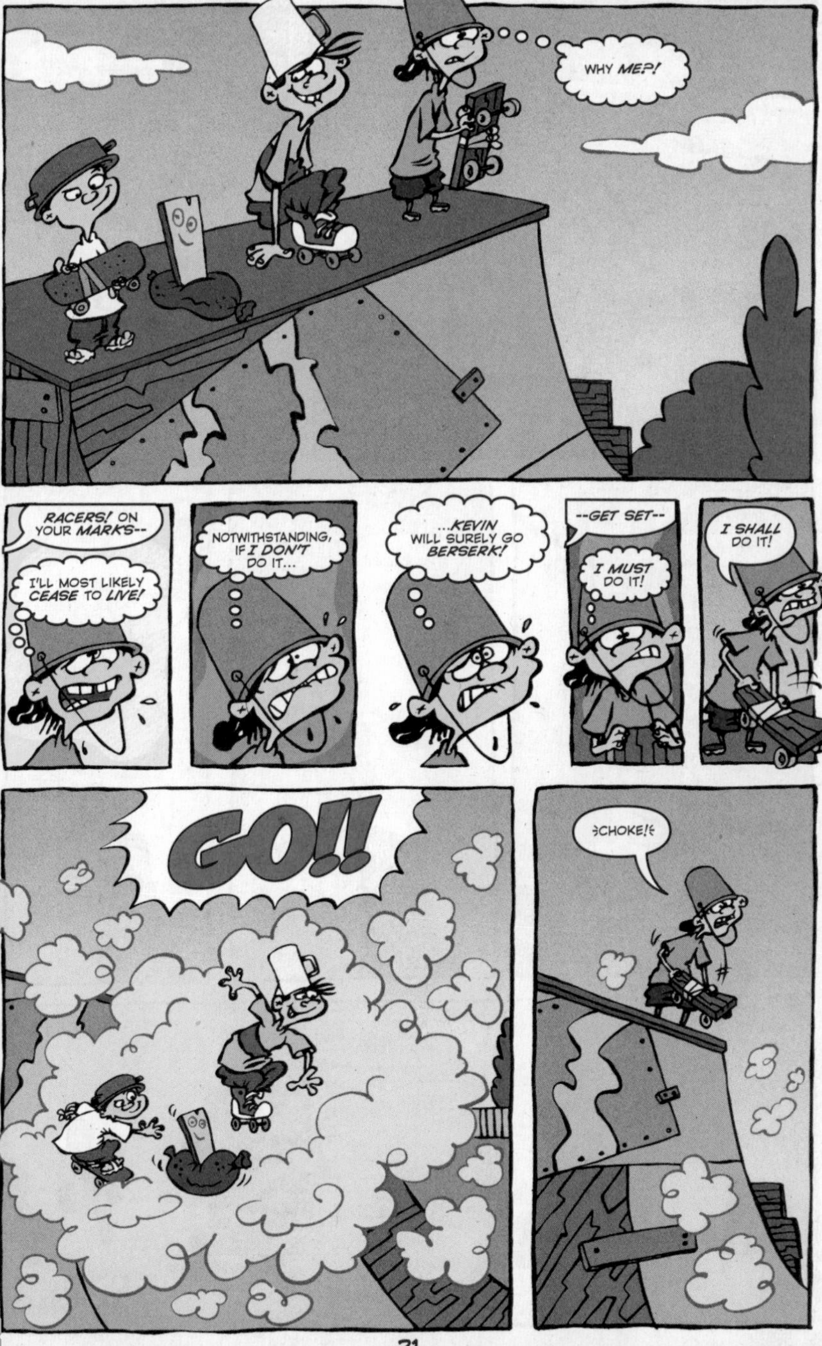
WHY ME?!
RACERS! ON YOUR MARKS--
I'LL MOST LIKELY CEASE TO LIVE!
NOTWITHSTANDING, IF I DON'T DO IT...
...KEVIN WILL SURELY GO BERSERK!
--GET SET--
I MUST DO IT!
I SHALL DO IT!
GO!!
CHOKE!

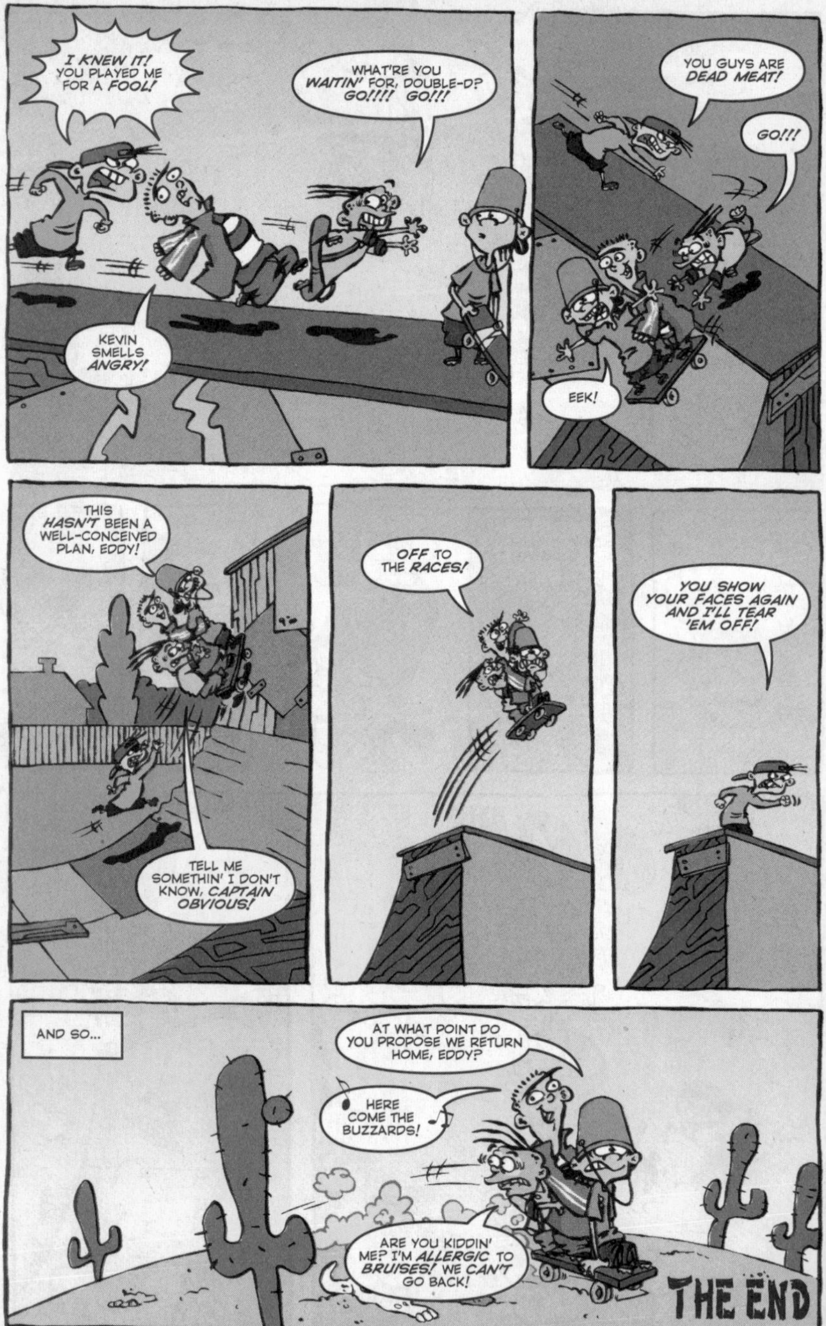
I KNEW IT! YOU PLAYED ME FOR A FOOL!
WHAT'RE YOU WAITIN' FOR, DOUBLE-D? GO!!!! GO!!!
KEVIN SMELLS ANGRY!
YOU GUYS ARE DEAD MEAT!
GO!!!
EEK!
THIS HASN'T BEEN A WELL-CONCEIVED PLAN, EDDY!
TELL ME SOMETHIN' I DON'T KNOW, CAPTAIN OBVIOUS!
OFF TO THE RACES!
YOU SHOW YOUR FACES AGAIN AND I'LL TEAR 'EM OFF!
AND SO...
AT WHAT POINT DO YOU PROPOSE WE RETURN HOME, EDDY?
HERE COME THE BUZZARDS!
ARE YOU KIDDIN' ME? I'M ALLERGIC TO BRUISES! WE CAN'T GO BACK!
THE END

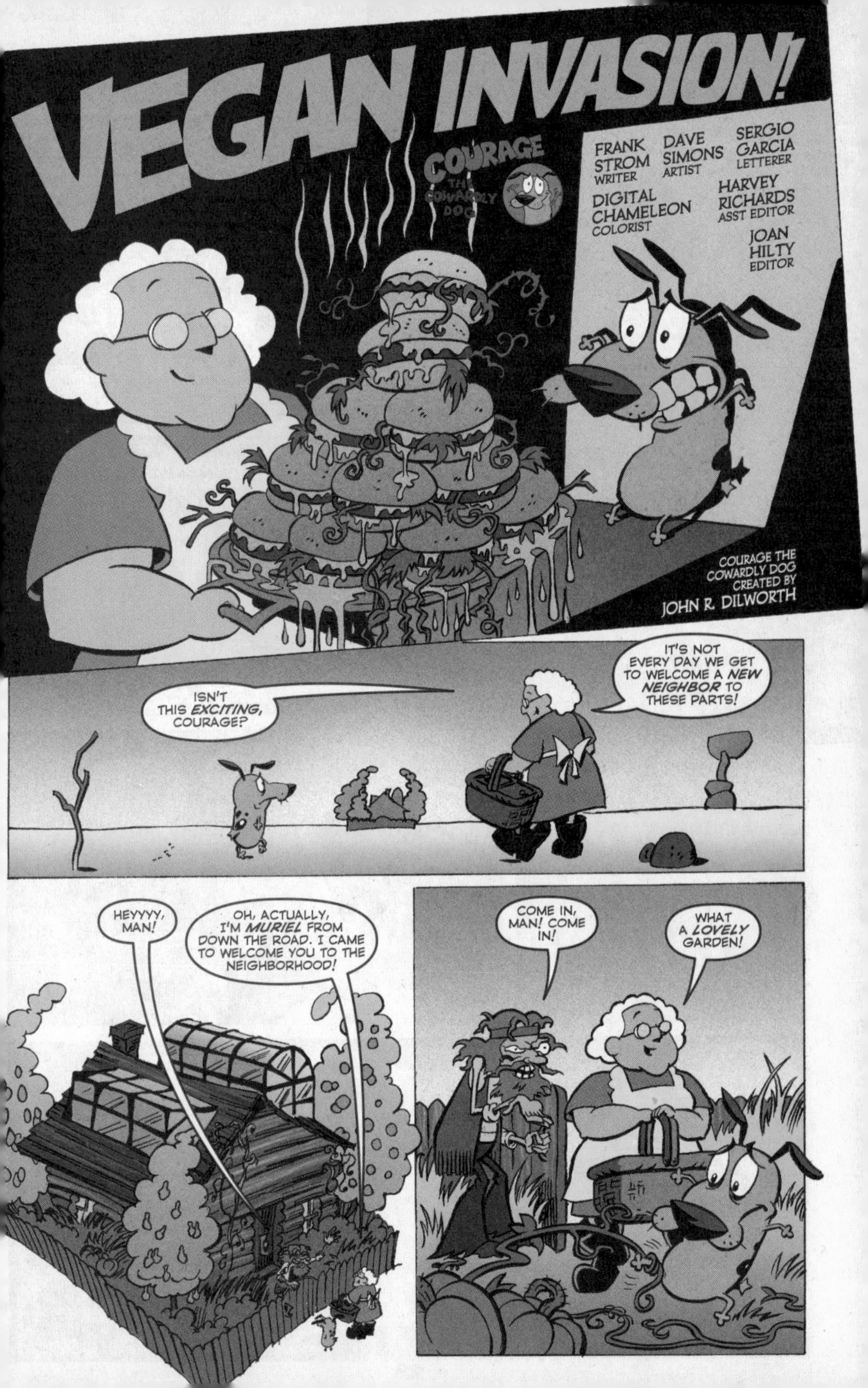
VEGAN INVASION!
COURAGE THE COWARDLY DOG
FRANK STROM WRITER
DAVE SIMONS ARTIST
SERGIO GARCIA LETTERER
DIGITAL CHAMELEON COLORIST
HARVEY RICHARDS ASST EDITOR
JOAN HILTY EDITOR
COURAGE THE COWARDLY DOG CREATED BY JOHN R. DILWORTH
ISN'T THIS EXCITING, COURAGE?
IT'S NOT EVERY DAY WE GET TO WELCOME A NEW NEIGHBOR TO THESE PARTS!
HEYYYY, MAN!
OH, ACTUALLY, I'M MURIEL FROM DOWN THE ROAD. I CAME TO WELCOME YOU TO THE NEIGHBORHOOD!
COME IN, MAN! COME IN!
WHAT A LOVELY GARDEN!

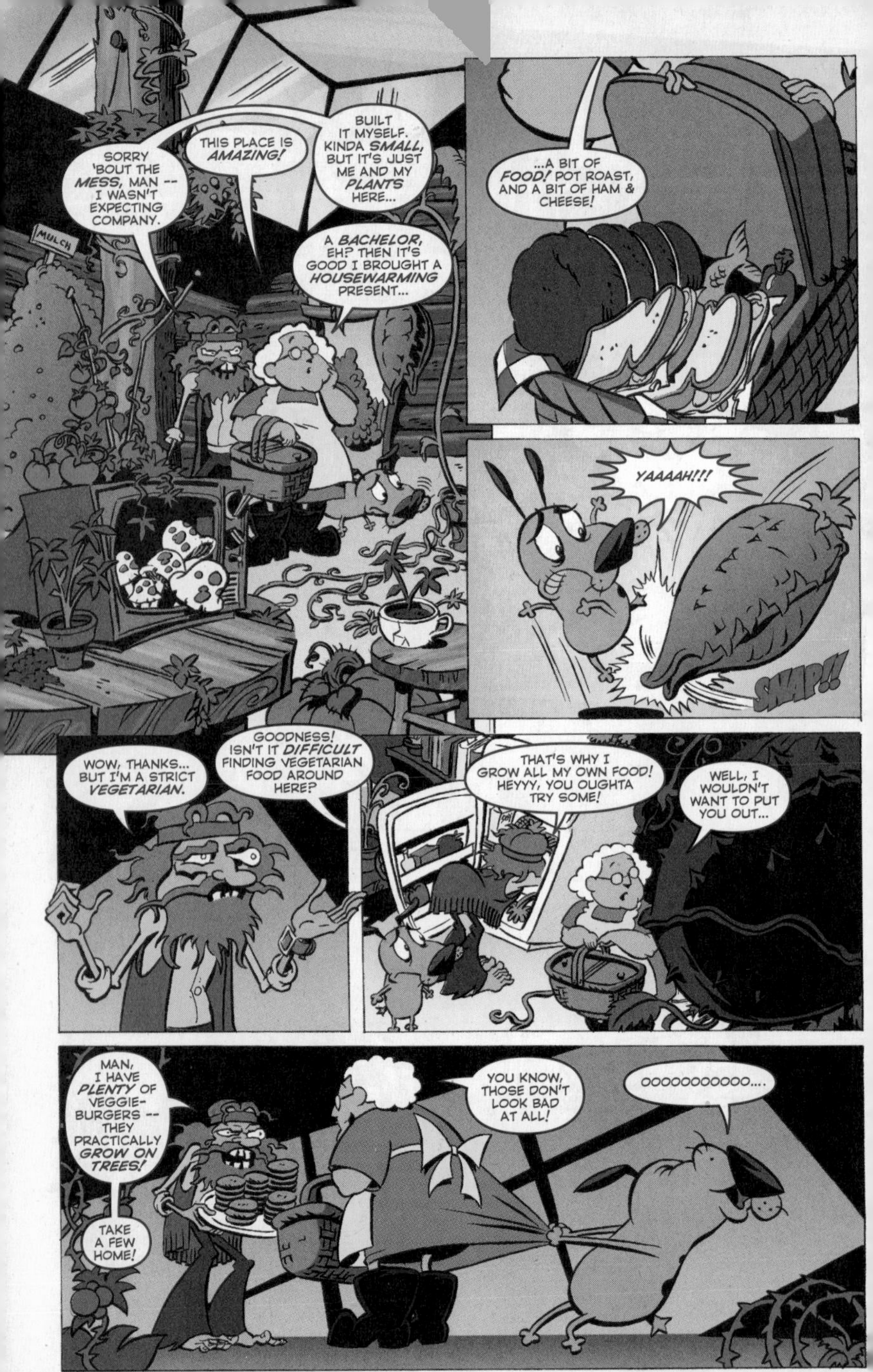
SORRY 'BOUT THE MESS, MAN -- I WASN'T EXPECTING COMPANY.
THIS PLACE IS AMAZING!
BUILT IT MYSELF. KINDA SMALL, BUT IT'S JUST ME AND MY PLANTS HERE...
A BACHELOR, EH? THEN IT'S GOOD I BROUGHT A HOUSEWARMING PRESENT...
MULCH
...A BIT OF FOOD! POT ROAST, AND A BIT OF HAM & CHEESE!
YAAAAH!!!
SNAP!!
WOW, THANKS... BUT I'M A STRICT VEGETARIAN.
GOODNESS! ISN'T IT DIFFICULT FINDING VEGETARIAN FOOD AROUND HERE?
THAT'S WHY I GROW ALL MY OWN FOOD! HEYYY, YOU OUGHTA TRY SOME!
WELL, I WOULDN'T WANT TO PUT YOU OUT...
MAN, I HAVE PLENTY OF VEGGIE-BURGERS -- THEY PRACTICALLY GROW ON TREES!
TAKE A FEW HOME!
YOU KNOW, THOSE DON'T LOOK BAD AT ALL!
OOOOOOOOOOO....

MMM! SOMETHIN' SURE SMELLS *GOOD!*

WHAT'S COOKIN'?

IT'S A TASTY TREAT FROM THAT NICE *VEGETARIAN* FELLOW WHO JUST MOVED IN DOWN THE ROAD!

VEGGIE-BURGERS?!? I AIN'T EATIN' *THOSE!*

WHY NOT? YOU JUST SAID THEY SMELLED GOOD!

SMELLIN' AND *TASTIN'* IS TWO DIFFERENT THINGS! GOLDURN THINGS PROBABLY TASTE LIKE *SWAMP MOSS!*

I THINK IT'S HIGH TIME WE STARTED EATING A *HEALTHY DIET,* EUSTACE!

MMMMMM!

ARR RRA ROOO!!!

GRUMMBBLE... GRUMMBBLE...

I DON'T *TRUST* 'EM! AIN'T NO TELLIN' *WHAT* THEY PUT IN THESE THINGS!

WELL, THERE'S NO HARM IN TRYING THEM! ISN'T THAT RIGHT, *COURAGE?*

RRA RRRA ROOO!!!

MUNCH... MUNCH... YOU SEE? THEY'RE *DELICIOUS!* THEY'RE... THEY'RE...

...MIND-NUMBING!

...MUST COOK...MORE... BURGERS...!

ROOP!?

ER...WE'RE OUTTA BUNS! I'LL GO GET SOME FROM TH' *CELLAR!*

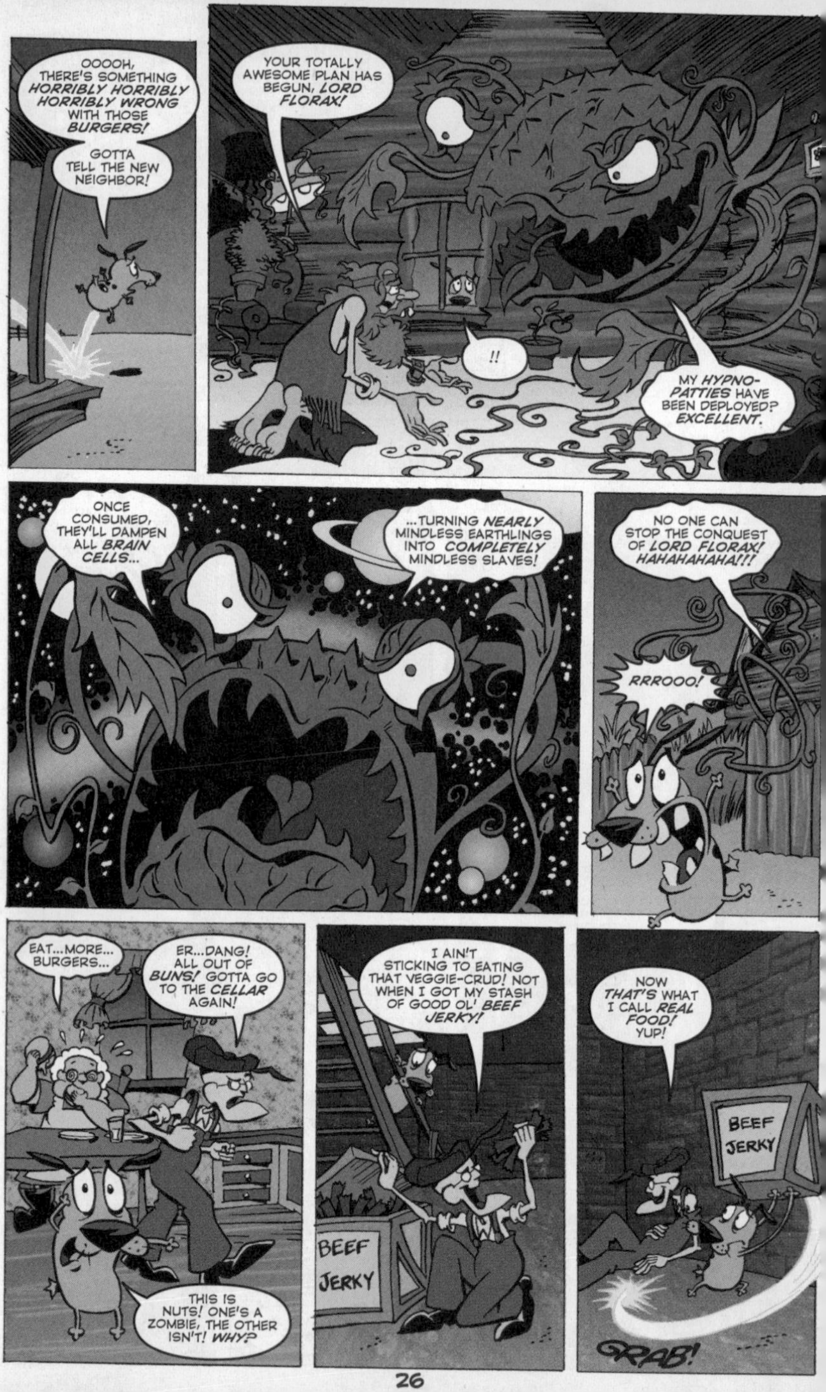
OOOOH, THERE'S SOMETHING HORRIBLY HORRIBLY HORRIBLY WRONG WITH THOSE BURGERS!
GOTTA TELL THE NEW NEIGHBOR!
YOUR TOTALLY AWESOME PLAN HAS BEGUN, LORD FLORAX!
!!
MY HYPNO-PATTIES HAVE BEEN DEPLOYED? EXCELLENT.
ONCE CONSUMED, THEY'LL DAMPEN ALL BRAIN CELLS...
...TURNING NEARLY MINDLESS EARTHLINGS INTO COMPLETELY MINDLESS SLAVES!
NO ONE CAN STOP THE CONQUEST OF LORD FLORAX! HAHAHAHAHA!!!
RRROOO!
EAT...MORE... BURGERS...
ER...DANG! ALL OUT OF BUNS! GOTTA GO TO THE CELLAR AGAIN!
THIS IS NUTS! ONE'S A ZOMBIE, THE OTHER ISN'T! WHY?
I AIN'T STICKING TO EATING THAT VEGGIE-CRUD! NOT WHEN I GOT MY STASH OF GOOD OL' BEEF JERKY!
BEEF JERKY
NOW THAT'S WHAT I CALL REAL FOOD! YUP!
BEEF JERKY
GRAB!

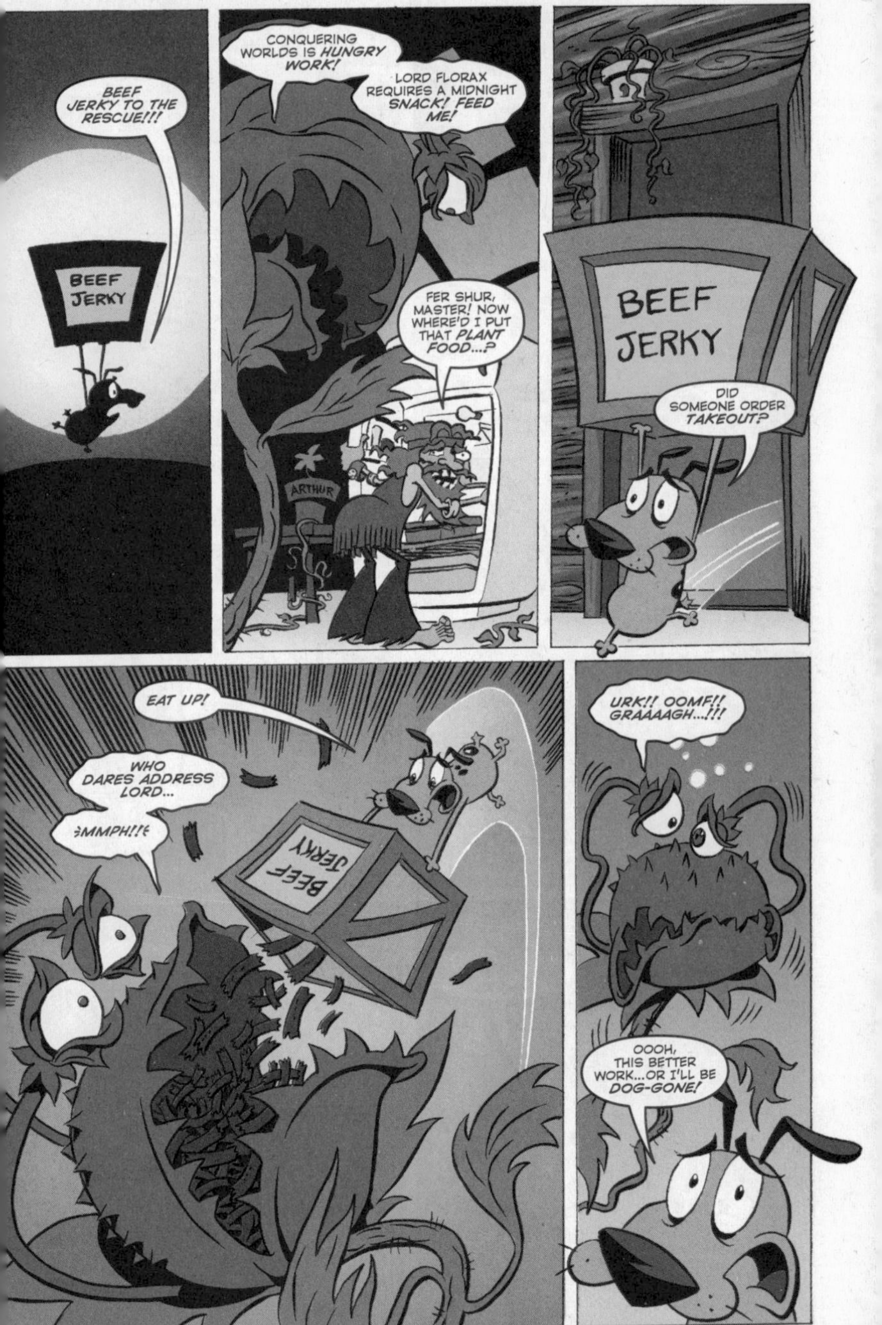
BEEF JERKY TO THE RESCUE!!!
BEEF JERKY
CONQUERING WORLDS IS HUNGRY WORK!
LORD FLORAX REQUIRES A MIDNIGHT SNACK! FEED ME!
FER SHUR, MASTER! NOW WHERE'D I PUT THAT PLANT FOOD...?
ARTHUR
BEEF JERKY
DID SOMEONE ORDER TAKEOUT?
EAT UP!
WHO DARES ADDRESS LORD...
MMPH!!
BEEF JERKY
URK!! OOMF!! GRAAAAGH...!!!
OOOH, THIS BETTER WORK...OR I'LL BE DOG-GONE!

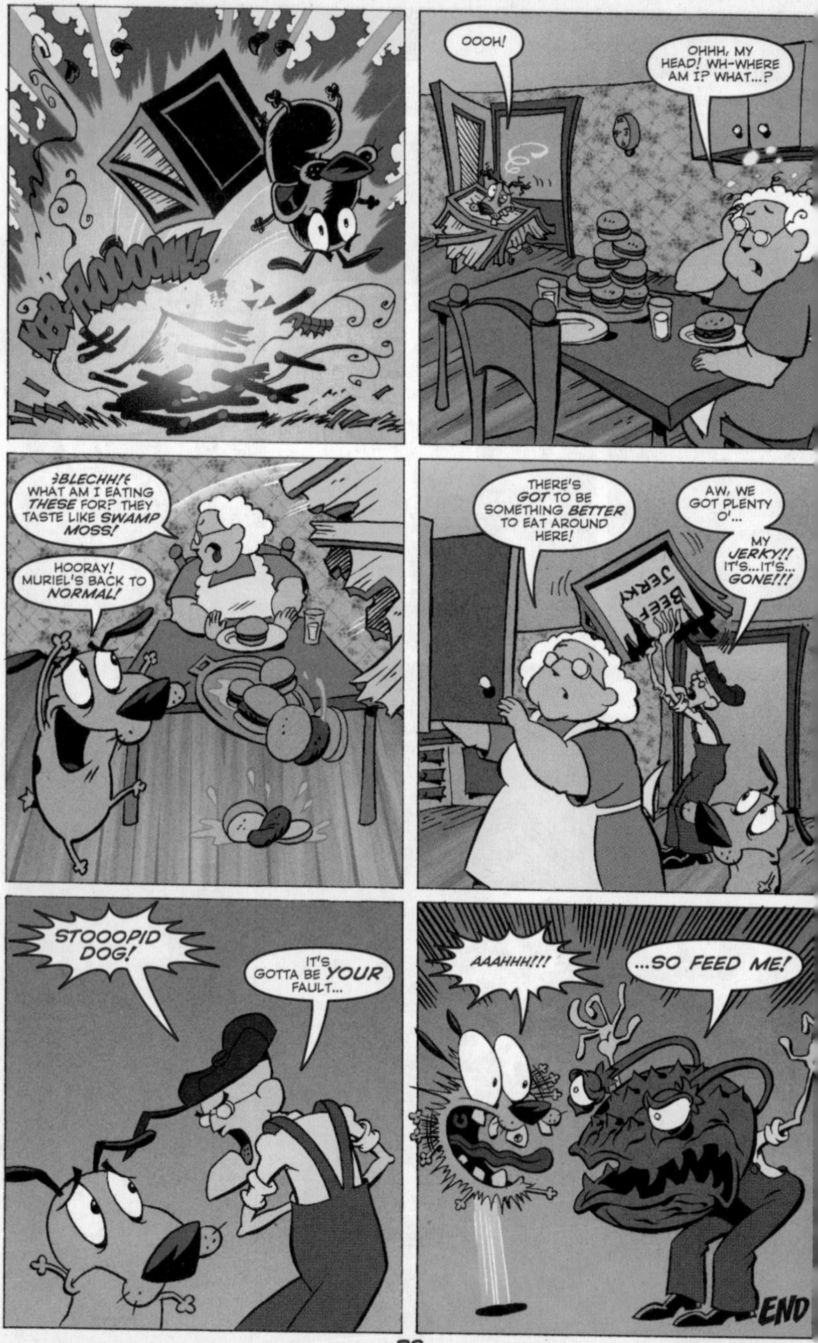
KA-FLOOOOM!!
OOOH!
OHHH, MY HEAD! WH-WHERE AM I? WHAT...?
BLECHH!
WHAT AM I EATING THESE FOR? THEY TASTE LIKE SWAMP MOSS!
HOORAY! MURIEL'S BACK TO NORMAL!
THERE'S GOT TO BE SOMETHING BETTER TO EAT AROUND HERE!
AW, WE GOT PLENTY O'...
BEEF JERKY
MY JERKY!! IT'S...IT'S... GONE!!!
STOOOPID DOG!
IT'S GOTTA BE YOUR FAULT...
AAAHHH!!!
...SO FEED ME!
END

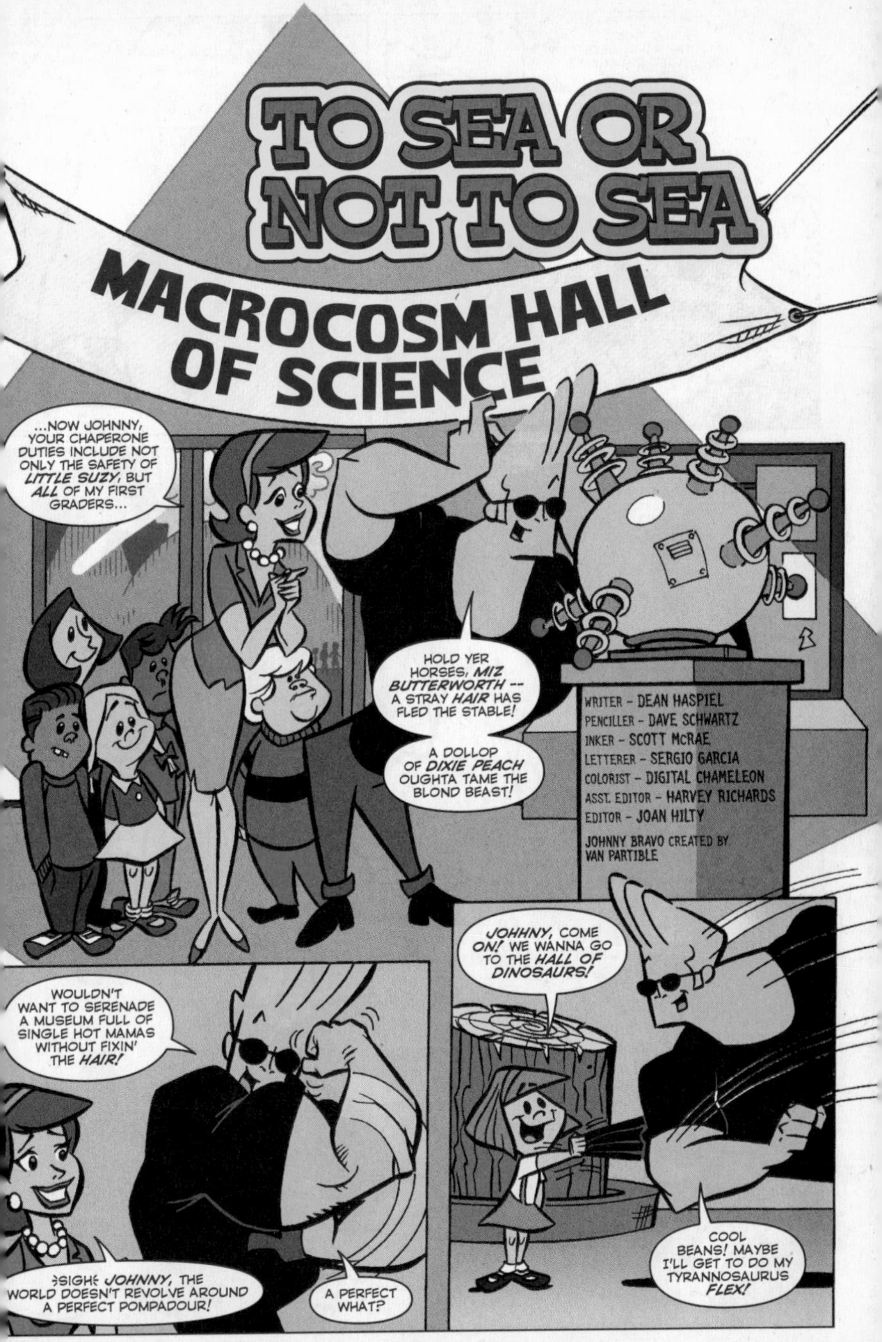
TO SEA OR NOT TO SEA
MACROCOSM HALL OF SCIENCE
...NOW JOHNNY, YOUR CHAPERONE DUTIES INCLUDE NOT ONLY THE SAFETY OF LITTLE SUZY, BUT ALL OF MY FIRST GRADERS...
HOLD YER HORSES, MIZ BUTTERWORTH -- A STRAY HAIR HAS FLED THE STABLE!
A DOLLOP OF DIXIE PEACH OUGHTA TAME THE BLOND BEAST!
WRITER - DEAN HASPIEL
PENCILLER - DAVE SCHWARTZ
INKER - SCOTT McRAE
LETTERER - SERGIO GARCIA
COLORIST - DIGITAL CHAMELEON
ASST. EDITOR - HARVEY RICHARDS
EDITOR - JOAN HILTY
JOHNNY BRAVO CREATED BY VAN PARTIBLE
WOULDN'T WANT TO SERENADE A MUSEUM FULL OF SINGLE HOT MAMAS WITHOUT FIXIN' THE HAIR!
SIGH JOHNNY, THE WORLD DOESN'T REVOLVE AROUND A PERFECT POMPADOUR!
A PERFECT WHAT?
JOHNNY, COME ON! WE WANNA GO TO THE HALL OF DINOSAURS!
COOL BEANS! MAYBE I'LL GET TO DO MY TYRANNOSAURUS FLEX!

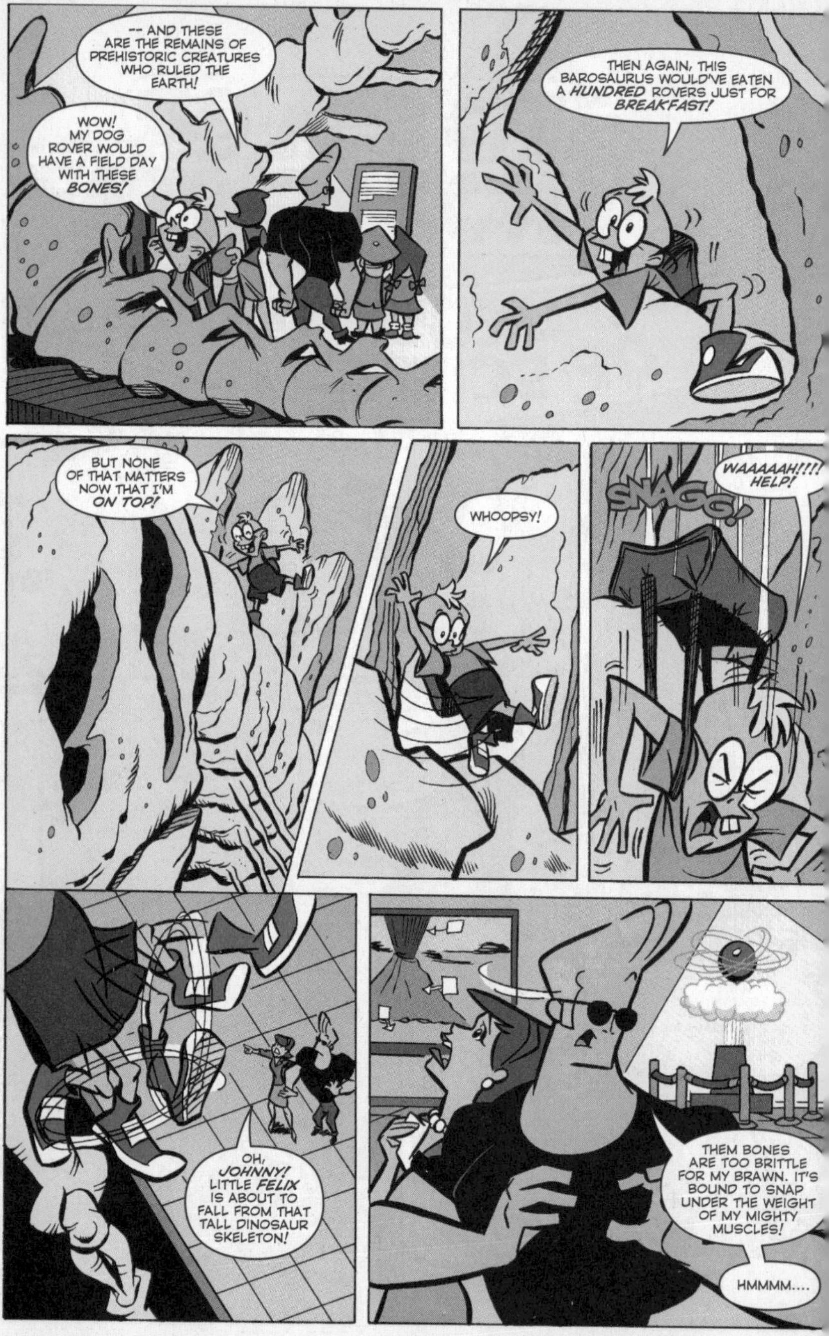
-- AND THESE ARE THE REMAINS OF PREHISTORIC CREATURES WHO RULED THE EARTH!
WOW! MY DOG ROVER WOULD HAVE A FIELD DAY WITH THESE BONES!
THEN AGAIN, THIS BAROSAURUS WOULD'VE EATEN A HUNDRED ROVERS JUST FOR BREAKFAST!
BUT NONE OF THAT MATTERS NOW THAT I'M ON TOP!
WHOOPSY!
SNAGG!
WAAAAAH!!!! HELP!
OH, JOHNNY! LITTLE FELIX IS ABOUT TO FALL FROM THAT TALL DINOSAUR SKELETON!
THEM BONES ARE TOO BRITTLE FOR MY BRAWN. IT'S BOUND TO SNAP UNDER THE WEIGHT OF MY MIGHTY MUSCLES!
HMMMM....

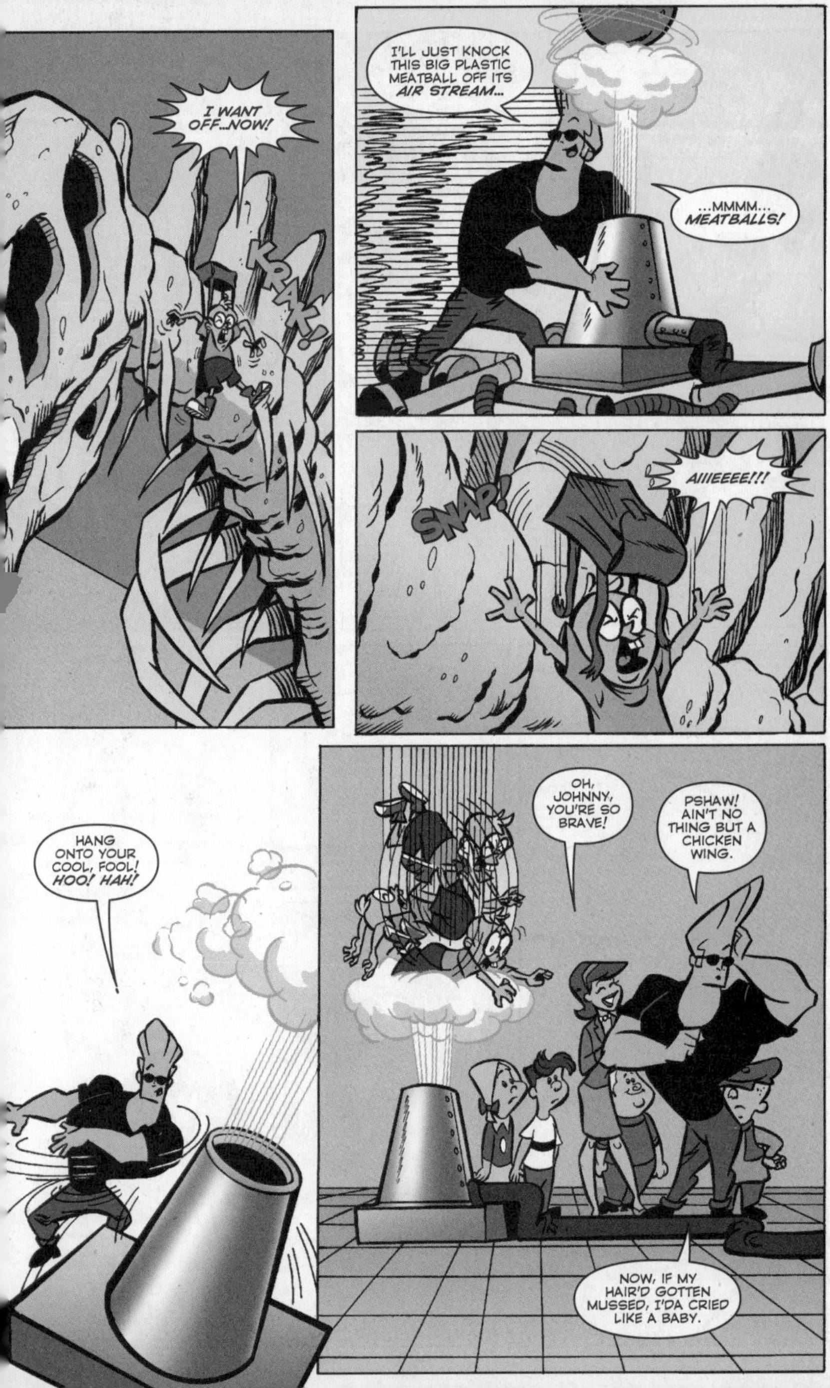
I WANT OFF...NOW!
KRAK!
I'LL JUST KNOCK THIS BIG PLASTIC MEATBALL OFF ITS AIR STREAM...
...MMMM... MEATBALLS!
SNAP!
AIIEEEE!!!
HANG ONTO YOUR COOL, FOOL! HOO! HAH!
OH, JOHNNY, YOU'RE SO BRAVE!
PSHAW! AIN'T NO THING BUT A CHICKEN WING.
NOW, IF MY HAIR'D GOTTEN MUSSED, I'DA CRIED LIKE A BABY.

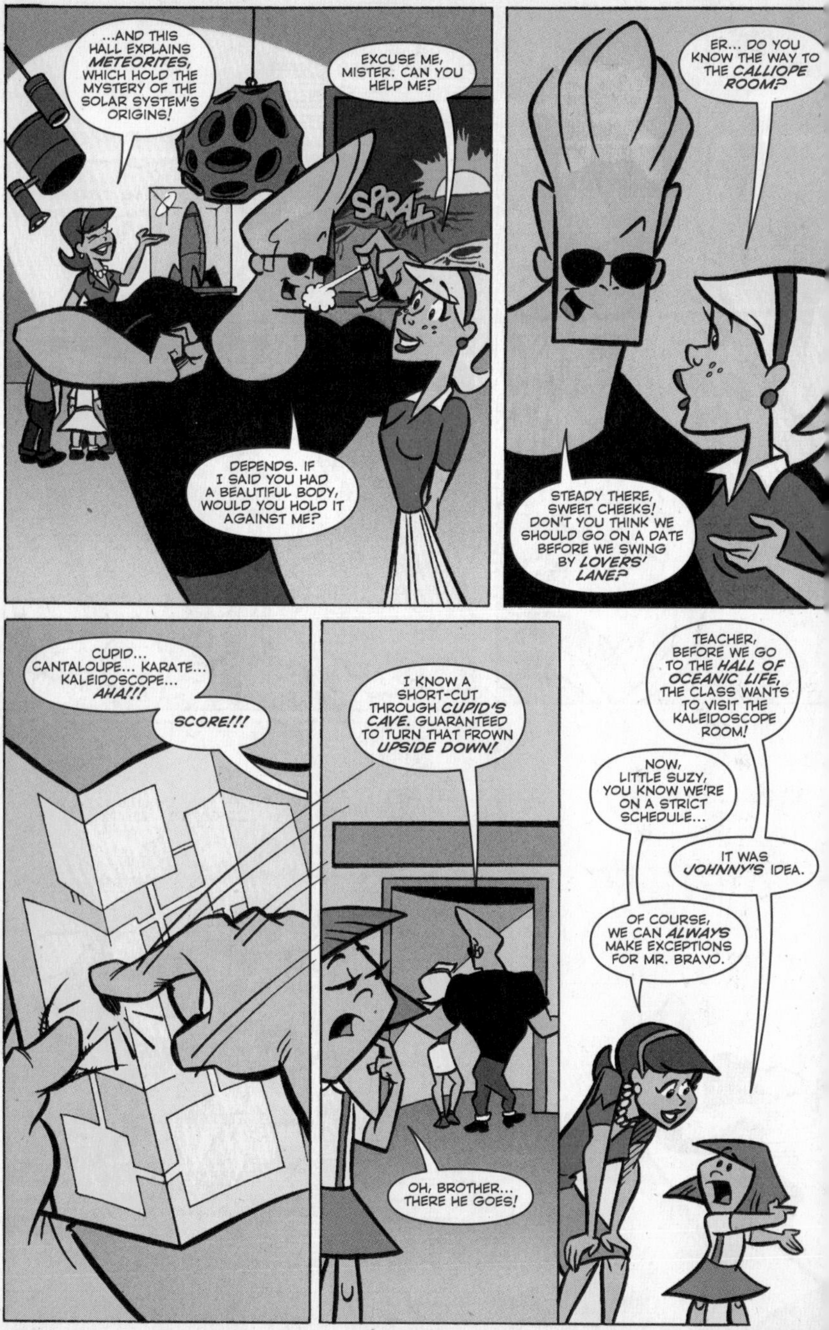
...AND THIS HALL EXPLAINS *METEORITES,* WHICH HOLD THE MYSTERY OF THE SOLAR SYSTEM'S ORIGINS!
EXCUSE ME, MISTER. CAN YOU HELP ME?
SPRAY
DEPENDS. IF I SAID YOU HAD A BEAUTIFUL BODY, WOULD YOU HOLD IT AGAINST ME?
ER... DO YOU KNOW THE WAY TO THE *CALLIOPE ROOM?*
STEADY THERE, SWEET CHEEKS! DON'T YOU THINK WE SHOULD GO ON A DATE BEFORE WE SWING BY *LOVERS' LANE?*
CUPID... CANTALOUPE... KARATE... KALEIDOSCOPE... *AHA!!!*
SCORE!!!
I KNOW A SHORT-CUT THROUGH *CUPID'S CAVE.* GUARANTEED TO TURN THAT FROWN *UPSIDE DOWN!*
OH, BROTHER... THERE HE GOES!
TEACHER, BEFORE WE GO TO THE *HALL OF OCEANIC LIFE,* THE CLASS WANTS TO VISIT THE KALEIDOSCOPE ROOM!
NOW, LITTLE SUZY, YOU KNOW WE'RE ON A STRICT SCHEDULE...
IT WAS *JOHNNY'S* IDEA.
OF COURSE, WE CAN *ALWAYS* MAKE EXCEPTIONS FOR MR. BRAVO.

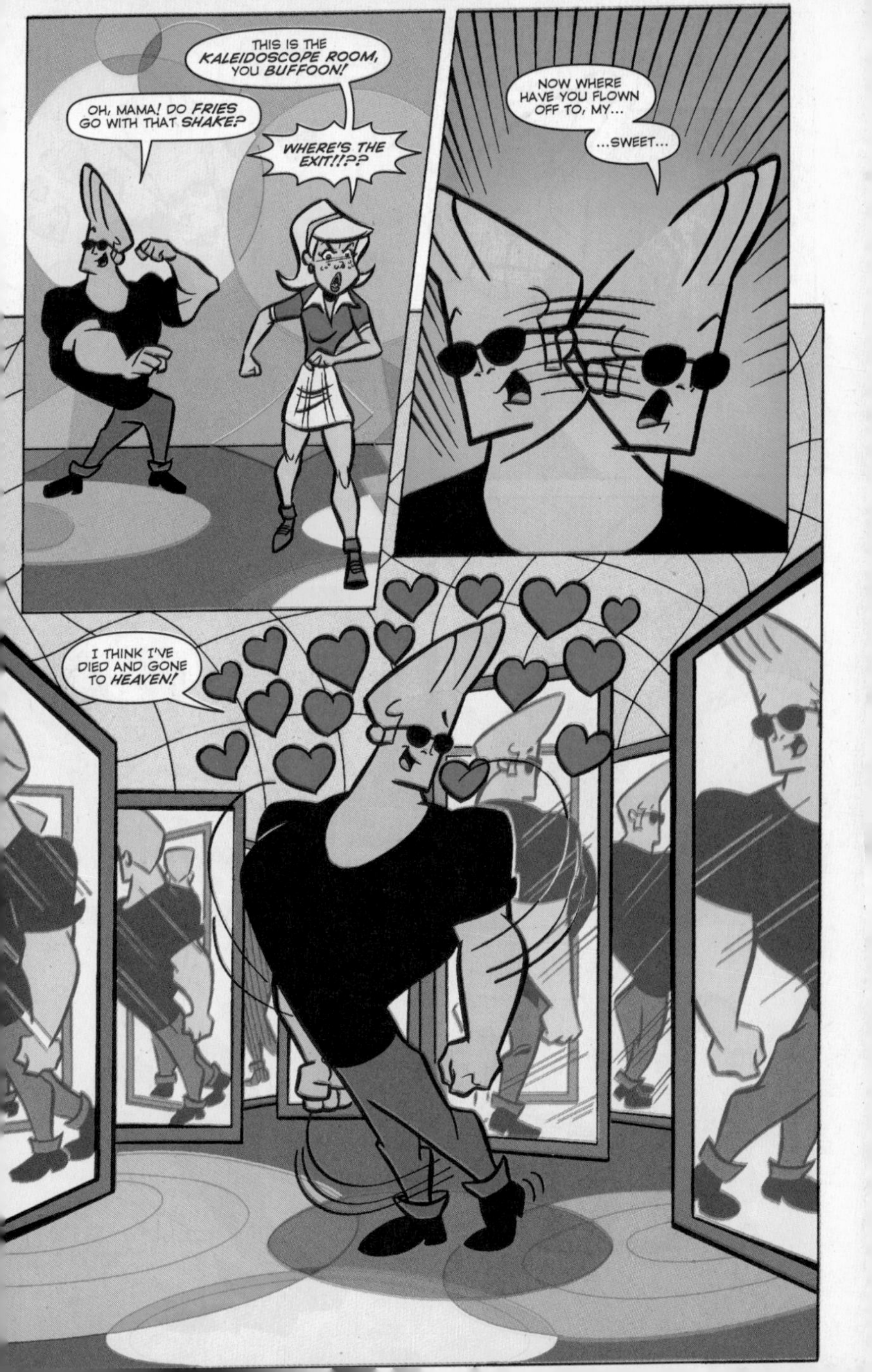

OH, MAMA! DO FRIES GO WITH THAT SHAKE?
THIS IS THE KALEIDOSCOPE ROOM, YOU BUFFOON!
WHERE'S THE EXIT!!??
NOW WHERE HAVE YOU FLOWN OFF TO, MY...
...SWEET...
I THINK I'VE DIED AND GONE TO HEAVEN!

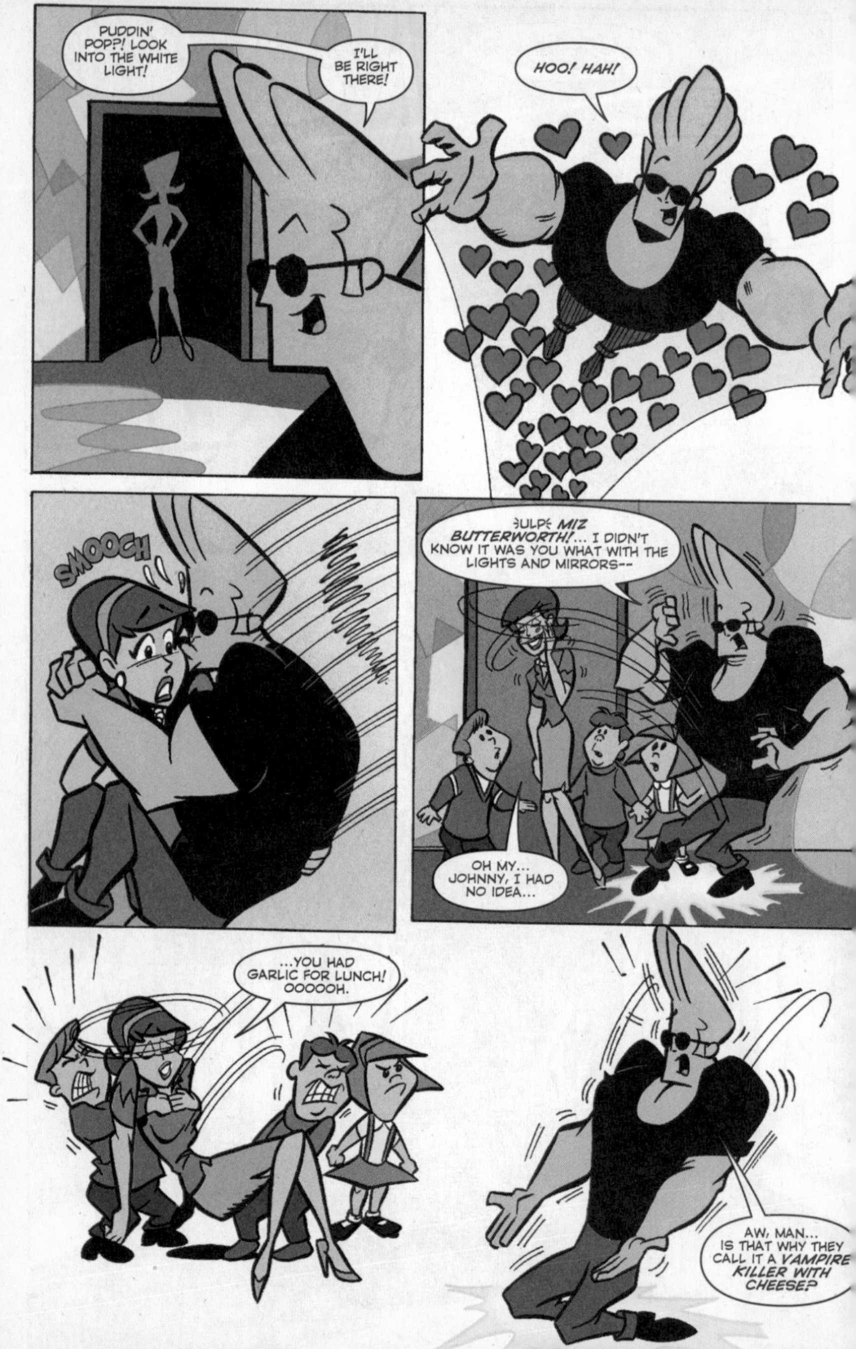
PUDDIN' POP?! LOOK INTO THE WHITE LIGHT!
I'LL BE RIGHT THERE!
HOO! HAH!
SMOOCH
GULP MIZ BUTTERWORTH!... I DIDN'T KNOW IT WAS YOU WHAT WITH THE LIGHTS AND MIRRORS--
OH MY... JOHNNY, I HAD NO IDEA...
...YOU HAD GARLIC FOR LUNCH! OOOOOH.
AW, MAN... IS THAT WHY THEY CALL IT A VAMPIRE KILLER WITH CHEESE?

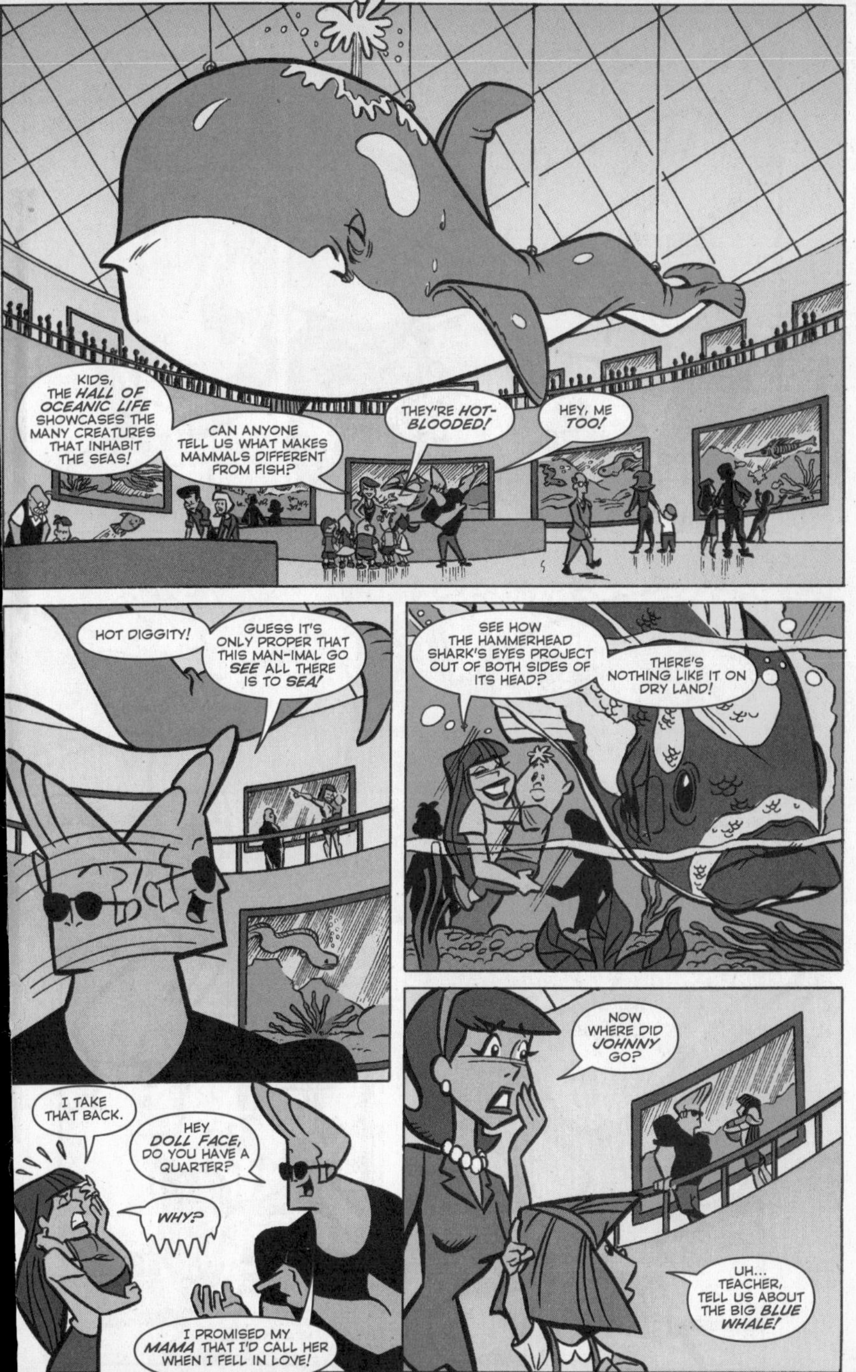
KIDS, THE HALL OF OCEANIC LIFE SHOWCASES THE MANY CREATURES THAT INHABIT THE SEAS!
CAN ANYONE TELL US WHAT MAKES MAMMALS DIFFERENT FROM FISH?
THEY'RE HOT-BLOODED!
HEY, ME TOO!
HOT DIGGITY!
GUESS IT'S ONLY PROPER THAT THIS MAN-IMAL GO SEE ALL THERE IS TO SEA!
SEE HOW THE HAMMERHEAD SHARK'S EYES PROJECT OUT OF BOTH SIDES OF ITS HEAD?
THERE'S NOTHING LIKE IT ON DRY LAND!
I TAKE THAT BACK.
HEY DOLL FACE, DO YOU HAVE A QUARTER?
WHY?
I PROMISED MY MAMA THAT I'D CALL HER WHEN I FELL IN LOVE!
NOW WHERE DID JOHNNY GO?
UH... TEACHER, TELL US ABOUT THE BIG BLUE WHALE!

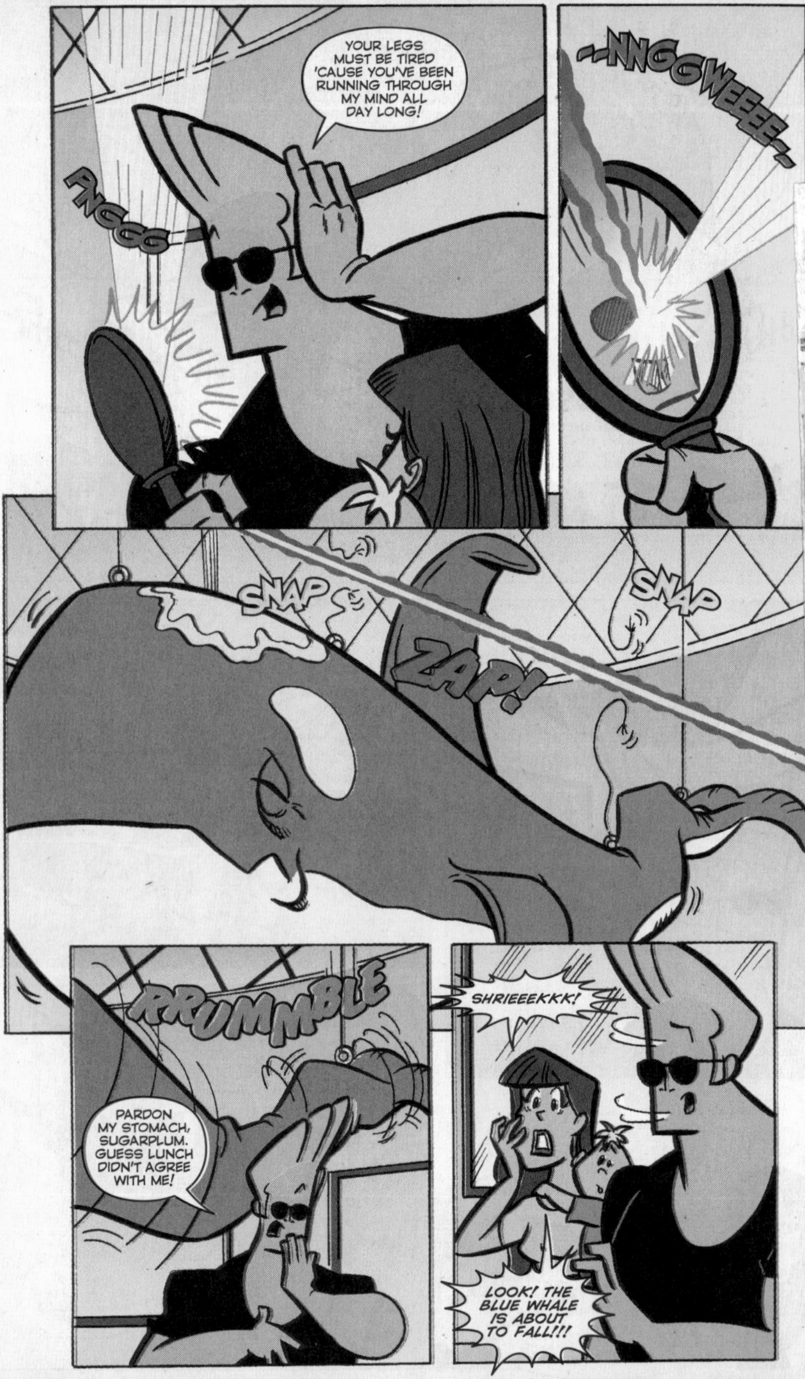
YOUR LEGS MUST BE TIRED 'CAUSE YOU'VE BEEN RUNNING THROUGH MY MIND ALL DAY LONG!
PNGGG
--NNGGWEEEEE--
SNAP
SNAP
ZAP!
PRUMMBLE
PARDON MY STOMACH, SUGARPLUM. GUESS LUNCH DIDN'T AGREE WITH ME!
SHRIEEEKKK!
LOOK! THE BLUE WHALE IS ABOUT TO FALL!!!

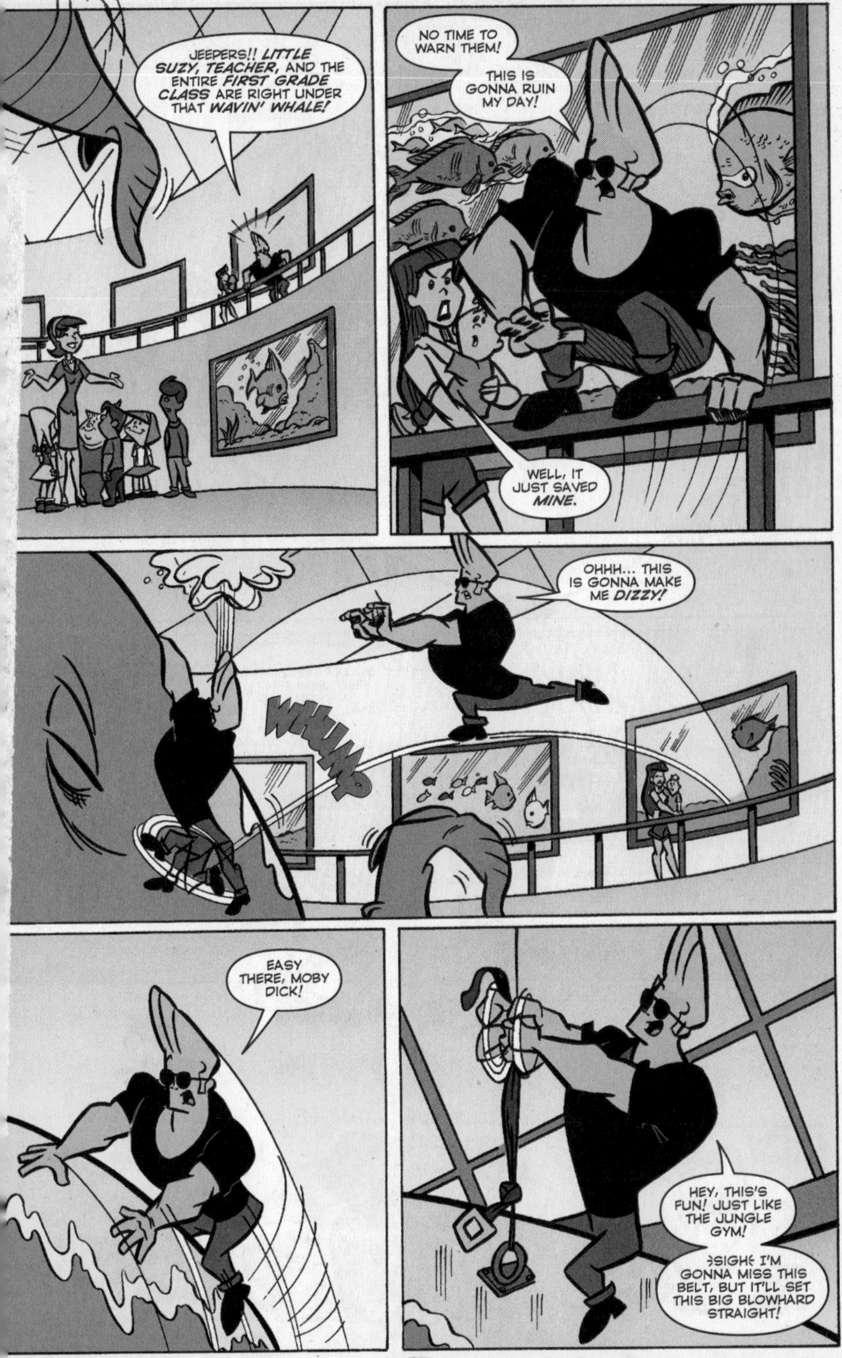
JEEPERS!! LITTLE SUZY, TEACHER, AND THE ENTIRE FIRST GRADE CLASS ARE RIGHT UNDER THAT WAVIN' WHALE!
NO TIME TO WARN THEM!
THIS IS GONNA RUIN MY DAY!
WELL, IT JUST SAVED MINE.
OHHH... THIS IS GONNA MAKE ME DIZZY!
WHUMP
EASY THERE, MOBY DICK!
HEY, THIS'S FUN! JUST LIKE THE JUNGLE GYM!
SIGH I'M GONNA MISS THIS BELT, BUT IT'LL SET THIS BIG BLOWHARD STRAIGHT!

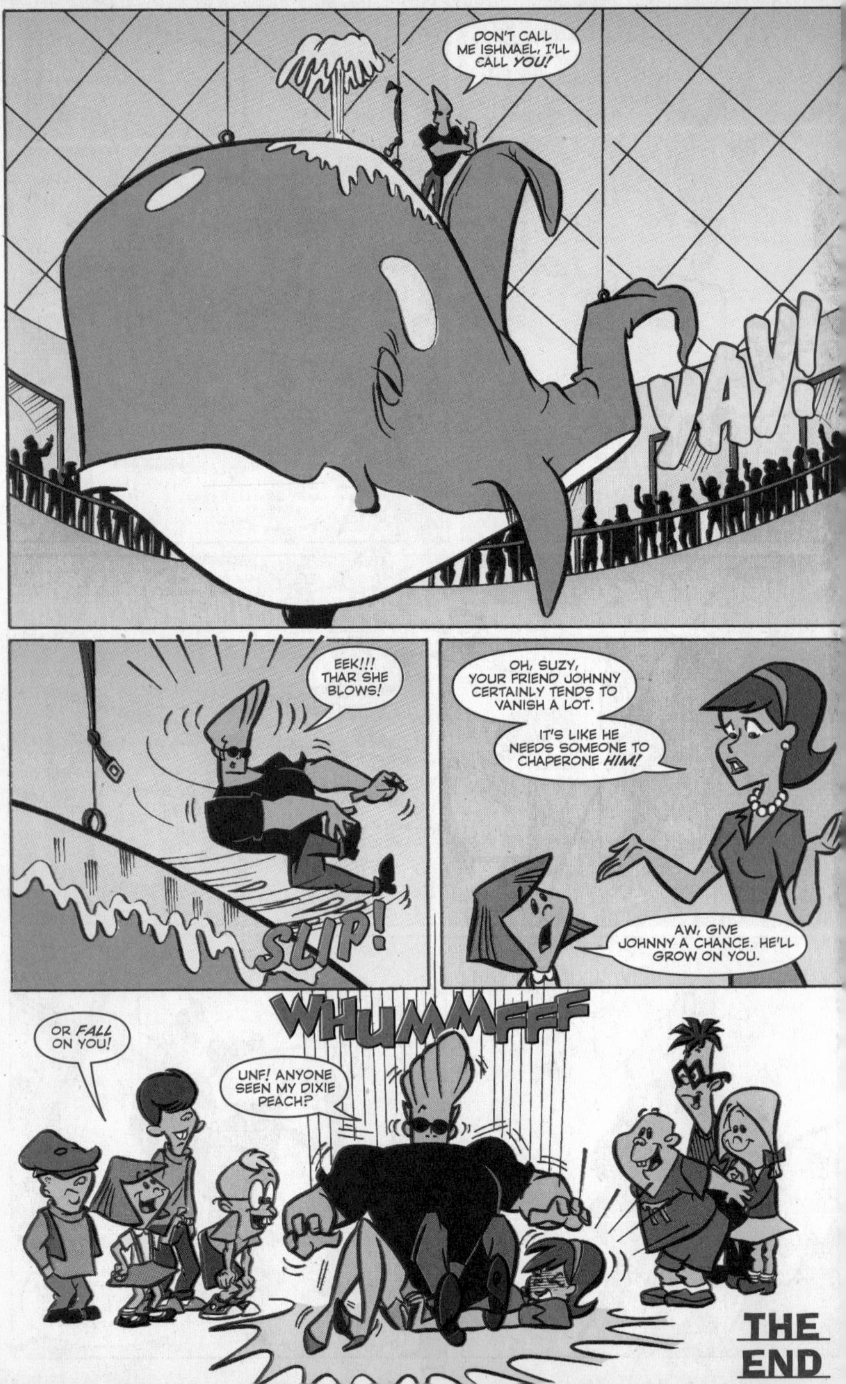
DON'T CALL ME ISHMAEL, I'LL CALL *YOU!*
YAY!
EEK!!! THAR SHE BLOWS!
SLIP!
OH, SUZY, YOUR FRIEND JOHNNY CERTAINLY TENDS TO VANISH A LOT.
IT'S LIKE HE NEEDS SOMEONE TO CHAPERONE *HIM!*
AW, GIVE JOHNNY A CHANCE. HE'LL GROW ON YOU.
WHUMMFFF
OR *FALL* ON YOU!
UNF! ANYONE SEEN MY DIXIE PEACH?
THE END

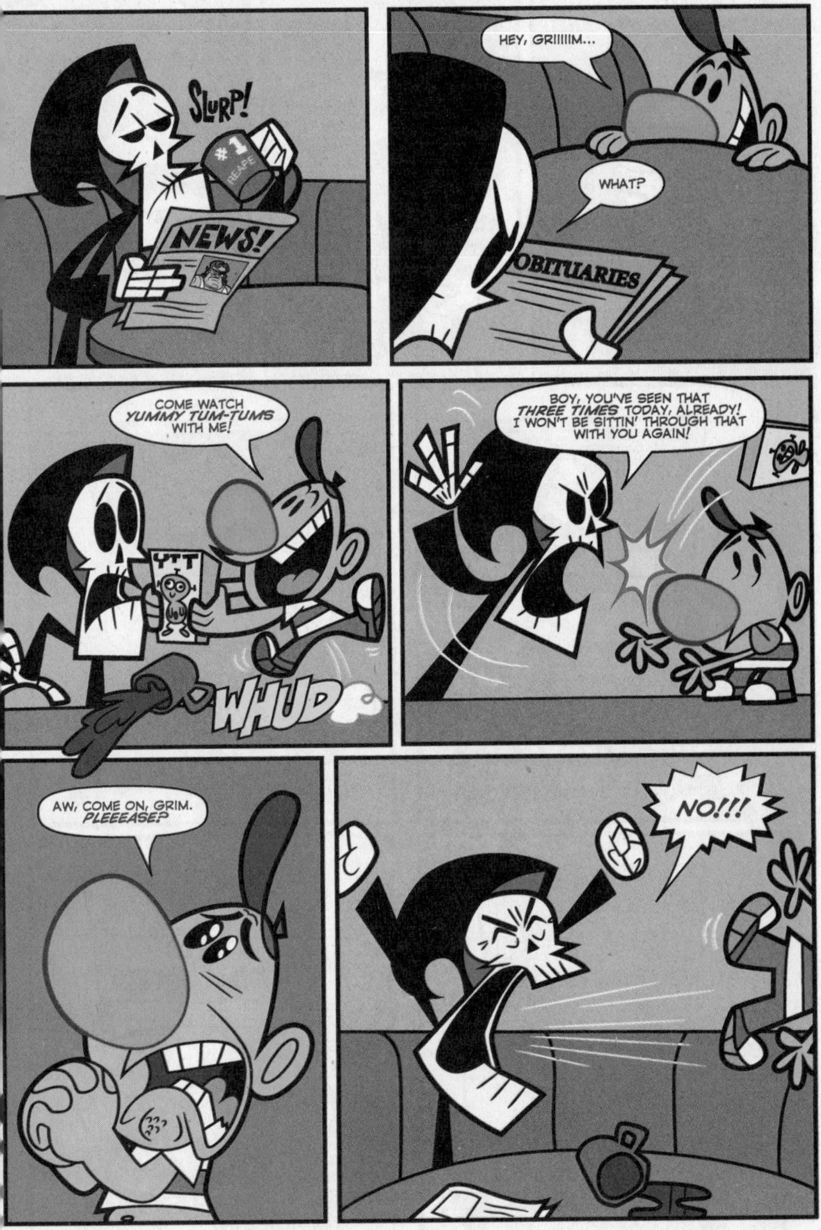

SLURP!
#1 REAPE
NEWS!
HEY, GRIIIIIM...
WHAT?
OBITUARIES
COME WATCH *YUMMY TUM-TUMS* WITH ME!
YTT
WHUD
BOY, YOU'VE SEEN THAT *THREE TIMES* TODAY, ALREADY! I WON'T BE SITTIN' THROUGH THAT WITH YOU AGAIN!
AW, COME ON, GRIM. *PLEEEASE?*
NO!!!

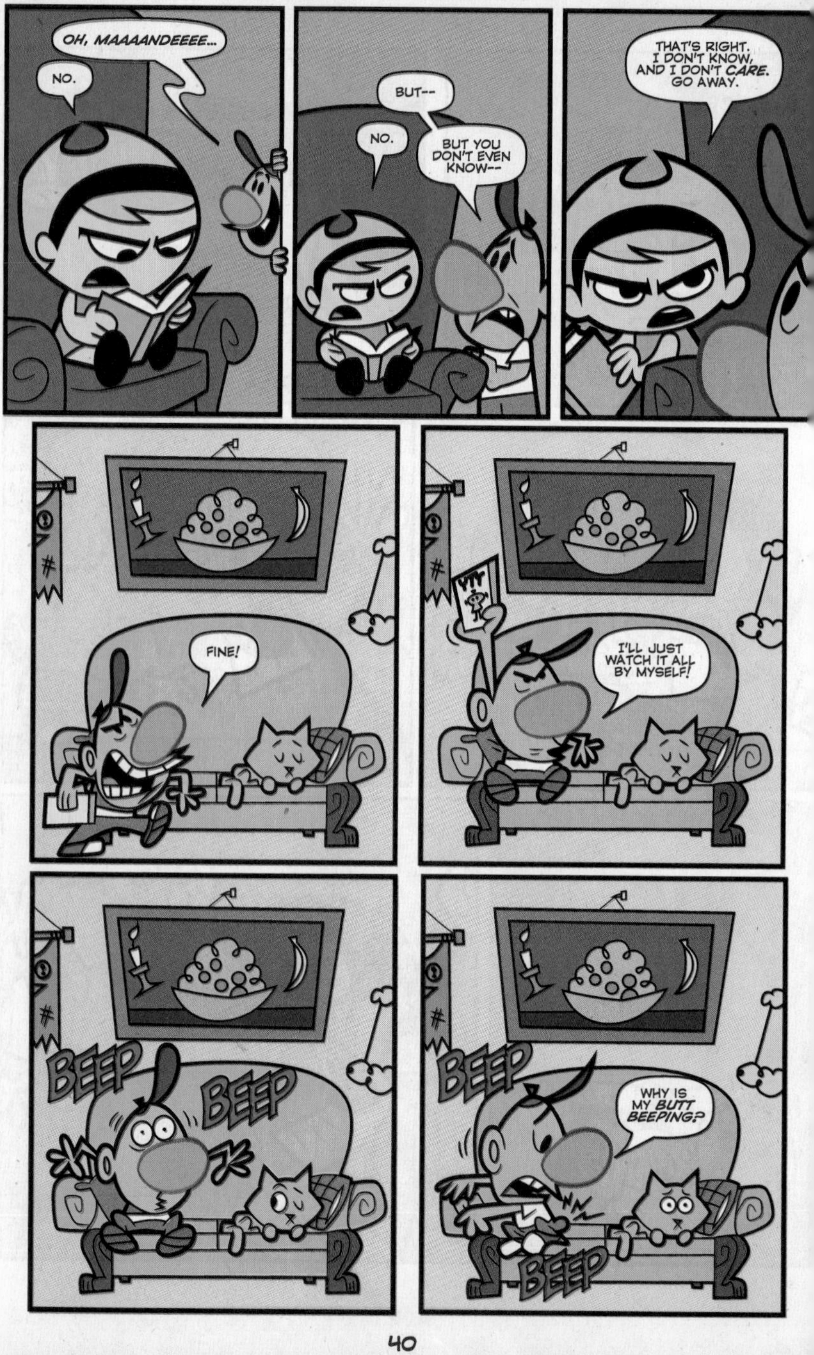
OH, MAAAANDEEEE...
NO.
BUT--
NO.
BUT YOU DON'T EVEN KNOW--
THAT'S RIGHT. I DON'T KNOW, AND I DON'T *CARE*. GO AWAY.
FINE!
I'LL JUST WATCH IT ALL BY MYSELF!
BEEP
BEEP
BEEP
WHY IS MY *BUTT* *BEEPING?*
BEEP

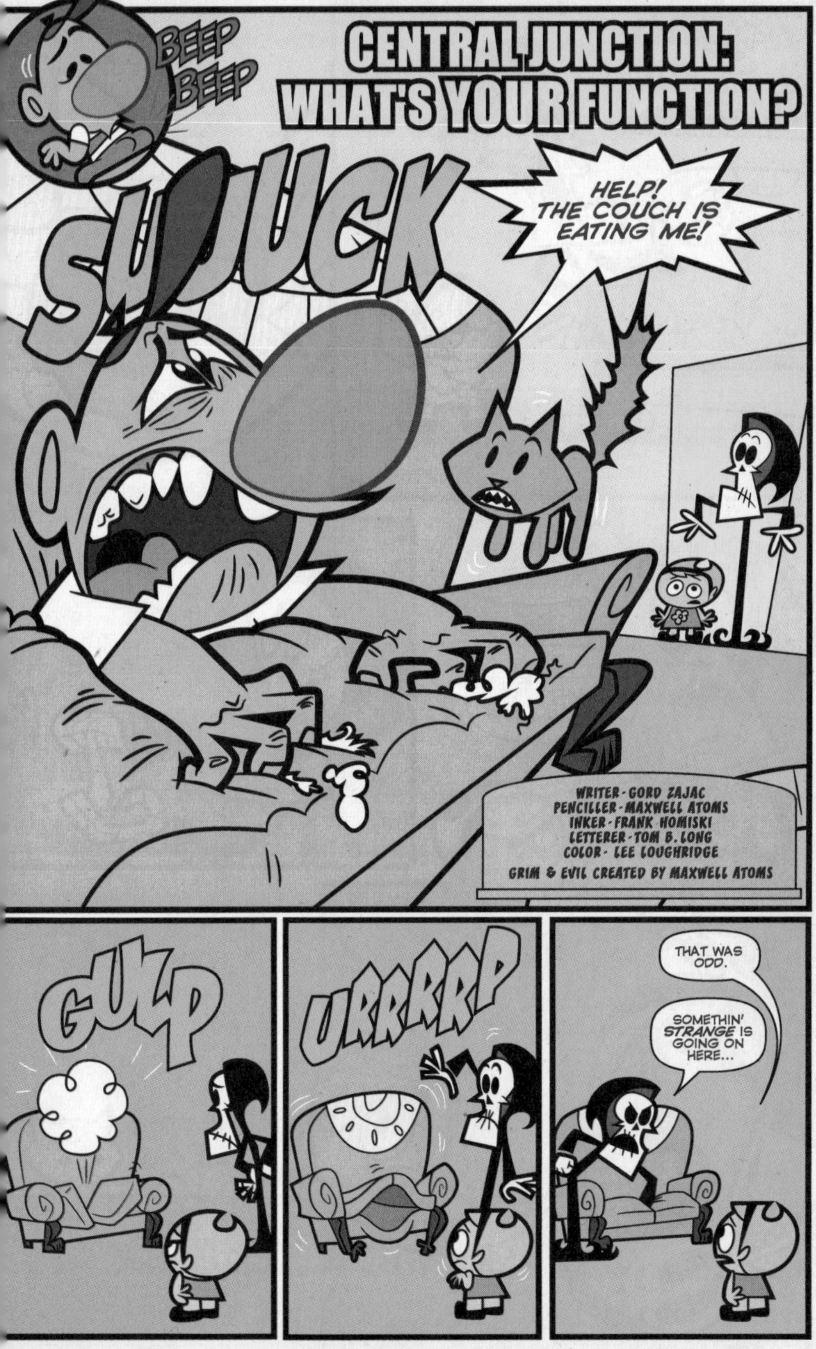
CENTRAL JUNCTION: WHAT'S YOUR FUNCTION?
BEEP BEEP
SUUCK
HELP! THE COUCH IS EATING ME!
WRITER - GORD ZAJAC
PENCILLER - MAXWELL ATOMS
INKER - FRANK HOMISKI
LETTERER - TOM B. LONG
COLOR - LEE LOUGHRIDGE
GRIM & EVIL CREATED BY MAXWELL ATOMS
GULP
URRRRP
THAT WAS ODD.
SOMETHIN' *STRANGE* IS GOING ON HERE...

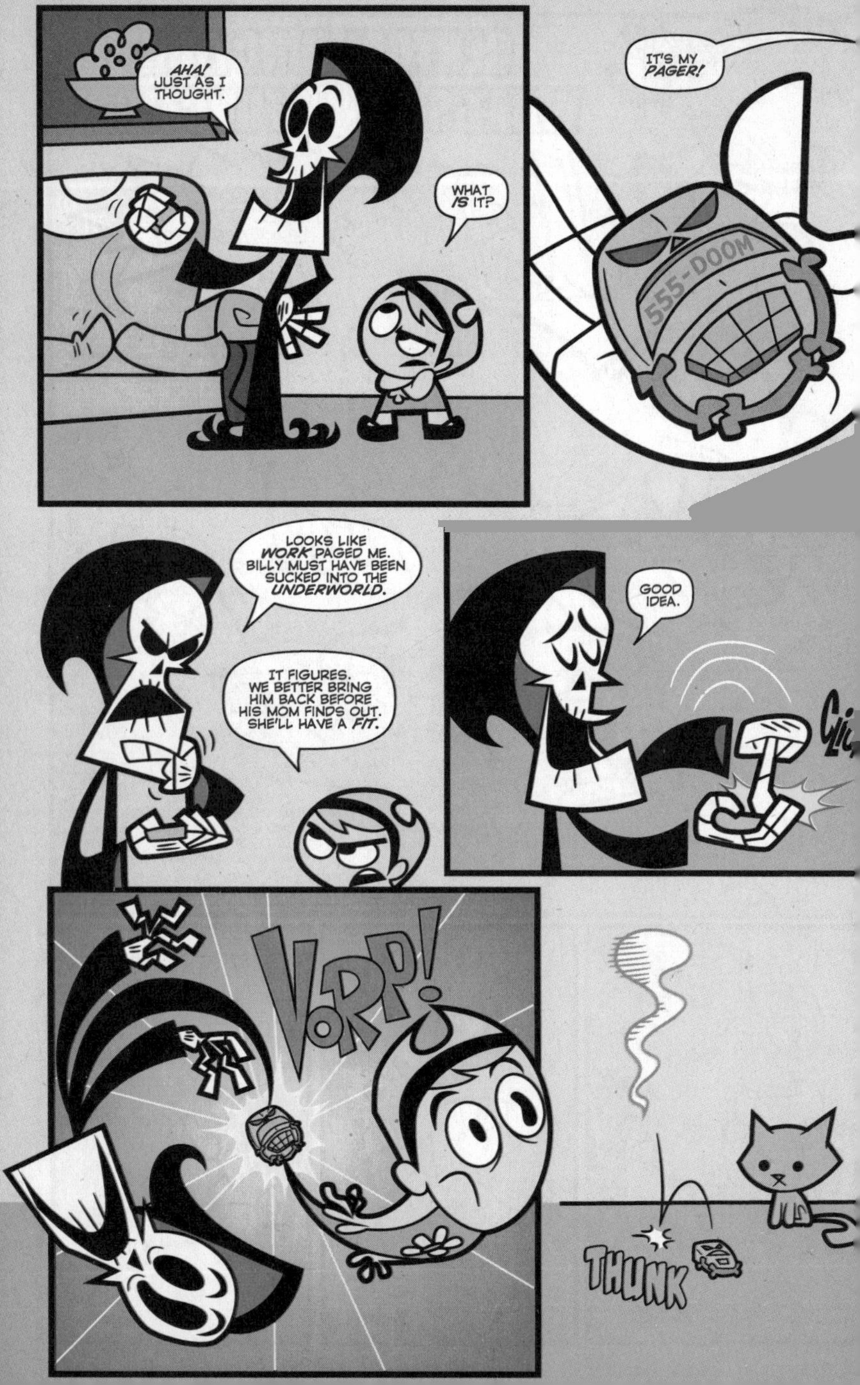
AHA! JUST AS I THOUGHT.
WHAT IS IT?
IT'S MY PAGER!
555-DOOM
LOOKS LIKE WORK PAGED ME. BILLY MUST HAVE BEEN SUCKED INTO THE UNDERWORLD.
IT FIGURES. WE BETTER BRING HIM BACK BEFORE HIS MOM FINDS OUT. SHE'LL HAVE A FIT.
GOOD IDEA.
VORP!
THUNK

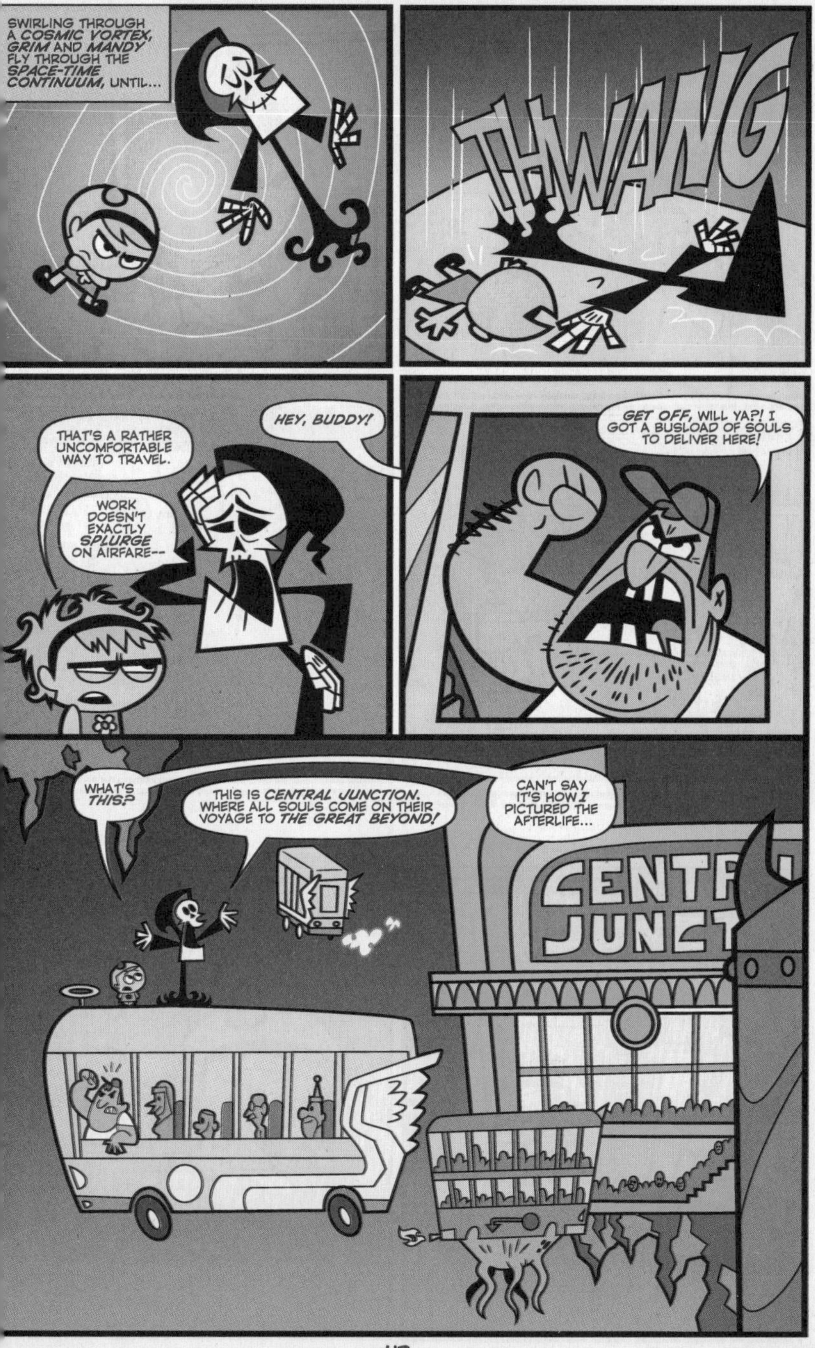
SWIRLING THROUGH A COSMIC VORTEX, GRIM AND MANDY FLY THROUGH THE SPACE-TIME CONTINUUM, UNTIL...
THWANG
HEY, BUDDY!
THAT'S A RATHER UNCOMFORTABLE WAY TO TRAVEL.
WORK DOESN'T EXACTLY SPLURGE ON AIRFARE--
GET OFF, WILL YA?! I GOT A BUSLOAD OF SOULS TO DELIVER HERE!
WHAT'S THIS?
THIS IS CENTRAL JUNCTION. WHERE ALL SOULS COME ON THEIR VOYAGE TO THE GREAT BEYOND!
CAN'T SAY IT'S HOW I PICTURED THE AFTERLIFE...
CENTR
JUNCT

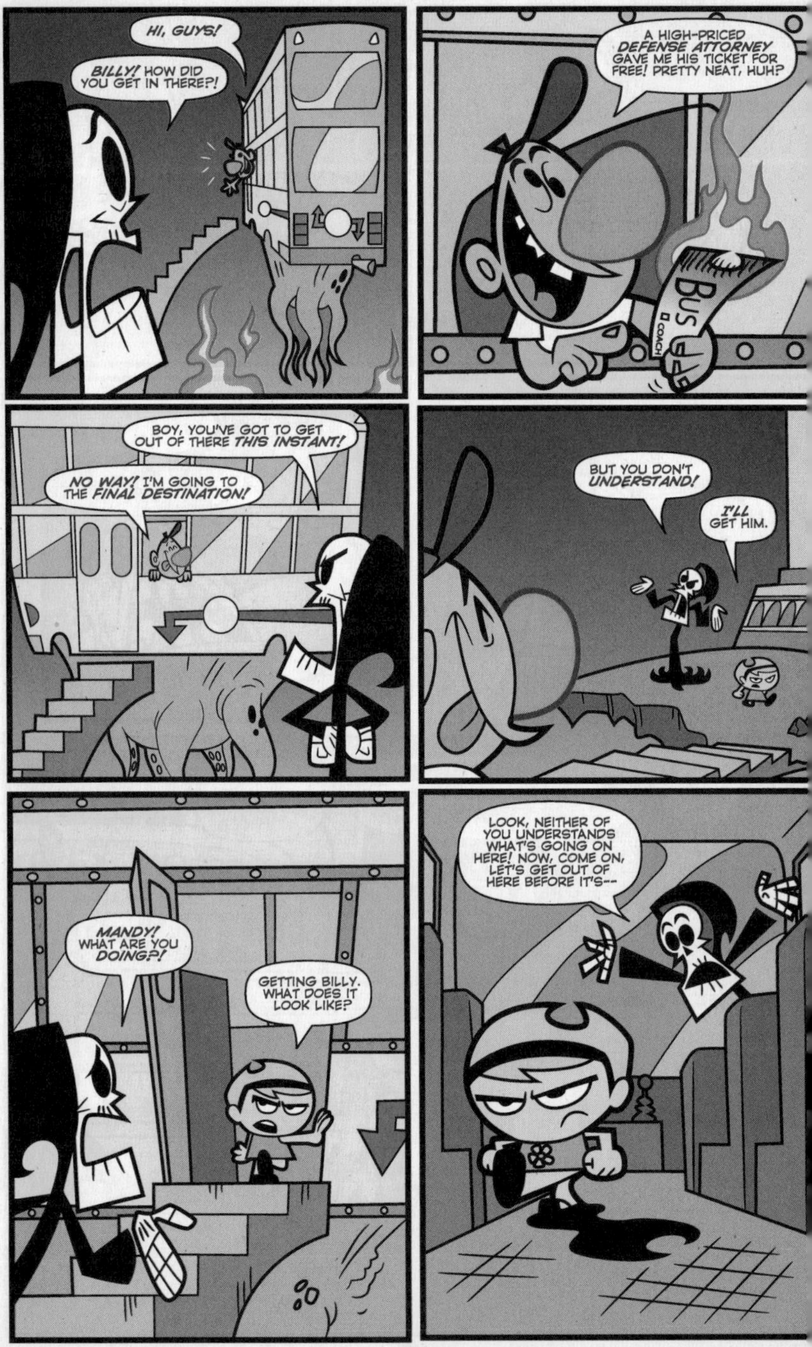
HI, GUYS!
BILLY! HOW DID YOU GET IN THERE?!
A HIGH-PRICED DEFENSE ATTORNEY GAVE ME HIS TICKET FOR FREE! PRETTY NEAT, HUH?
BUS
COACH
BOY, YOU'VE GOT TO GET OUT OF THERE THIS INSTANT!
NO WAY! I'M GOING TO THE FINAL DESTINATION!
BUT YOU DON'T UNDERSTAND!
I'LL GET HIM.
MANDY! WHAT ARE YOU DOING?!
GETTING BILLY. WHAT DOES IT LOOK LIKE?
LOOK, NEITHER OF YOU UNDERSTANDS WHAT'S GOING ON HERE! NOW, COME ON, LET'S GET OUT OF HERE BEFORE IT'S--

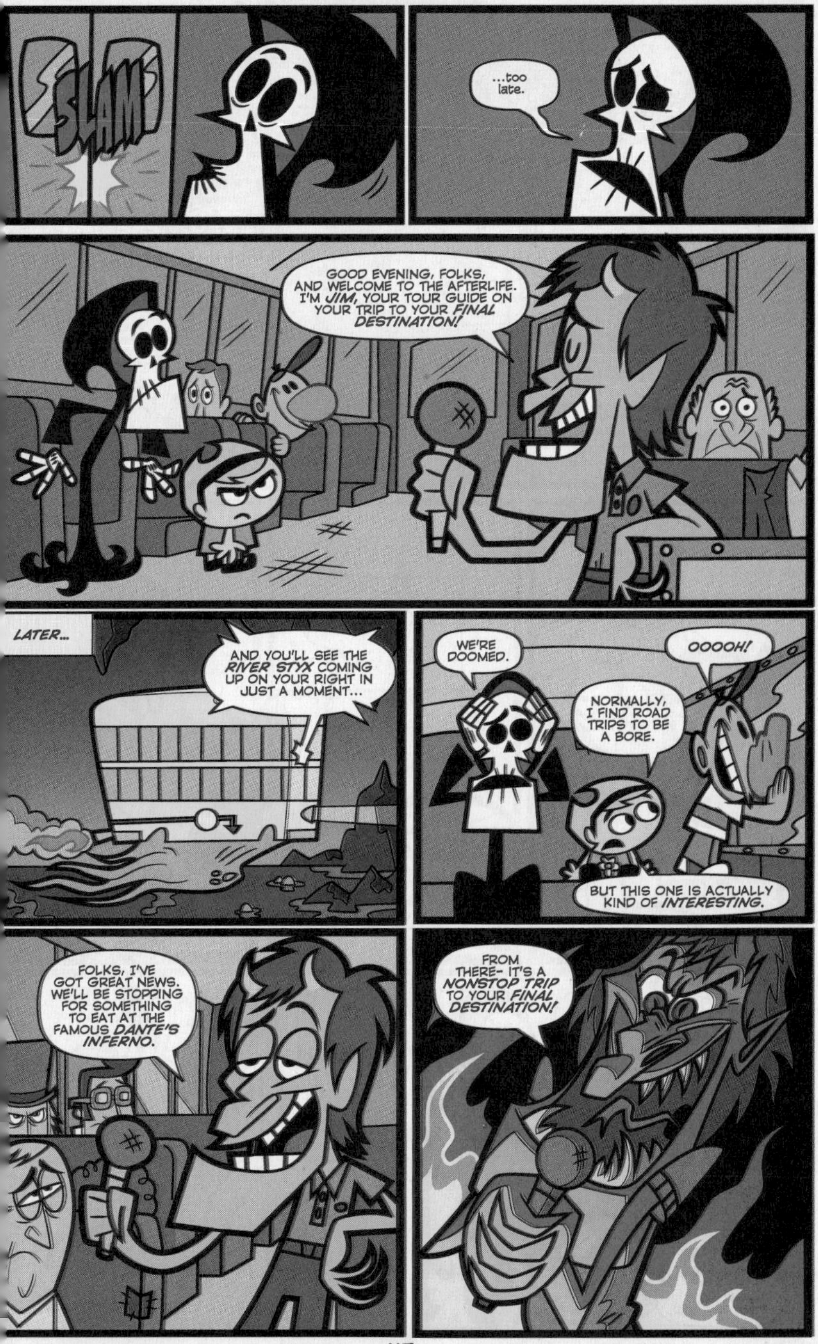
SLAM
...too late.
GOOD EVENING, FOLKS, AND WELCOME TO THE AFTERLIFE. I'M JIM, YOUR TOUR GUIDE ON YOUR TRIP TO YOUR FINAL DESTINATION!
LATER...
AND YOU'LL SEE THE RIVER STYX COMING UP ON YOUR RIGHT IN JUST A MOMENT...
WE'RE DOOMED.
OOOOH!
NORMALLY, I FIND ROAD TRIPS TO BE A BORE.
BUT THIS ONE IS ACTUALLY KIND OF INTERESTING.
FOLKS, I'VE GOT GREAT NEWS. WE'LL BE STOPPING FOR SOMETHING TO EAT AT THE FAMOUS DANTE'S INFERNO.
FROM THERE- IT'S A NONSTOP TRIP TO YOUR FINAL DESTINATION!

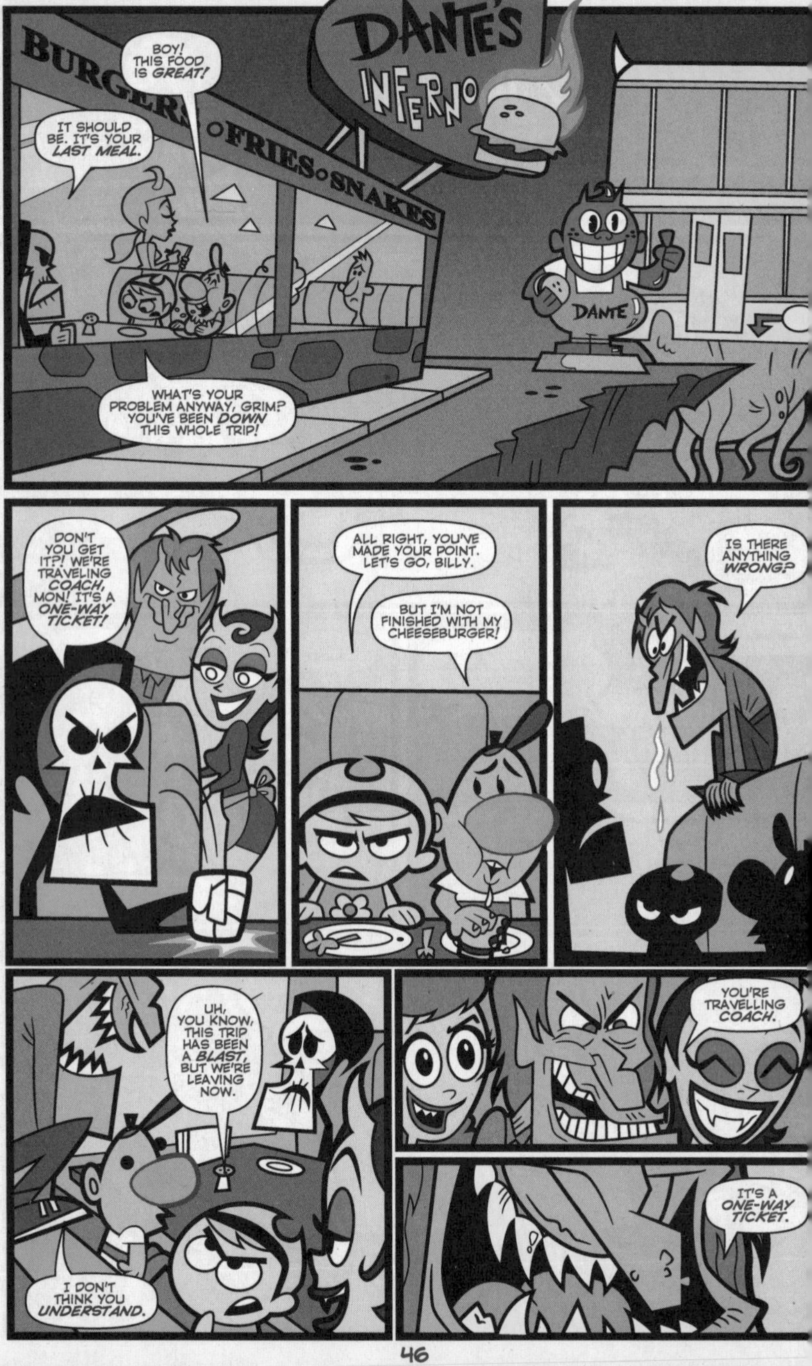
BURGERS FRIES SNAKES
DANTE'S INFERNO
DANTE
BOY! THIS FOOD IS *GREAT!*
IT SHOULD BE. IT'S YOUR *LAST MEAL.*
WHAT'S YOUR PROBLEM ANYWAY, GRIM? YOU'VE BEEN *DOWN* THIS WHOLE TRIP!
DON'T YOU GET IT?! WE'RE TRAVELING *COACH,* MON! IT'S A *ONE-WAY TICKET!*
ALL RIGHT, YOU'VE MADE YOUR POINT. LET'S GO, BILLY.
BUT I'M NOT FINISHED WITH MY CHEESEBURGER!
IS THERE ANYTHING *WRONG?*
UH, YOU KNOW, THIS TRIP HAS BEEN A *BLAST,* BUT WE'RE LEAVING NOW.
I DON'T THINK YOU *UNDERSTAND.*
YOU'RE TRAVELLING *COACH.*
IT'S A *ONE-WAY TICKET.*

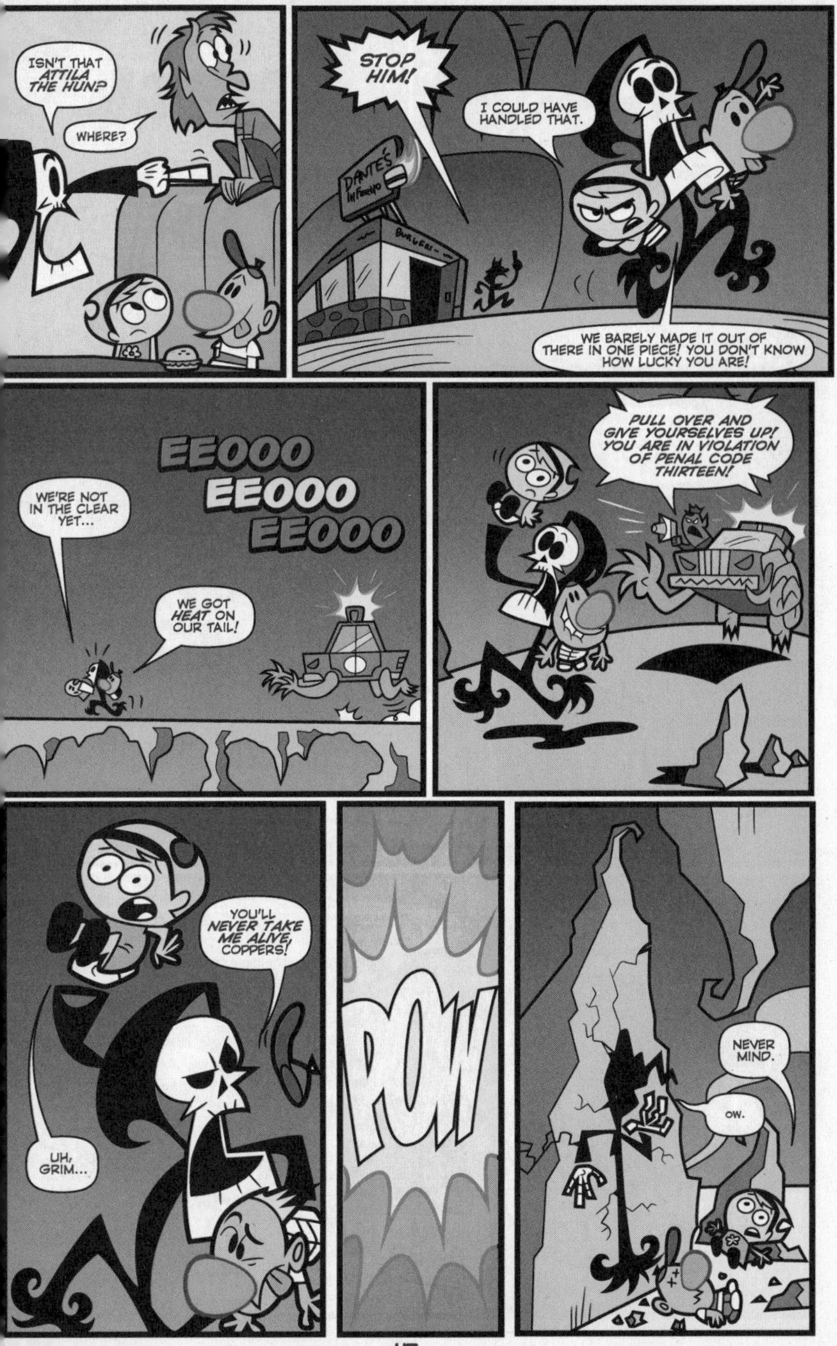
ISN'T THAT ATTILA THE HUN?
WHERE?
STOP HIM!
DANTE'S INFERNO
BURGERS
I COULD HAVE HANDLED THAT.
WE BARELY MADE IT OUT OF THERE IN ONE PIECE! YOU DON'T KNOW HOW LUCKY YOU ARE!
EEOOO EEOOO EEOOO
WE'RE NOT IN THE CLEAR YET...
WE GOT HEAT ON OUR TAIL!
PULL OVER AND GIVE YOURSELVES UP! YOU ARE IN VIOLATION OF PENAL CODE THIRTEEN!
YOU'LL NEVER TAKE ME ALIVE, COPPERS!
UH, GRIM...
POW
NEVER MIND.
OW.

SOON...

ALL RISE! THE HONORABLE *JUDGE GABBY* PRESIDING!

WAY TO GO, *GRIM!* NOT ONLY DID YOU GET US ARRESTED, BUT I NEVER GOT TO SEE THE *FINAL DESTINATION!*

OH, *SHUT UP!*

YOUR HONOR, THIS CASE IS THE *UNDERWORLD* VS. *BILLY AND MANDY.*

BALIFF

DO THE DEFENDANTS HAVE ANYTHING *IMPORTANT* TO SAY BEFORE I PASS JUDGMENT?

YOUR HONOR, IF I MAY ADDRESS THE—

bob

IN THAT CASE, I'LL PASS MY JUDGMENT.

THEY'RE NOT BEING FAIR.

THAT'S BECAUSE THEY DON'T HAVE TO BE.

I'M AFRAID I HAVE NO CHOICE BUT TO LET THEM GO *FREE.*

REALLY!?

THEY'VE GOT A GOOD *70 YEARS* BEFORE THEY'RE SCHEDULED TO ARRIVE.

DOES THIS MEAN I DON'T GET TO SEE THE *FINAL DESTINATION?*

WELL, KID, MAYBE YOU WON'T SEE IT *NOW*— BUT IF YOU WORK *REALLY HARD* AT IT, YOU MAY JUST *EARN* YOURSELF A COACH TICKET ONE DAY.

OH *BOY!*

OH, *BROTHER!*

ENDSVILLE BAB

48

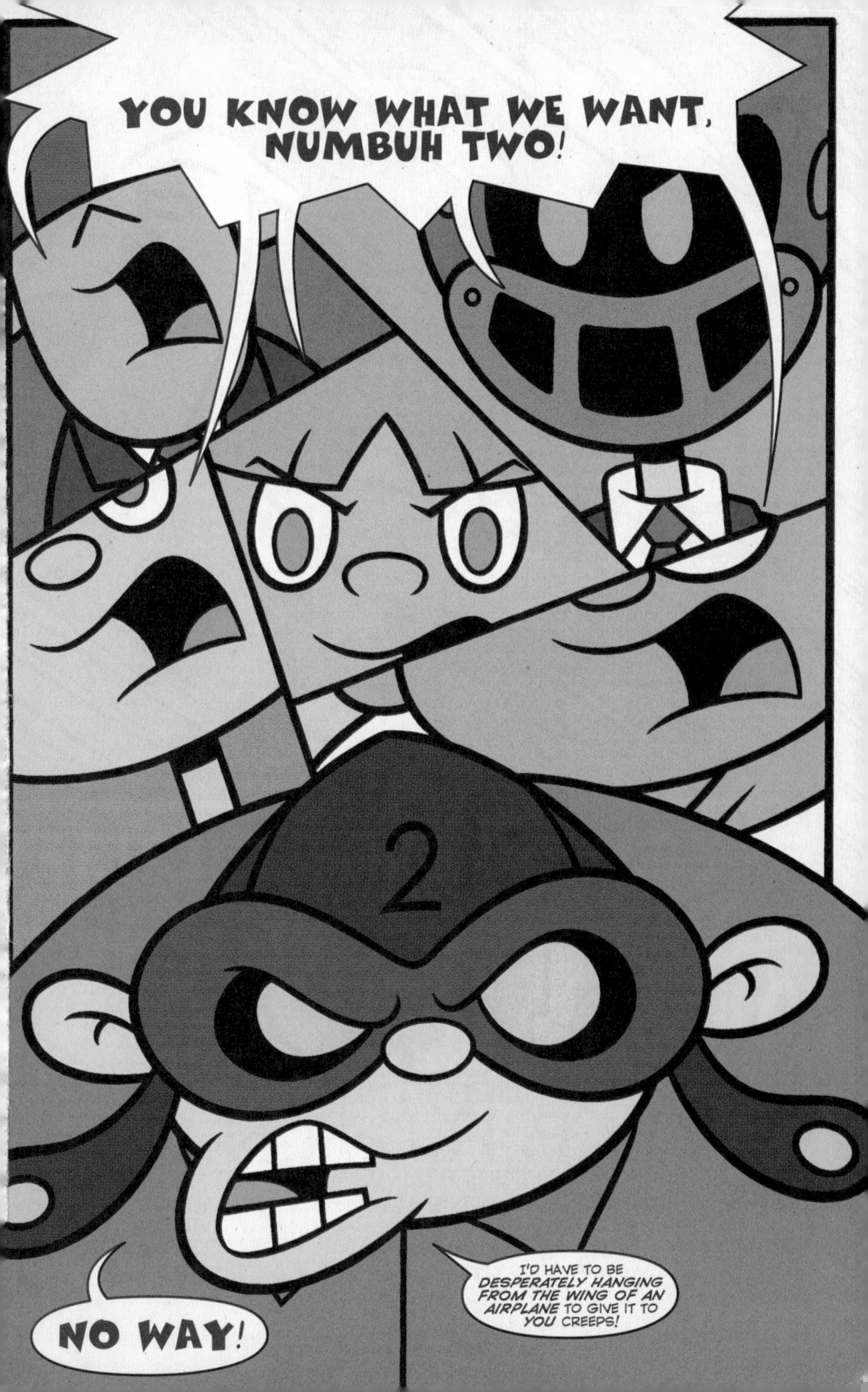
YOU KNOW WHAT WE WANT, NUMBUH TWO!
NO WAY!
I'D HAVE TO BE DESPERATELY HANGING FROM THE WING OF AN AIRPLANE TO GIVE IT TO YOU CREEPS!

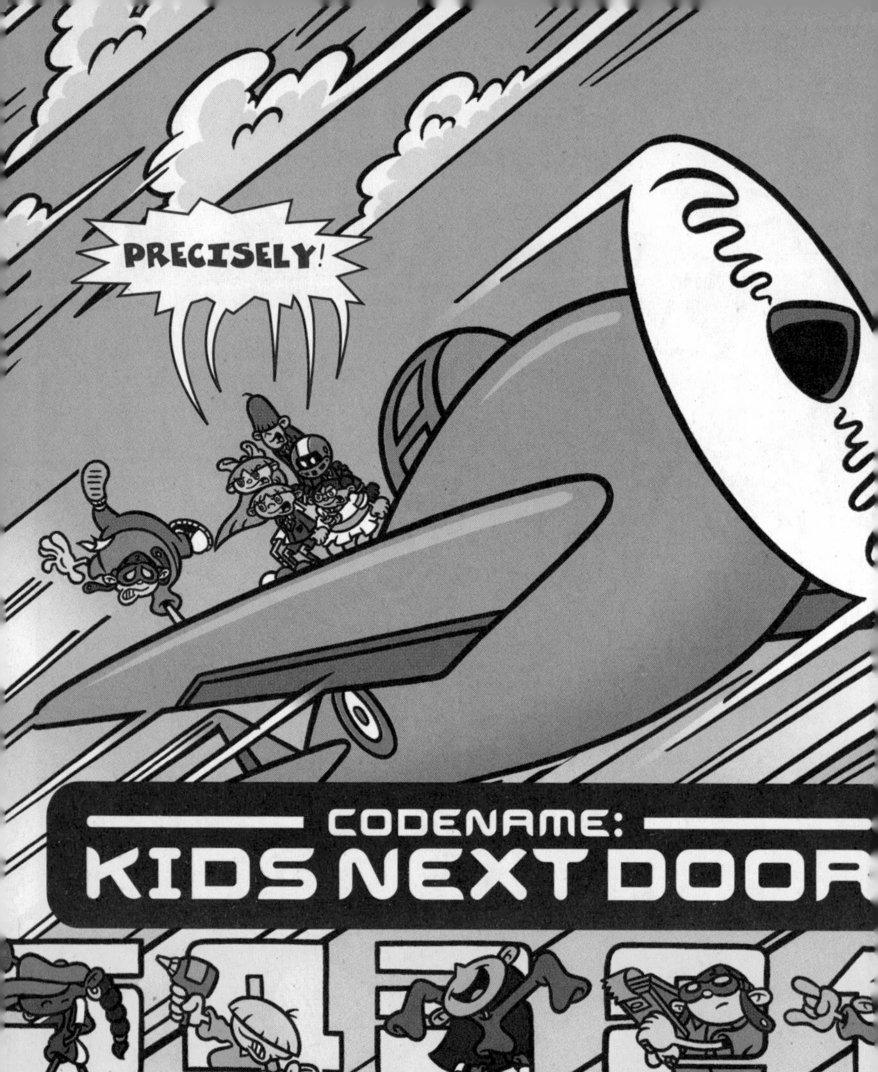
PRECISELY!
CODENAME:
KIDS NEXT DOOR

OPERATION: A.I.R.P.L.A.N.E.*

*AIRCRAFT IS RATHER PROBLEMATIC LOCALE AGAINST NEFARIOUS ENEMIE

writing operative: **MR. WARBURTON** • pencilling patrol: **MAURICE FONTENOT**
inking agent: **JARED DEAL** • letterer lieutenant: **JENNA GARCIA** •
color commando: **SNO CONE** • auto-pilot: **HARVEY RICHARDS** • pilot: **JOAN HIL**
KIDS NEXT DOOR created by **MR. WARBURTON**

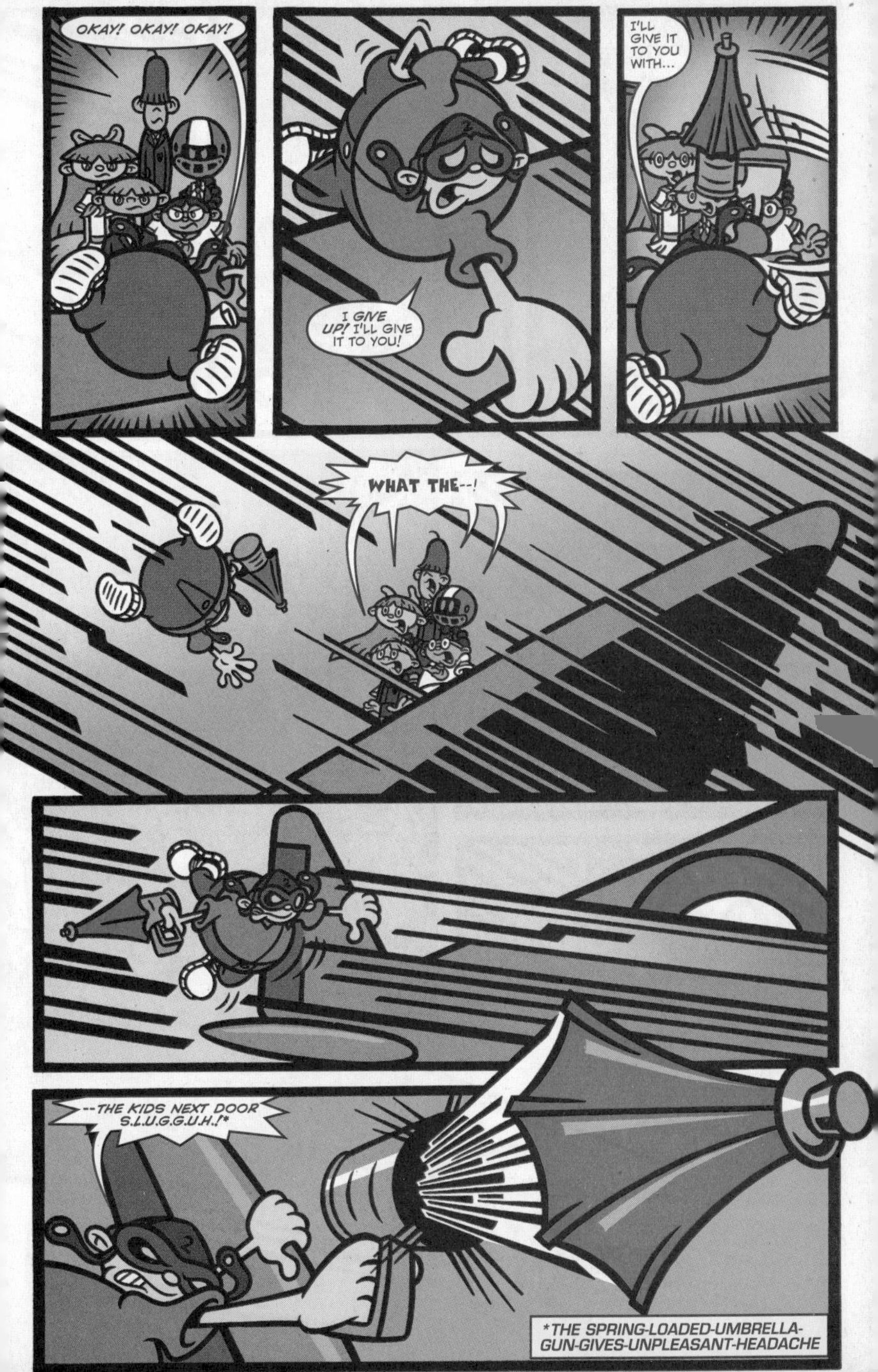
OKAY! OKAY! OKAY!
I GIVE UP! I'LL GIVE IT TO YOU!
I'LL GIVE IT TO YOU WITH...
WHAT THE--!
--THE KIDS NEXT DOOR S.L.U.G.G.U.H.!*
*THE SPRING-LOADED-UMBRELLA-GUN-GIVES-UNPLEASANT-HEADACHE

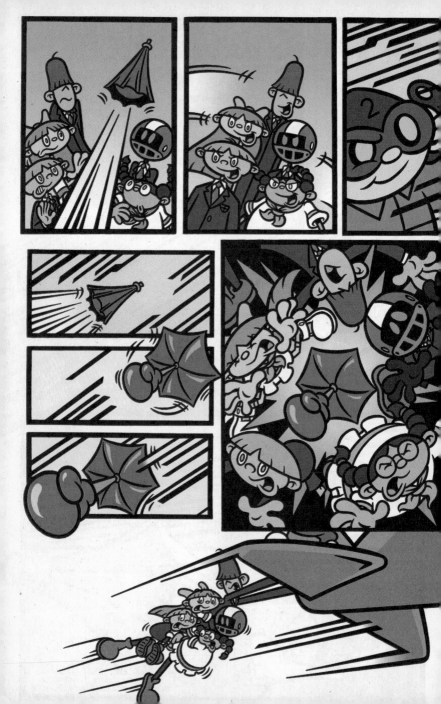

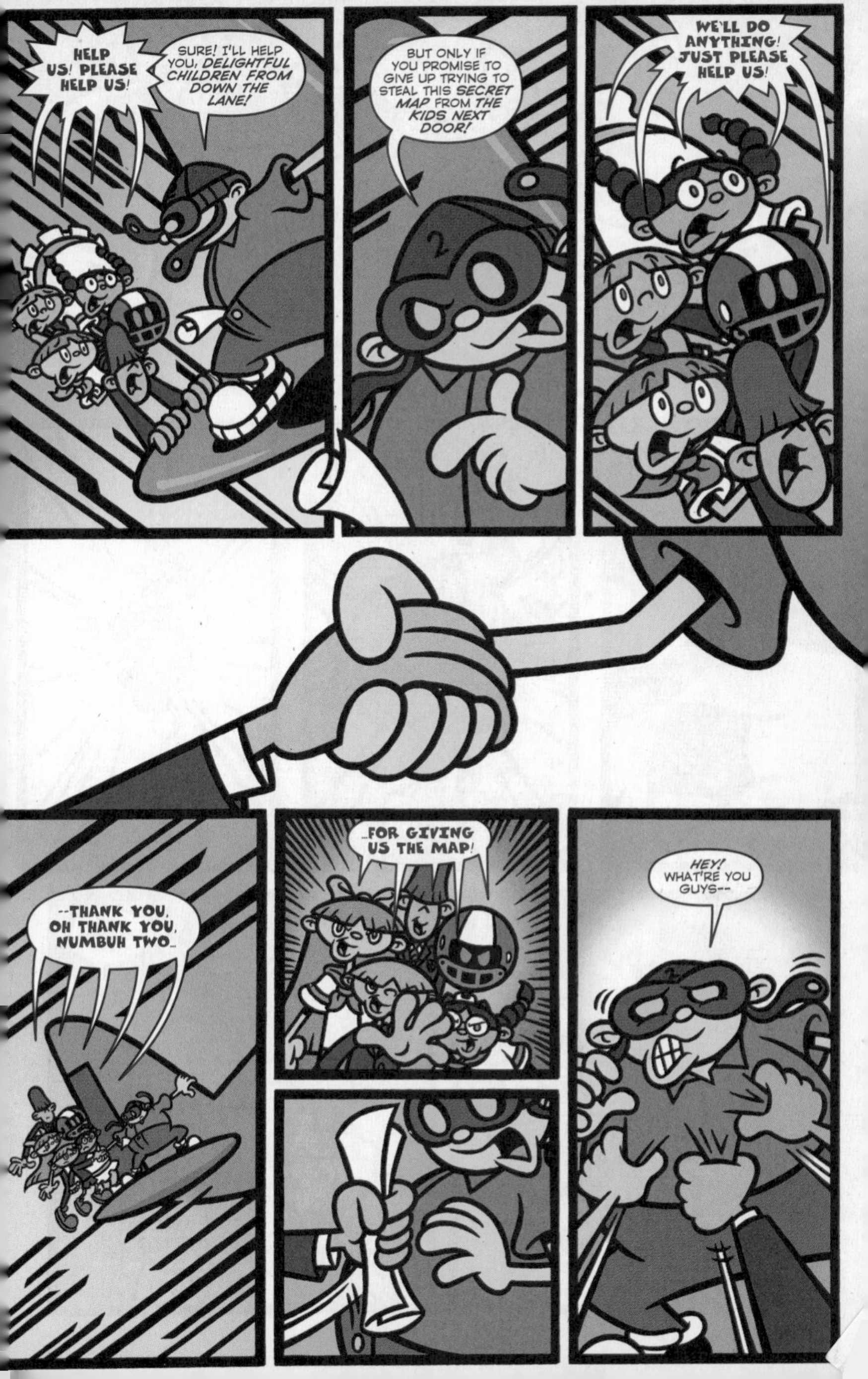
HELP US! PLEASE HELP US!
SURE! I'LL HELP YOU, DELIGHTFUL CHILDREN FROM DOWN THE LANE!
BUT ONLY IF YOU PROMISE TO GIVE UP TRYING TO STEAL THIS SECRET MAP FROM THE KIDS NEXT DOOR!
WE'LL DO ANYTHING! JUST PLEASE HELP US!
--THANK YOU. OH THANK YOU. NUMBUH TWO...
...FOR GIVING US THE MAP!
HEY! WHAT'RE YOU GUYS--

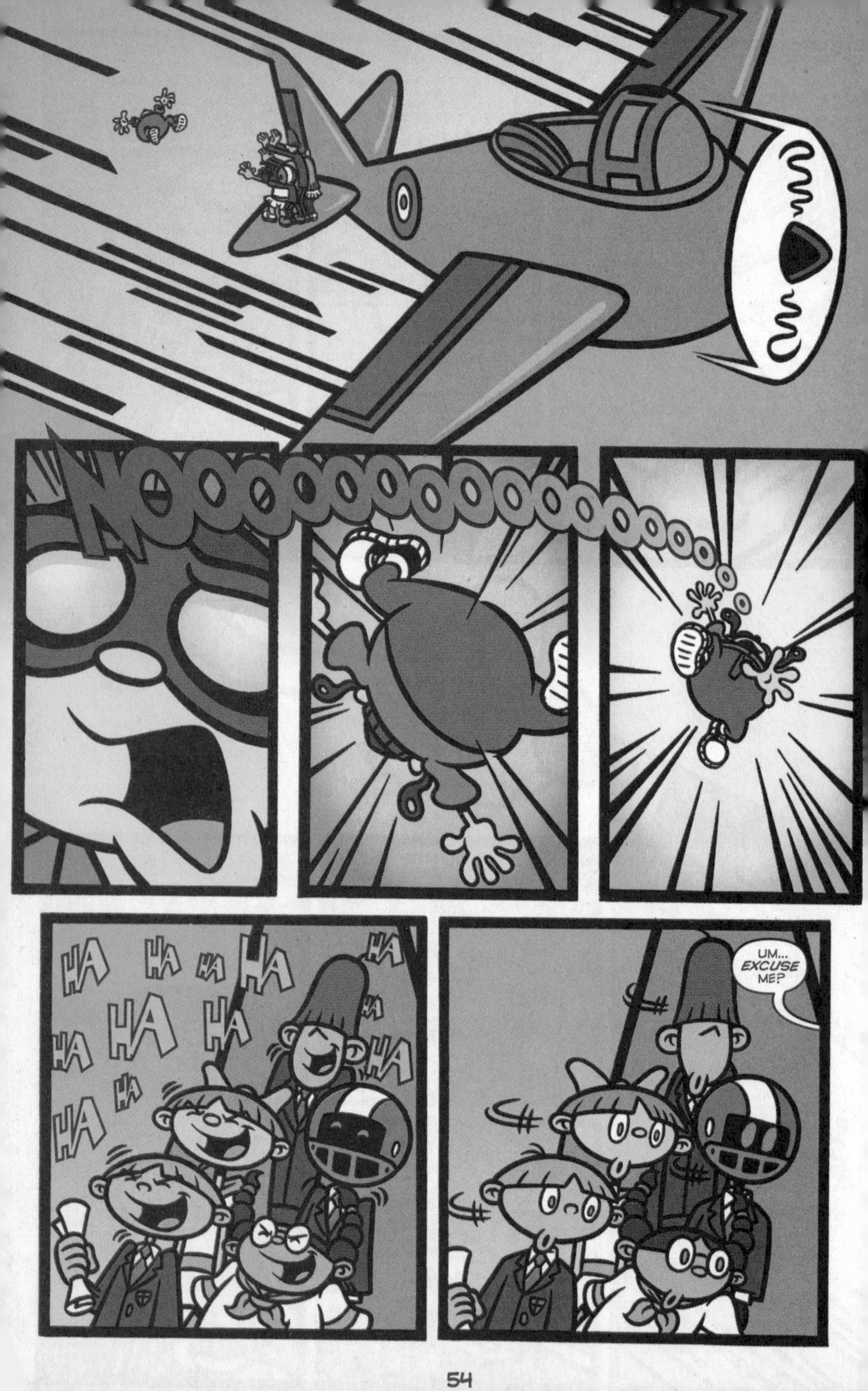
NOOOOOOOOOOOOOOOOOOO
HA HA HA HA HA HA HA HA HA HA HA HA HA
UM... *EXCUSE* ME?

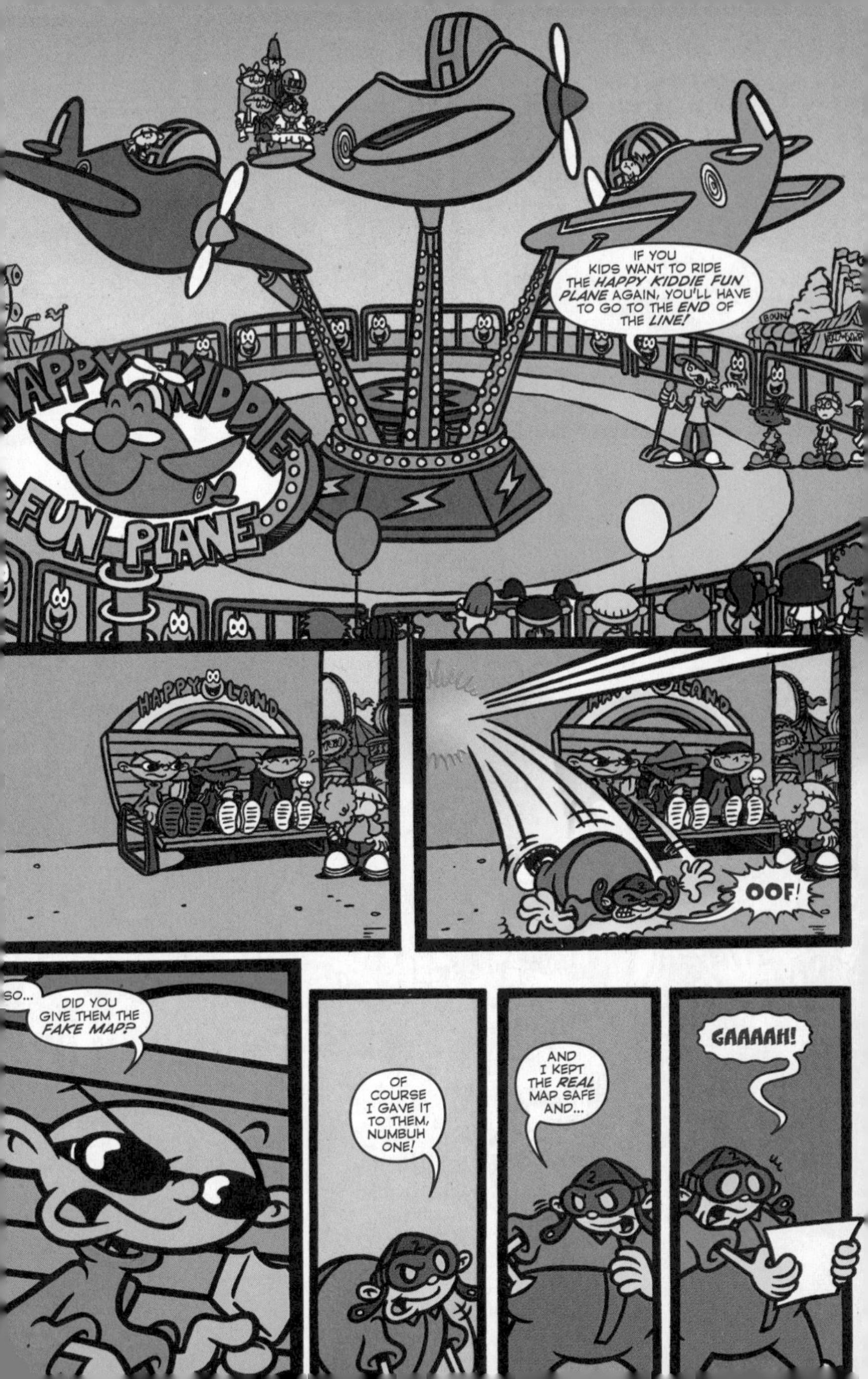
IF YOU KIDS WANT TO RIDE THE *HAPPY KIDDIE FUN PLANE* AGAIN, YOU'LL HAVE TO GO TO THE *END* OF THE *LINE!*
HAPPY KIDDIE FUN PLANE
HAPPY LAND
OOF!
SO... DID YOU GIVE THEM THE *FAKE MAP?*
OF COURSE I GAVE IT TO THEM, NUMBUH ONE!
AND I KEPT THE *REAL* MAP SAFE AND...
GAAAAH!

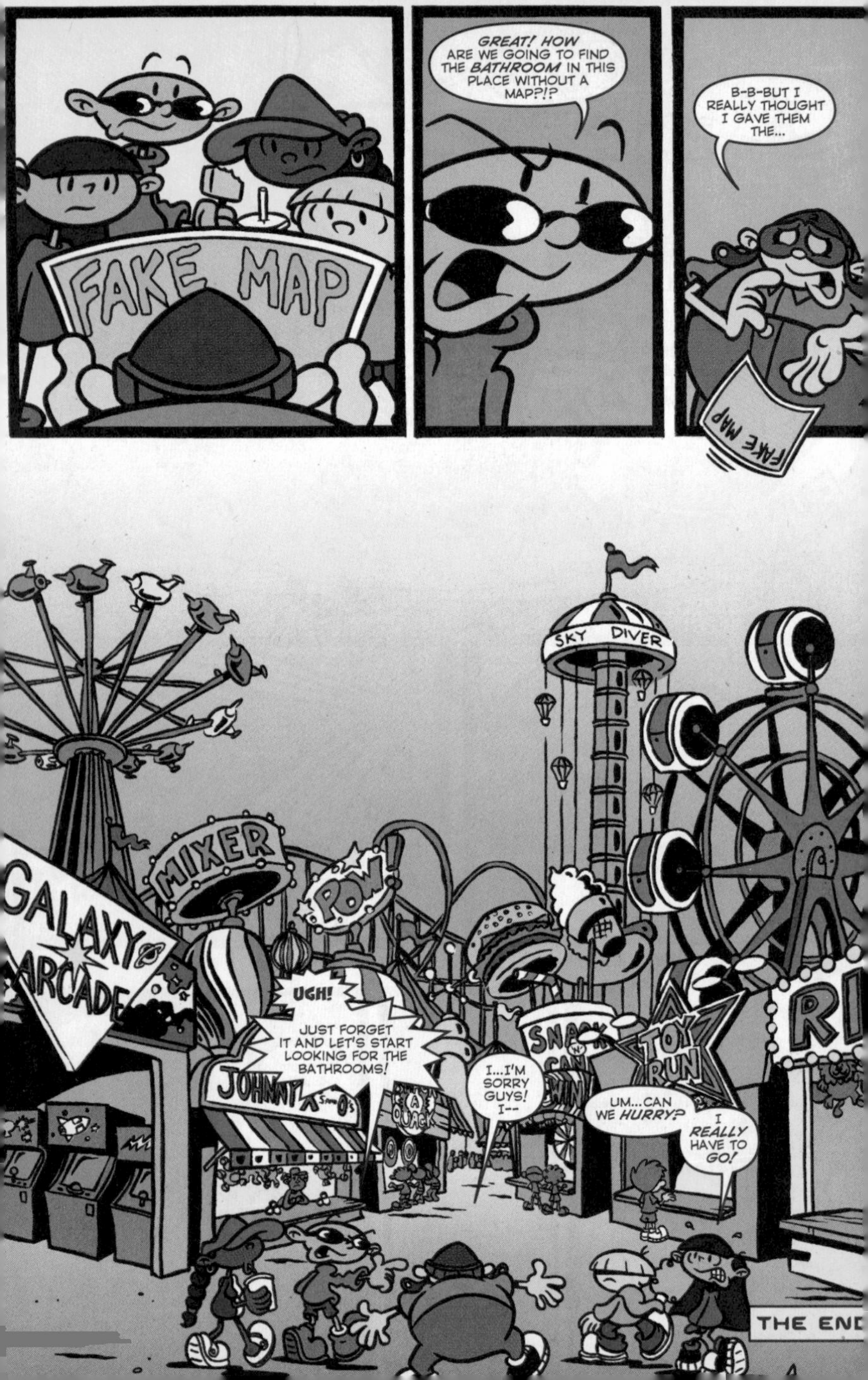
FAKE MAP
GREAT! HOW ARE WE GOING TO FIND THE BATHROOM IN THIS PLACE WITHOUT A MAP?!?
B-B-BUT I REALLY THOUGHT I GAVE THEM THE...
FAKE MAP
SKY DIVER
MIXER
POW!
GALAXY ARCADE
UGH!
JUST FORGET IT AND LET'S START LOOKING FOR THE BATHROOMS!
I...I'M SORRY GUYS! I--
UM...CAN WE HURRY?
I REALLY HAVE TO GO!
TOY RUN
THE END

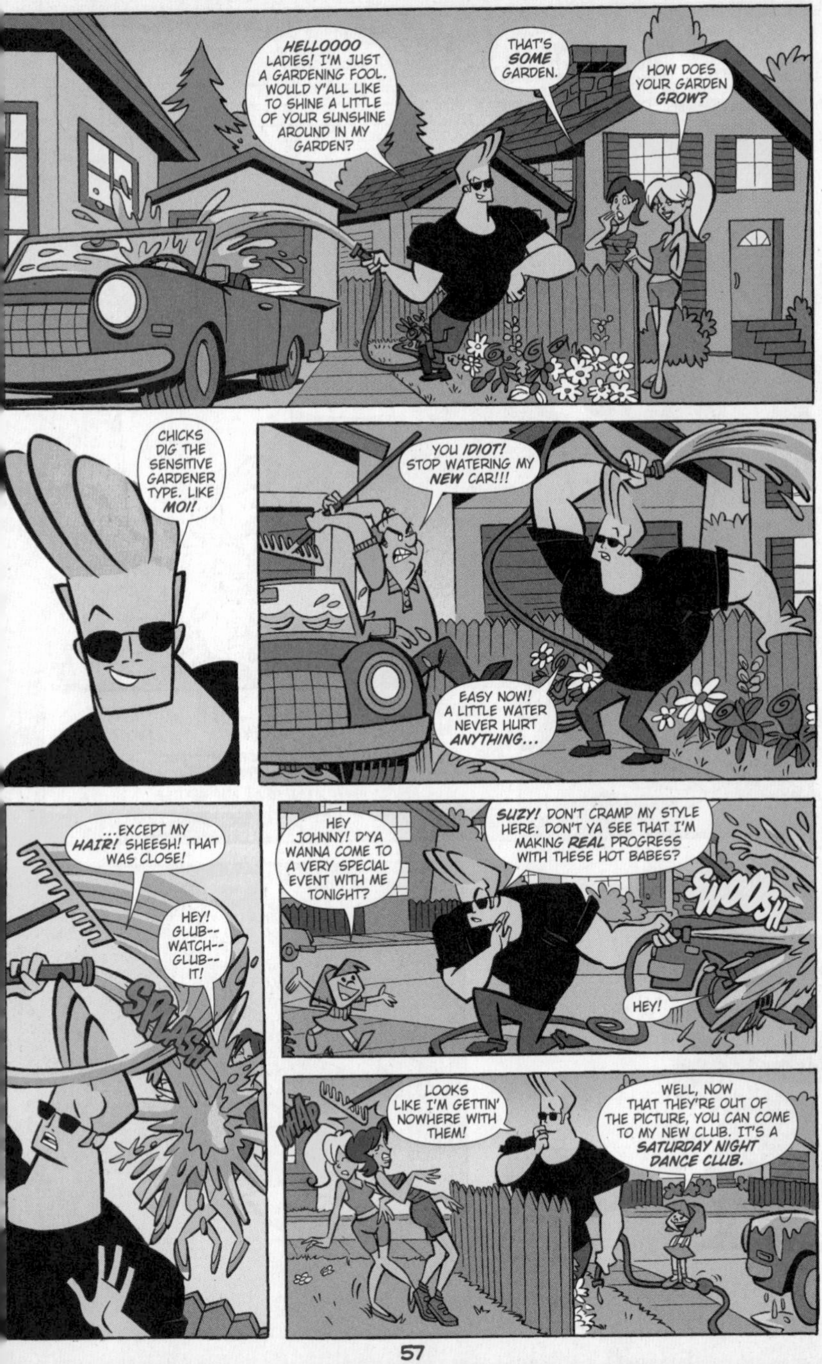
HELLOOOO LADIES! I'M JUST A GARDENING FOOL. WOULD Y'ALL LIKE TO SHINE A LITTLE OF YOUR SUNSHINE AROUND IN MY GARDEN?
THAT'S SOME GARDEN.
HOW DOES YOUR GARDEN GROW?
CHICKS DIG THE SENSITIVE GARDENER TYPE. LIKE MOI!
YOU IDIOT! STOP WATERING MY NEW CAR!!!
EASY NOW! A LITTLE WATER NEVER HURT ANYTHING...
...EXCEPT MY HAIR! SHEESH! THAT WAS CLOSE!
HEY! GLUB-- WATCH-- GLUB-- IT!
SPLASH
HEY JOHNNY! D'YA WANNA COME TO A VERY SPECIAL EVENT WITH ME TONIGHT?
SUZY! DON'T CRAMP MY STYLE HERE. DON'T YA SEE THAT I'M MAKING REAL PROGRESS WITH THESE HOT BABES?
SWOOSH
HEY!
WHAP
LOOKS LIKE I'M GETTIN' NOWHERE WITH THEM!
WELL, NOW THAT THEY'RE OUT OF THE PICTURE, YOU CAN COME TO MY NEW CLUB. IT'S A SATURDAY NIGHT DANCE CLUB.

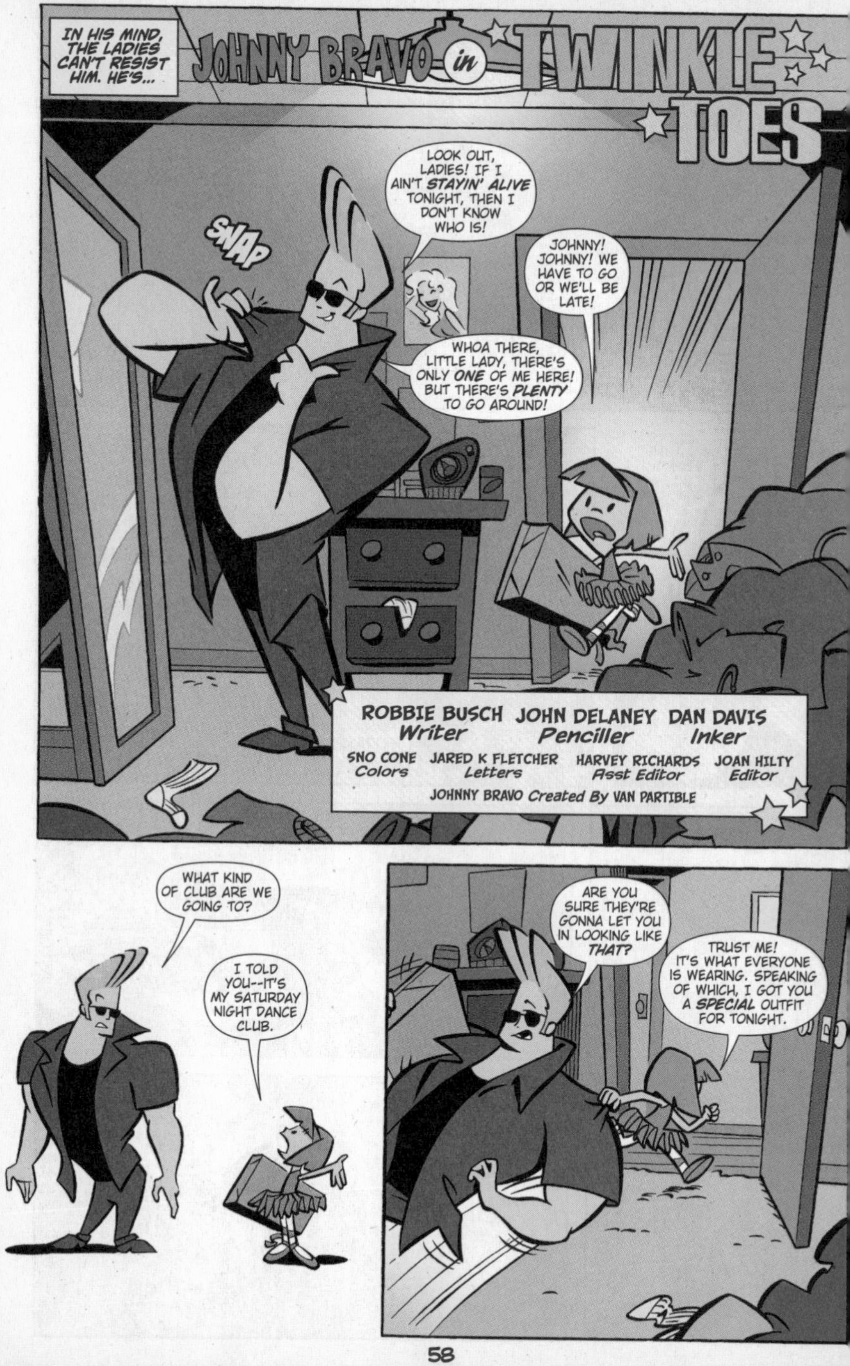
IN HIS MIND, THE LADIES CAN'T RESIST HIM. HE'S...
JOHNNY BRAVO in TWINKLE TOES
LOOK OUT, LADIES! IF I AIN'T STAYIN' ALIVE TONIGHT, THEN I DON'T KNOW WHO IS!
SNAP
JOHNNY! JOHNNY! WE HAVE TO GO OR WE'LL BE LATE!
WHOA THERE, LITTLE LADY, THERE'S ONLY ONE OF ME HERE! BUT THERE'S PLENTY TO GO AROUND!
ROBBIE BUSCH Writer JOHN DELANEY Penciller DAN DAVIS Inker
SNO CONE Colors JARED K FLETCHER Letters HARVEY RICHARDS Asst Editor JOAN HILTY Editor
JOHNNY BRAVO Created By VAN PARTIBLE
WHAT KIND OF CLUB ARE WE GOING TO?
I TOLD YOU--IT'S MY SATURDAY NIGHT DANCE CLUB.
ARE YOU SURE THEY'RE GONNA LET YOU IN LOOKING LIKE THAT?
TRUST ME! IT'S WHAT EVERYONE IS WEARING. SPEAKING OF WHICH, I GOT YOU A SPECIAL OUTFIT FOR TONIGHT.

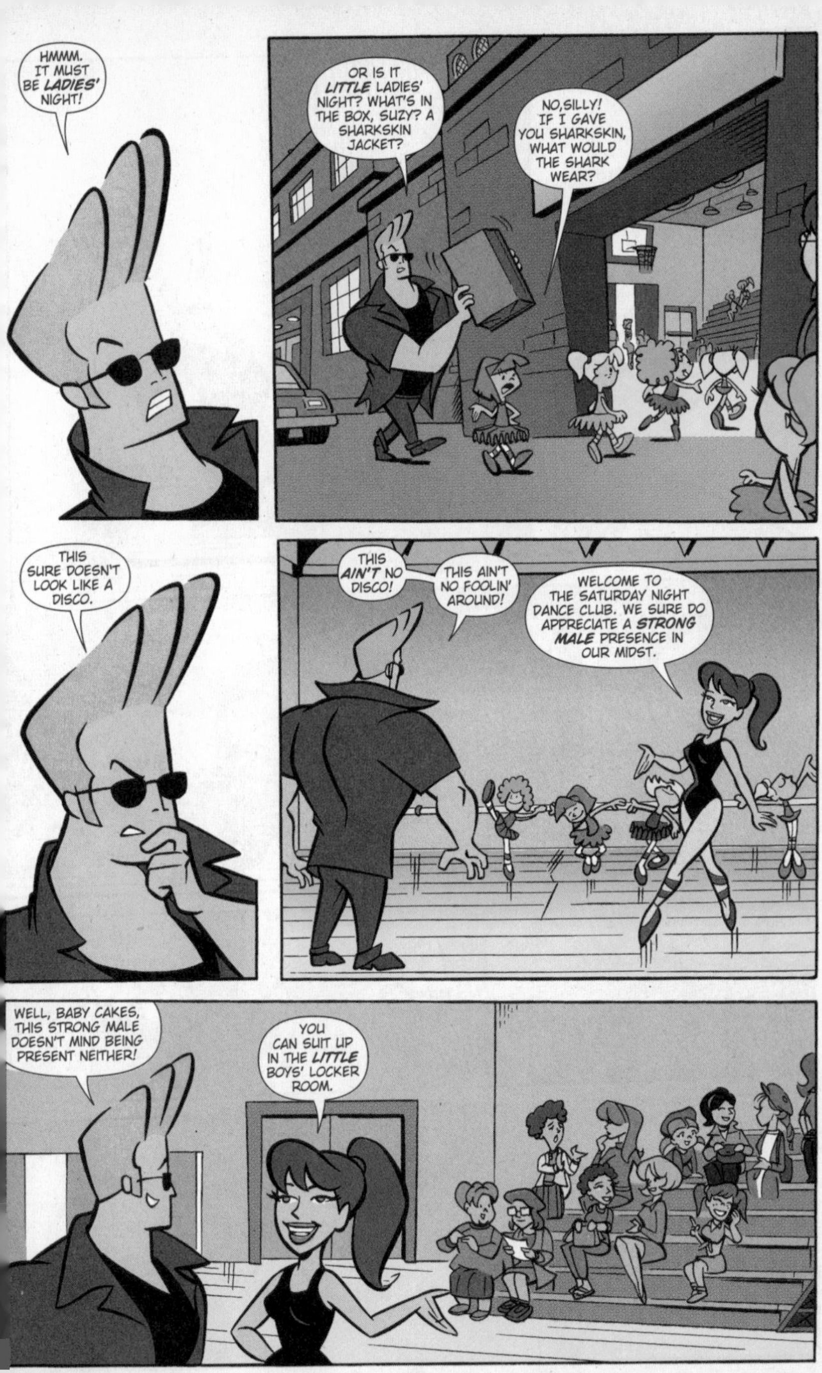
HMMM. IT MUST BE LADIES' NIGHT!
OR IS IT LITTLE LADIES' NIGHT? WHAT'S IN THE BOX, SUZY? A SHARKSKIN JACKET?
NO,SILLY! IF I GAVE YOU SHARKSKIN, WHAT WOULD THE SHARK WEAR?
THIS SURE DOESN'T LOOK LIKE A DISCO.
THIS AIN'T NO DISCO!
THIS AIN'T NO FOOLIN' AROUND!
WELCOME TO THE SATURDAY NIGHT DANCE CLUB. WE SURE DO APPRECIATE A STRONG MALE PRESENCE IN OUR MIDST.
WELL, BABY CAKES, THIS STRONG MALE DOESN'T MIND BEING PRESENT NEITHER!
YOU CAN SUIT UP IN THE LITTLE BOYS' LOCKER ROOM.

SUIT UP?

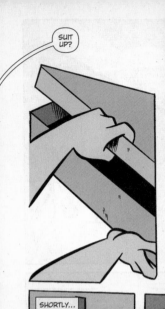

OH MAMA, HELP ME!

BU-BU-BU...

NO BUTS ABOUT IT! NOW GET YOUR BUTT IN THERE AND CHANGE.

SHORTLY...

I FEEL LIKE A TEN-POUND HAM IN A FIVE-POUND BAG! ÷GULP!÷

WELL, COME BE OUR HAM...

AND STOP BEING SUCH A CHICKEN!

HMMM. MAYBE THIS CHICKEN IS REALLY A PEACOCK!

CLAP

WHY, THANK YOU VERY MUCH!

HI-YA!

CLAP CLAP CLAP

I'LL BE HERE ALL NIGHT, LADIES.

I'M IMPRESSED BY YOUR COMFORT WITH YOUR MASCULINITY. TAKE YOUR PLACE WITH OUR LITTLE DANCERS, PLEASE.

WELL, IF YOU PUT IT THAT WAY... MY MASCULINITY HAS NEVER BEEN MORE COMFORTABLE.

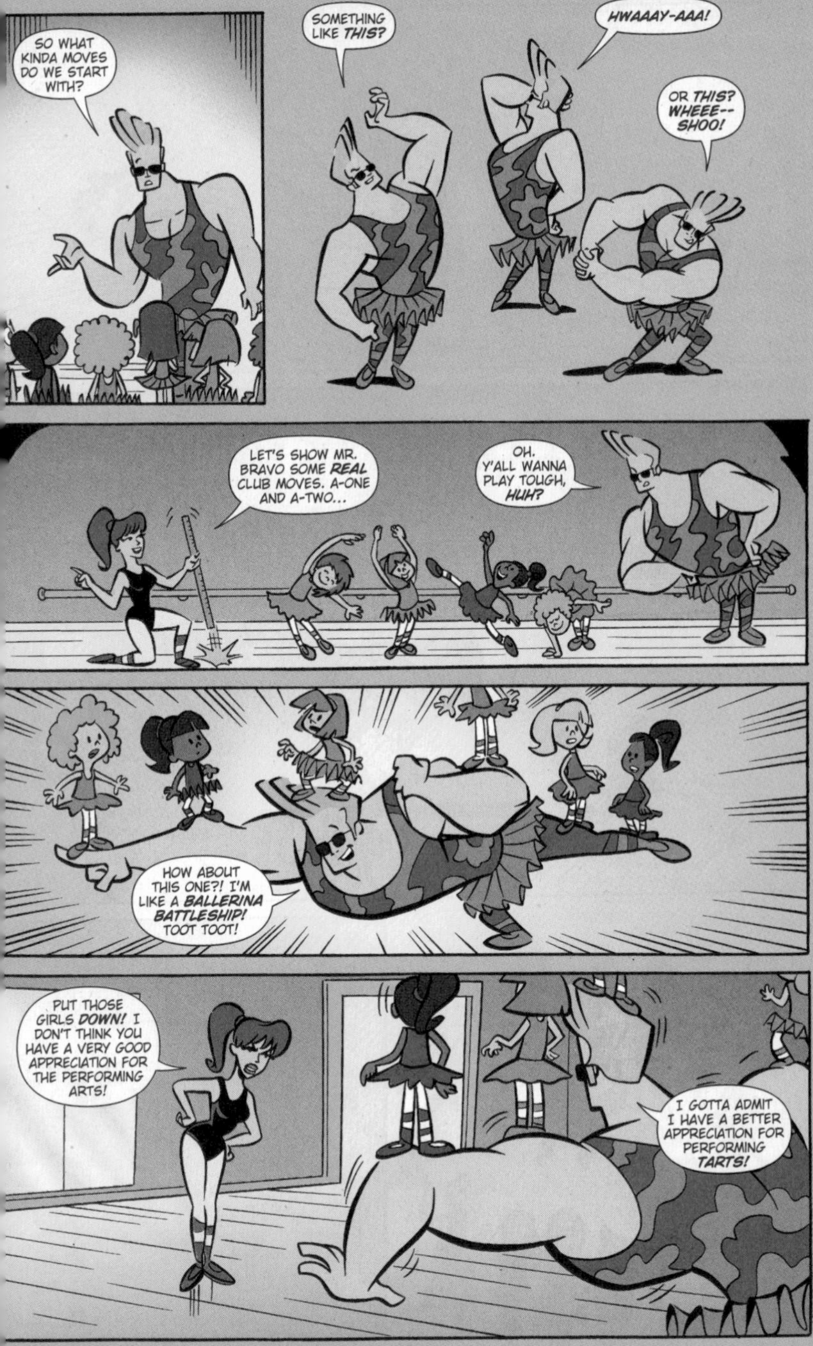
SO WHAT KINDA MOVES DO WE START WITH?
SOMETHING LIKE *THIS?*
HWAAAY-AAA!
OR *THIS? WHEEE-- SHOO!*
LET'S SHOW MR. BRAVO SOME *REAL* CLUB MOVES. A-ONE AND A-TWO...
OH. Y'ALL WANNA PLAY TOUGH, *HUH?*
HOW ABOUT THIS ONE?! I'M LIKE A *BALLERINA BATTLESHIP!* TOOT TOOT!
PUT THOSE GIRLS *DOWN!* I DON'T THINK YOU HAVE A VERY GOOD APPRECIATION FOR THE PERFORMING ARTS!
I GOTTA ADMIT I HAVE A BETTER APPRECIATION FOR PERFORMING *TARTS!*

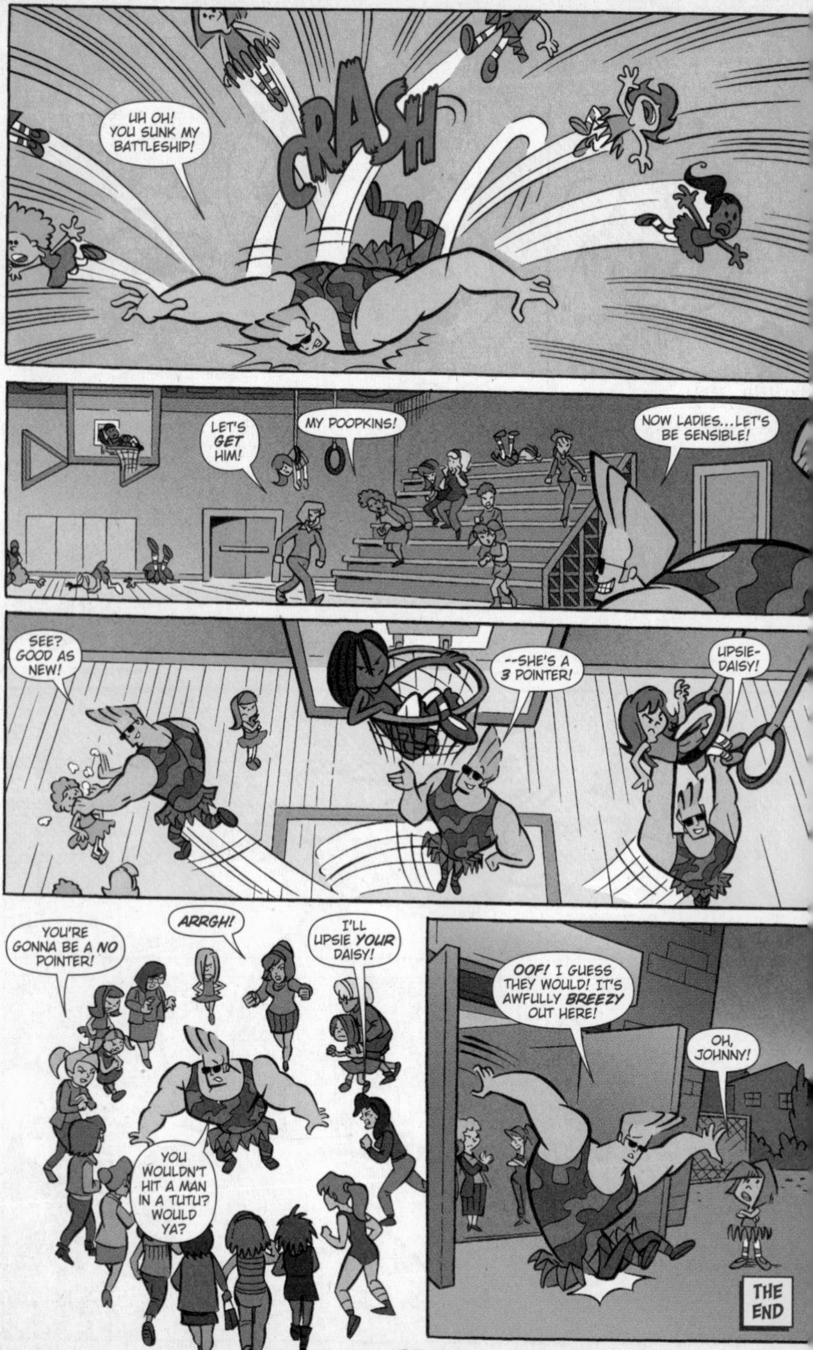
UH OH! YOU SUNK MY BATTLESHIP!
CRASH
LET'S GET HIM!
MY POOPKINS!
NOW LADIES...LET'S BE SENSIBLE!
SEE? GOOD AS NEW!
--SHE'S A 3 POINTER!
UPSIE-DAISY!
YOU'RE GONNA BE A NO POINTER!
ARRGH!
I'LL UPSIE YOUR DAISY!
YOU WOULDN'T HIT A MAN IN A TUTU? WOULD YA?
OOF! I GUESS THEY WOULD! IT'S AWFULLY BREEZY OUT HERE!
OH, JOHNNY!
THE END

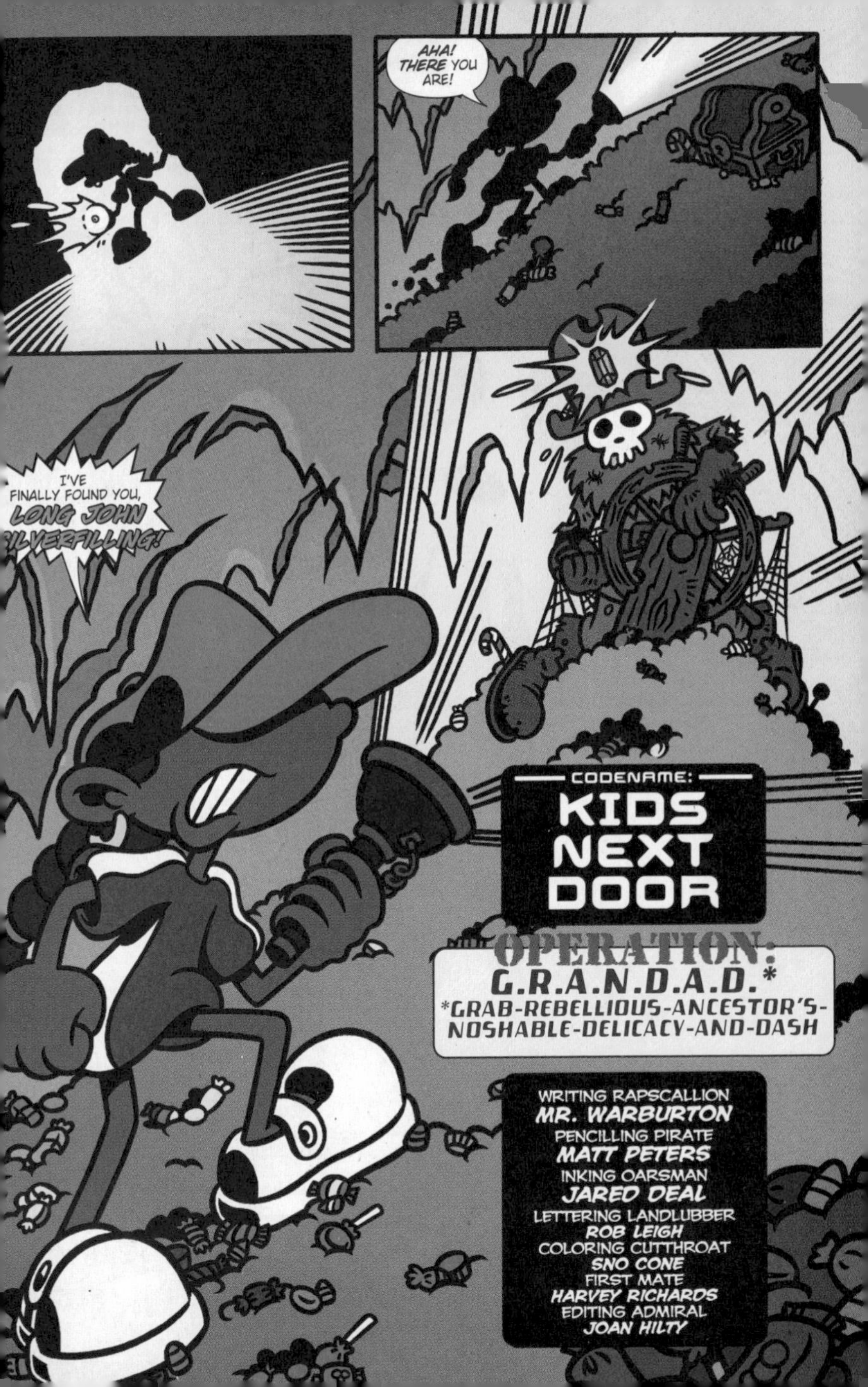
AHA! THERE YOU ARE!
I'VE FINALLY FOUND YOU, LONG JOHN SILVERFILLING!
CODENAME: KIDS NEXT DOOR
OPERATION: G.R.A.N.D.A.D.*
*GRAB-REBELLIOUS-ANCESTOR'S-NOSHABLE-DELICACY-AND-DASH
WRITING RAPSCALLION MR. WARBURTON
PENCILLING PIRATE MATT PETERS
INKING OARSMAN JARED DEAL
LETTERING LANDLUBBER ROB LEIGH
COLORING CUTTHROAT SNO CONE
FIRST MATE HARVEY RICHARDS
EDITING ADMIRAL JOAN HILTY

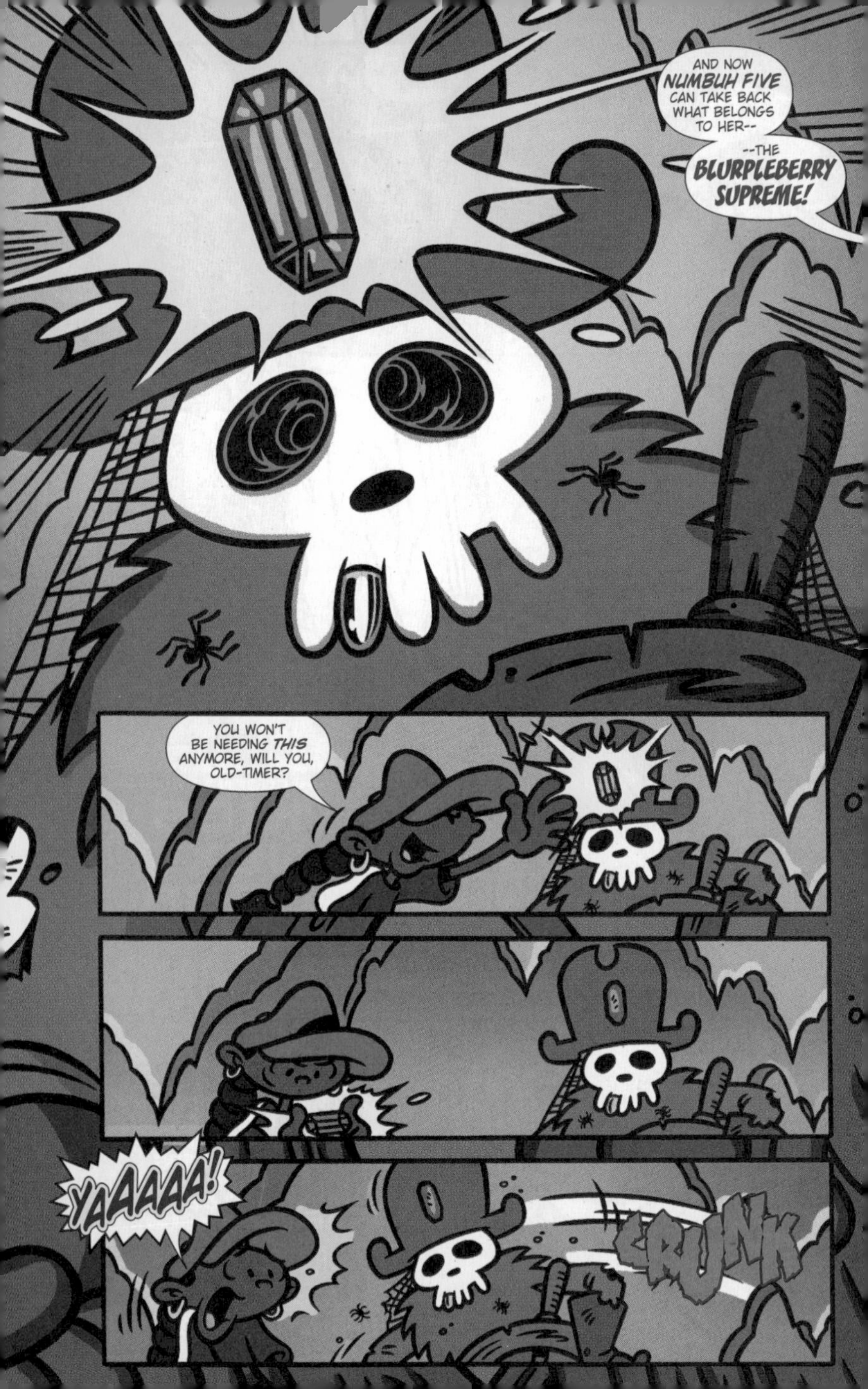
AND NOW NUMBUH FIVE CAN TAKE BACK WHAT BELONGS TO HER--
--THE BLURPLEBERRY SUPREME!
YOU WON'T BE NEEDING THIS ANYMORE, WILL YOU, OLD-TIMER?
YAAAAA!
CRUNK

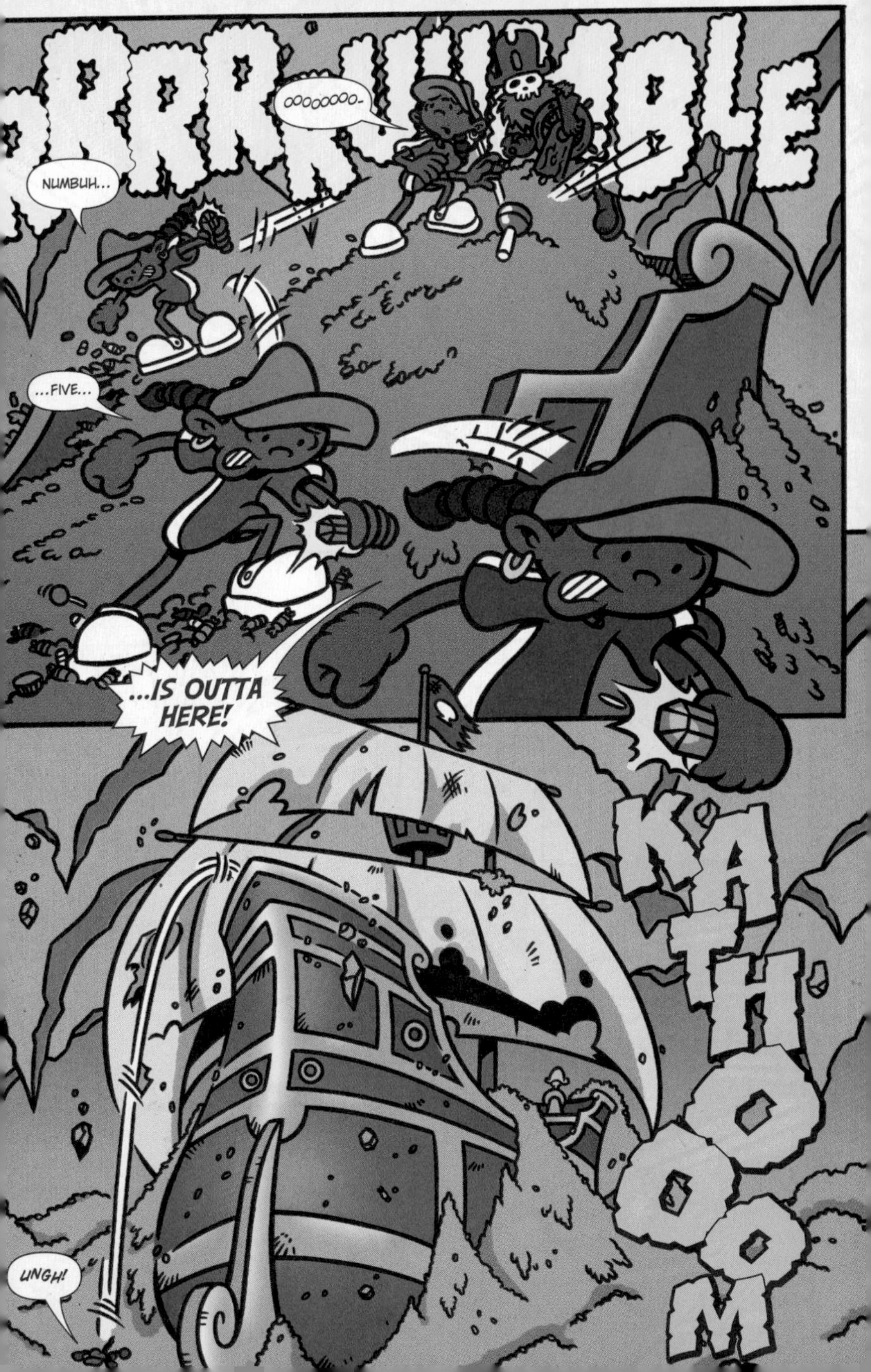

RRRUUUMBLE
NUMBUH...
OOOOOOOO-
...FIVE...
...IS OUTTA HERE!
KATHOOOOM
UNGH!

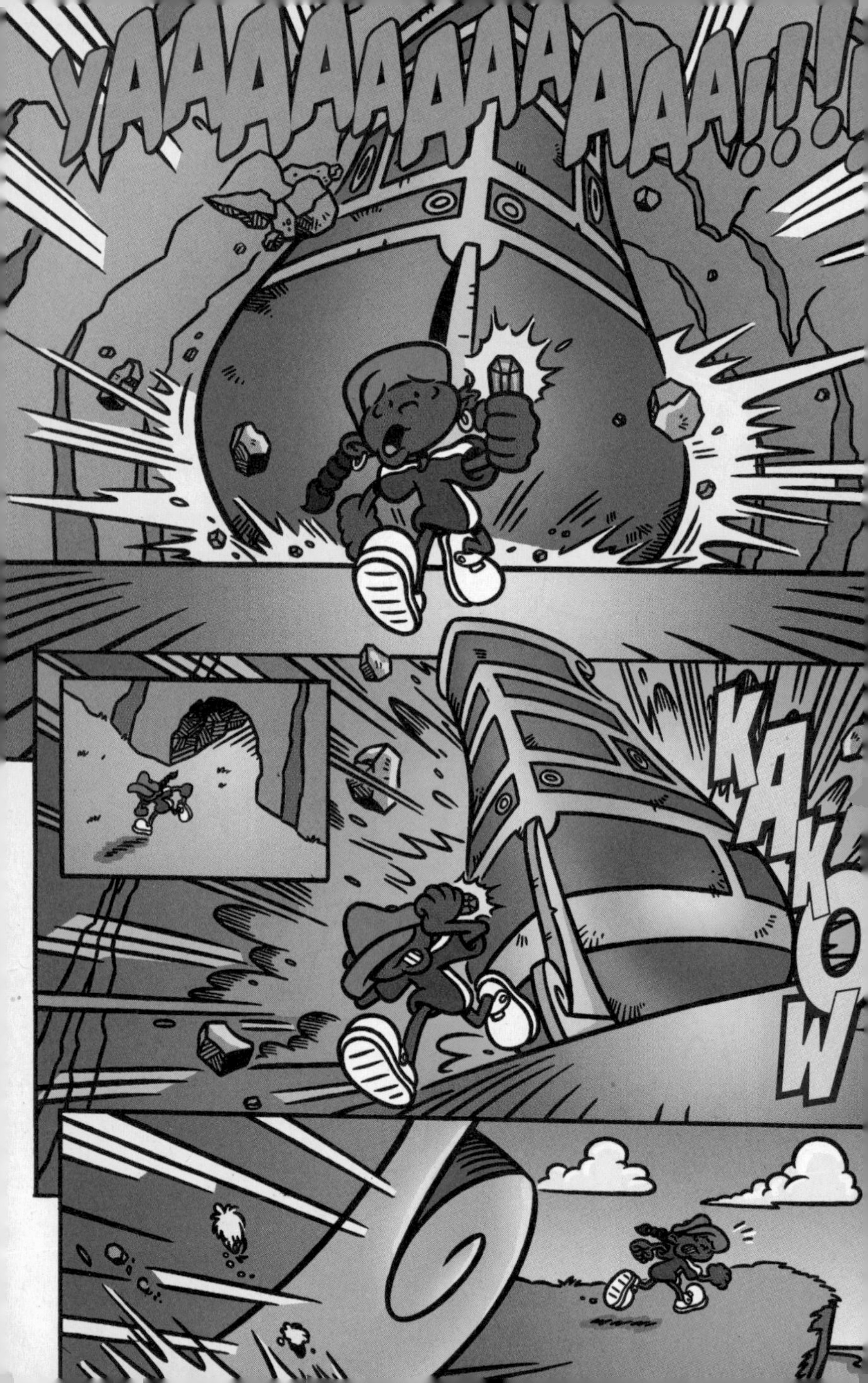
YAAAAAAAAAAA!!!!
KAKOW

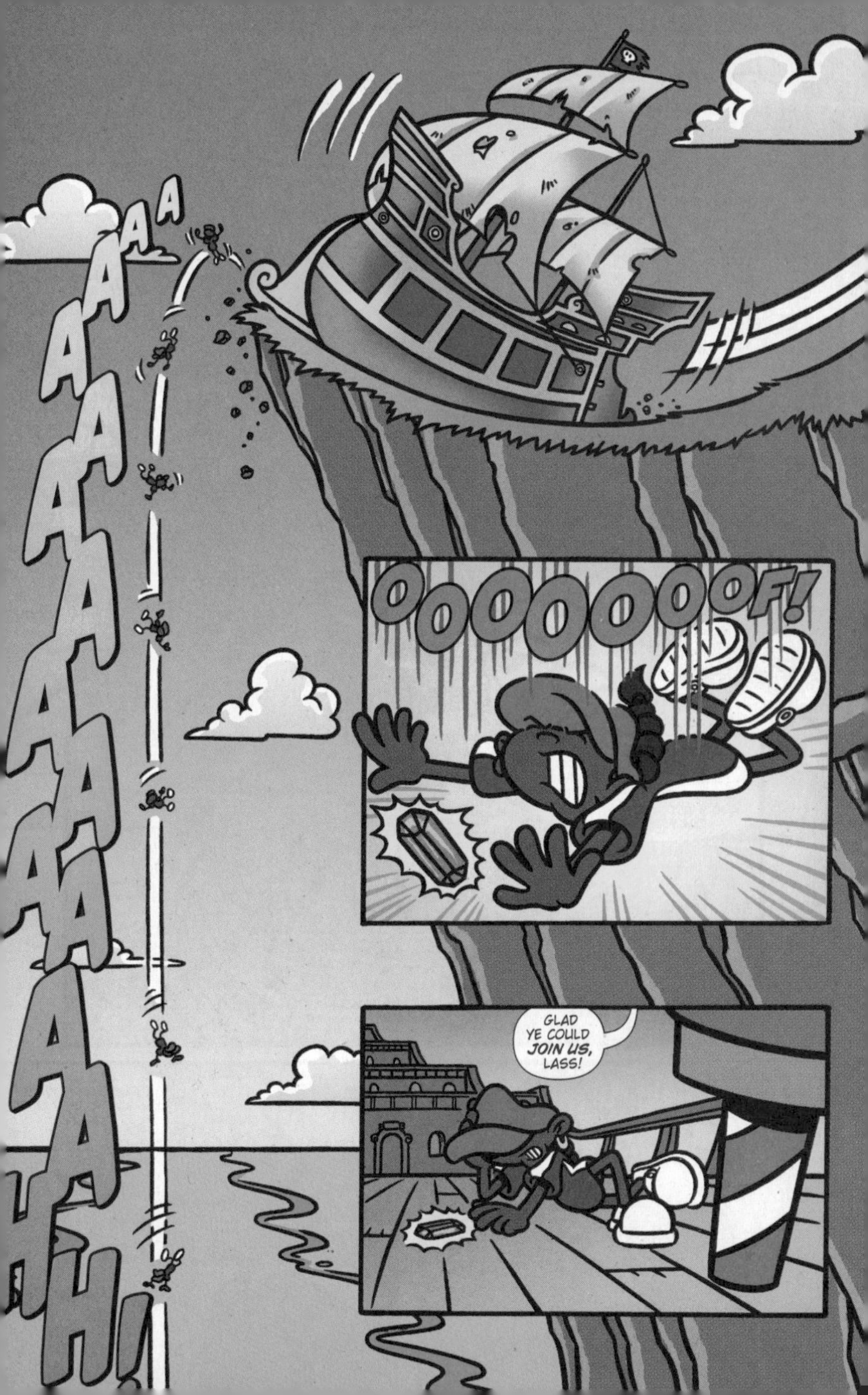
AAAAAAAAAAAAAAAAAAH!
OOOOOOOOF!
GLAD YE COULD JOIN US, LASS!

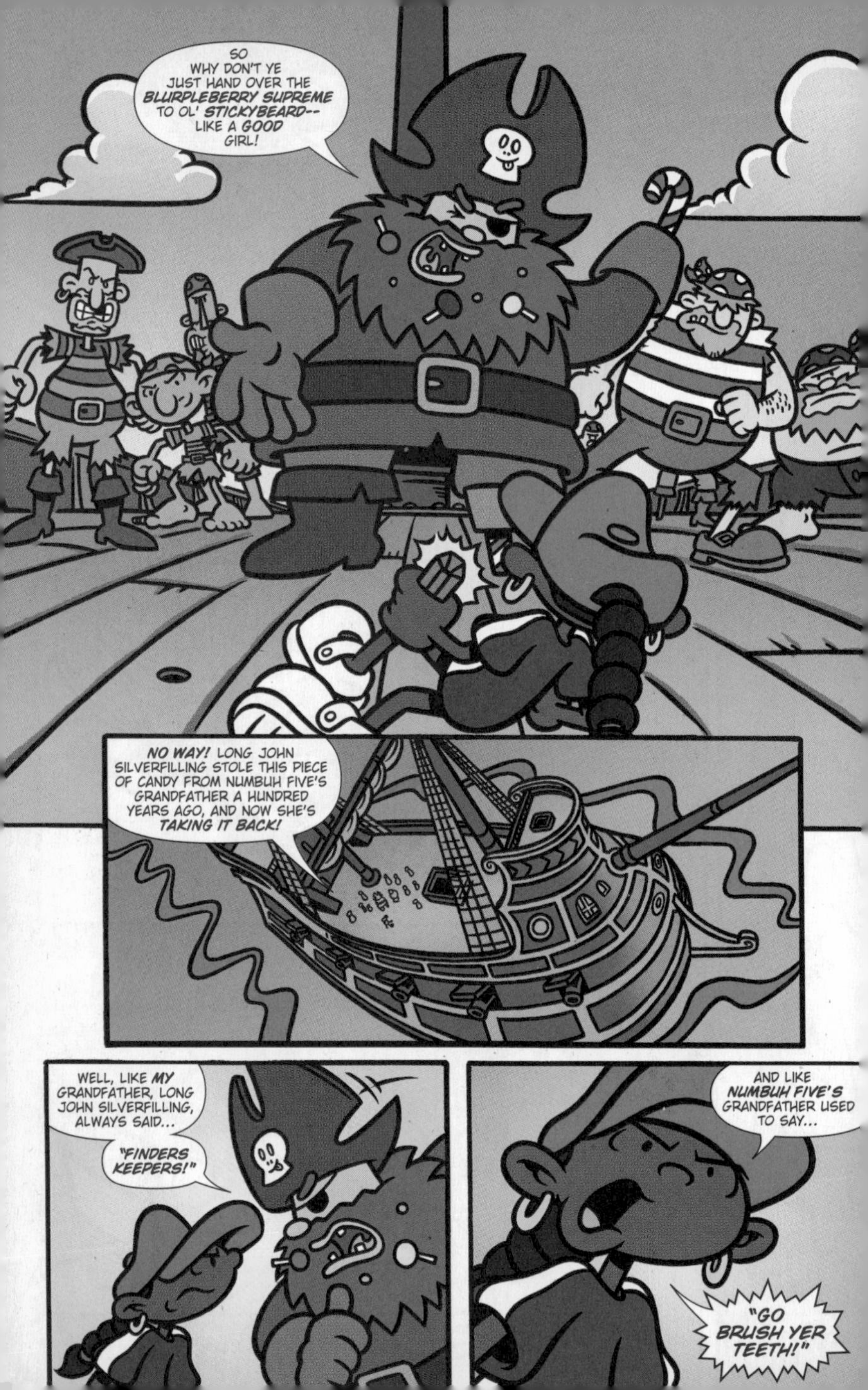
SO WHY DON'T YE JUST HAND OVER THE BLURPLEBERRY SUPREME TO OL' STICKYBEARD-- LIKE A GOOD GIRL!
NO WAY! LONG JOHN SILVERFILLING STOLE THIS PIECE OF CANDY FROM NUMBUH FIVE'S GRANDFATHER A HUNDRED YEARS AGO, AND NOW SHE'S TAKING IT BACK!
WELL, LIKE MY GRANDFATHER, LONG JOHN SILVERFILLING, ALWAYS SAID...
"FINDERS KEEPERS!"
AND LIKE NUMBUH FIVE'S GRANDFATHER USED TO SAY...
"GO BRUSH YER TEETH!"

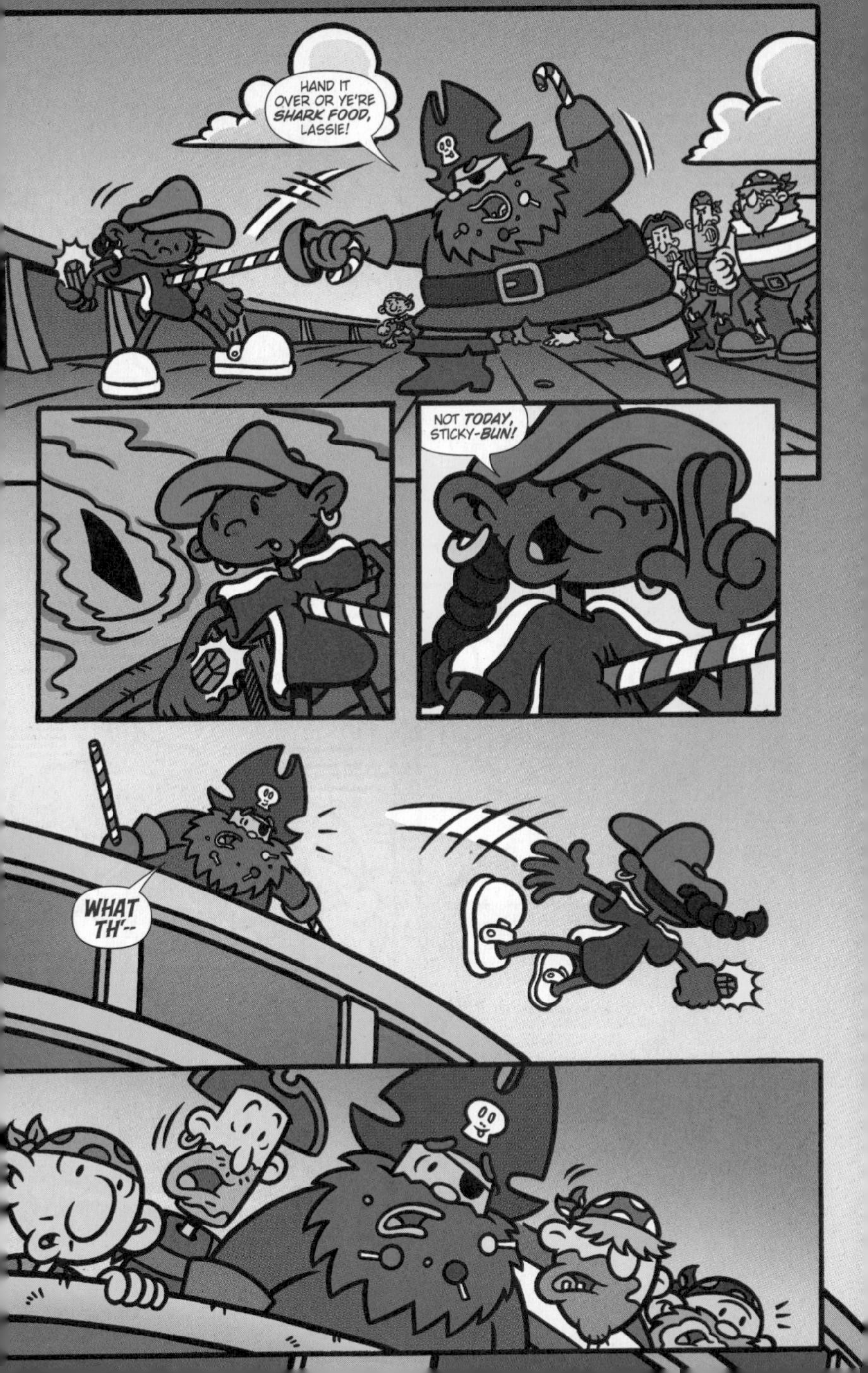
HAND IT OVER OR YE'RE SHARK FOOD, LASSIE!
NOT TODAY, STICKY-BUN!
WHAT TH'--

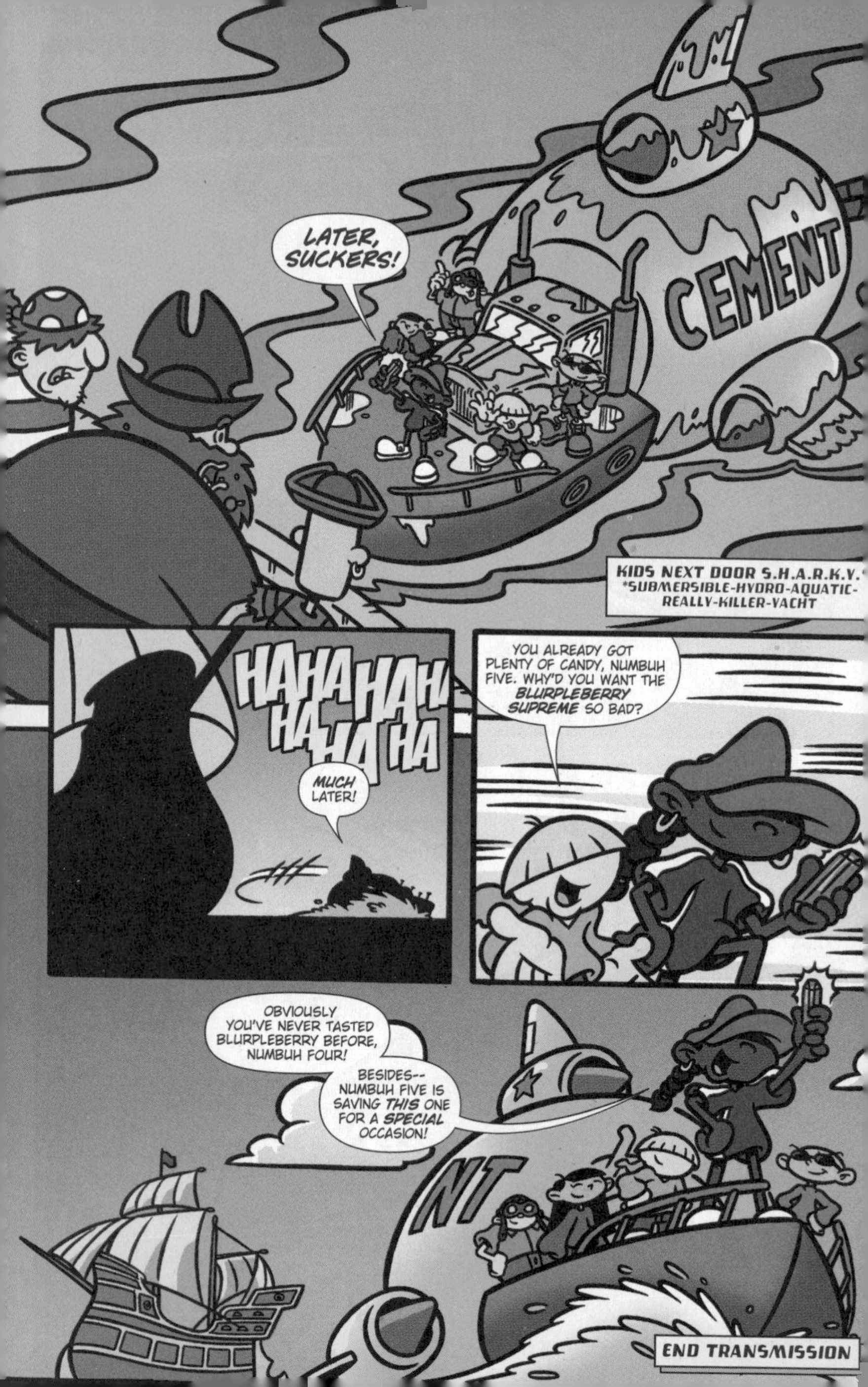
LATER, SUCKERS!
CEMENT
KIDS NEXT DOOR S.H.A.R.K.Y.*
*SUBMERSIBLE-HYDRO-AQUATIC-REALLY-KILLER-YACHT
HAHAHAHAHAHAHA HA
MUCH LATER!
YOU ALREADY GOT PLENTY OF CANDY, NUMBUH FIVE. WHY'D YOU WANT THE BLURPLEBERRY SUPREME SO BAD?
OBVIOUSLY YOU'VE NEVER TASTED BLURPLEBERRY BEFORE, NUMBUH FOUR!
BESIDES-- NUMBUH FIVE IS SAVING THIS ONE FOR A SPECIAL OCCASION!
NT
END TRANSMISSION

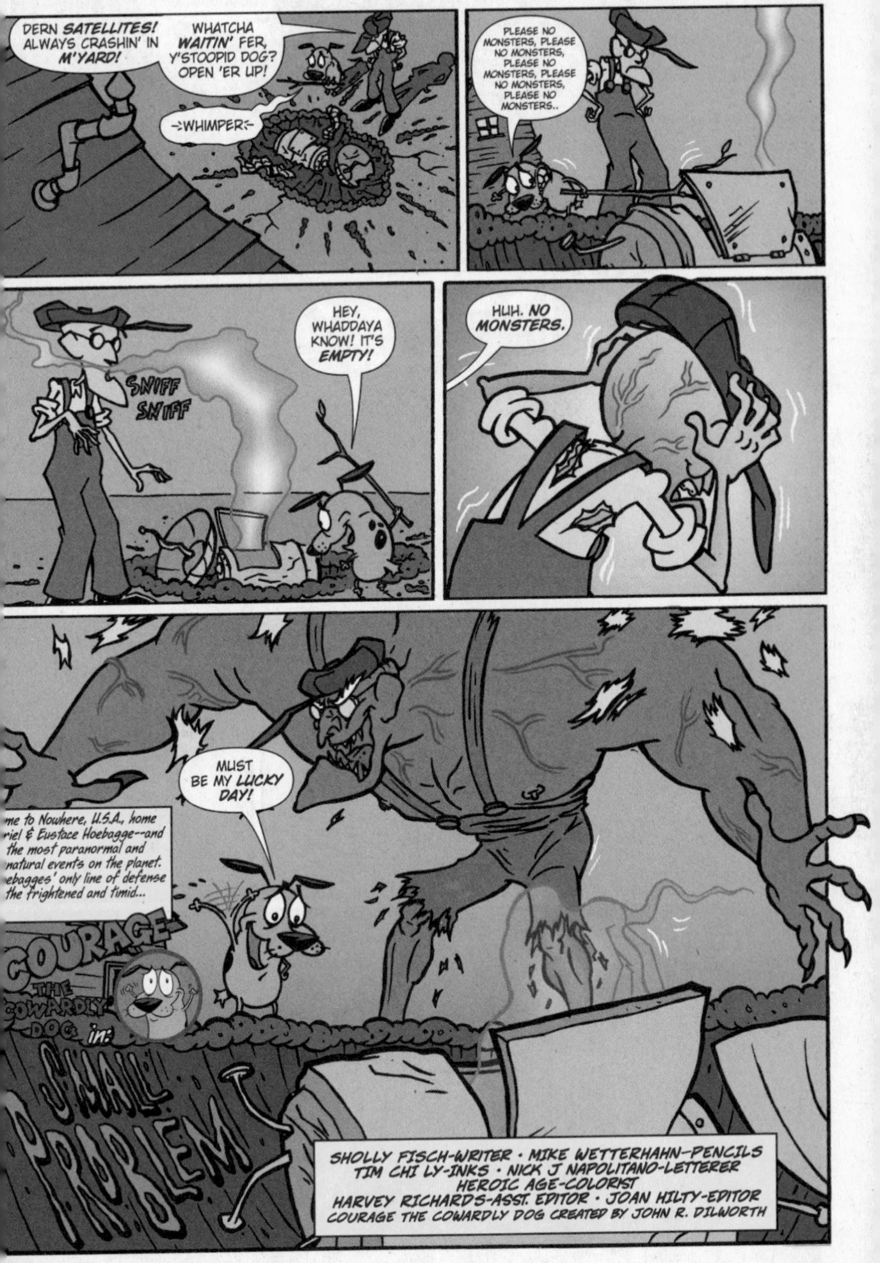
DERN SATELLITES! ALWAYS CRASHIN' IN M'YARD!
WHATCHA WAITIN' FER, Y'STOOPID DOG? OPEN 'ER UP!
WHIMPER
PLEASE NO MONSTERS, PLEASE NO MONSTERS, PLEASE NO MONSTERS, PLEASE NO MONSTERS, PLEASE NO MONSTERS..
SNIFF SNIFF
HEY, WHADDAYA KNOW! IT'S EMPTY!
HUH. NO MONSTERS.
MUST BE MY LUCKY DAY!
me to Nowhere, U.S.A., home
riel & Eustace Hoebagge--and
the most paranormal and
natural events on the planet.
ebagges' only line of defense
the frightened and timid...
COURAGE THE COWARDLY DOG in:
SNAIL PROBLEM
SHOLLY FISCH-WRITER • MIKE WETTERHAHN-PENCILS
TIM CHI LY-INKS • NICK J NAPOLITANO-LETTERER
HEROIC AGE-COLORIST
HARVEY RICHARDS-ASST. EDITOR • JOAN HILTY-EDITOR
COURAGE THE COWARDLY DOG CREATED BY JOHN R. DILWORTH

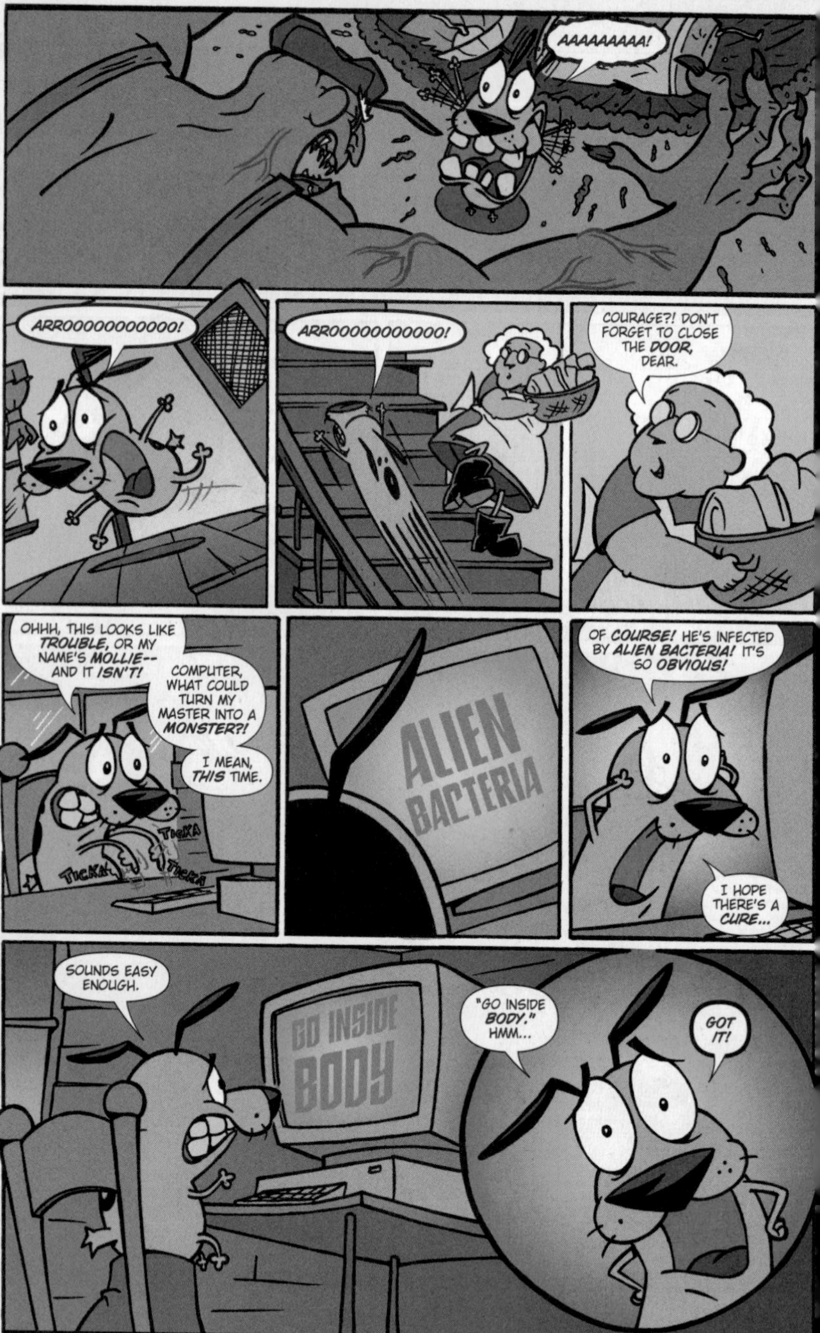
AAAAAAAAA!
ARROOOOOOOOOOO!
ARROOOOOOOOOOO!
COURAGE?! DON'T FORGET TO CLOSE THE DOOR, DEAR.
OHHH, THIS LOOKS LIKE TROUBLE, OR MY NAME'S MOLLIE-- AND IT ISN'T!
COMPUTER, WHAT COULD TURN MY MASTER INTO A MONSTER?!
I MEAN, THIS TIME.
TICKA
TICKA
TICKA
ALIEN BACTERIA
OF COURSE! HE'S INFECTED BY ALIEN BACTERIA! IT'S SO OBVIOUS!
I HOPE THERE'S A CURE...
SOUNDS EASY ENOUGH.
GO INSIDE BODY
"GO INSIDE BODY." HMM...
GOT IT!

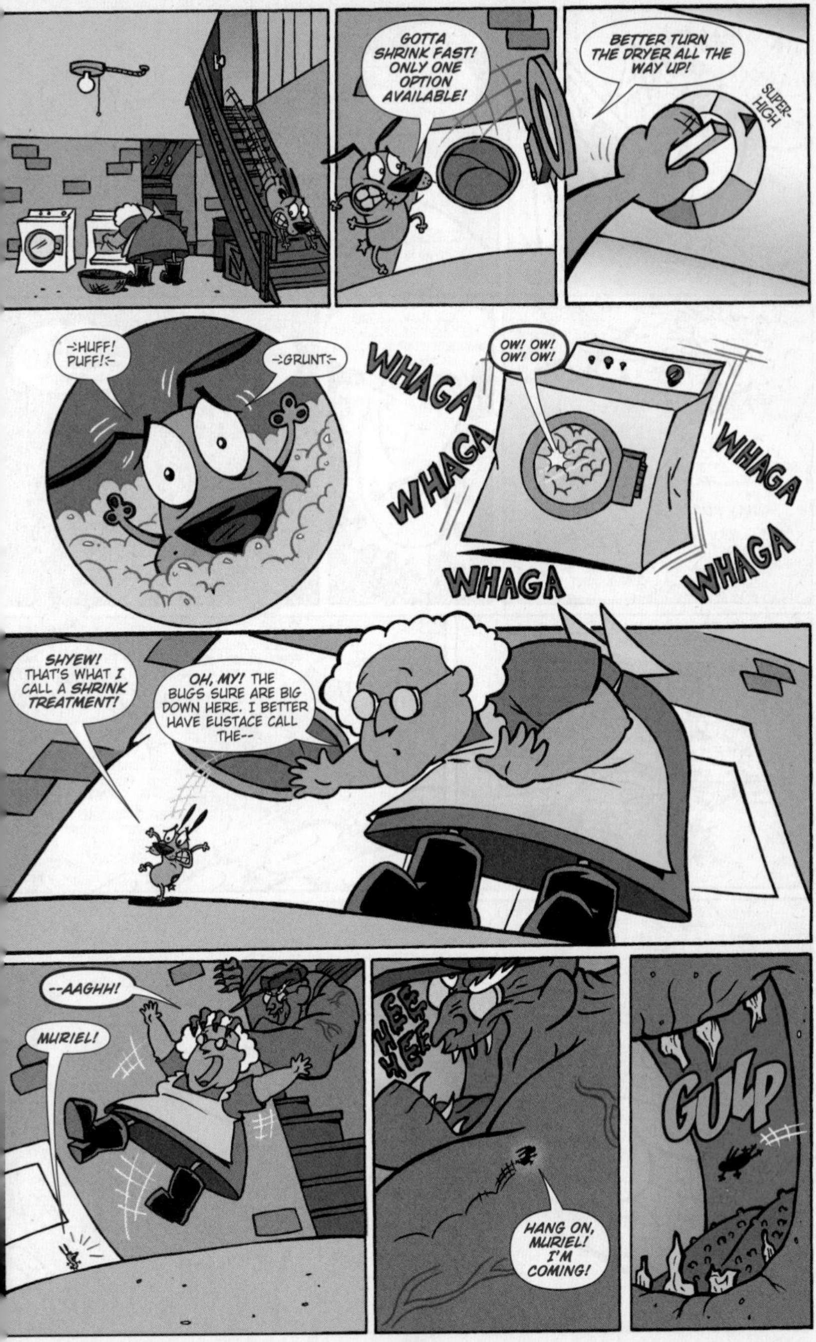
GOTTA SHRINK FAST! ONLY ONE OPTION AVAILABLE!
BETTER TURN THE DRYER ALL THE WAY UP!
SUPER-HIGH
-HUFF! PUFF!-
-GRUNT-
WHAGA
WHAGA
OW! OW! OW! OW!
WHAGA
WHAGA
WHAGA
SHYEW! THAT'S WHAT I CALL A SHRINK TREATMENT!
OH, MY! THE BUGS SURE ARE BIG DOWN HERE. I BETTER HAVE EUSTACE CALL THE--
--AAGHH!
MURIEL!
HEE HEE
HANG ON, MURIEL! I'M COMING!
GULP

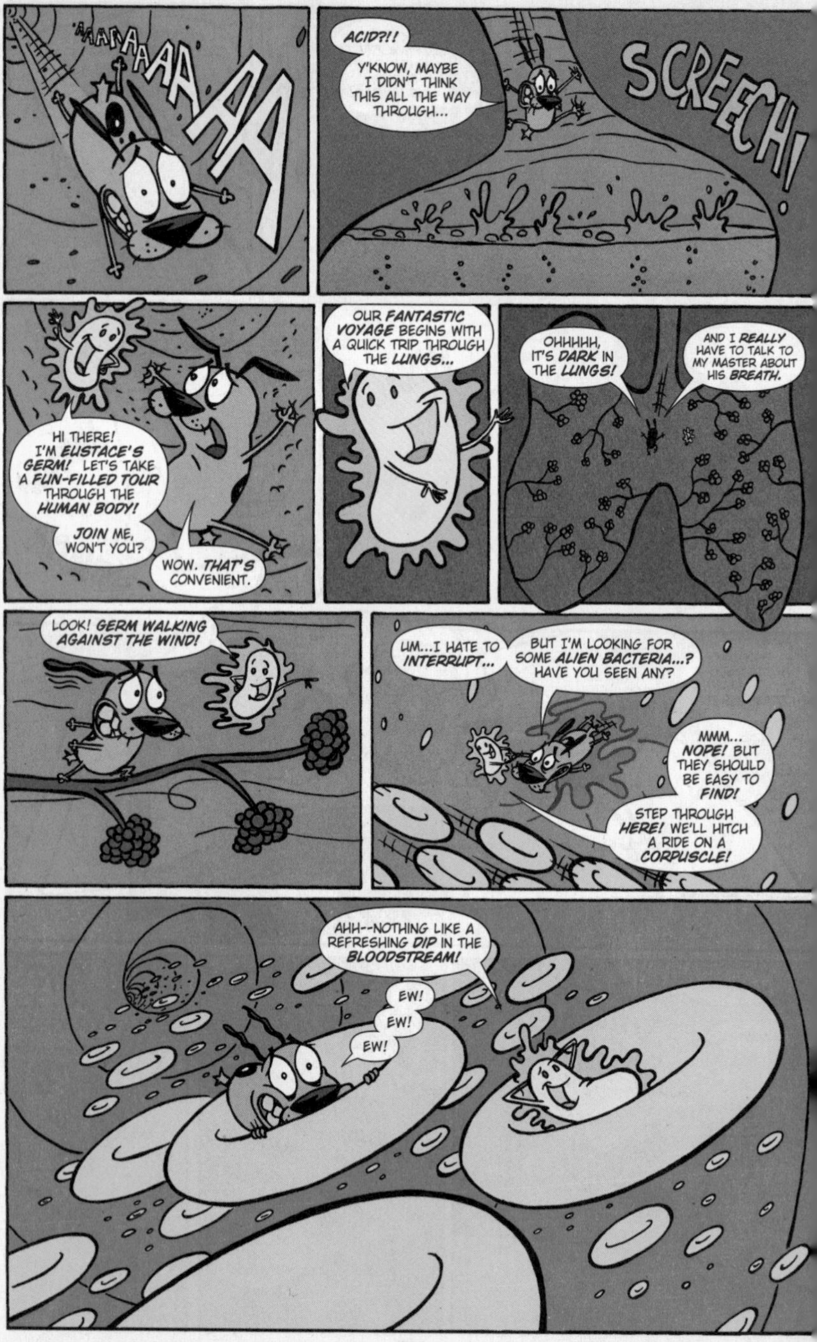
AAAAAAAAAA
ACID?!!
Y'KNOW, MAYBE I DIDN'T THINK THIS ALL THE WAY THROUGH...
SCREECH!
HI THERE! I'M EUSTACE'S GERM! LET'S TAKE A FUN-FILLED TOUR THROUGH THE HUMAN BODY!
JOIN ME, WON'T YOU?
WOW. THAT'S CONVENIENT.
OUR FANTASTIC VOYAGE BEGINS WITH A QUICK TRIP THROUGH THE LUNGS...
OHHHHH, IT'S DARK IN THE LUNGS!
AND I REALLY HAVE TO TALK TO MY MASTER ABOUT HIS BREATH.
LOOK! GERM WALKING AGAINST THE WIND!
UM...I HATE TO INTERRUPT...
BUT I'M LOOKING FOR SOME ALIEN BACTERIA...? HAVE YOU SEEN ANY?
MMM... NOPE! BUT THEY SHOULD BE EASY TO FIND!
STEP THROUGH HERE! WE'LL HITCH A RIDE ON A CORPUSCLE!
AHH--NOTHING LIKE A REFRESHING DIP IN THE BLOODSTREAM!
EW!
EW!
EW!

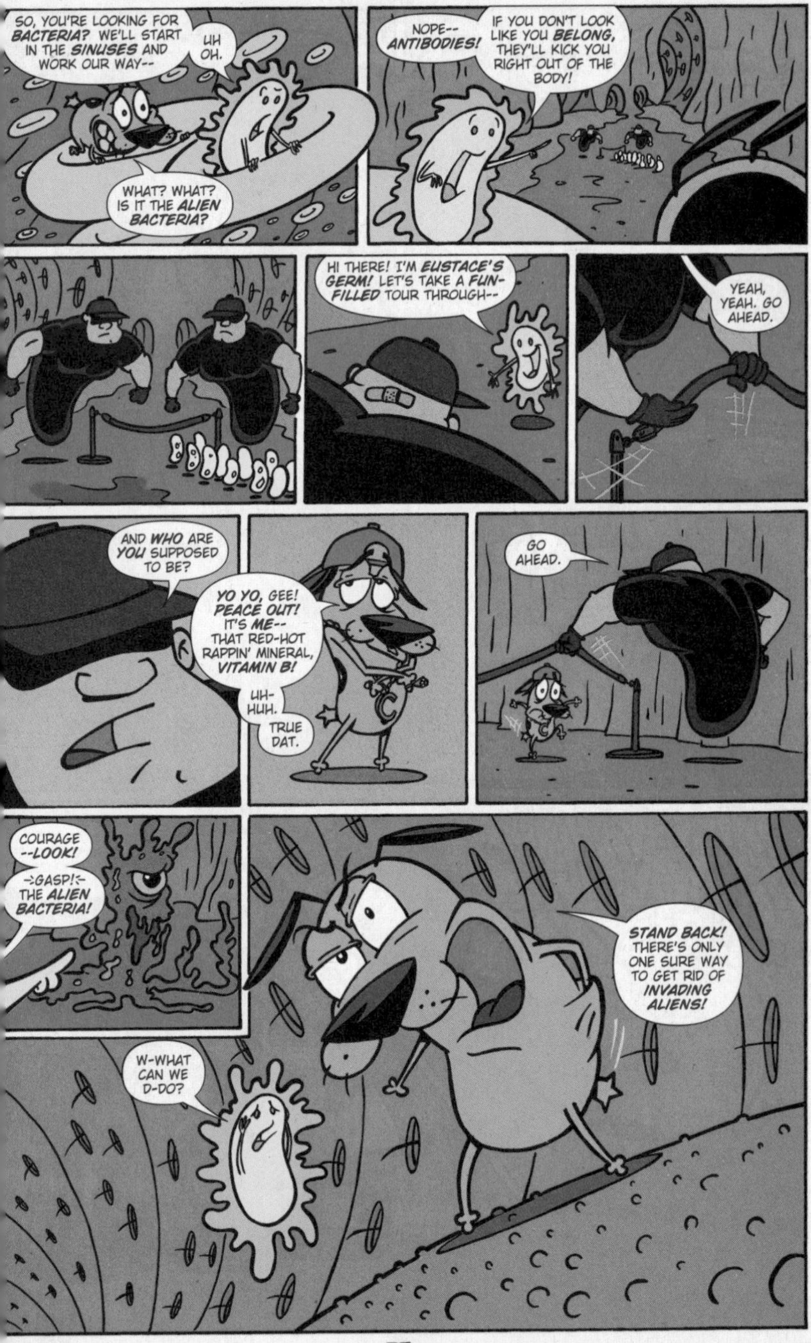
SO, YOU'RE LOOKING FOR BACTERIA? WE'LL START IN THE SINUSES AND WORK OUR WAY--
UH OH.
WHAT? WHAT? IS IT THE ALIEN BACTERIA?
NOPE-- ANTIBODIES!
IF YOU DON'T LOOK LIKE YOU BELONG, THEY'LL KICK YOU RIGHT OUT OF THE BODY!
HI THERE! I'M EUSTACE'S GERM! LET'S TAKE A FUN-FILLED TOUR THROUGH--
YEAH, YEAH. GO AHEAD.
AND WHO ARE YOU SUPPOSED TO BE?
YO YO, GEE! PEACE OUT! IT'S ME-- THAT RED-HOT RAPPIN' MINERAL, VITAMIN B!
UH-HUH.
TRUE DAT.
GO AHEAD.
COURAGE --LOOK!
-GASP!- THE ALIEN BACTERIA!
STAND BACK! THERE'S ONLY ONE SURE WAY TO GET RID OF INVADING ALIENS!
W-WHAT CAN WE D-DO?

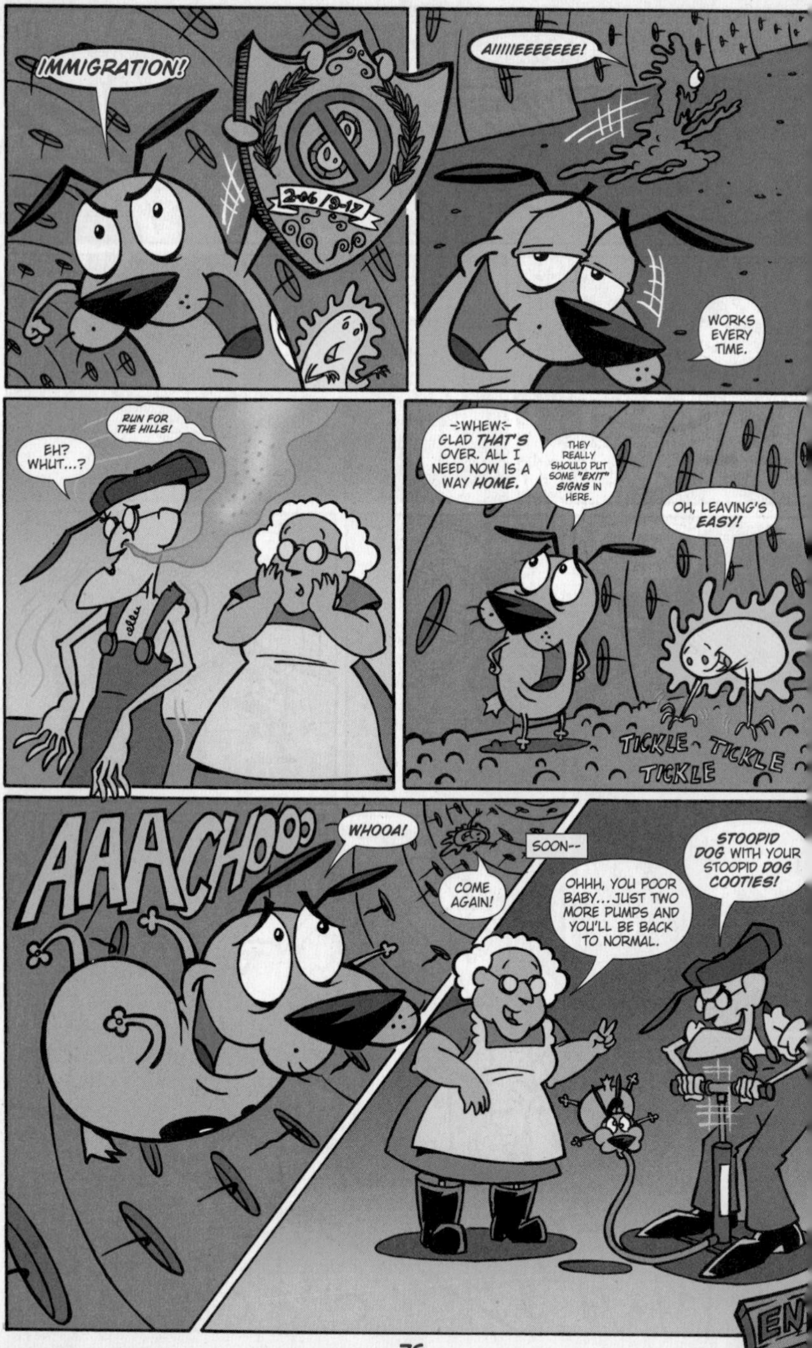

IMMIGRATION!
2-06/9-17
AIIIIIEEEEEEE!
WORKS EVERY TIME.
EH? WHUT...?
RUN FOR THE HILLS!
-WHEW- GLAD THAT'S OVER. ALL I NEED NOW IS A WAY HOME.
THEY REALLY SHOULD PUT SOME "EXIT" SIGNS IN HERE.
OH, LEAVING'S EASY!
TICKLE TICKLE TICKLE
AAACHOOO
WHOOA!
COME AGAIN!
SOON--
OHHH, YOU POOR BABY... JUST TWO MORE PUMPS AND YOU'LL BE BACK TO NORMAL.
STOOPID DOG WITH YOUR STOOPID DOG COOTIES!

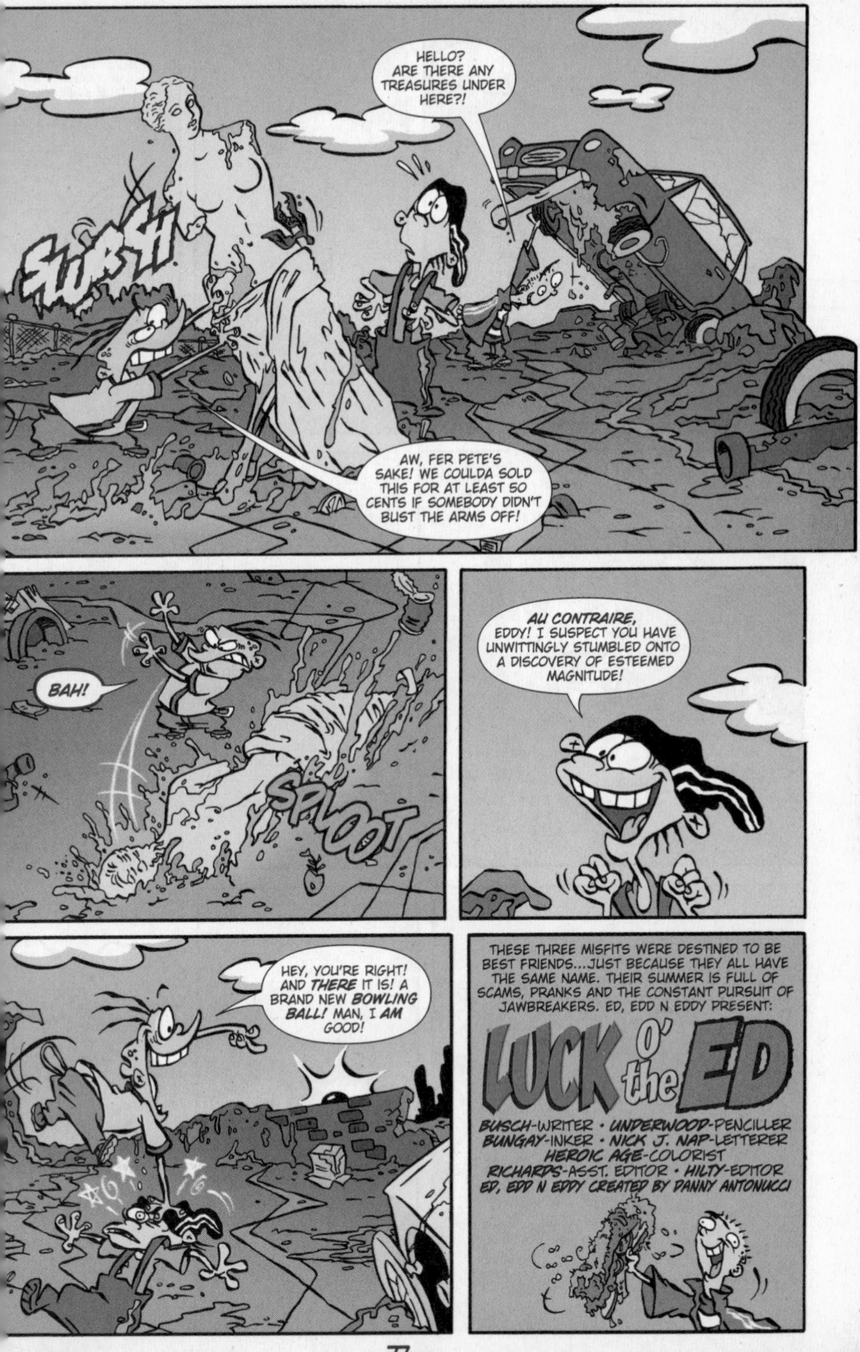
HELLO? ARE THERE ANY TREASURES UNDER HERE?!
AW, FER PETE'S SAKE! WE COULDA SOLD THIS FOR AT LEAST 50 CENTS IF SOMEBODY DIDN'T BUST THE ARMS OFF!
BAH!
SPLOOT
AU CONTRAIRE, EDDY! I SUSPECT YOU HAVE UNWITTINGLY STUMBLED ONTO A DISCOVERY OF ESTEEMED MAGNITUDE!
HEY, YOU'RE RIGHT! AND THERE IT IS! A BRAND NEW BOWLING BALL! MAN, I AM GOOD!
THESE THREE MISFITS WERE DESTINED TO BE BEST FRIENDS...JUST BECAUSE THEY ALL HAVE THE SAME NAME. THEIR SUMMER IS FULL OF SCAMS, PRANKS AND THE CONSTANT PURSUIT OF JAWBREAKERS. ED, EDD N EDDY PRESENT:
LUCK O' the ED
BUSCH-WRITER • UNDERWOOD-PENCILLER
BUNGAY-INKER • NICK J. NAP-LETTERER
HEROIC AGE-COLORIST
RICHARDS-ASST. EDITOR • HILTY-EDITOR
ED, EDD N EDDY CREATED BY DANNY ANTONUCCI

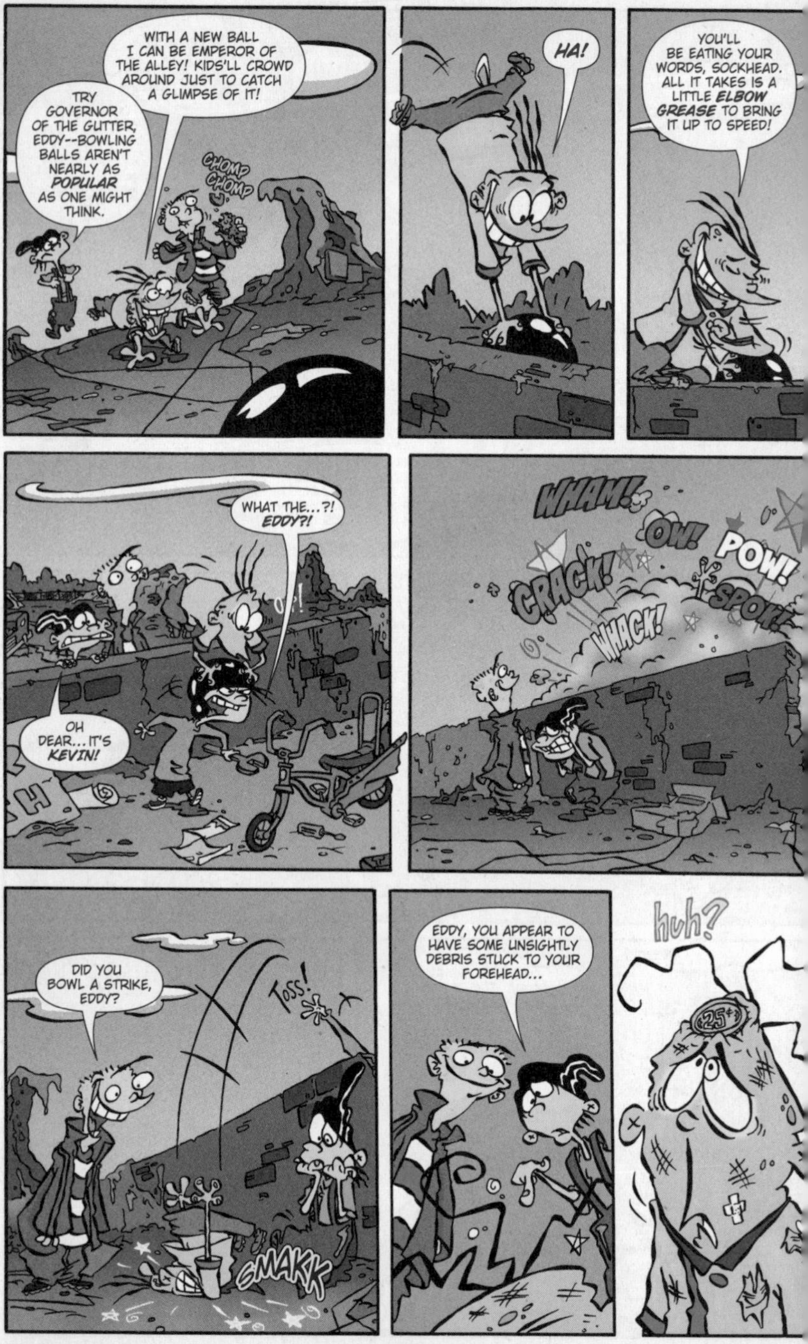
WITH A NEW BALL I CAN BE EMPEROR OF THE ALLEY! KIDS'LL CROWD AROUND JUST TO CATCH A GLIMPSE OF IT!
TRY GOVERNOR OF THE GUTTER, EDDY--BOWLING BALLS AREN'T NEARLY AS POPULAR AS ONE MIGHT THINK.
CHOMP CHOMP
HA!
YOU'LL BE EATING YOUR WORDS, SOCKHEAD. ALL IT TAKES IS A LITTLE ELBOW GREASE TO BRING IT UP TO SPEED!
WHAT THE...?! EDDY?!
OH DEAR...IT'S KEVIN!
WHAM!
OW!
POW!
CRACK!
SPOK!
WHACK!
DID YOU BOWL A STRIKE, EDDY?
TOSS!
SMAKK
EDDY, YOU APPEAR TO HAVE SOME UNSIGHTLY DEBRIS STUCK TO YOUR FOREHEAD...
huh?
25¢

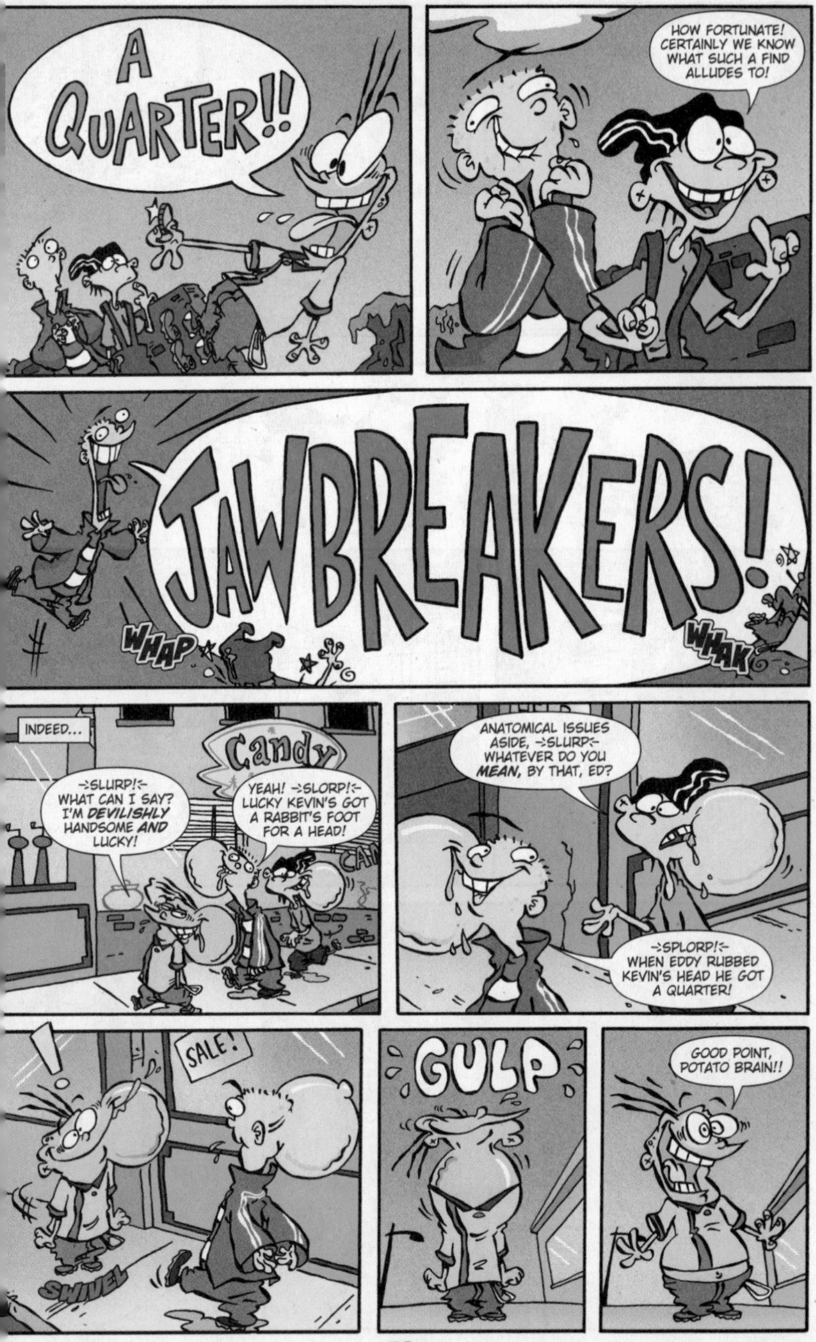
A QUARTER!!
HOW FORTUNATE! CERTAINLY WE KNOW WHAT SUCH A FIND ALLUDES TO!
JAWBREAKERS!
WHAP
WHAK
INDEED...
Candy
-SLURP!- WHAT CAN I SAY? I'M DEVILISHLY HANDSOME AND LUCKY!
YEAH! -SLORP!- LUCKY KEVIN'S GOT A RABBIT'S FOOT FOR A HEAD!
ANATOMICAL ISSUES ASIDE, -SLURP- WHATEVER DO YOU MEAN, BY THAT, ED?
-SPLORP!- WHEN EDDY RUBBED KEVIN'S HEAD HE GOT A QUARTER!
!
SALE!
SWIVEL
GULP
GOOD POINT, POTATO BRAIN!!

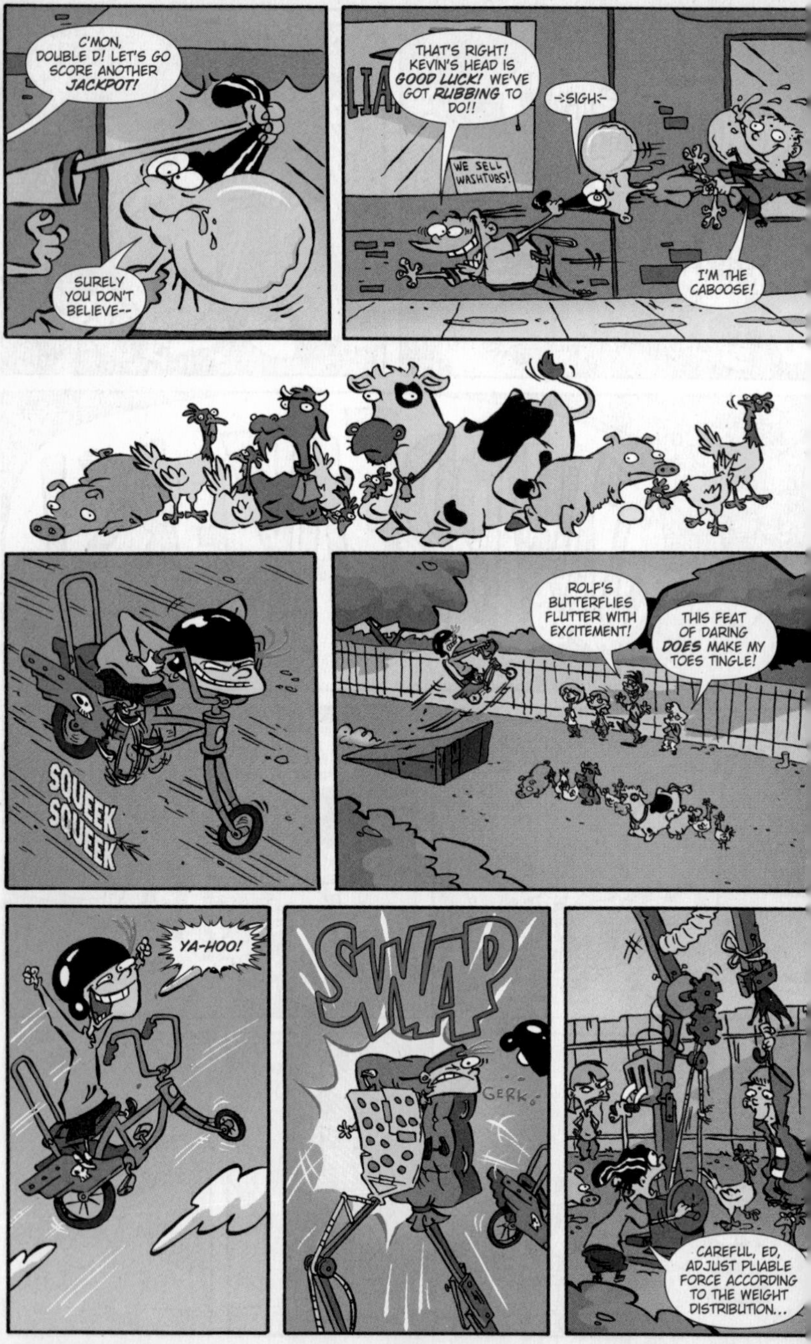
C'MON, DOUBLE D! LET'S GO SCORE ANOTHER JACKPOT!
SURELY YOU DON'T BELIEVE--
THAT'S RIGHT! KEVIN'S HEAD IS GOOD LUCK! WE'VE GOT RUBBING TO DO!!
WE SELL WASHTUBS!
-SIGH-
I'M THE CABOOSE!
SQUEEK SQUEEK
ROLF'S BUTTERFLIES FLUTTER WITH EXCITEMENT!
THIS FEAT OF DARING DOES MAKE MY TOES TINGLE!
YA-HOO!
SWAP
GERK
CAREFUL, ED, ADJUST PLIABLE FORCE ACCORDING TO THE WEIGHT DISTRIBUTION...

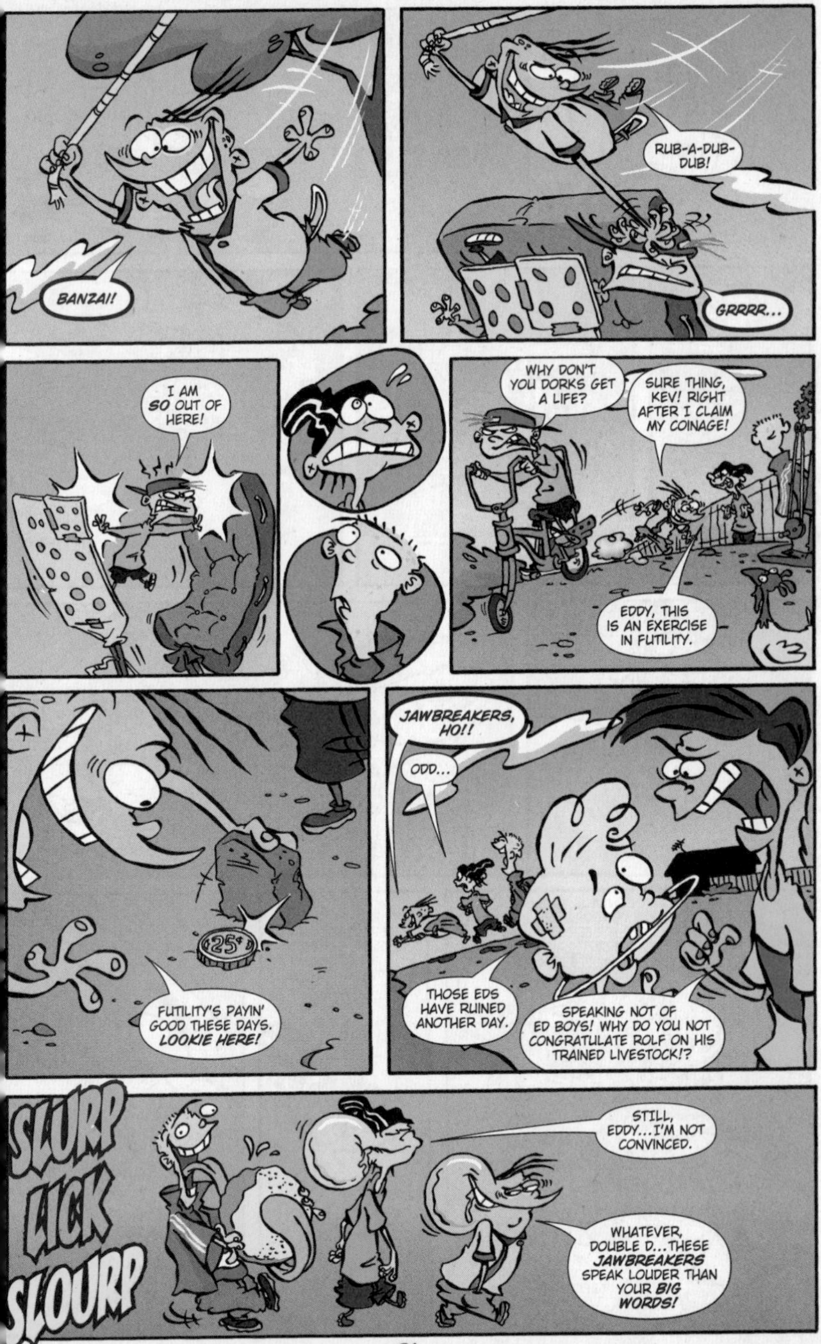
BANZAI!
RUB-A-DUB-DUB!
GRRRR...
I AM SO OUT OF HERE!
WHY DON'T YOU DORKS GET A LIFE?
SURE THING, KEV! RIGHT AFTER I CLAIM MY COINAGE!
EDDY, THIS IS AN EXERCISE IN FUTILITY.
FUTILITY'S PAYIN' GOOD THESE DAYS. LOOKIE HERE!
25¢
JAWBREAKERS, HO!!
ODD...
THOSE EDS HAVE RUINED ANOTHER DAY.
SPEAKING NOT OF ED BOYS! WHY DO YOU NOT CONGRATULATE ROLF ON HIS TRAINED LIVESTOCK!?
SLURP LICK SLOURP
STILL, EDDY...I'M NOT CONVINCED.
WHATEVER, DOUBLE D...THESE JAWBREAKERS SPEAK LOUDER THAN YOUR BIG WORDS!

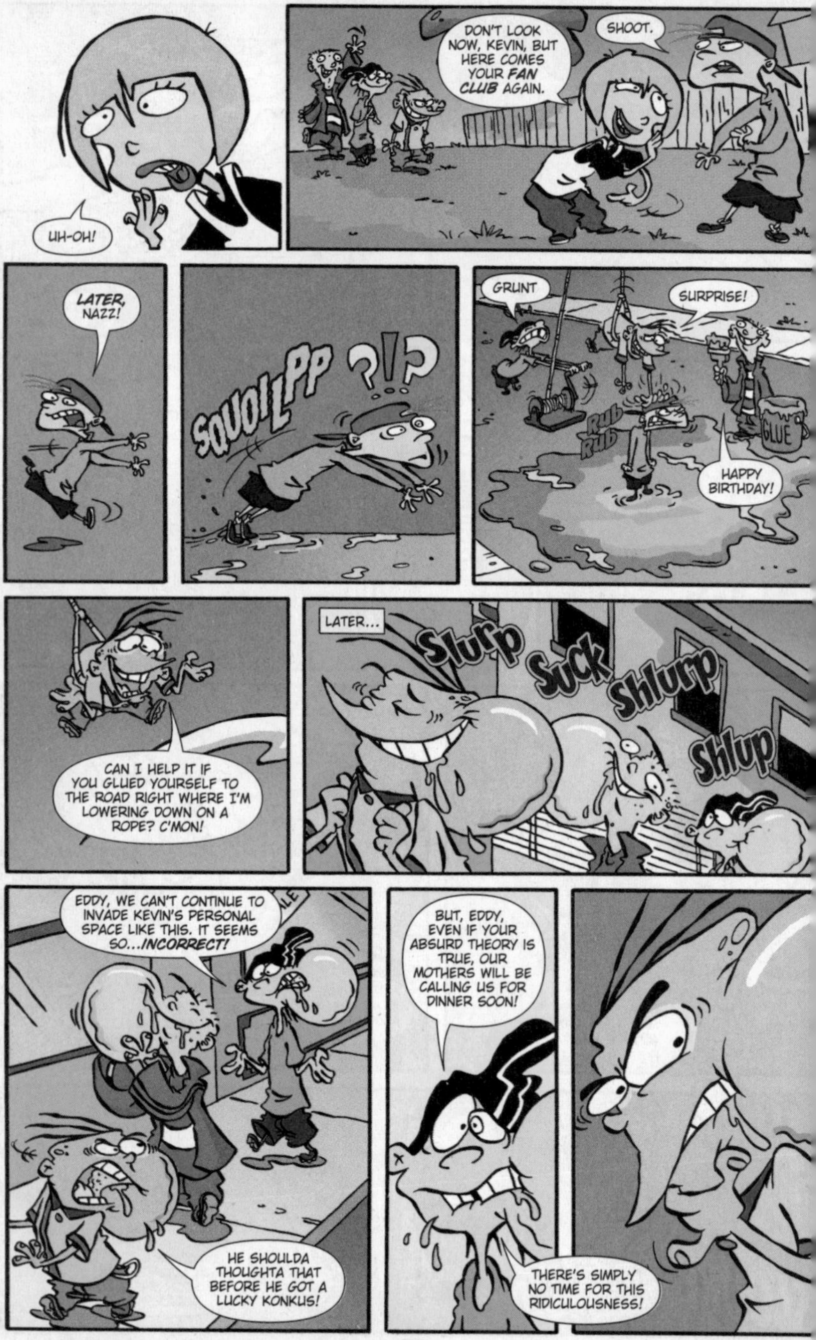
UH-OH!
DON'T LOOK NOW, KEVIN, BUT HERE COMES YOUR FAN CLUB AGAIN.
SHOOT.
LATER, NAZZ!
SQUOILLPP
?!?
GRUNT
SURPRISE!
Rub Rub
GLUE
HAPPY BIRTHDAY!
CAN I HELP IT IF YOU GLUED YOURSELF TO THE ROAD RIGHT WHERE I'M LOWERING DOWN ON A ROPE? C'MON!
LATER...
Slurp
Suck
Shlurp
Shlup
EDDY, WE CAN'T CONTINUE TO INVADE KEVIN'S PERSONAL SPACE LIKE THIS. IT SEEMS SO...INCORRECT!
HE SHOULDA THOUGHTA THAT BEFORE HE GOT A LUCKY KONKUS!
BUT, EDDY, EVEN IF YOUR ABSURD THEORY IS TRUE, OUR MOTHERS WILL BE CALLING US FOR DINNER SOON!
THERE'S SIMPLY NO TIME FOR THIS RIDICULOUSNESS!

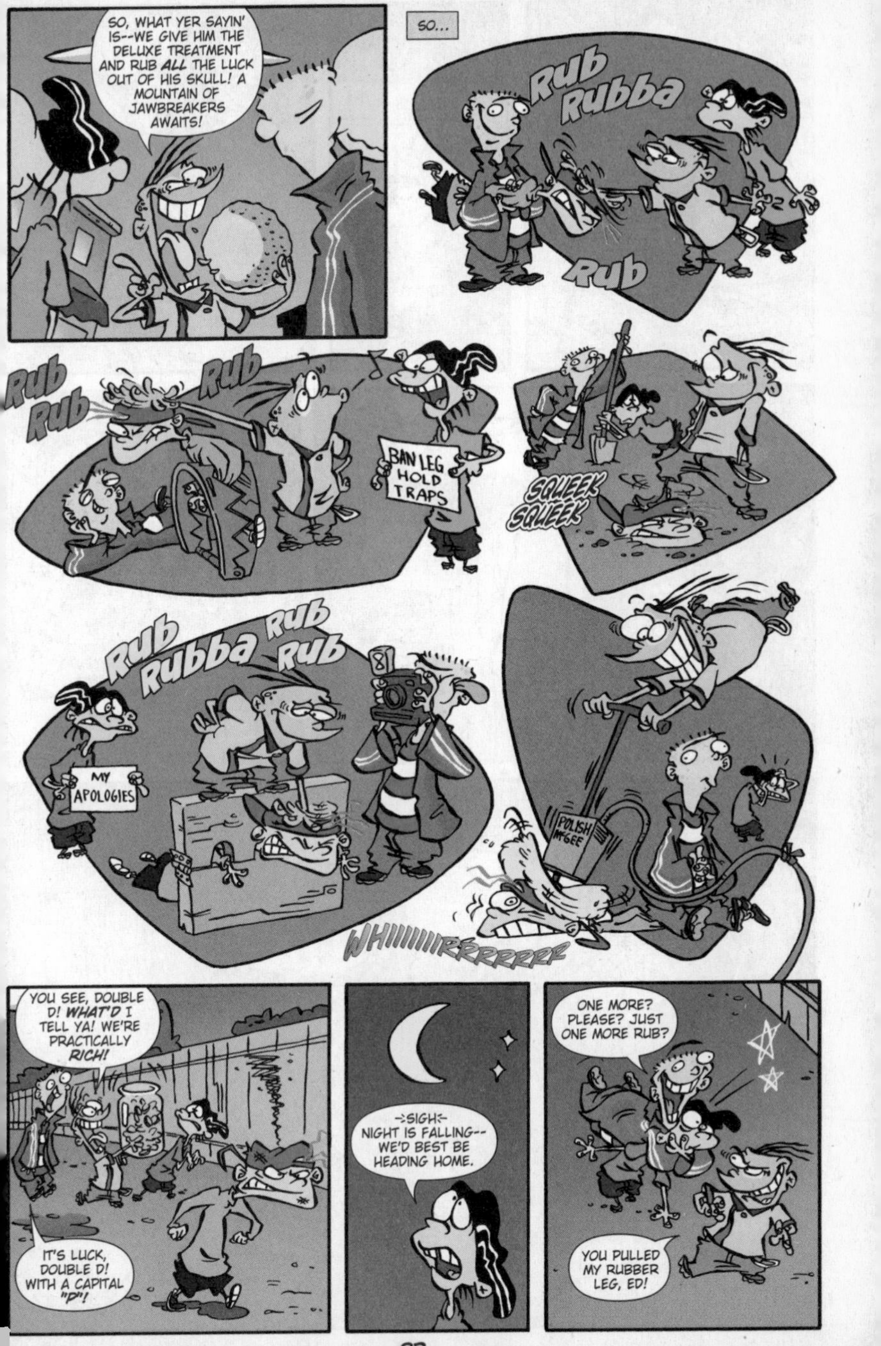
SO, WHAT YER SAYIN' IS--WE GIVE HIM THE DELUXE TREATMENT AND RUB ALL THE LUCK OUT OF HIS SKULL! A MOUNTAIN OF JAWBREAKERS AWAITS!
SO...
Rub Rubba
Rub
Rub Rub
Rub
BAN LEG HOLD TRAPS
SQUEEK SQUEEK
Rub Rubba Rub Rub
MY APOLOGIES
POLISH McGEE
WHIIIIIIIIRRRRRRR
YOU SEE, DOUBLE D! WHAT'D I TELL YA! WE'RE PRACTICALLY RICH!
IT'S LUCK, DOUBLE D! WITH A CAPITAL "P"!
-SIGH- NIGHT IS FALLING-- WE'D BEST BE HEADING HOME.
ONE MORE? PLEASE? JUST ONE MORE RUB?
YOU PULLED MY RUBBER LEG, ED!

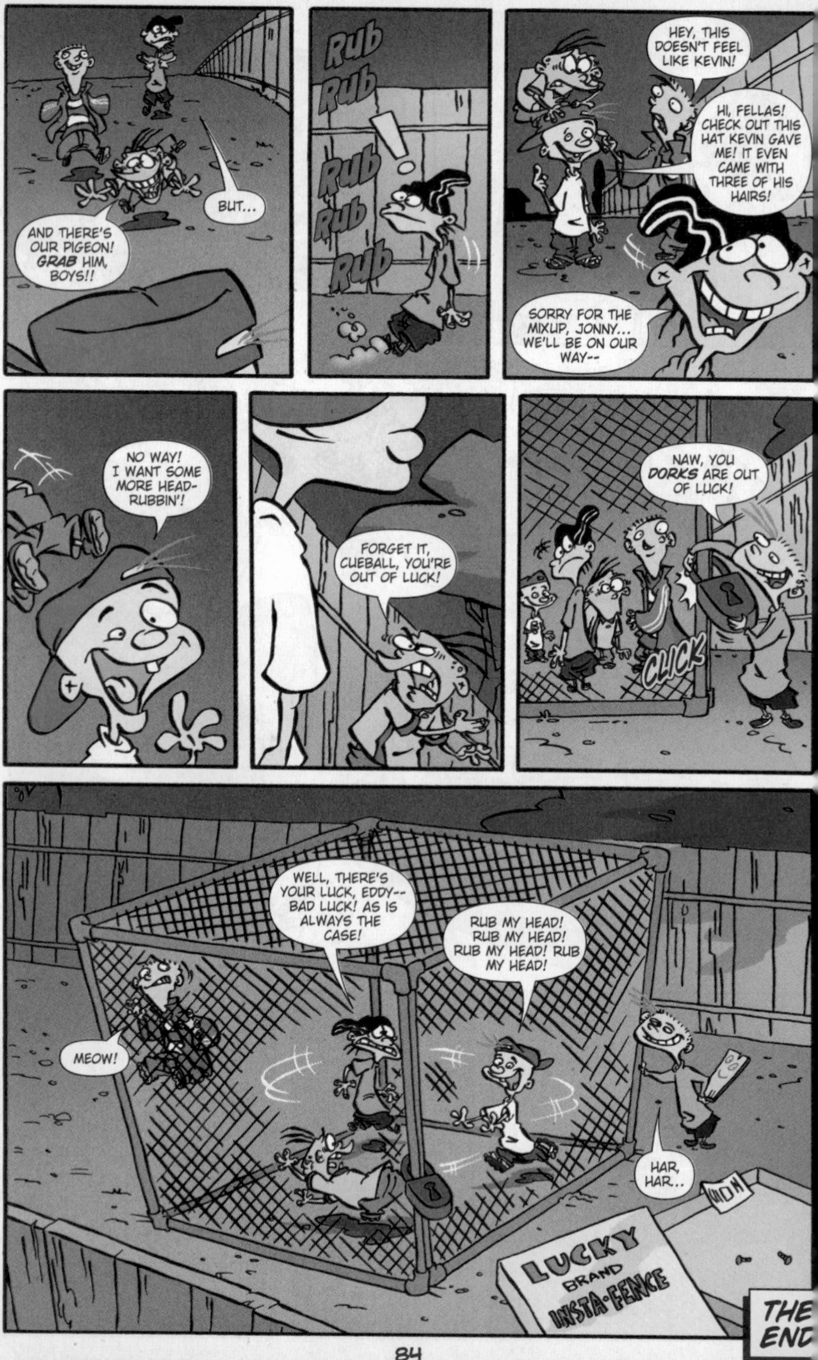
BUT...
AND THERE'S OUR PIGEON! GRAB HIM, BOYS!!
Rub
Rub
Rub
Rub
Rub
HEY, THIS DOESN'T FEEL LIKE KEVIN!
HI, FELLAS! CHECK OUT THIS HAT KEVIN GAVE ME! IT EVEN CAME WITH THREE OF HIS HAIRS!
SORRY FOR THE MIXUP, JONNY... WE'LL BE ON OUR WAY--
NO WAY! I WANT SOME MORE HEAD-RUBBIN'!
FORGET IT, CUEBALL, YOU'RE OUT OF LUCK!
NAW, YOU DORKS ARE OUT OF LUCK!
CLICK
WELL, THERE'S YOUR LUCK, EDDY--BAD LUCK! AS IS ALWAYS THE CASE!
RUB MY HEAD! RUB MY HEAD! RUB MY HEAD! RUB MY HEAD!
MEOW!
HAR, HAR..
LUCKY BRAND INSTA-FENCE
THE END

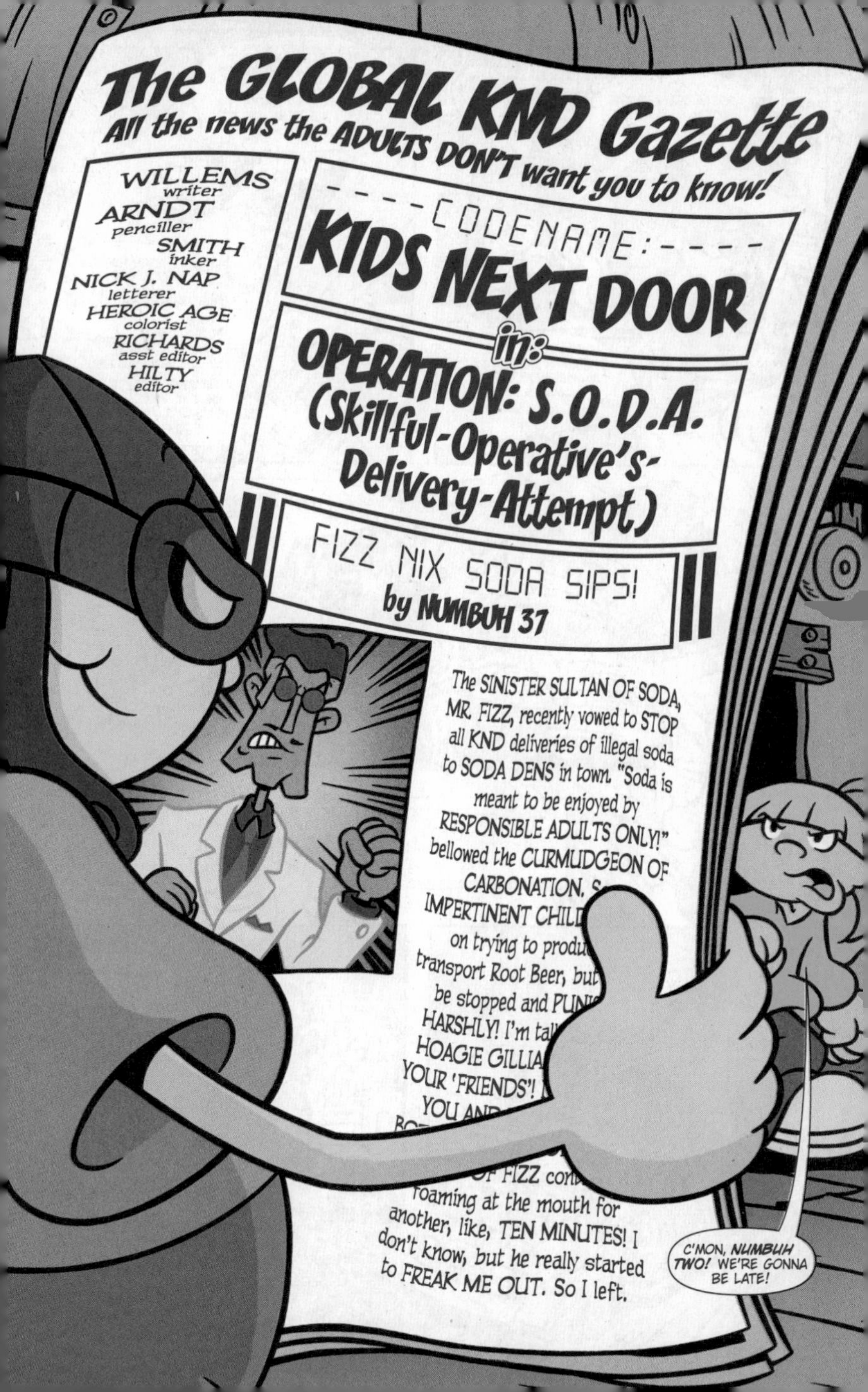
The GLOBAL KND Gazette
All the news the ADULTS DON'T want you to know!
WILLEMS writer
ARNDT penciller
SMITH inker
NICK J. NAP letterer
HEROIC AGE colorist
RICHARDS asst editor
HILTY editor
----CODENAME:----
KIDS NEXT DOOR
in:
OPERATION: S.O.D.A.
(Skillful-Operative's-Delivery-Attempt)
FIZZ NIX SODA SIPS!
by NUMBUH 37
The SINISTER SULTAN OF SODA, MR. FIZZ, recently vowed to STOP all KND deliveries of illegal soda to SODA DENS in town. "Soda is meant to be enjoyed by RESPONSIBLE ADULTS ONLY!" bellowed the CURMUDGEON OF CARBONATION.
IMPERTINENT CHILD
on trying to produ
transport Root Beer, but
be stopped and PUN
HARSHLY! I'm tal
HOAGIE GILLIA
YOUR 'FRIENDS'!
YOU AN
OF FIZZ con
foaming at the mouth for another, like, TEN MINUTES! I don't know, but he really started to FREAK ME OUT. So I left.
C'MON, NUMBUH TWO! WE'RE GONNA BE LATE!

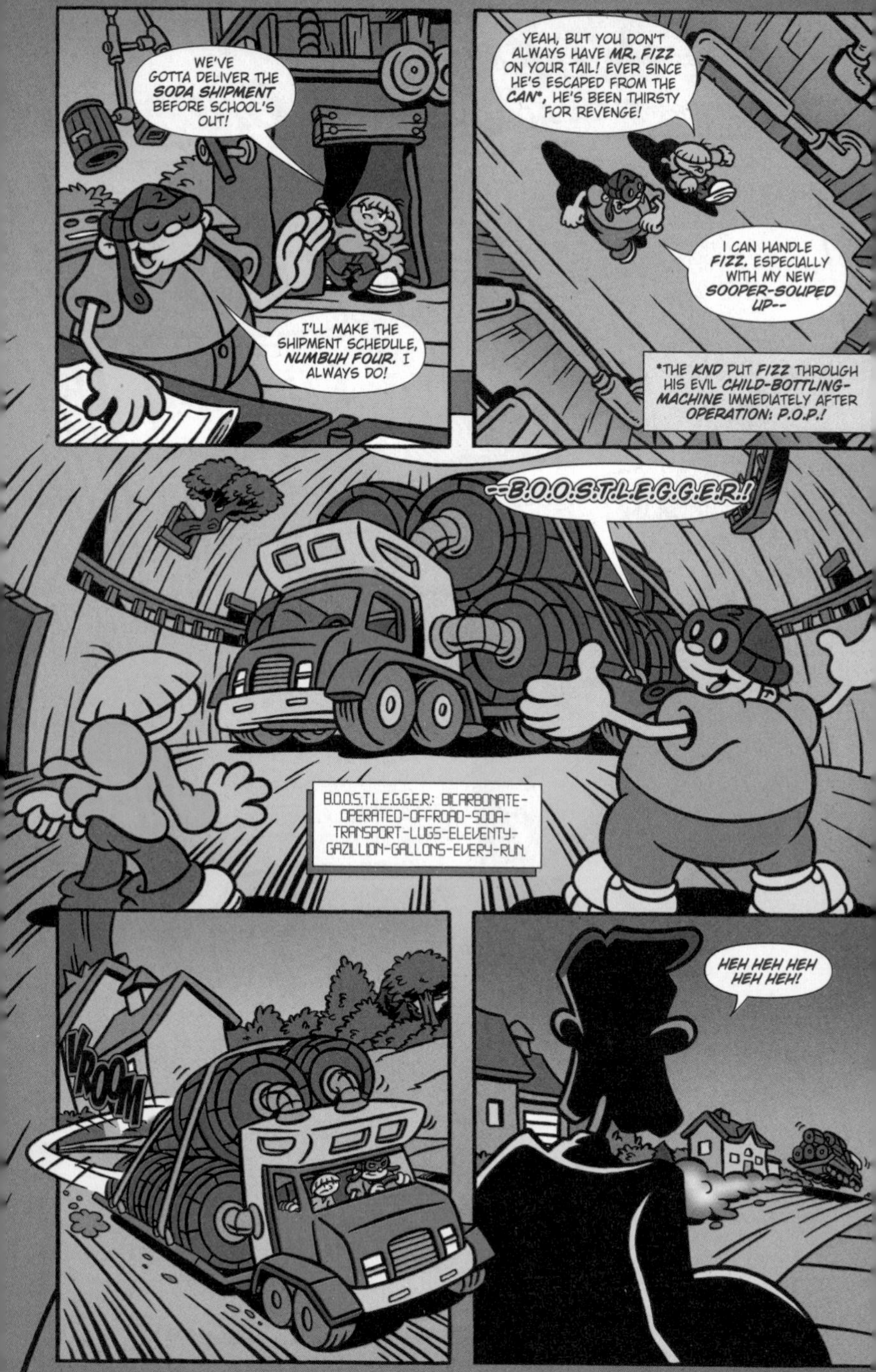
WE'VE GOTTA DELIVER THE SODA SHIPMENT BEFORE SCHOOL'S OUT!
I'LL MAKE THE SHIPMENT SCHEDULE, NUMBUH FOUR. I ALWAYS DO!
YEAH, BUT YOU DON'T ALWAYS HAVE MR. FIZZ ON YOUR TAIL! EVER SINCE HE'S ESCAPED FROM THE CAN*, HE'S BEEN THIRSTY FOR REVENGE!
I CAN HANDLE FIZZ. ESPECIALLY WITH MY NEW SOOPER-SOUPED UP--
*THE KND PUT FIZZ THROUGH HIS EVIL CHILD-BOTTLING-MACHINE IMMEDIATELY AFTER OPERATION: P.O.P.!
--B.O.O.S.T.L.E.G.G.E.R.!
B.O.O.S.T.L.E.G.G.E.R.: BICARBONATE-OPERATED-OFFROAD-SODA-TRANSPORT-LUGS-ELEVENTY-GAZILLION-GALLONS-EVERY-RUN.
VROOM
HEH HEH HEH HEH HEH!

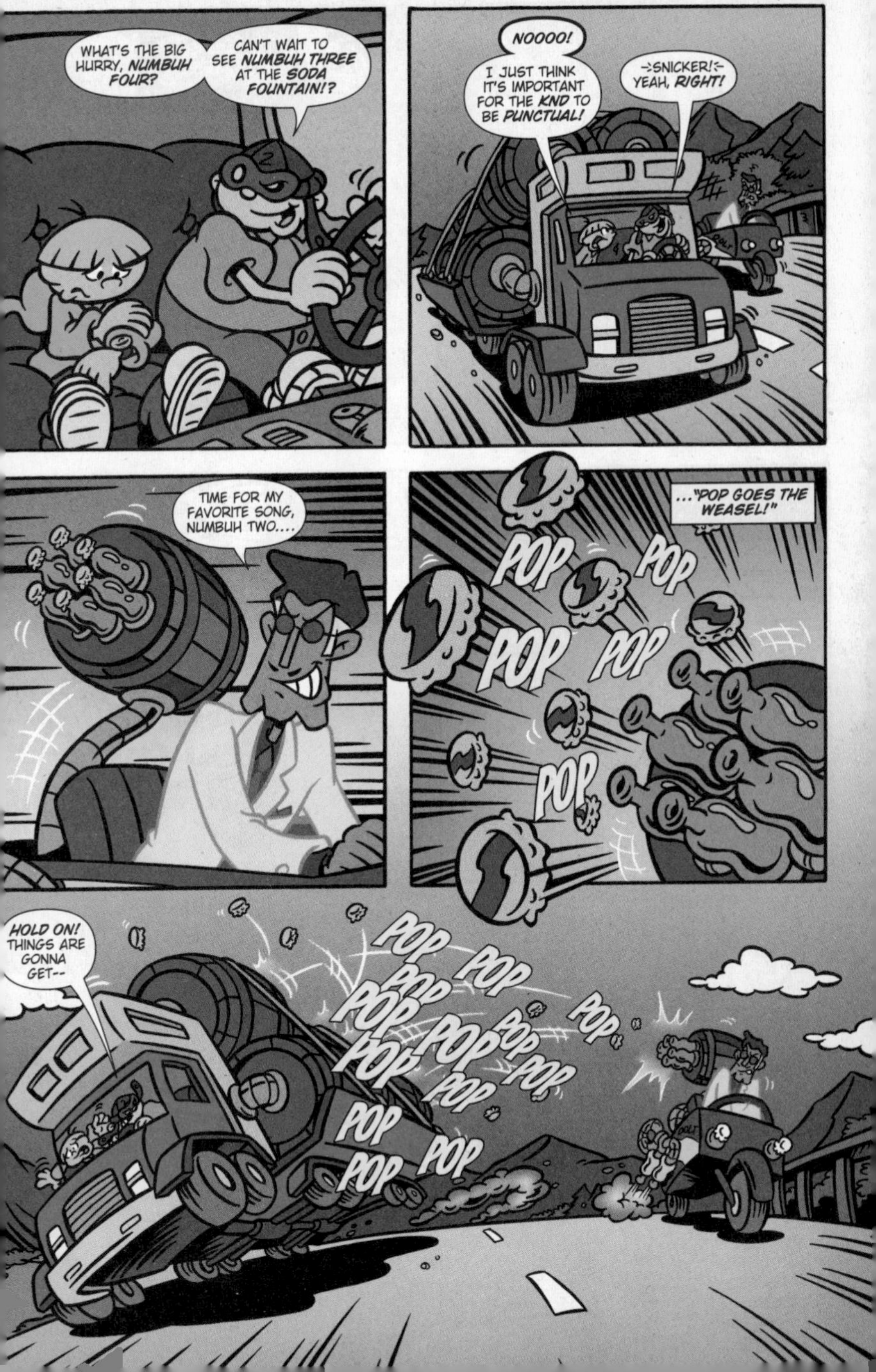
WHAT'S THE BIG HURRY, NUMBUH FOUR?
CAN'T WAIT TO SEE NUMBUH THREE AT THE SODA FOUNTAIN!?
NOOOO!
I JUST THINK IT'S IMPORTANT FOR THE KND TO BE PUNCTUAL!
-SNICKER!- YEAH, RIGHT!
TIME FOR MY FAVORITE SONG, NUMBUH TWO....
..."POP GOES THE WEASEL!"
POP POP POP POP POP
HOLD ON! THINGS ARE GONNA GET--
POP POP POP POP POP POP POP POP POP POP POP POP POP

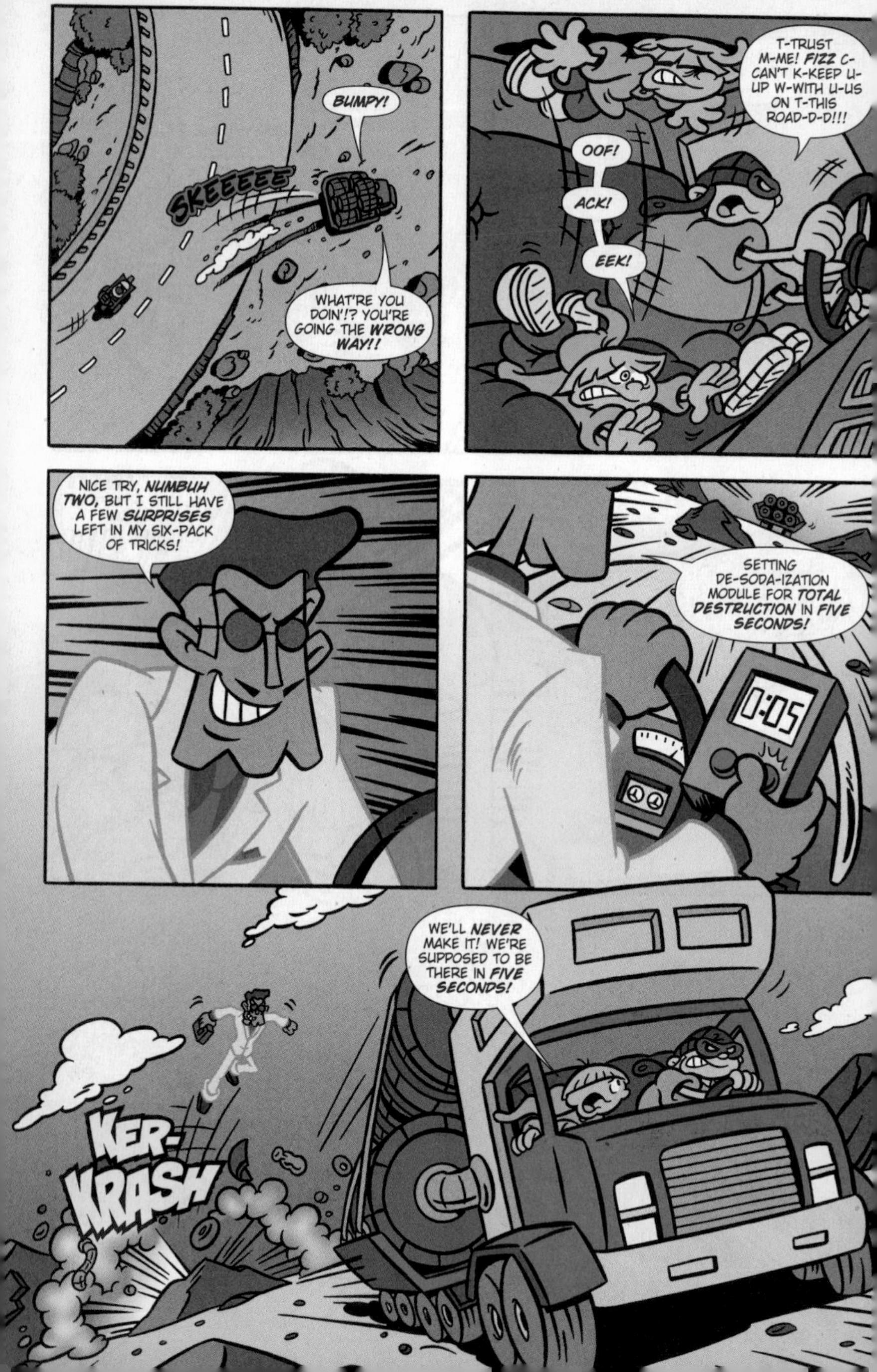
BUMPY!
SKEEEEEE
WHAT'RE YOU DOIN'!? YOU'RE GOING THE WRONG WAY!!
T-TRUST M-ME! FIZZ C-CAN'T K-KEEP U-UP W-WITH U-US ON T-THIS ROAD-D-D!!!
OOF!
ACK!
EEK!
NICE TRY, NUMBUH TWO, BUT I STILL HAVE A FEW SURPRISES LEFT IN MY SIX-PACK OF TRICKS!
SETTING DE-SODA-IZATION MODULE FOR TOTAL DESTRUCTION IN FIVE SECONDS!
0:05
WE'LL NEVER MAKE IT! WE'RE SUPPOSED TO BE THERE IN FIVE SECONDS!
KER-KRASH

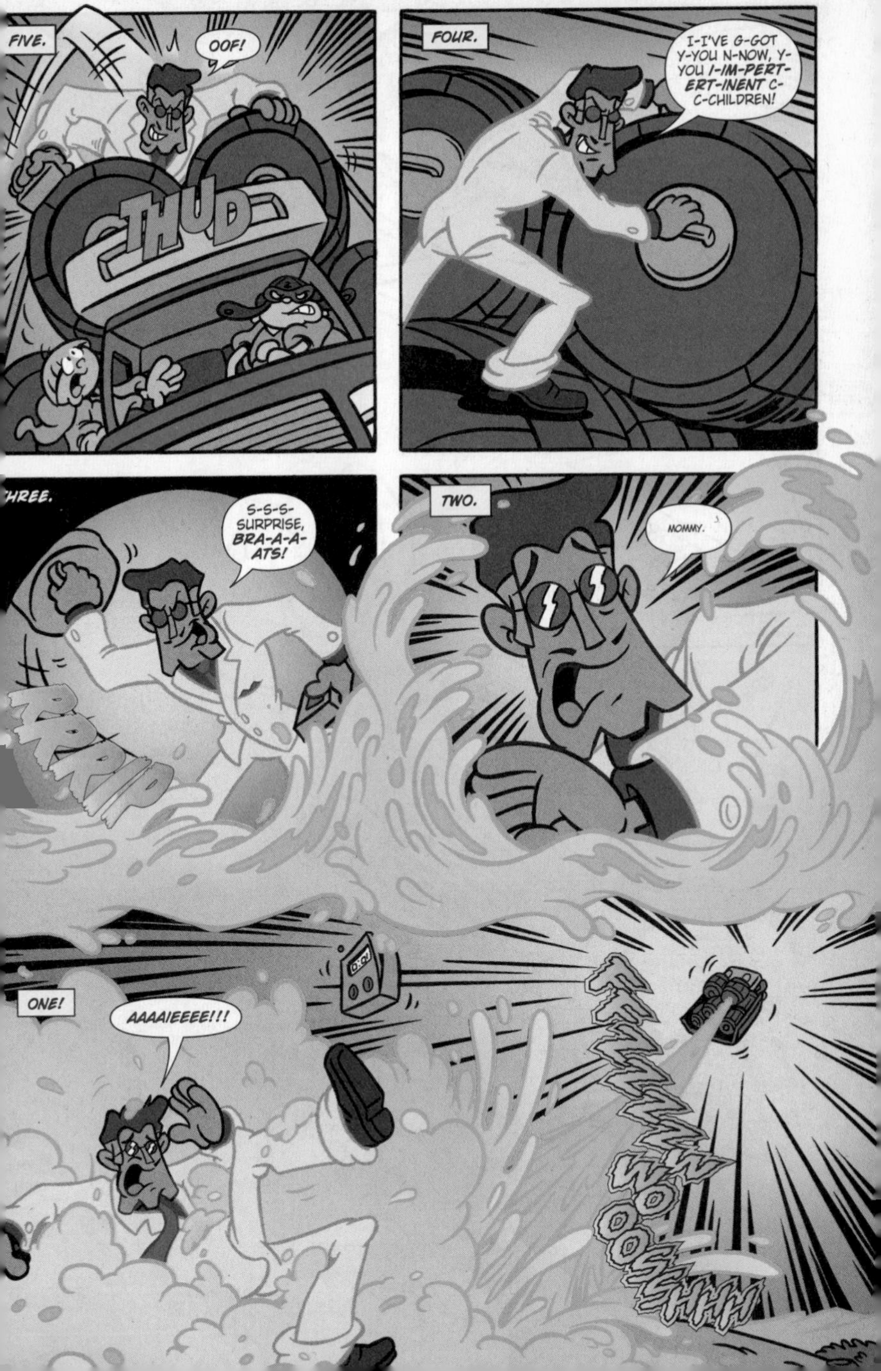
FIVE.
OOF!
THUD
FOUR.
I-I'VE G-GOT Y-YOU N-NOW, Y-YOU I-IM-PERT-ERT-INENT C-C-CHILDREN!
THREE.
S-S-S-SURPRISE, BRA-A-A-ATS!
RRRIP
TWO.
MOMMY.
ONE!
AAAAIEEEE!!!
WOOOSHHH

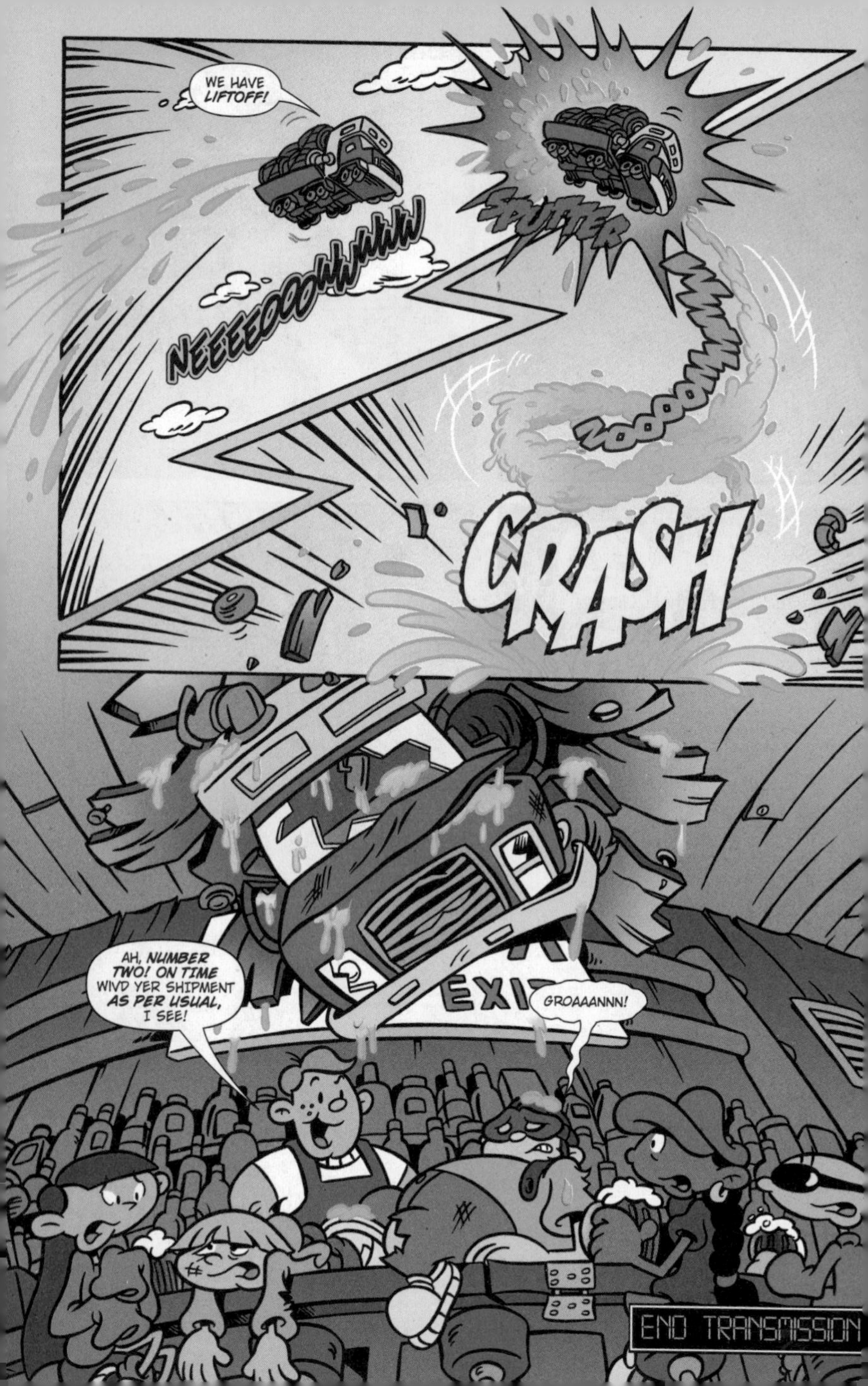
WE HAVE LIFTOFF!
NEEEEOOOWWWWW
SPUTTER
ZOOOOOWWWWW
CRASH
AH, NUMBER TWO! ON TIME WIVD YER SHIPMENT AS PER USUAL, I SEE!
GROAAANNN!
EXIT
END TRANSMISSION

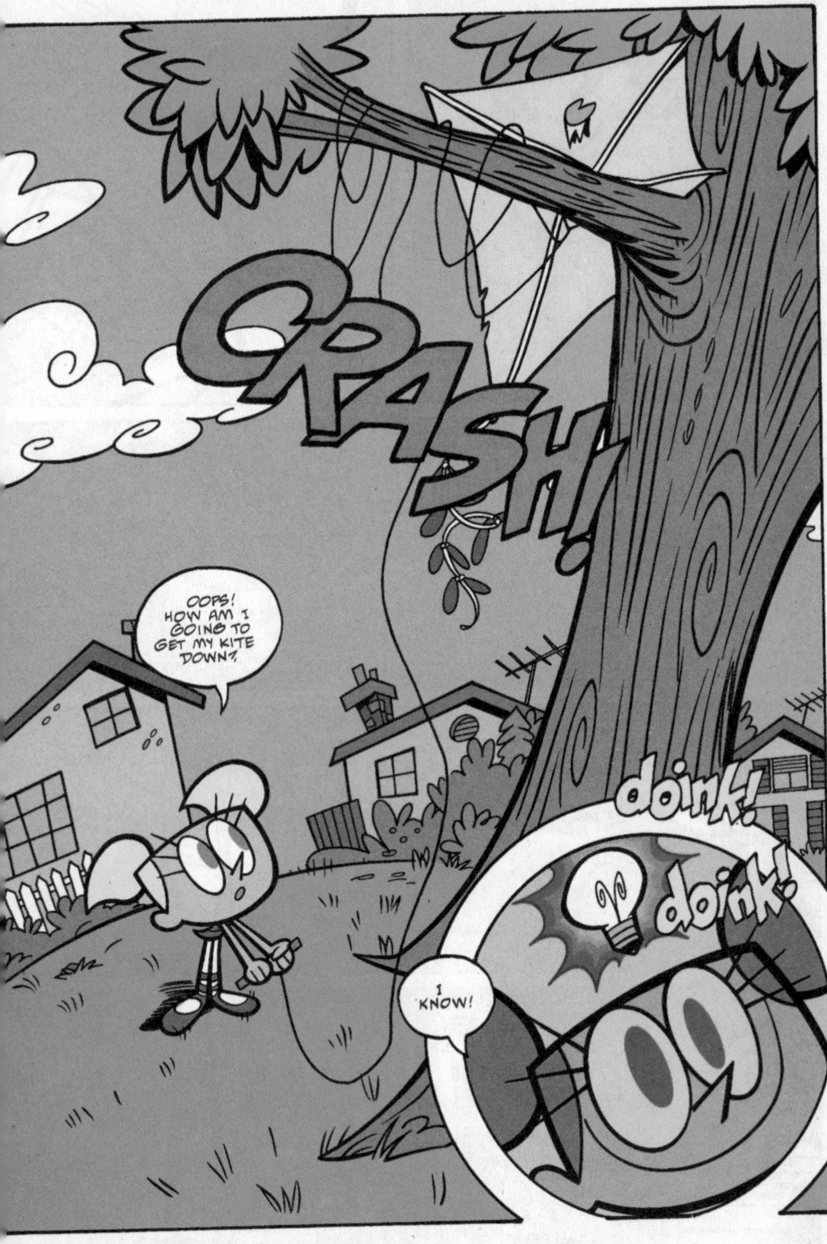
CRASH!
OOPS! HOW AM I GOING TO GET MY KITE DOWN?
doink!
doink!
I KNOW!

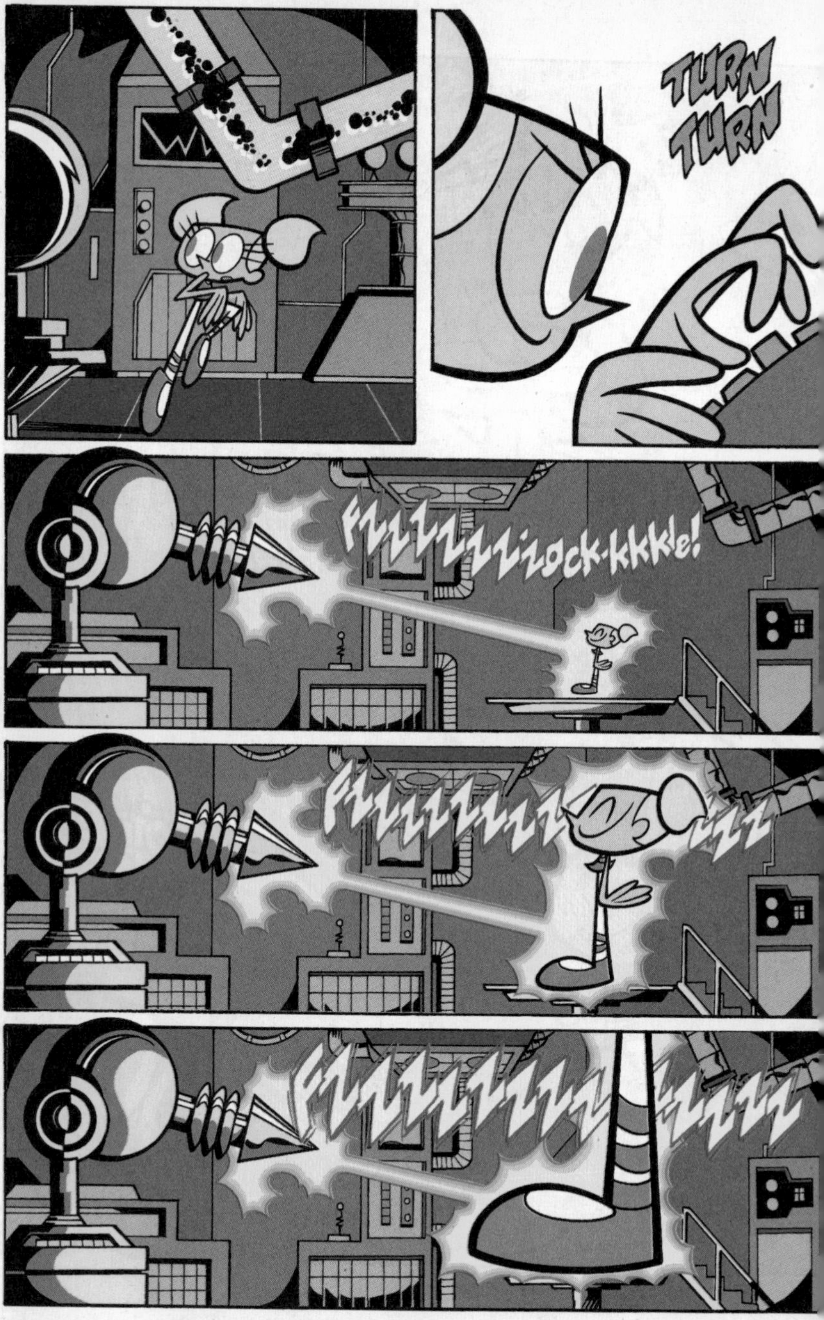
TURN TURN
FZZZZZZZZZOCK-KKKLE!

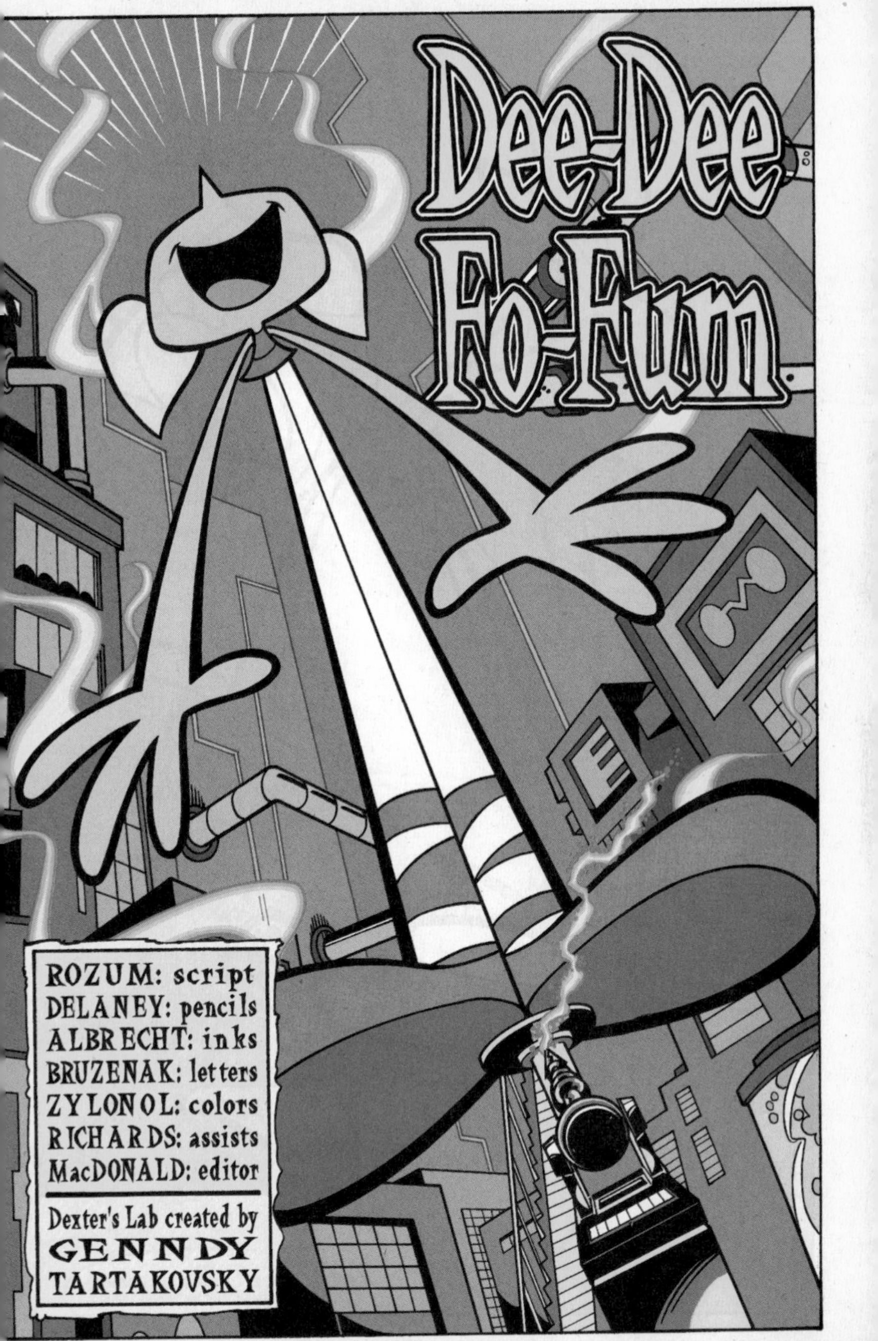
Dee-Dee Fo-Fum
ROZUM: script
DELANEY: pencils
ALBRECHT: inks
BRUZENAK: letters
ZYLONOL: colors
RICHARDS: assists
MacDONALD: editor
Dexter's Lab created by
GENNDY
TARTAKOVSKY

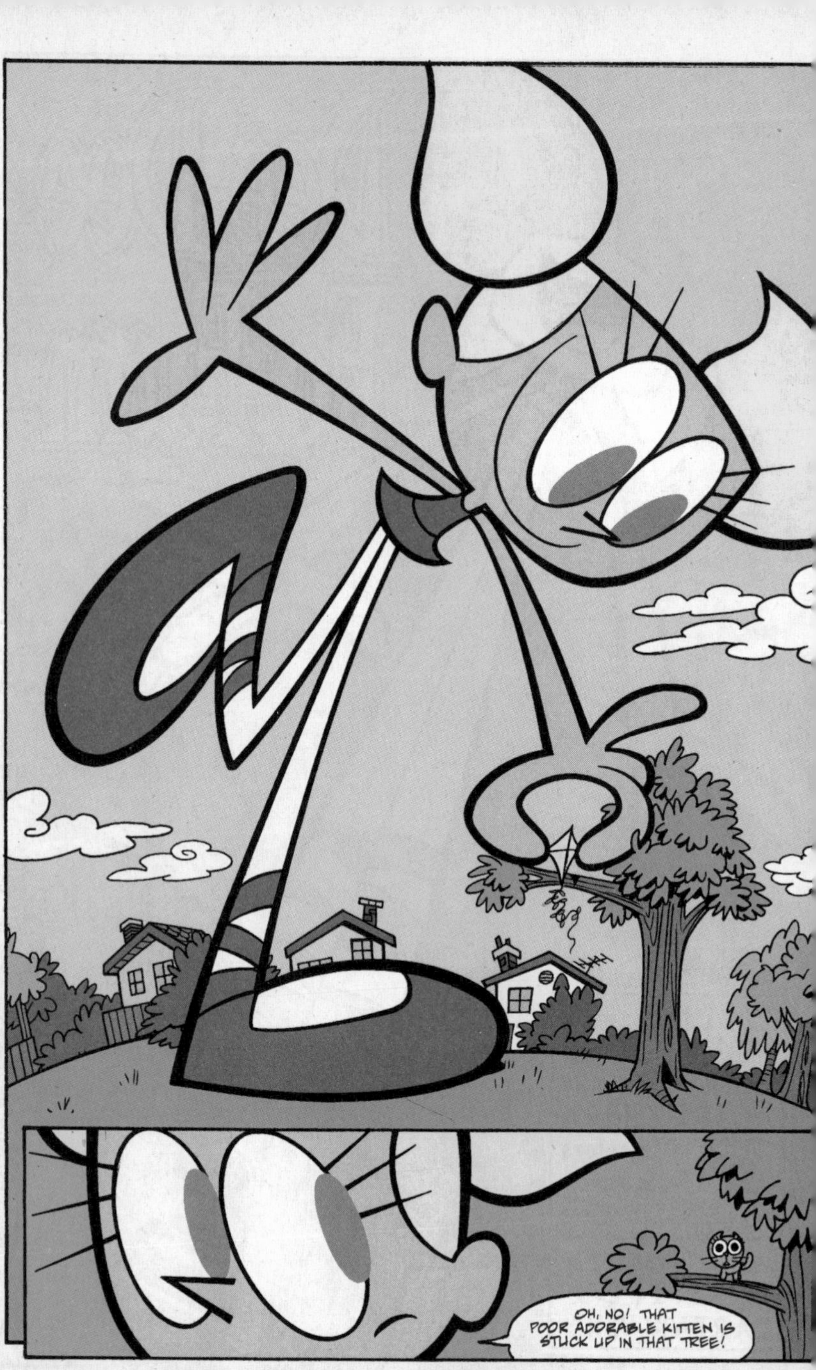
OH, NO! THAT POOR ADORABLE KITTEN IS STUCK UP IN THAT TREE!

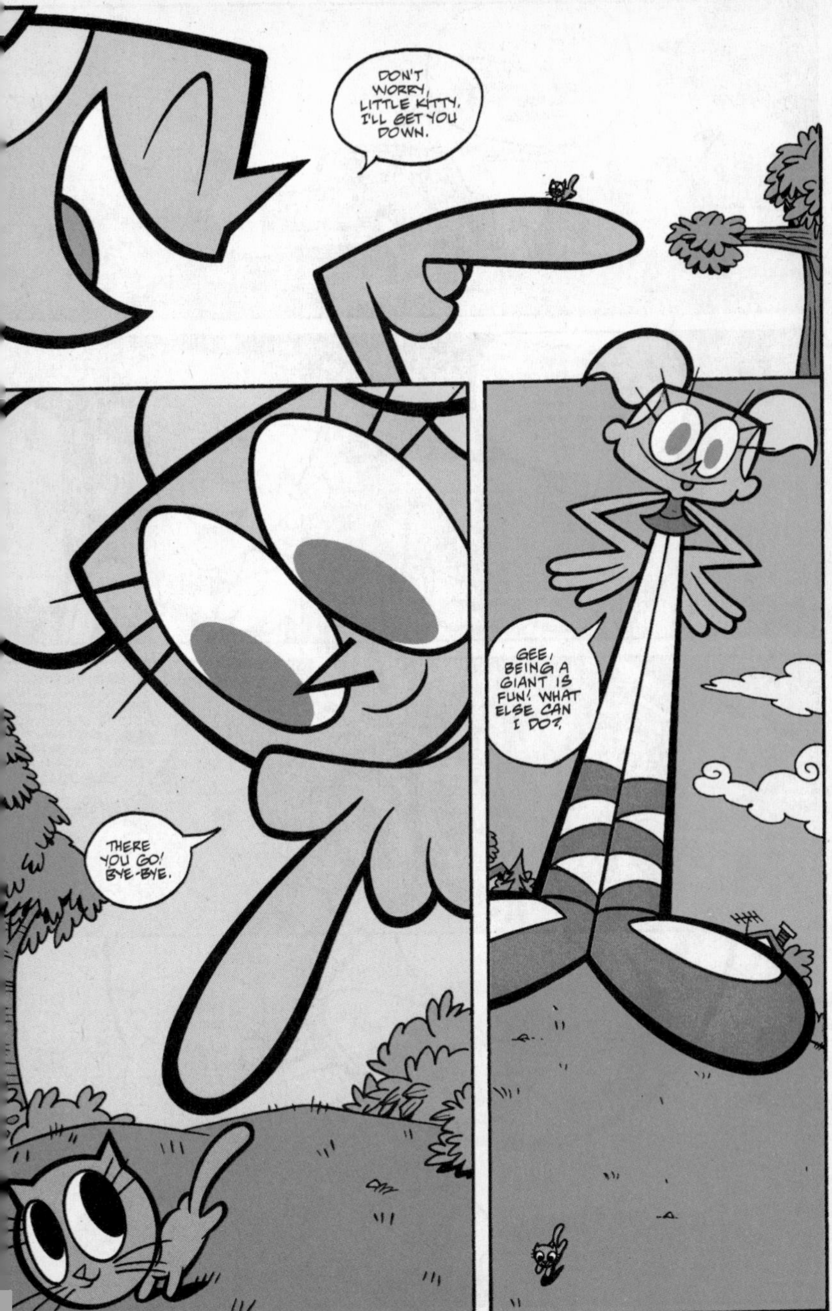
DON'T WORRY, LITTLE KITTY, I'LL GET YOU DOWN.
THERE YOU GO! BYE-BYE.
GEE, BEING A GIANT IS FUN! WHAT ELSE CAN I DO?

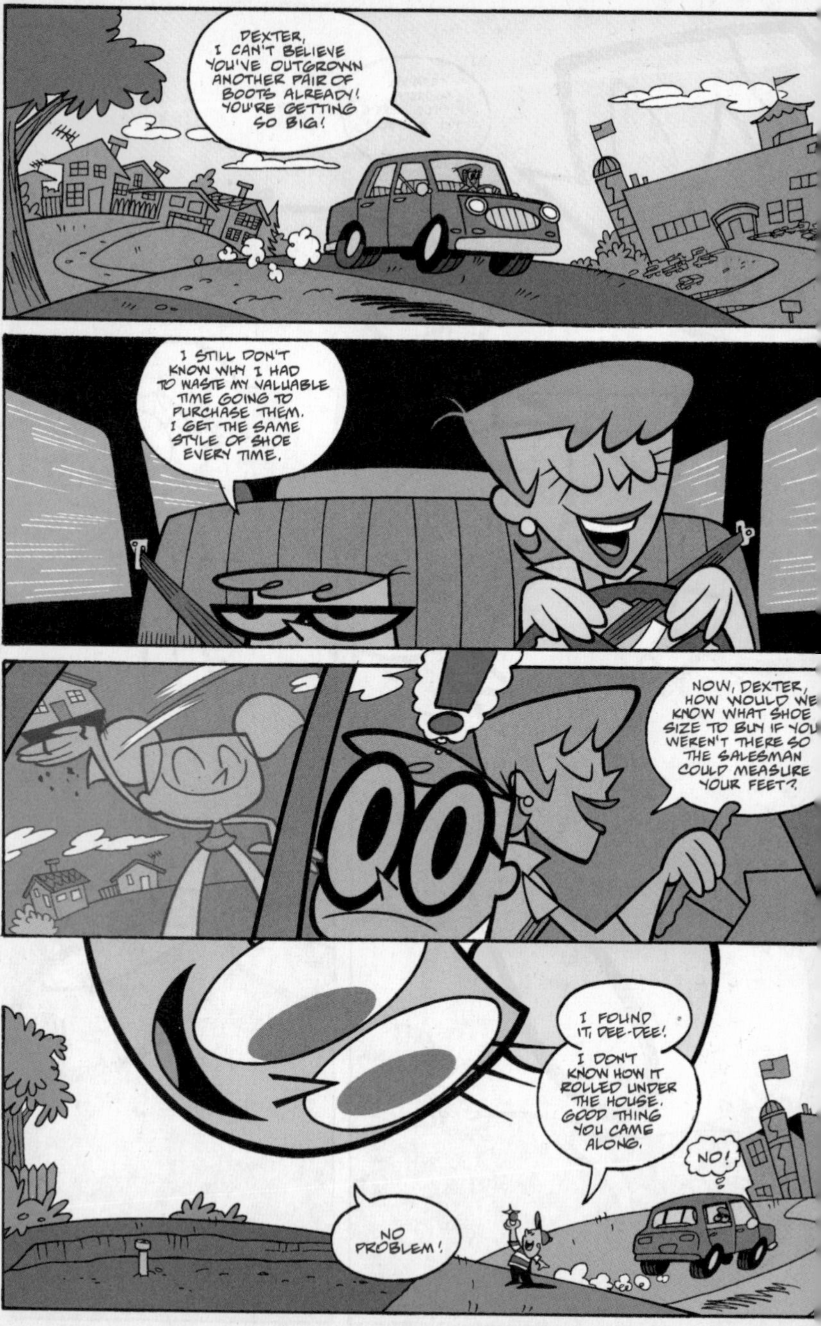
DEXTER, I CAN'T BELIEVE YOU'VE OUTGROWN ANOTHER PAIR OF BOOTS ALREADY! YOU'RE GETTING SO BIG!
I STILL DON'T KNOW WHY I HAD TO WASTE MY VALUABLE TIME GOING TO PURCHASE THEM. I GET THE SAME STYLE OF SHOE EVERY TIME.
NOW, DEXTER, HOW WOULD WE KNOW WHAT SHOE SIZE TO BUY IF YOU WEREN'T THERE SO THE SALESMAN COULD MEASURE YOUR FEET?
I FOUND IT, DEE-DEE!
I DON'T KNOW HOW IT ROLLED UNDER THE HOUSE. GOOD THING YOU CAME ALONG.
NO!
NO PROBLEM!

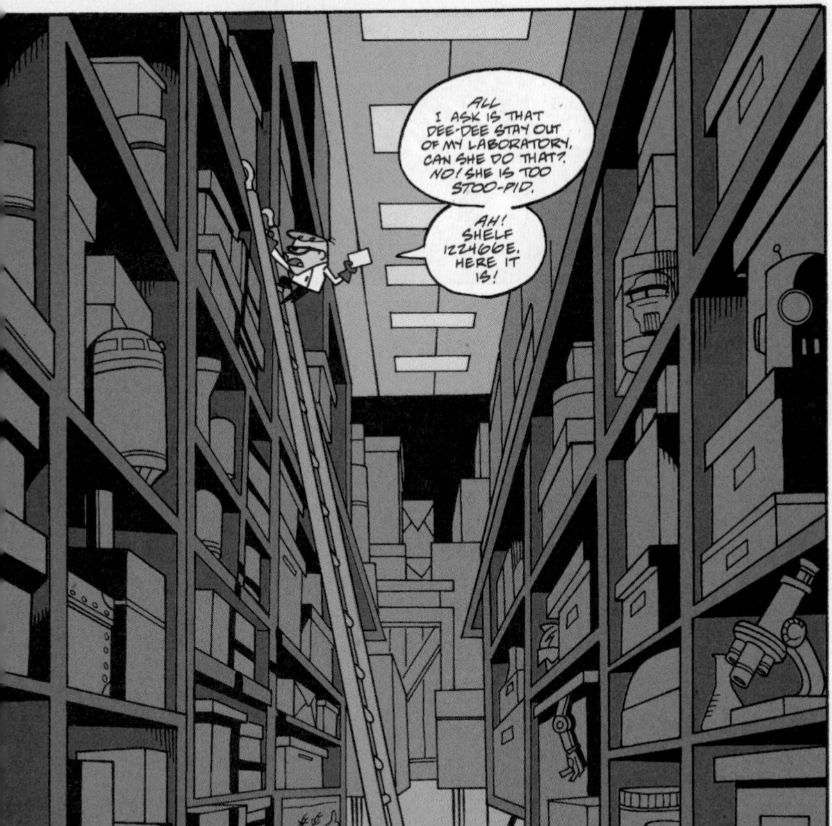
ALL I ASK IS THAT DEE-DEE STAY OUT OF MY LABORATORY. CAN SHE DO THAT? NO! SHE IS TOO STOO-PID.
AH! SHELF 122466E. HERE IT IS!

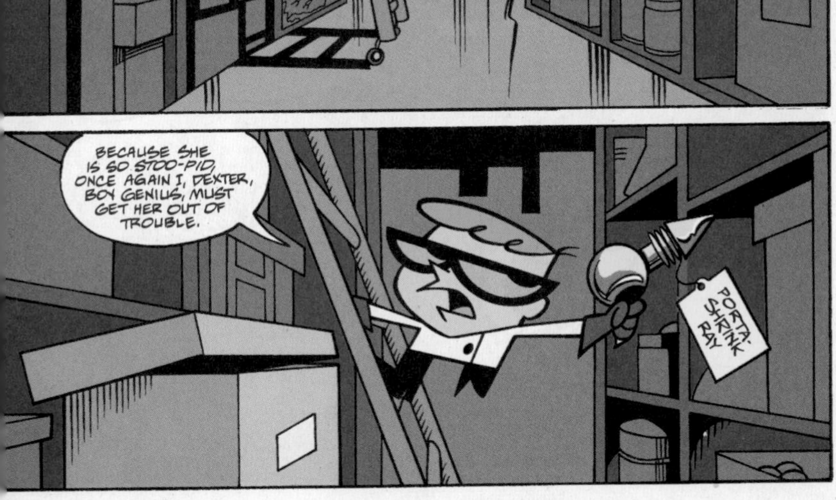
BECAUSE SHE IS SO STOO-PID, ONCE AGAIN I, DEXTER, BOY GENIUS, MUST GET HER OUT OF TROUBLE.
PORTA-SHRINK RAY

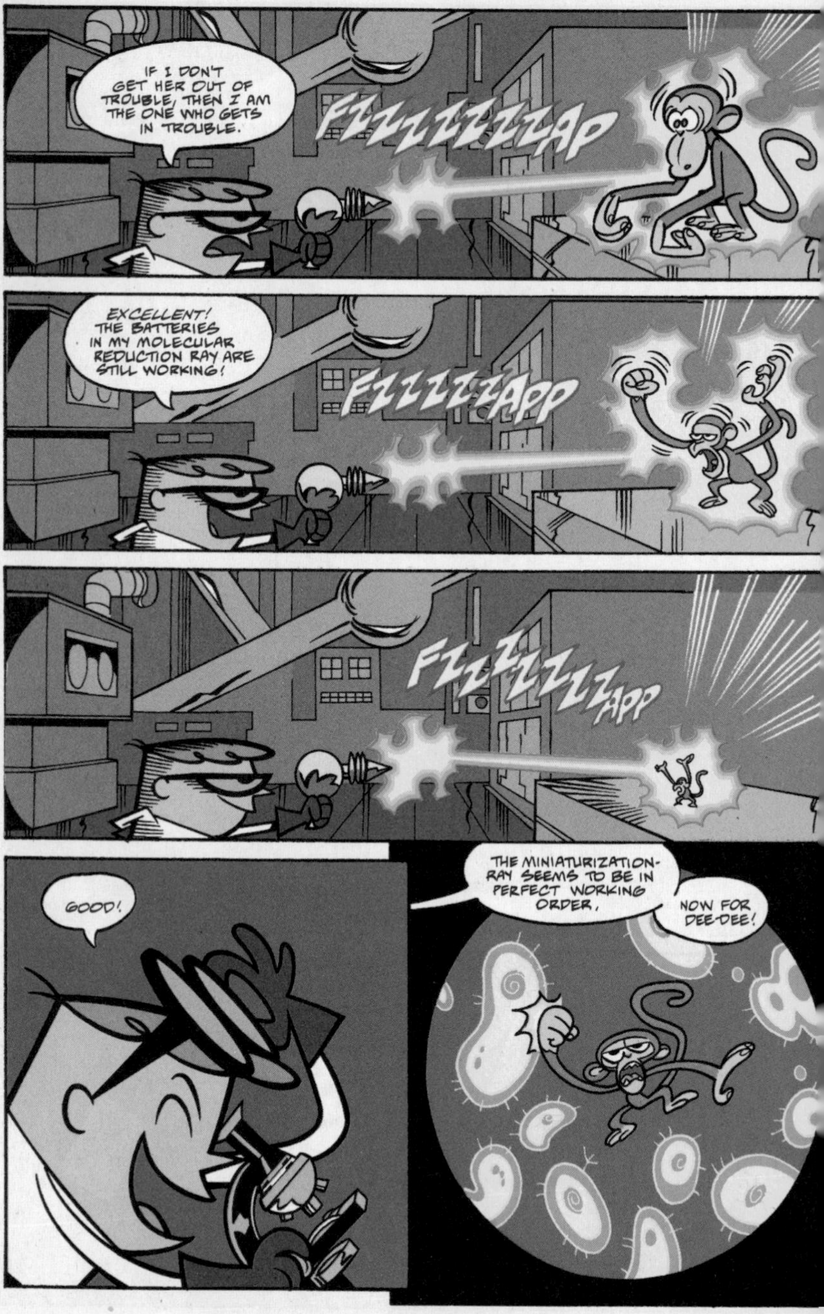
IF I DON'T GET HER OUT OF TROUBLE, THEN I AM THE ONE WHO GETS IN TROUBLE.
FZZZZZZZZAP
EXCELLENT! THE BATTERIES IN MY MOLECULAR REDUCTION RAY ARE STILL WORKING!
FZZZZZZAPP
FZZZZZZZAPP
GOOD!
THE MINIATURIZATION-RAY SEEMS TO BE IN PERFECT WORKING ORDER.
NOW FOR DEE-DEE!

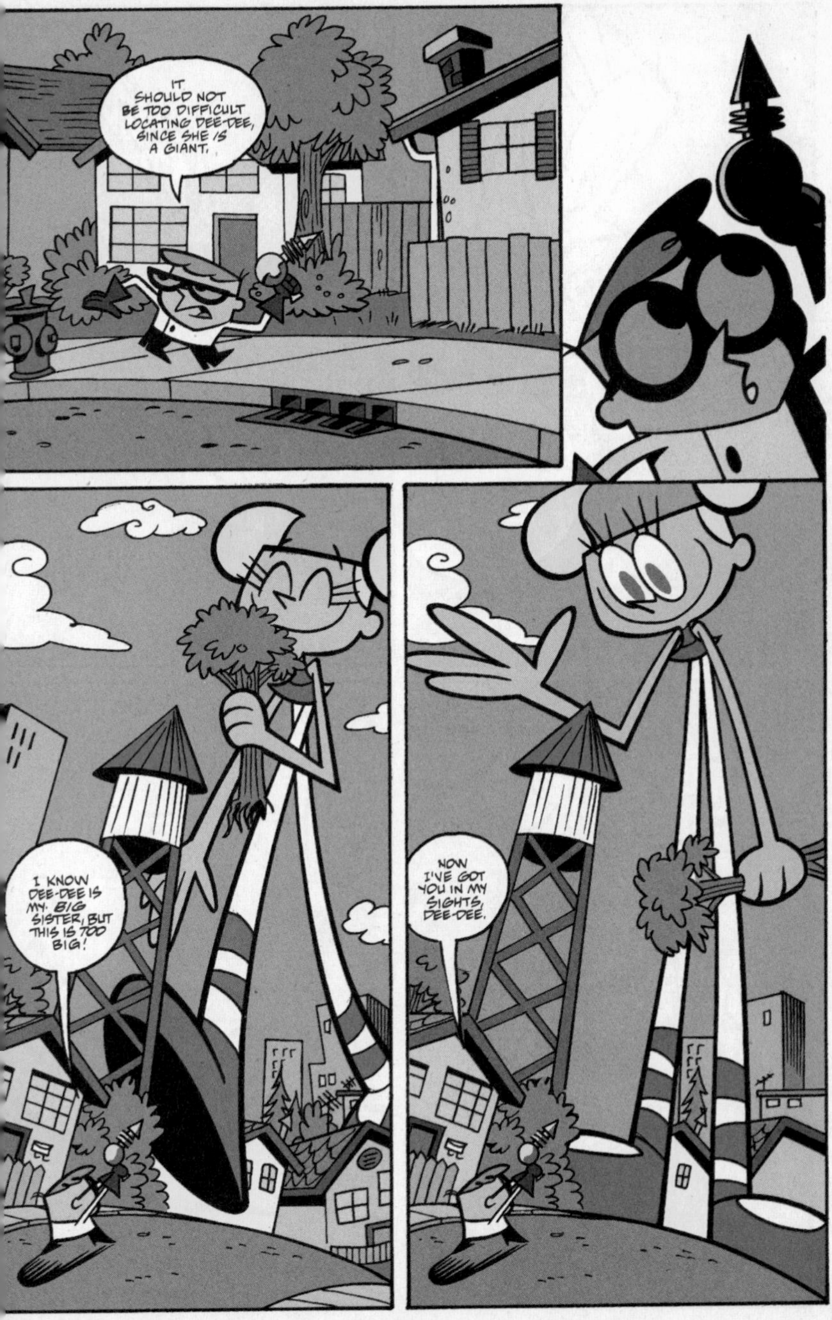
IT SHOULD NOT BE TOO DIFFICULT LOCATING DEE-DEE, SINCE SHE IS A GIANT.
I KNOW DEE-DEE IS MY BIG SISTER, BUT THIS IS TOO BIG!
NOW I'VE GOT YOU IN MY SIGHTS, DEE-DEE.

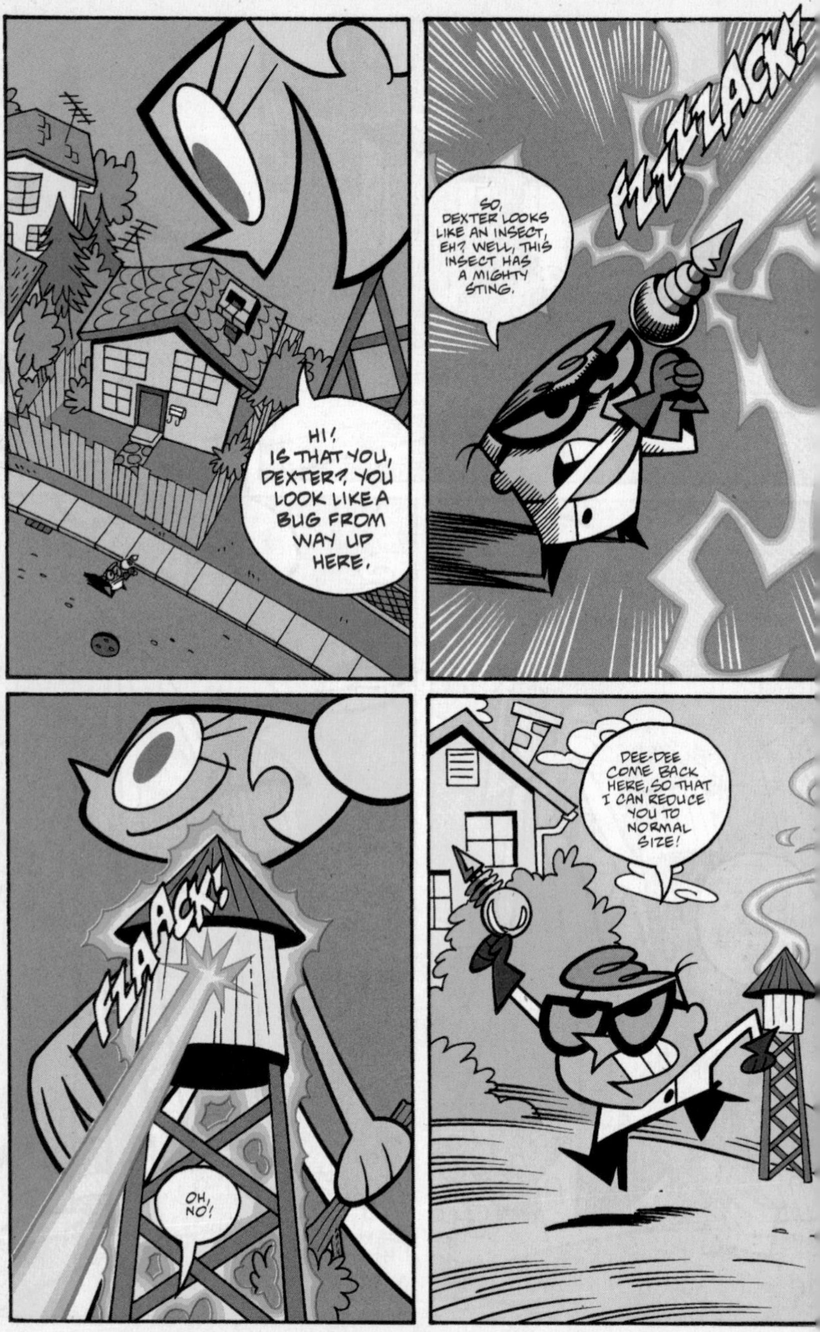
HI! IS THAT YOU, DEXTER? YOU LOOK LIKE A BUG FROM WAY UP HERE.
FZZZZACK!
SO, DEXTER LOOKS LIKE AN INSECT, EH? WELL, THIS INSECT HAS A MIGHTY STING.
FZAACK!
OH, NO!
DEE-DEE COME BACK HERE, SO THAT I CAN REDUCE YOU TO NORMAL SIZE!

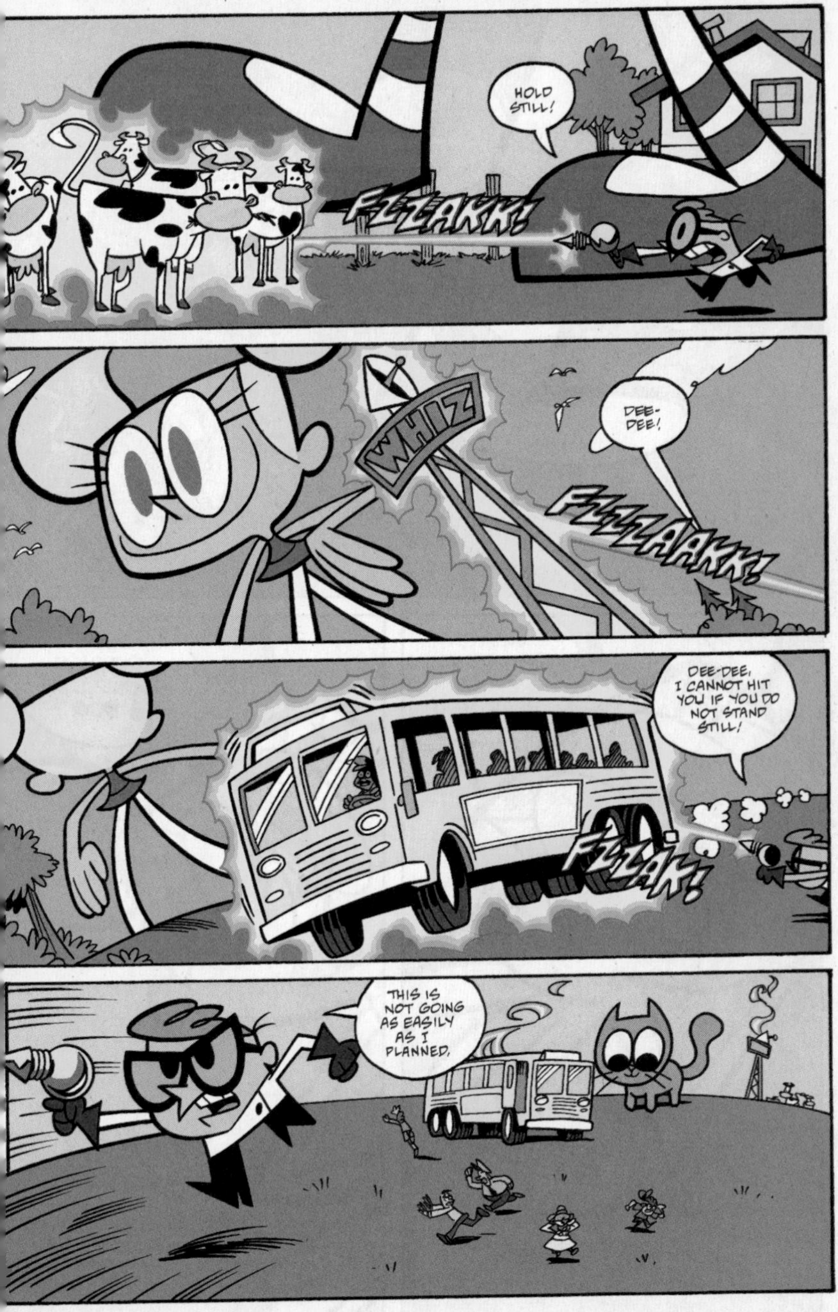
HOLD STILL!
FZZZAKK!
WHIZ
DEE-DEE!
FZZZAAKK!
DEE-DEE, I CANNOT HIT YOU IF YOU DO NOT STAND STILL!
FZZAK!
THIS IS NOT GOING AS EASILY AS I PLANNED.

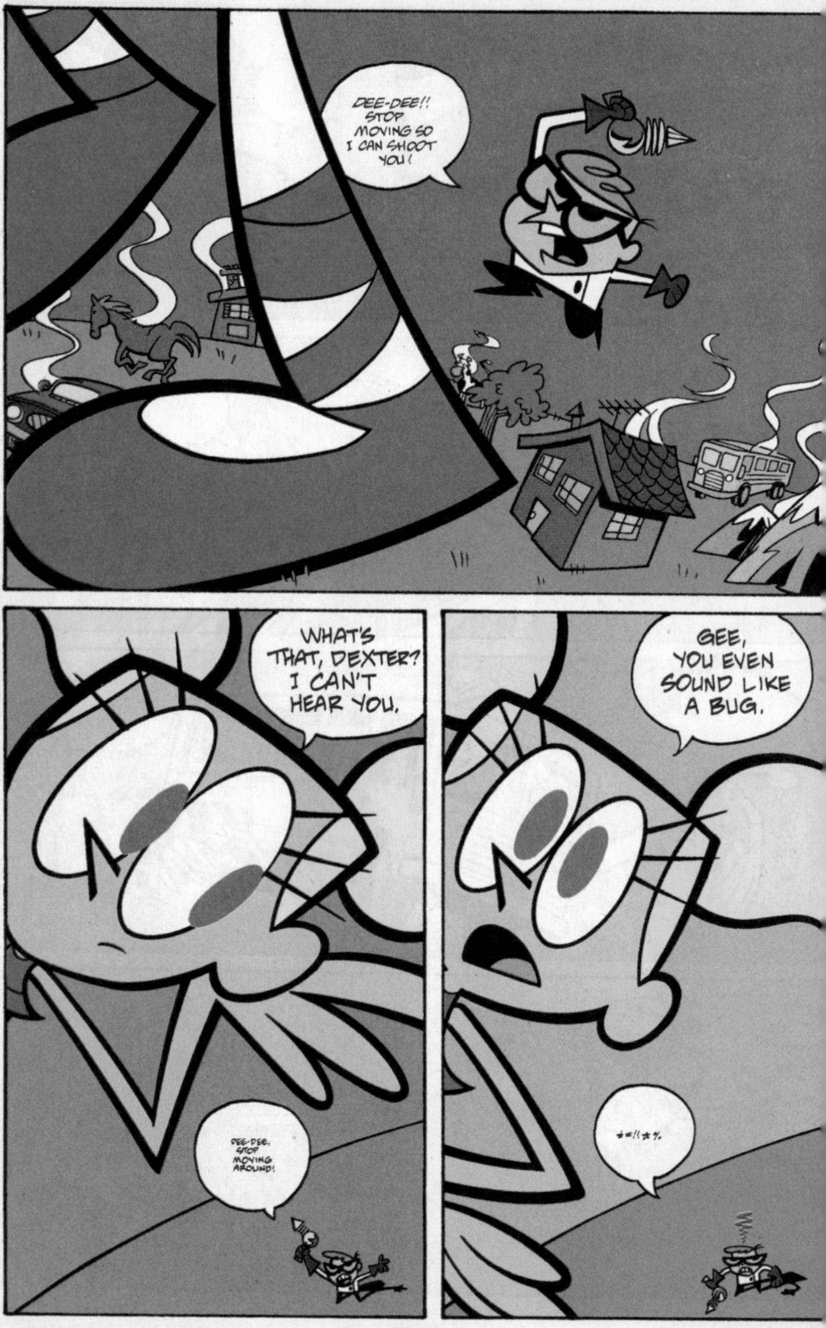
DEE-DEE!! STOP MOVING SO I CAN SHOOT YOU!
WHAT'S THAT, DEXTER? I CAN'T HEAR YOU.
DEE-DEE, STOP MOVING AROUND!
GEE, YOU EVEN SOUND LIKE A BUG.
=!!%

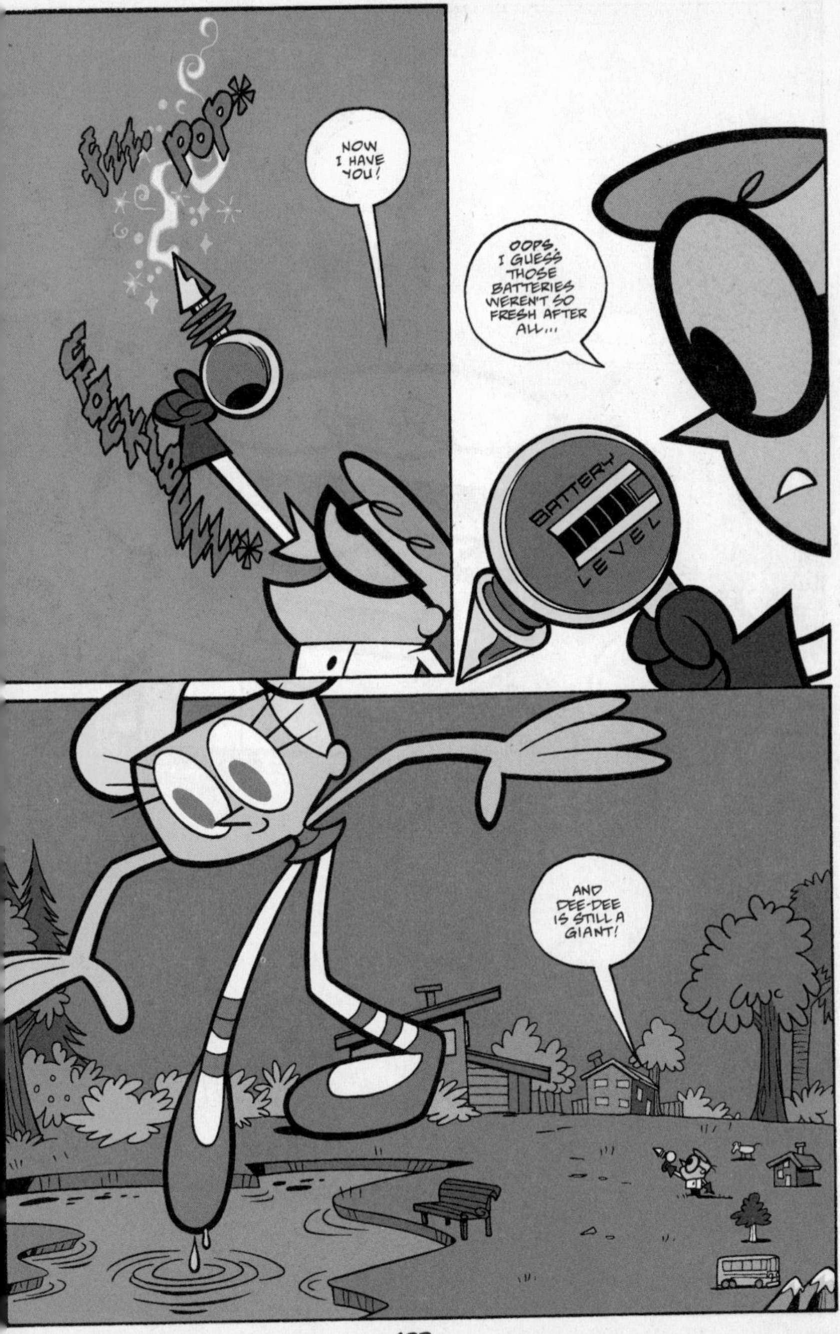
POP
NOW I HAVE YOU!
OOPS. I GUESS THOSE BATTERIES WEREN'T SO FRESH AFTER ALL...
BATTERY LEVEL
AND DEE-DEE IS STILL A GIANT!

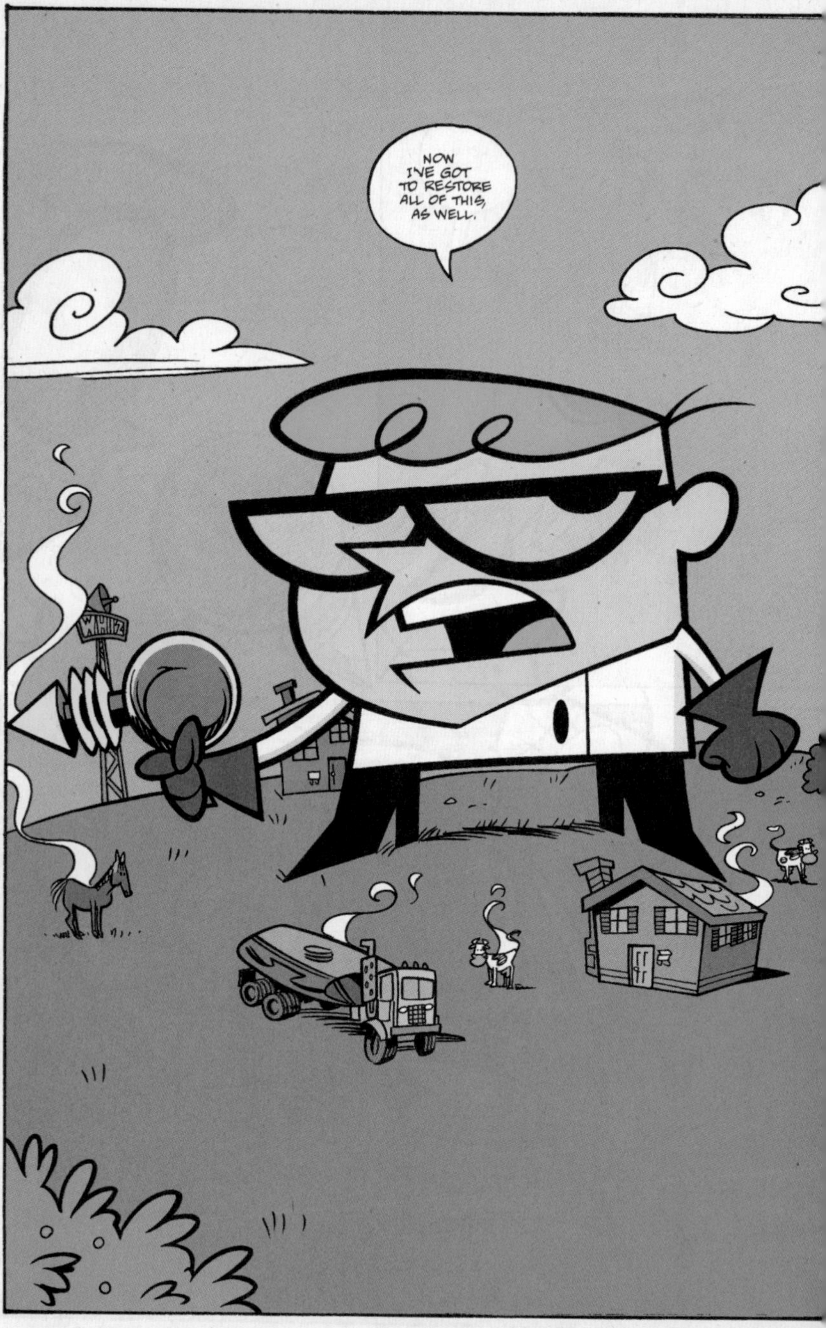
NOW I'VE GOT TO RESTORE ALL OF THIS, AS WELL.
WHHZ

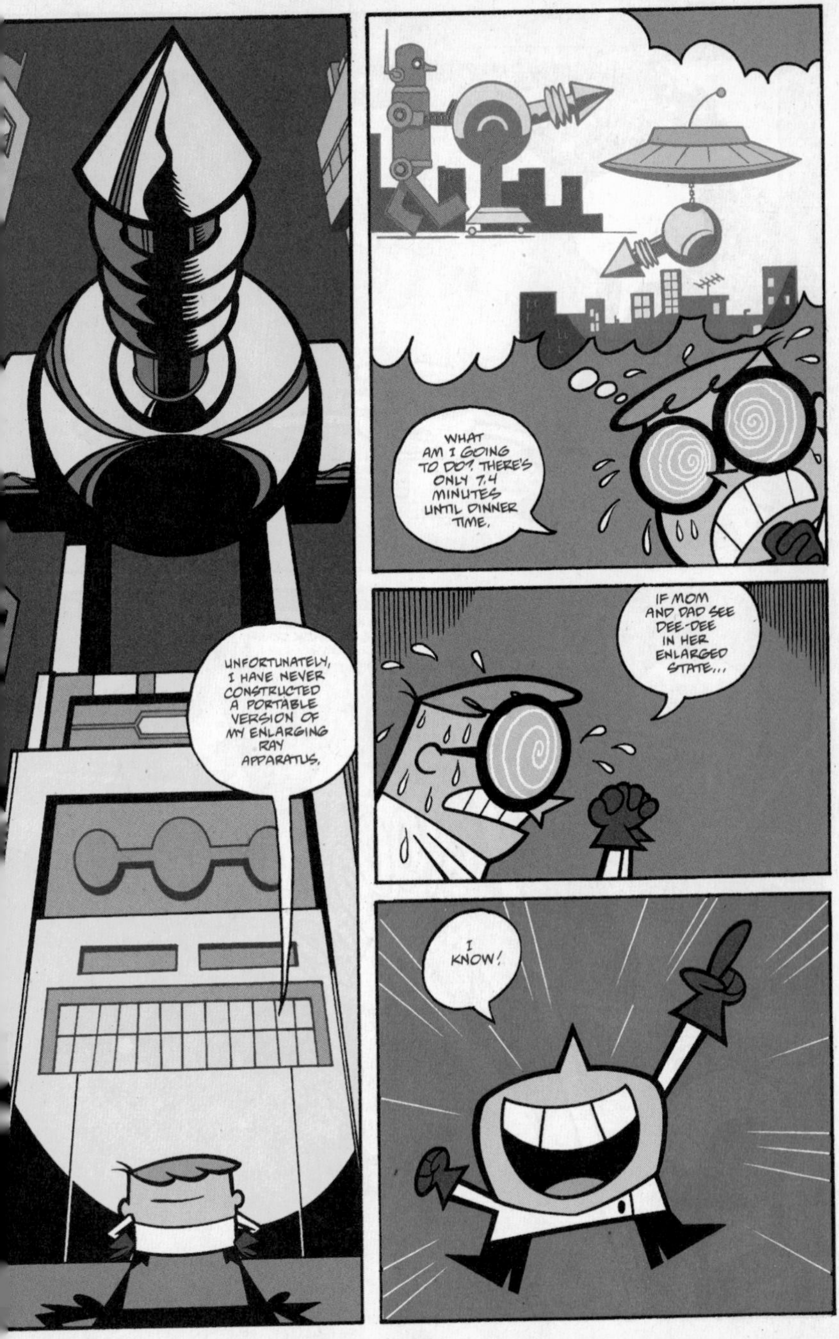
UNFORTUNATELY, I HAVE NEVER CONSTRUCTED A PORTABLE VERSION OF MY ENLARGING RAY APPARATUS.
WHAT AM I GOING TO DO? THERE'S ONLY 7.4 MINUTES UNTIL DINNER TIME.
IF MOM AND DAD SEE DEE-DEE IN HER ENLARGED STATE...
I KNOW!

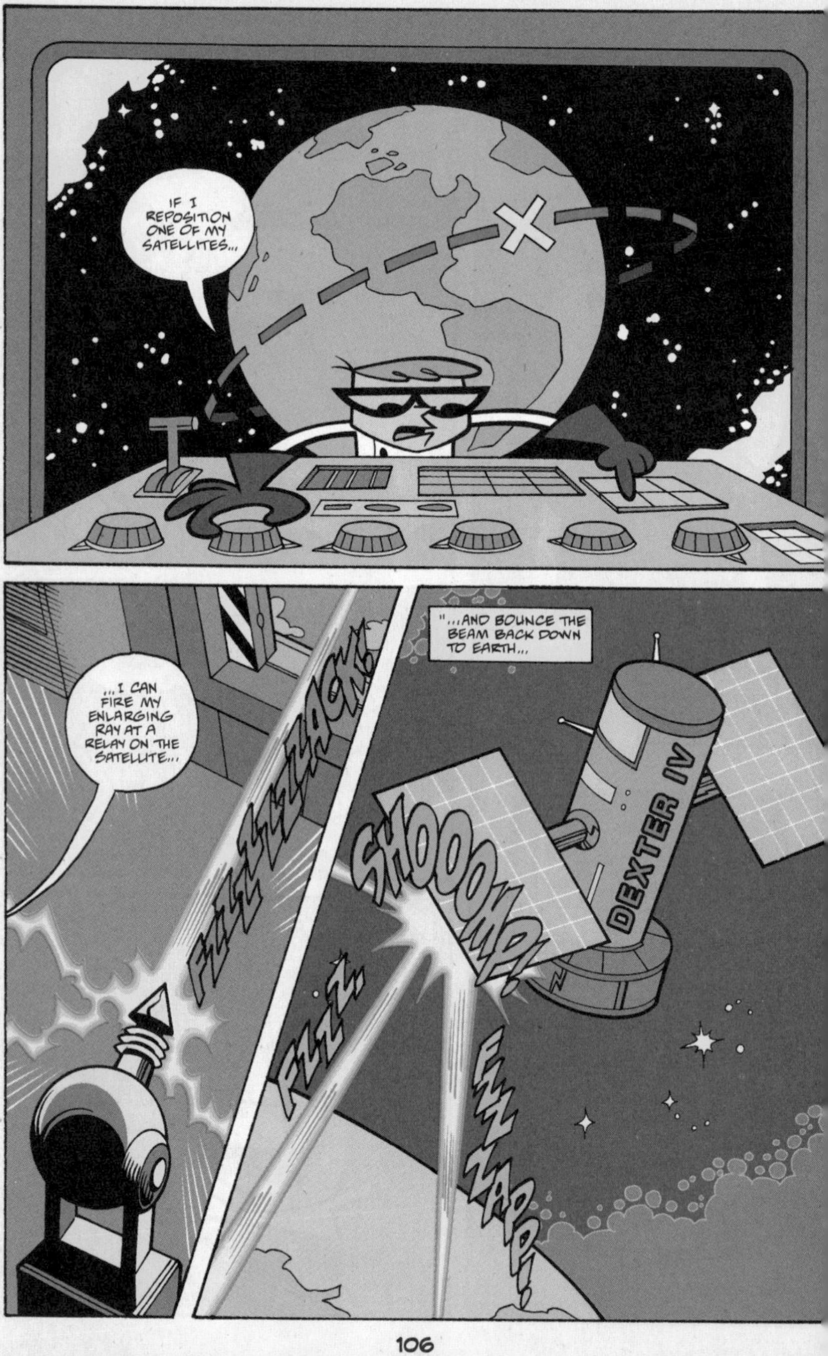

IF I REPOSITION ONE OF MY SATELLITES...
...I CAN FIRE MY ENLARGING RAY AT A RELAY ON THE SATELLITE...
"...AND BOUNCE THE BEAM BACK DOWN TO EARTH...
FZZZZZZZACK!
SHOOOOMP!
DEXTER IV
FZZZZ.
FZZZZAPP!

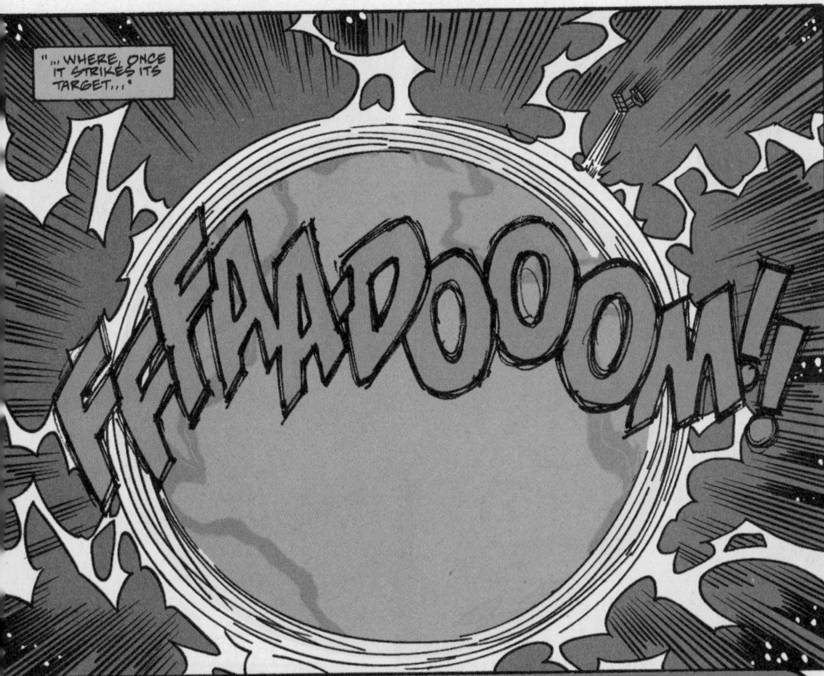
"...WHERE, ONCE IT STRIKES ITS TARGET..."
FFFAADOOOM!!

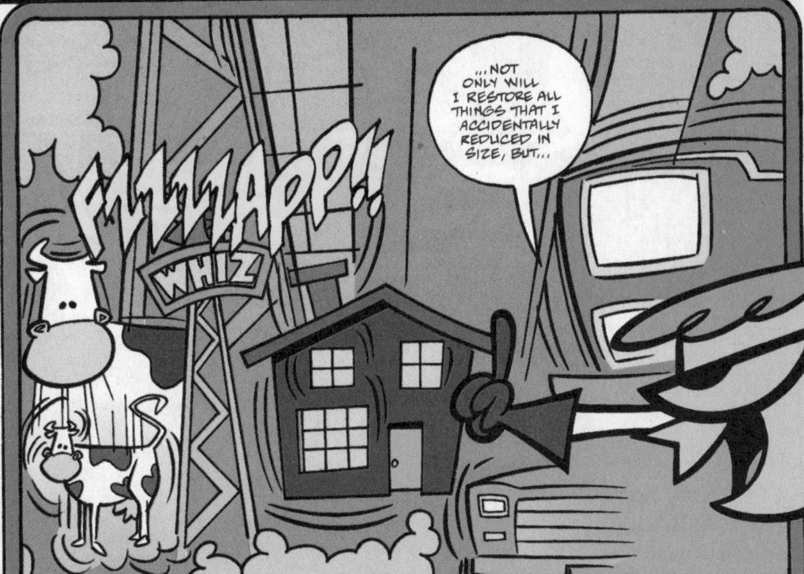
...NOT ONLY WILL I RESTORE ALL THINGS THAT I ACCIDENTALLY REDUCED IN SIZE, BUT...
FZZZAPP!!
WHIZ

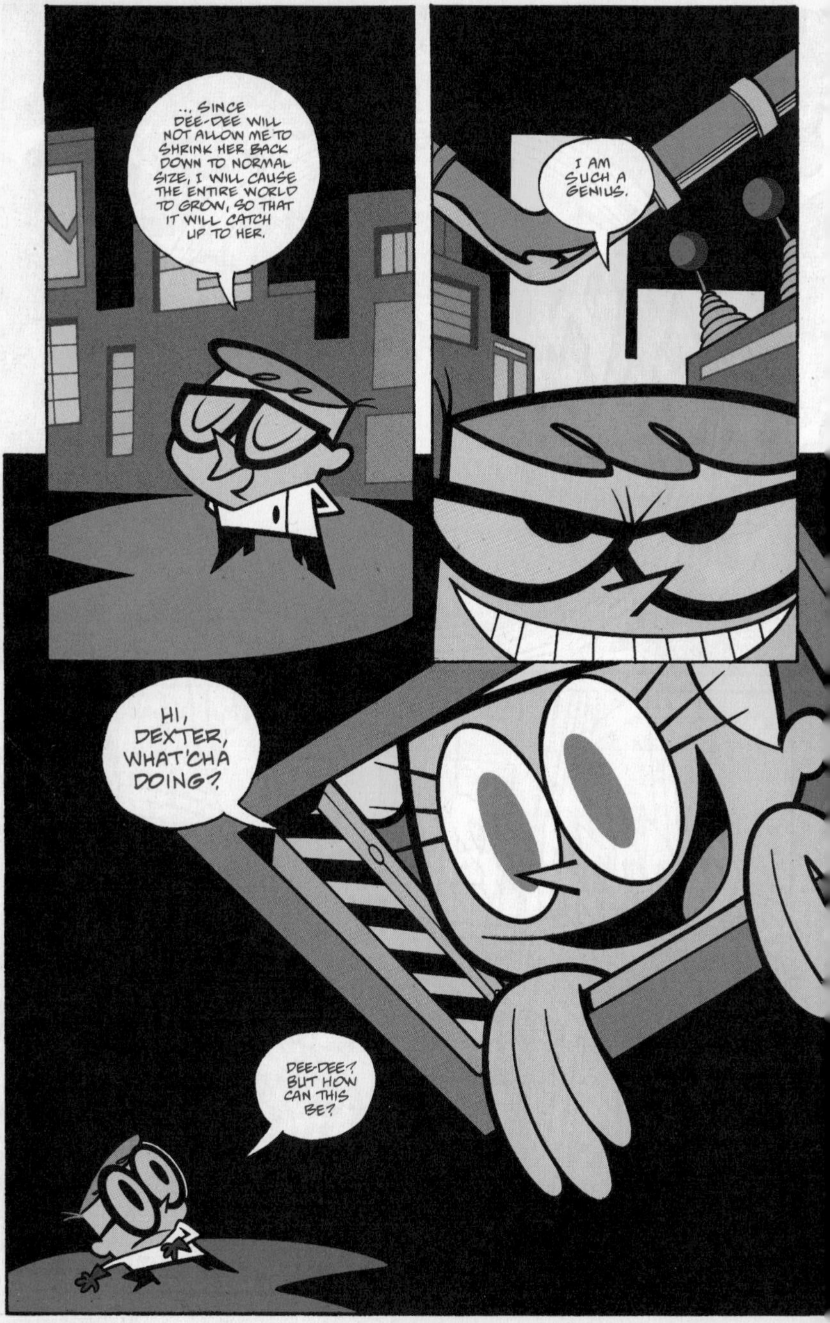
... SINCE DEE-DEE WILL NOT ALLOW ME TO SHRINK HER BACK DOWN TO NORMAL SIZE, I WILL CAUSE THE ENTIRE WORLD TO GROW, SO THAT IT WILL CATCH UP TO HER.
I AM SUCH A GENIUS.
HI, DEXTER, WHAT'CHA DOING?
DEE-DEE? BUT HOW CAN THIS BE?

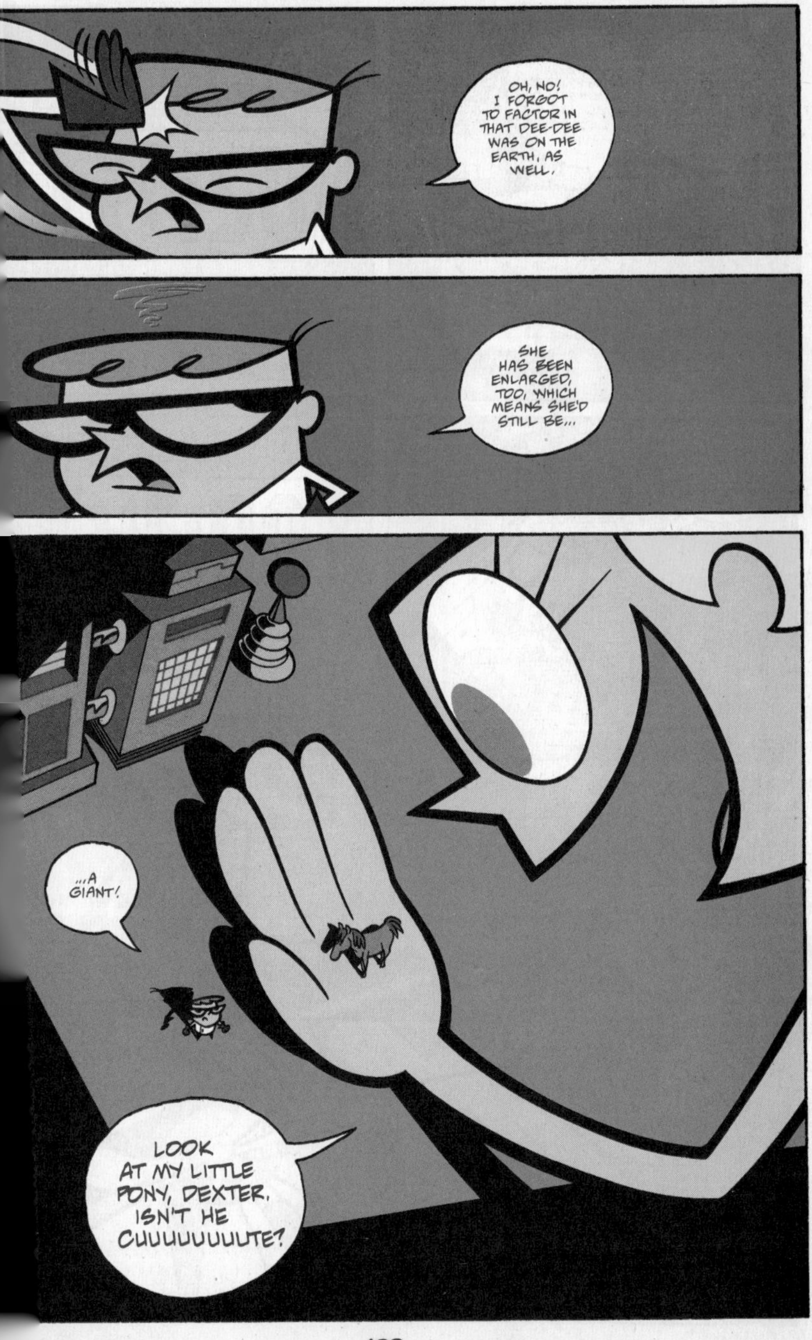
OH, NO! I FORGOT TO FACTOR IN THAT DEE-DEE WAS ON THE EARTH, AS WELL.
SHE HAS BEEN ENLARGED, TOO, WHICH MEANS SHE'D STILL BE...
...A GIANT!
LOOK AT MY LITTLE PONY, DEXTER. ISN'T HE CUUUUUUUUTE?

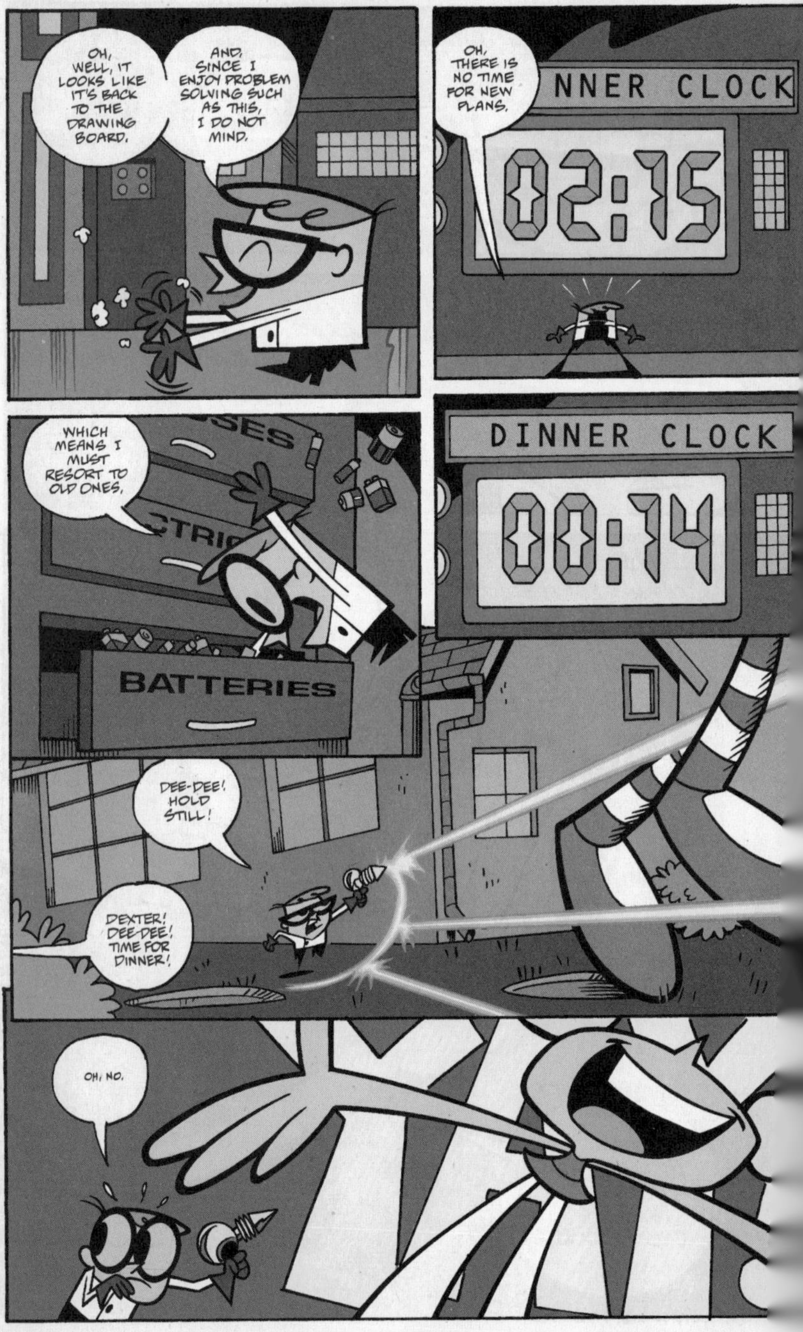
OH, WELL, IT LOOKS LIKE IT'S BACK TO THE DRAWING BOARD.
AND, SINCE I ENJOY PROBLEM SOLVING SUCH AS THIS, I DO NOT MIND.
OH, THERE IS NO TIME FOR NEW PLANS.
NNER CLOCK
02:75
WHICH MEANS I MUST RESORT TO OLD ONES.
BATTERIES
DINNER CLOCK
00:74
DEE-DEE! HOLD STILL!
DEXTER! DEE-DEE! TIME FOR DINNER!
OH, NO.

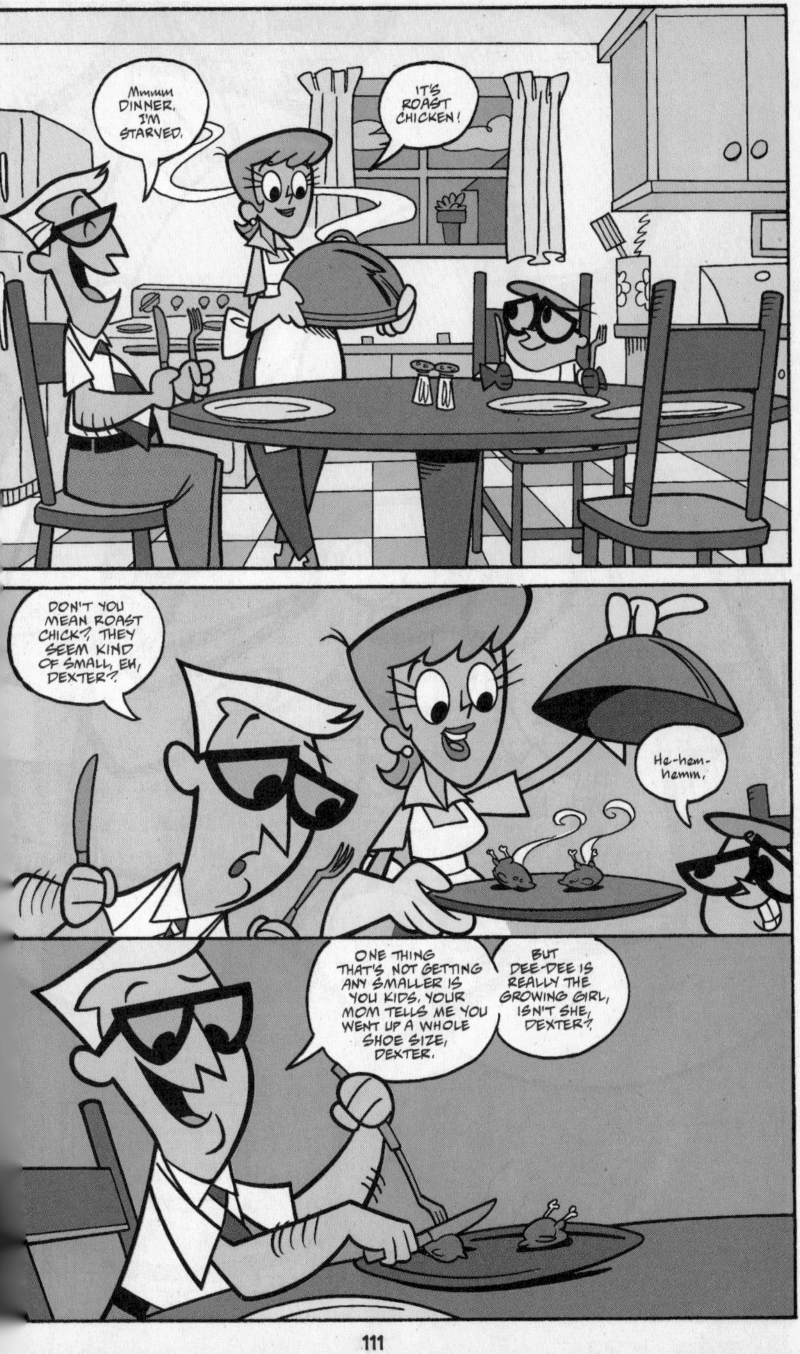
Mmmm DINNER. I'M STARVED.
IT'S ROAST CHICKEN!
DON'T YOU MEAN ROAST CHICK? THEY SEEM KIND OF SMALL, EH, DEXTER?
He-hem-hemm.
ONE THING THAT'S NOT GETTING ANY SMALLER IS YOU KIDS. YOUR MOM TELLS ME YOU WENT UP A WHOLE SHOE SIZE, DEXTER.
BUT DEE-DEE IS REALLY THE GROWING GIRL, ISN'T SHE, DEXTER?

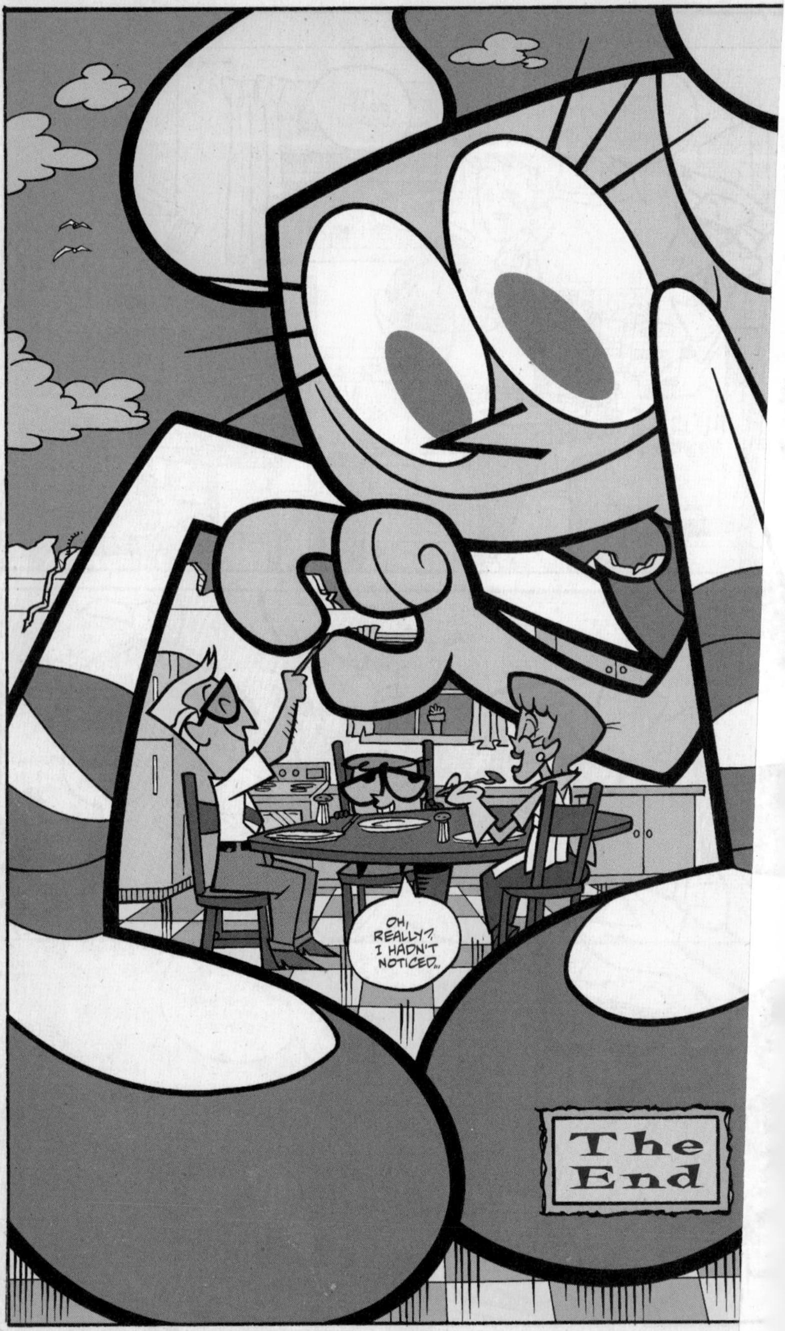
OH, REALLY?! I HADN'T NOTICED...
The End